Zero

An *Orbit* Novel

Ø

J.S Collyer

Legal Notice

Dagda Publishing Ltd
85 St Stephens Road, Nottingham, UK NG2 4JR
Company Number: 9073900, Registered in the UK
dagdapublishing.co.uk
facebook.com/dagdapublishing
twitter.com/dagdapublishing

All enquiries: info@dagdapublishing.co.uk

For Mum and Dad, who always believed.
For Adam and Cheryl, who always encouraged.
And for Christopher, who always laughed.

Theirs not to make reply,
theirs not to reason why,
theirs but to do and die.

- The Charge of the Light Brigade,
Alfred Lord Tennyson

CONTENTS

Prologue

Hugo had admitted to himself long ago that death was something he'd accepted into his life like a friend. Or a lover. It was loyal and consistent. It followed him like a phantom. The cold part of his brain knew it was part of his job. The warmer part, well...that tempted him to believe that he liked it that way.

It was real. It was certain.

Even civilian casualties didn't stir more than the odd pang deep inside him whilst he lay awake at night staring at the bulkhead. If existence had taught him anything, it was that nothing worth having came without cost.

But this was different.

Hugo's hand was trembling as he pressed the gun to the temple of the man who had been his friend. A lifetime's training was screaming at him to fire. But his hand shook. The other man looked up at him through the blood and dirt and all Hugo could feel was breakers of shame and confusion crashing up against his insides. A bitter taste washed up his throat. He cursed everything he could think of: the Service, fate, the *Zero*. The blood pounded in his ears as he raged. How had it come to this?

/

"Gamma, turn to point 5-5-9."

"Commander?"

"There's a break in the defence. Turn in and advance."

"Issue the retreat order, Commander," the cool tones of an Analyst hummed in his headset. "Acknowledge."

"I'm repeating, Fraser," Hugo growled. "And there's no time for repeating. Advance. Take the break. Engage and destroy."

"Yes, Commander." Fraser's voice sounded strained over the comm. Hugo watched the lights on the screen displaying Gamma Company's approach to the resource satellite and the enemy beyond. The Black Dawn Foundation were numerous, but scattered and rudderless. He'd seen it a hundred times before. All ideals and no tactics. They were moving in on the satellite, firing wildly with no cohesive formation or definable strategy.

"Commander," the Analyst hummed in his ear again. "Issue the order to retreat to your unit and acknowledge."

"Negative. X4-18 is at risk."

"Satellite X4-18 is an acceptable loss," the Analyst replied smoothly. "Issue the order to retreat and acknowledge."

Hugo scowled and leaned over the display. The lights reached the black mass of the satellite, swung round and smashed right into the enemy line. Five red dots disappeared, reports from the scanners scrolling along the side of the screen as they did so. Three green dots also vanished.

"Fall back at point 7-5-6," Hugo mumbled to five of his pilots remaining and he saw the dots on the screen move to obey. "Take position. Engage."

Three more red dots disappeared, as did another green. The remaining red dots were forced far apart by the Service fighters. The Analyst had been replaced by a furious captain in his ear, but by the time someone came to pull him from his workstation the remaining rebel fighters had been heavily damaged or destroyed.

Ø

Hugo sat up straight on the bench in the Command Centre brig, staring at the wall. His hands were on his knees and he sat perfectly still and balanced. He played the battle over and over in his head but only moved when the door opened and someone entered his cell. The Service officer, another commander by her pips, looked down at him with a curious expression on her face.

"Commander Hugo?" Hugo didn't bother answering. His name was on the door. He scowled at her. She looked momentarily apprehensive then gathered herself. "Someone hasn't been playing well with others," she said with a smile. Hugo deepened his scowl. Her smile broadened. "I'm Hudson, Colonel Marcus Luscombe's aide," she said. "You've been reassigned."

She held out an envelope. Hugo stared at it for a moment, trying to remember the last time he'd seen anything in hard-copy.

"Don't open it until you're back in your cabin," Hudson continued. "Your contact will meet you at Command Spaceport, terminal 10, tomorrow at the allotted time. Good luck, Captain." And then she turned and left, leaving Hugo blinking in her wake and taking a couple of minutes to process the fact that she had called him *captain*.

Ø

He stood at the meeting point with his pack containing everything he owned, and a plastic cup of coffee from one of the dispensers that tasted like it had engine fuel in it. He glowered around the terminal. Most people moving about were uniformed in the black and grey of Service officers, or the ubiquitous grey jumpsuits of technicians and pilots. They all looked like they had somewhere important to get to. Standing there in plain combat trousers, civilian shirt, and jacket, Hugo ground his teeth as the rush of indignation rose inside him once again.

He swallowed the rest of the sour coffee and scoured the throng, hoping the contact wouldn't turn up, but he did. And on time, Hugo noted with mild surprise.

"Captain Hugo?" The young man was tall, perhaps even a hairs-breadth taller than Hugo, with clear, pale eyes and a broad smile. There was scarring over one eyebrow and a notch missing from one of his ears. He wasn't in uniform either, but worn and practical garments and sturdy boots. His black jacket looked like it had once been part of some sort of uniform but was faded and scuffed beyond recognition and had no trace of insignia. He held out his hand. There was oil under his fingernails. "Commander Ezekiel Webb. Good to meet you." His smile only faltered slightly when Hugo didn't take the offered hand. He gave a slight shrug. "This way," he said.

Hugo followed the commander, noting with disapproval that the other man wore his black hair long. What didn't fall across his face was bound in a thick ponytail down his back. There was also a spacer tattoo on the back of his neck. Hugo felt his reservations broaden.

"You'll like the Zero," Webb said. He had an odd tang to his voice, the remnants of an accent that had the afterthought of American. It had been a long time since he'd heard a Lunar 1 accent. It did not stir happy memories. "She's pulled us through more than our share of shit-storms."

Hugo grunted. Webb seemed impervious to his mood and prattled on, voice light and hands gesturing easily as they paced down the space station's corridor. Hugo slid a sideways glance at his new commander, noting his easy stride, so unlike Hugo's regimented gait which was the result of years of drilling.

"There she is." Webb paused at a viewscreen and pointed. Hugo stepped up and peered out. A craft was docked at the end of the next walkway. Against the vast, star-specked nothingness beyond, she looked tiny. She was also angular, ugly and extremely battered. There was carbon scoring all over her hull and parts of her had clearly once belonged to another, or even several other vessels.

"Don't be fooled, Captain," Webb said and Hugo realised too late that his thoughts must be showing on his face. "Most of that's for show. She's a little hellcat. Trust me."

Hugo suppressed a snort.

"This way," Webb said needlessly, turning down the walkway. Hugo followed, a prickling spreading over his skin as they arrived at the hatch. Webb keyed in a code and it clunked, then slid open. "After you, Captain."

As Hugo stepped onto his first command, the prickling intensified. He blinked. After the dimness of the walkway the ship's corridor was almost too bright.

"Kinjo," Webb called out as the hatch slid shut behind them. Further down the corridor a small figure pulled its head out of a service panel and blinked back at them. "Come and meet the new captain. Captain Hugo, Midshipman Iena Kinjo."

Kinjo came forward cautiously, a computer panel clutched tightly in her hands, and eyes wide as saucers. Her boiler suit was too big for her and there was a smudge of oil across one cheek. Her glance flicked to Webb and then back to Hugo. "Captain Hugo," she said. Her voice was small but she managed a half-decent salute.

"At ease," Hugo said and she relaxed slightly.

"Sir..." she said in a small voice then coughed, straightened her back and tried again. "Sir, is it true you served aboard the *Resolution*?"

Hugo gritted his teeth but hoped his face remained neutral. "That's correct."

Her eyes widened. "Wow…sorry, it's just…uh…"

"Kinjo was in Haven when she was being built," Webb put in, a warm smile on his face.

"My father worked on her, sir," Kinjo continued, still staring at him. "The finest flagship the Service ever commissioned, he said. What's she like, sir?"

"Kinjo," Webb interrupted, possibly seeing the look on Hugo's face. "Take the captain's pack to his cabin, would you?"

"Yes, sir," she said, taking it and throwing curious glances back over her shoulder as she left.

"She's training with our medic and helps out the engineers. I think she's going to be better at taking machines apart than humans, personally, but you gotta give a kid a chance to learn. This way."

Hugo followed Webb down the corridor. Their steps rung on the metal grill floor. He had to admit it looked better on the inside than he had dared hope. All the wall panels were a shining white polyfibre and the lighting was uniform and clear, though the air did have that metallic tang of an older model oxygen generator.

"Research lab and medbay." Webb had paused at a double doorway. The door hissed open and Webb stood aside, letting Hugo precede him into the room. If anything it was even brighter than the corridor. The ceiling was made up entirely of lighting panels and the walls and work surfaces were the same white as the corridor. One bulkhead was made up entirely of wall display screens and blinking equipment. There were bunks embedded in the opposite bulkhead and through glass doors at the end of the room he saw a darkened surgery bay. Two people were bent over one of the workstations, but straightened up as they entered.

"Our researcher, Dr. Spinn," Webb said and the small man with thinning hair blinked at Hugo. His eyes were shining and he swallowed as he took Hugo in. "And this is Anita Rami. Lieutenant Rami," Webb quickly corrected, like he wasn't in the habit of using her rank. "Medic, strategist and has a way with a computer system you wouldn't believe."

Rami stood with the bearing of an actual soldier, arms clasped behind her back and eyes sharp as split glass.

"Captain Kaleb Hugo," Webb introduced him and she bowed slightly, though Hugo could see her giving him an equally appraising glance as he was giving her.

Hugo spared them a nod and turned to leave, Webb at his heels. Webb talked on as they continued down the corridor, pointing out workstations, emergency hatches, stashes of lenslights and medkits. Hugo, having already familiarised himself with the schematics, bit his tongue. But then, he thought bitterly, maybe this kind of crew wasn't aware of the professional methods of trained officers of the Service.

Next was the galley. Like the rest of the ship, it was clean but cluttered, overly-stuffed cupboards of equipment and supplies, hard-copy pictures and posters of sports teams and vintage vehicles tacked to the walls. There was another crew member sat at the table. He was frowning at a computer panel but looked up as they entered. Hugo was pleased to see him get to his feet.

"Sub-Lieutenant More," Webb said. "Chief engineer and technician, maintenance, weapons expert and almost as good a pilot as me." Webb grinned but More just stood there, carefully blank. "Thomas, this is Captain Hugo." More nodded, not speaking, just looking Hugo up and down. Hugo took a deep breath, liking the examination less and less. "How's the port thruster doing?" Webb asked.

"It's sorted, Zeek... Commander," More corrected himself, catching Hugo's eye. He was a broad-shouldered man, dark hair just starting to silver at the temples and with two days' worth of growth on his chin. At least he didn't wear his hair long, Hugo thought. "We were able to get replacement driver plugs this morning."

"Good. Make sure it's all connected in for launch."

"Aye, Commander," More acknowledged, eyes still on Hugo.

Next was the cargo hold and, even though Hugo knew what was there from the reports, he couldn't help but acknowledge a grudging admiration as Webb carried on his commentary.

"Three stealth fighters, all in top notch condition," Webb said as his boots clanged onto deck at the bottom of the ladder. "And if you think you know fast, wait until you see these in action. Damn things move like the devil."

Hugo eyed the fighters. They were newer model one-man fighter craft and, as Webb said, gleaming and expertly maintained, even to Hugo's critical eye. There wasn't even any carbon scoring around the barrels of the pulse cannons. Hugo felt his spirits climb back up a rung. If the Service saw fit to furnish the *Zero* with craft like this, then its missions surely had to have some credibility after all.

"Handy for aiding a retreat as well as an assault. Saved my ass more times than I care to admit," Webb said, patting the side of the nearest one like an old friend.

Hugo heard movement from behind the furthest fighter and the metallic clank of tools being stowed.

"Sub? Bolt?" Webb called. Two men emerged, wiping hands on oily cloths. Big men these were too, broad shouldered and both even taller than Webb. They walked with the wide gait of men used to space decks and both had dark hair cropped close to their heads, making it difficult for Hugo to tell them apart at first glance. When they got closer he could see one engineer had a livid scar across his brow, starting at the left eyebrow and arching up his scalp, pulling his face into a permanent questioning expression. Hugo had two more pairs of eyes look him up and down but at least these men had the decency to mumble, "Cap'n," as they did so. Hugo once again noted how they looked to Webb for guidance and wondered if he should be annoyed or reassured by all this suspicion.

Webb made introductions, and Hugo found out that scar-face was Crewman Subune, or Sub, and the one with the square jaw and black eyes was Crewman Bolt.

"We're about done here," Bolt said, after a pause.

"I still want to replace some of the supports in *Father's* harness," Sub muttered. "But they didn't have the right resistance straps in supply."

"Dolgorukov will have what we need," Webb said.

"*Father?*" Hugo asked.

"The fighter furthest to port," he gestured. "The middle one is *Son* and this one is *Ghost.*" He patted the fighter next to him again. "Our very own Holy Trinity."

"Who pilots them?"

"We're all trained, even Spinn. You never know when and where you might need a pulse cannon or six backing you up." Webb was grinning but the engineers just stood trying to steal glances at Hugo. "And over here, Captain. These are my pride and joy." Webb moved deeper into the hold.

"Land transports?" Hugo ventured, sullenly.

"Not just any land transports," Webb said, pulling a cover off the first shapeless bundle that rested against the hull. "This here's my baby."

Hugo had to admit the motorcycle was impressive. He hadn't seen many in his life apart from in pictures. Like *Father, Son* and *Ghost* it was in pristine condition, not a speck of oil grimed the metal and the chassis was black as space. The tyres were off-road, Hugo noted, and Webb stroked the handles fondly.

"I call her *Sin,*" he grinned.

"You're a baptised Nova, I'm guessing?" Hugo asked.

The bluntness of the question didn't seem to faze Webb who just shrugged. "I couldn't tell you. Most kids on Lunar 1 are that's for sure. I don't remember it if I was. Baptised or not, I figure I'm going to Hell anyway. Might as well have a decent ride." Webb laughed before showing Hugo the other three motorcycles battened down under protective covers against the aft bulkhead.

In the last corner hunkered an ancient four-by-four, dented and battered but with new tyres and gleaming metal work.

"You wouldn't think they would blend in," Webb said. "But most surface-types still use transports like this. On Earth anyway. Moon's a different ball game but dirt-side...fighters and flyers stick out like sore thumbs anywhere but the spaceport cities. And even there it's best we keep a low profile. Now come on, I know you want to see the bridge."

Hugo followed Webb back up the ladder. A couple of twists and turns, and one stairway later, they emerged into a dim space with walls lined by the blinking lights of controls, dominated at one end by a plexiglass viewscreen. The vastness of space yawned beyond it, pinprick stars glinting in the blackness. A control panel spanned the width of the viewscreen with two harnessed chairs bolted in front of it.

"I like to have a co-pilot plus a couple more crew up here on the monitors when we're in drift," Webb said, "depending on the mission. But you can pilot her single-handed if needs be."

Hugo noted with relief that at least the bridge was free of the clutter. All the workstations were clear, even if the chairs and harnesses were worn and every display and command pad he saw was functional and high-quality.

"So, I think that's everything?" Webb span round one of the chairs and dropping himself into it. "Anything I've left out?"

Hugo gave him a narrow glance. "You."

"Me?" Webb blinked. "Well, let me see," he said, counting off on his long fingers. "Pilot, navigator, infiltrator, gunner...know a fair amount about computer systems though not as much as Rami. Munitions I'm good at." He quirked another easy grin. Hugo didn't return it. "Go on then, Captain. You've read the files. What am I missing?" Webb leaned back again, hands interlaced across his chest.

"The files aren't real."

Webb shrugged. "Our Service profiles don't exist. Officially. But you read the public profiles, surely?"

Hugo crossed his arms. "All I could rely on in your public profile was your age. And all that told me was that you are far too young to be in such a commanding position of any vessel. Even a sneak-tub such as this."

Webb's smile took on a frozen look. "Technically, you can't even rely on that, Captain. I have no idea when I was born."

"Commander -"

"Look, Hugo. I'm not all that much younger than you -"

"There's a difference between age and experience. I've been trained since I was six. But you already know that. I do have a Service profile."

"If I were being pedantic, *Captain*, I would say I've been learning what I know longer."

"I meant formal training. Academy training," Hugo countered, feeling his temper flare. "Not picking up tricks from the streets of the colonies. This crew -"

Webb was on his feet. "You can say what you like about me, Captain," he said, leaning in, voice low and smile gone. "But I won't hear a word against this crew. They have fought and bled for the Service every bit as much as any fleet officer, except at a higher cost because they did it in the dark."

"Commander, I suggest you watch your tone."

"And I suggest, Captain, that you pull your head out of your Academy-trained ass before we land at Tranquillity. I'm not about to have another captain screw up a mission trying to prove he's too good for the job."

They stood almost toe-to-toe. Hugo felt heat broiling inside him. If it hadn't been for the years of discipline that had beaten his resolve stiff he would have struck the Commander. As it was, he stood, eyes locked with Webb's, until he trusted his voice to be steady.

"Since I don't assume full command of this vessel until we launch, I'm going to let that slide, Commander. But I would like it noted that any future insubordination will not be tolerated." Webb leant back out of the confrontational stance and folded his arms, still watching him, but didn't respond. Hugo eventually let his eyes slide from the exchange and paced over to the viewscreen. "You will relay my first set of orders to the crew."

"Yes, sir," Webb responded and Hugo heard the smile was back in his voice. This made Hugo bridle but he surpassed it.

"We depart for Tranquillity on the hour," he said, checking the time on his wrist panel. "I want to leave on time. Make sure everything is checked and ready." Hugo looked up at Webb, who carried on gazing at him for a moment longer than was comfortable. Then he made a slight bow.

"Aye, Captain," he said, then paced back to the hatch and left.

Hugo was left alone on the bridge. His bridge. He sighed, feeling something rattle out of him, and dropped himself into a control chair. He stared out at the spread of stars, trying to ignore the chill of nerves warring with the heat of anger inside him. He was so engrossed in trying not to think, that the beeping of an incoming message startled him. "On screen," he said when he'd gathered himself.

Part of the viewscreen opened itself up to display a video feed of an older man with close-cut grey hair, heavy brow and a pristine Service uniform with a spread of pips across the shoulder. "Captain Hugo," he said, nodding. "I'm glad I caught you."

"Colonel Luscombe. Sir," Hugo replied, straightening himself in the chair.

"I was hoping to catch you at Command, but you'd gone by the time I arrived."

"Apologies, sir," Hugo said. "If I'd known you were wanting to see me-"

The colonel shook his head. "No matter. I just wanted to clarify a few things."

"Yes, sir?" Hugo said, fighting back a scowl.

Luscombe paused, eyeing him a minute as if guessing his thoughts. "Firstly," he said. "I will remind you again that every mission report must be made directly to me, and only me. If it's not a Red-Level mission a skeleton report can be made to my aide, but otherwise you find me or you wait. Is that clear?"

"Yes, Colonel."

"Good. I want you to report to me in person after your Tranquillity trip."

"In person, sir?"

"Yes, Captain," Luscombe said. "I have your first Red-Level assignment. And I think it wise we meet in person to go over a few things. I don't have to tell you again about the highly sensitive nature of the responsibility you've been given?"

"No, sir," Hugo said. "You don't."

"I didn't think so. Take my advice. Use this moon trip to get to know the ship and the crew. Not many Zero captains have had that chance before. Listen and learn. This is not an unworthy command, but neither is it an easy one. But Admiral Pharos thinks you're up to it. I don't think I'll be surprising you by saying I'll be reserving my judgement."

"No, Colonel." He ground his teeth for a moment. "Sir?"

The colonel's face was stone again. "Yes?"

"About Black Dawn...I didn't -"

"I can't go through that with you now, Hugo," Luscombe said.

"I just wanted to clarify -"

"We will talk more when you return."

Hugo swallowed. "Yes, sir."

Luscombe nodded. "Good. And one last bit of advice for you..."

"Sir?"

"Take Webb's lead until you get your head in the right place. It's the best way. Trust me."

Hugo managed a stiff nod. "Yes, sir."

"Congratulations again, Captain. See you shortly."

"Yes, sir."

And the screen went blank.

"Knows what he's talking about, does Luscombe. For a Service type, anyway."

Hugo jumped. Webb was leaning against the hatch, his infernal grin back in place.

"Is everything ready?" Hugo asked, recovering and fighting back the surge of temper.

"Sir, yes sir," Hugo couldn't quite determine if the salute Webb gave him was respectful or not. "Shall we cast off? I've yet to know cargo that has delivered itself."

"Begin launch sequences," Hugo said, getting up from the chair. Webb nodded, grinned and took the seat Hugo vacated just as More came onto the bridge and took the other. Rami and Spinn were close behind him. They all gave him nods and wary glances as they filed past. Rami and the researcher settled themselves at workstations and began running checks. Hugo looked around.

"Where's the command chair?" he asked.

"Er," Webb looked over his shoulder, though his hands didn't stop moving over the control panel. "My ass is in it. Sorry, Captain. Guess we've never had need for a proper captain's chair before."

"You've had captains before me," Hugo gritted. "What did they do?"

"They died," Webb muttered.

"Zeek," More said, and Hugo could swear it sounded like the older man was scolding his commander. "Captain," he said, turning to Hugo. "There is a harness on the spare workstation at the back. Would you like me to have a command chair fitted?"

Hugo tore his glare from the back of Webb's head to look at More. "Thank you, Sub-Lieutenant. We also need to have a word about your oxygen generator."

"Yes sir," More nodded. "I've been wanting to upgrade it for some time."

"What's stopped you?"

More swallowed, glanced at Webb and then turned back to his panel.

"Pirates don't need oxygen like everyone else, Commander?"

"Privateers, if we're talking labels, Captain." The fact that there seemed to be genuine amusement in the commander's voice made Hugo want to snarl. "And yes, we need oxygen. But where would pirates, as you say, get a Service-grade generator?"

"We'll pretend we stole it," Hugo muttered.

Webb shook his head. "Whatever you say, Captain. Permission to contact control."

Hugo sighed and started buckling himself into the last remaining chair. "Permission granted."

Hugo watched his crew complete the pre-launch checks and contact spaceport control, looking out for anything missed or any corners cut but all he saw was a group of people so familiar with their ship it was like an extension of their own bodies. Whatever else happened, Hugo reasoned, at least it was looking less likely he'd be blown up or drifted by his own crew.

"Checks complete and control has cleared us, sir," More said.

"Set a course for Tranquillity and take us away."

"Yes, sir."

There was a clang and a slight rumble in the metal under his feet as the Zero detached from her walkway. The stars out the front viewscreen dipped and then levelled out. Webb and More's hands skated over the panel without them having to look and the ship glided away from the Command Centre. As soon as they were at a safe distance Hugo commanded full thrusters. The ship shuddered around him and Hugo dug his fingers into his harness. The juddering smoothed out as the engines reached capacity. The ship turned, and a creamy curve of the Earth came into view, the fingernail of the moon beyond it. "Course set in, sir. Approximate arrival at Tranquillity in six hours."

"Good," Hugo said, taking lead from the others and unbuckling his harness. "Now, tell me more about this contact we're going to meet."

"Point."

"I'm sorry?" Hugo said, turning to Spinn with a frown.

Spinn turned in his chair, eyes wide as if just realising who he had corrected. "Sorry, sir. *Point*, sir. Not 'contact'."

"What?"

"He means, 'contact' is Service-speak, Captain Hugo," More explained. "It's best to refer to our connections as 'points'."

Hugo ground his teeth. "Very well. Tell me more about this point."

"Anton Dolgorukov, Captain," Webb said, leaning back in his control chair and idly steering the ship with twitches of his fingers. "He's a no-one. We trade machine parts with him."

"Does he have a record?"

Webb snorted and everyone else looked away. There was a pause before Webb looked over his shoulder at him. "Sorry, sir. It's just...everyone has a record. Even you do, now. It's the ones without records you need to watch out for."

"Tell me more about him."

"Rami?" Webb asked. "What's Dolgorukov's sheet look like at the moment?"

Rami tapped on her keypad, eyes skimming text on the display. "Nothing new from last time. Theft. Fraud. Aiding fugitives. Nothing proved, it's all Service Analyst data."

"Okay, Captain?"

"Not really," Hugo said. "What does he steal?"

Webb sighed. "Trust me, Captain. He's not dangerous. He's a mechanic. He cobbles together oxygen units, mopeds, repairs transports. He buys the odd load of stolen parts but he makes and sells cheap things that people on the outskirts of Tranquillity would never normally be able to afford."

"Thief with honour, then?" Hugo drawled.

Webb actually laughed. "Don't let him hear you accusing him of having honour. Look, Captain: Rami, Bolt and I will drive out to his yard, give him the cargo of parts and then we're out. We're keeping up appearances and maintaining goodwill. We'll probably not even have to pay a second cycle's berthing."

"I'm coming with you."

Webb span his seat round, eyes a little wide. "Uh, Captain?"

"What?"

"It's just..." Webb blinked, exchanged looks with More.

"Is there a problem, Commander?"

Webb shrugged. "No problem, Captain. It's just greenguns usually..."

"I am not a greengun Commander Webb," Hugo grated.

"No sir," Webb said, having the decency to look a little embarrassed. "What I meant to say, sir, is that all...all newcomers...I mean..." He scratched his head. "All the other captains took on more of an...observatory role, if you get me. For the first few missions at least."

"And where did that get them?"

Webb blinked. "Good point."

"I'm coming with you," Hugo stated. "If I am to command this ship and these missions I need to know and understand them. Lieutenant?"

"Yes, sir?" Rami said.

"Have everything we've got on Dolgorukov and our trade sent to the display in my cabin, please."

"Yes, sir," said Rami, turning back to her workstation and started entering commands.

"Let me know when we're preparing to dock." Hugo didn't wait for a response but left down the corridor toward the cabins.

When the door to the captain's cabin slid shut behind him he leant against it with a sigh and rubbed his temples against a rising headache. When he felt able to face it he lifted his head. The cabin was tiny. There was one narrow bunk sunk into the port bulkhead, a foldaway table with a chair bolted to the floor beside it and a couple of lockers. His pack was on the bed. There was a wall display above the table with a little blinking light in the corner showing waiting information.

He pulled the pack up onto the table and began unpacking whilst queuing up Rami's data. It didn't take him long to stow the couple of hard-copy books he'd brought with him and the little clothing he had. He would have to find time to get some more. He'd spent so long in uniform that he had pitifully little civilian clothing and even less that was suitable for this assignment.

Last of all he pulled out the lockbox that contained his guns. He keyed in the combination and took them out, laying them on the table side by side. They hadn't let him bring his Service-issue semis with him. These were new, unmarked and probably with no official licence anywhere. They were black, not silver like his service guns, and Hugo felt they carried more weight than the ones he had before.

He sat down at the table to clean them whilst flicking through the data from Lieutenant Rami. There was pitifully little there: a copy of Dolgorukov's criminal record (nothing proven, as Rami has said) and a little information on his repair and maintenance business. There was also a copy of the Zero's manifest, including the consignment of parts they were to deliver to their point.

It only took him a few minutes to go through it all but Hugo went through it backwards and forwards anyway and then searched for whatever else he could find in public records that might be relevant. He found little and tried searching Service records and found even less. He chewed his lip for a minute then shook his head. Webb seemed confident enough. Then again, he was beginning to wonder whether Webb wasn't confident about everything.

He finished reassembling the guns, strapped them into his shoulder holster and set it aside. Then he lay down on the bunk, threw his arm over his eyes to block out the view of the cabin, and continued trying not to think.

II

"Captain?"

Hugo started, hardly believing he'd fallen asleep. For a moment he was horribly disoriented, the metal walls of the bunk swirling and refusing to solidify into something real. Then everything came screaming back along with his headache.

"Hugo here," he mumbled.

More's face appeared on the cabin display. "We're entering moon space now, Captain."

Hugo sighed and sat up. "Do we have a dock?"

"Not yet, sir. Webb's just on the comm with harbour control."

"Fine. Is the Jeep ready and loaded?"

"Yes, sir."

"I'll be up in a minute."

The display went blank. Hugo pushed back the clench of nerves in his belly and heaved himself upright, straightened his clothes, strapped on his holster and shrugged his coat over the top. The ship was shuddering again as he made his way back onto the bridge. Hugo got himself back to the workstation chair and strapped himself in just as the *Zero* lurched as it came under the influence of the moon's artificial gravity.

Webb and More were at the controls. Hugo watched as the two men mumbled to each other and used the thrusters and dampers to steer the ship between the skyways towards the harbour. He watched the space-scraper towers of Tranquillity, a thousand bright lights against the or-ange-tinged sky, rise out of the view screen. Flashes of flyers zoomed back and forth, and soon the entire viewscreen was taken up with sheet metal and blinking lights.

"Shit, More, watch out on your left."

"I see it," More mumbled.

"Where exactly are we?"

Webb turned in his seat, making Hugo extremely nervous. "Tranquil-lity Northside harbour, Captain. Don't tell me you've only ever been to the classy ports?"

"Are there any classy ports on the moon?"

Webb barked a laugh and turned back to the panel, much to Hugo's relief. "Not a fan of the moon, huh?" The ship shuddered and lurched but Webb's hands danced on the controls and it smoothed out. A flyer passed dangerously close to the viewscreen but neither of the pilots flinched. "Relax, Captain. Could be worse. Could be Haven."

With a clang the ship settled into its berth. Webb stretched and More set about running shut down checks. Hugo unbuckled his harness and went for a better look out the viewscreen. Despite himself, he was impressed. The Northside Harbour was a clamorous and jumbled affair and the berth they'd been given was only just big enough. There was a hulking freighter on one side of them and a barque on the other that wasn't big, but was badly berthed. Webb and More had brought them right down in between with room to spare.

He glanced at Webb and saw he was grinning.

"Right. Shall we get this over with?"

"Sir, yes, sir," Webb said a little too cheerfully. Hugo noticed he had changed into a scruffier t-shirt and that there was knife in a sheath strapped to his forearm. He'd also put on a battered baseball cap, pulled it down low on his face, his long black tail of hair pulled through at the back. He gave Hugo a glance up and down as he pulled his jacket on. "Urm, sir... you're really coming with us?"

"Yes."

Webb sighed, glanced at More for support, but More was still purposefully running diagnostics on the control panel and not looking up. Hugo saw Webb steel himself.

"Very well sir. But... can I just.." He reached out.

"What are you doing?"

"Not everyone knows you're ex-Service. Word'll get around fast, especially if Dolgorukov has anything to do with it. But until then it's probably best not to look too... regimented."

"What are you going to do?"

"Just.. hold still."

Gritting his teeth Hugo begrudgingly allowed Webb to mess up his hair, turn up the collar on his jacket and untuck his shirt. The commander stood back with an appraising look.

"That will have to do. Don't shave for a couple of days. And try not to stand so straight. You're disenfranchised, remember."

Hugo glared and ran his hands through his hair. "I can't believe this. Come on then. Let's go."

"Sir," Webb nodded and gestured towards the door.

Rami and Bolt were waiting in the hold with the loaded four-by-four.

Webb climbed into the driver's seat and Hugo climbed up next to him. Rami and Bolt clambered into the back, sitting either side of a large metal cargo container on a lifter. There was a rush of cold air as the hold hatch opened and the ramp lowered, bringing with it a tangy and metallic smell of oil and mass-produced air. A wall of noise rushed in, the clanking of motors and the whining of flyers, the hum of electricity and the clatter of a million people and machines.

"Here we go, Captain. Still sure you wanna come and play?"

"Just drive."

Webb sniggered and the started the engine. The Jeep rumbled down the hold ramp and hit the tarmac of the harbour. Hugo felt a little light headed and took a few deep breaths to try and adjust to the air. They wove between other ships' landing gear and made it out onto the exitway.

"Let me know if you're gonna hurl, Captain," Webb said. "I can pull over."

"Just keep going," he snapped again, breathing deeply until the dizziness passed.

Ships of all shapes and sizes were crammed into the berths on either side of them and people were moving everywhere, zooming around on mopeds or shouting orders, clanking tools and wrestling with cargo. Their Jeep joined the queue of other vehicles on the exitway waiting to leave the harbour and Hugo craned his neck for a better look ahead. There were distinctly few hovercraft. He'd never seen a place with so many wheeled vehicles that wasn't Earth.

"Here's the manifest, Zeek," Rami said, handing a panel through to Webb as they waited in the queue. Hugo took it before Webb could and glanced at it, but it looked exactly the same as the copy he'd seen in his cabin.

"See, Captain," Webb smiled, taking the panel off him. "We're legitimate businessmen here."

"Do you even know what it is your selling?"

"We're not selling him anything," Webb replied, easing the four-by-four forward as the queue moved. "We're giving it to him."

"You're *giving*...what, no credit?"

Webb shook his head. "We owe Dolgorukov. This'll keep him sweet until we need the next favour."

"So we're *giving* him Service-level machine parts...in case we ever need a favour?"

"It pays to stay in Anton's good graces," Webb said. "You wouldn't believe what he can get his hands on."

"Captain...?" Hugo twisted in his seat to face Rami. She glanced at Webb and then back. "In all seriousness, sir. Dolgorukov's not dangerous. As far as points go he's got to be one of the lowest risk. But, even so..."

"Yes, Lieutenant?"

She swallowed. "No disrespect, sir. I just think its important you realise that we've spent a long time building up our relationship with him -"

"Rami," Webb warned.

"I just think the captain shouldn't -"

"Rami," he said again. "It's fine. Like the Captain said, learn by doing."

Rami nodded. Hugo didn't say anything, just turned in his seat to look back out the windscreen, trying the ignore the prickle that crept up his spine. They were nearing the exit terminal. The flyer in front moved forward and the gates of the terminal creaked shut behind it. Out of the corner of his eye he saw Webb pull his cap down lower on his face and slouch further in his seat, fingers drumming on the wheel. A glance in the rear view showed Rami and Bolt with backs straight and arms folded. No one seemed nervous exactly, but there was tension strung between them like wire and it seemed they were all purposely not looking at him. He shifted in his seat and glared ahead.

The exit terminal gates heaved open. Webb moved the Jeep into the bay and they clanged shut behind them. A bored looking customs agent took a swipe of all their ID cards and glanced at the manifest on Webb's panel. They were then waved back out the other side. Hugo let out a gust of breath when the gates of the harbour closed behind them.

"Piece of cake, eh Captain?" Webb said.

They went down the ramp onto a very busy groundway. Webb steered them amongst the mass of traffic easily enough but it was still an odd sensation to be in amongst so many ground vehicles. Hugo leaned forward to see the towering spacescrapers blink up into the darkness above. The lights from the skyways snaked between the towering buildings and made him feel very low down.

The rest of the journey went by in silence. Hugo watched the thronging streets of Northside Tranquillity pass by. The neon was not helping his headache, but he didn't close his eyes. He kept sneaking glances at Webb and at Rami and Bolt in the back. Rami tapped away on the computer panel, the light washing her skin sickly white. Bolt sat straight and stared out the window. Then he had to look back out the front again because the unfamiliar motion of the wheeled vehicle was making him nauseous. He blinked as the Jeep climbed to the apex of a ramp and emerged onto a better-lit level of the city. The traffic was thinner and they picked up speed.

Finally they turned another corner onto a virtually empty side street and pulled up beside some unmarked gates. There was no sign of any control panel or comm unit. They just sat there for a moment before Webb leaned out the driver window, grinned and waved up at one of the cameras mounted on the wall.

"Hey, Anton," he yelled. Hugo cringed. "Long time no see." Nothing happened. "Come on, Anton. We've got presents." Still nothing. Webb slumped back into his seat with a frown.

"You don't suppose he's still mad at us do you?" Rami asked.

Hugo glared at Webb. "Mad?"

"Nah," Webb said, waving his hand. "He couldn't still be mad..."

"Want me to try and get him on his personal comm?" Rami said.

Webb opened his mouth to reply just as there was a clunk and a hiss and the gates started to open. Webb cast Hugo a glance but the smile on his face was a little *too* relieved. "See?"

"I suppose there's no chance there's an ambush waiting?" Hugo said.

"Not Anton's style," Webb said and drove the car through the gates and into the cluttered yard beyond. Twisted metal and broken machinery were piled high against the walls. There were a couple of gutted flyers and more sheet metal than Hugo could quite believe was all legitimate scrap. There were a couple of people in overalls in amongst the piles of junk but they had stopped work to watch them as they parked up.

"Ezekiel Webb, you god-damned asshole," bellowed a voice from across the yard. "Where the hell have you been?"

"We'd've been here sooner, Anton, if you'd opened the gates," Webb said as he climbed out. Hugo got out too and stood close to the Jeep, getting a good look at the point as he came over the oil-stained yard towards them. He certainly didn't look threatening, even storming towards them brandishing a computer panel. He was short and round, hair thinning on the top and his skin had the pale, doughy look of someone who had spent their entire life under artificial light.

"*Baszódj meg*. You're a cheeky sonabitch, Webb," Dolgorukov drew level and folded his arms over his ample paunch. "You're lucky I don't... who's this?" His sharp eyes looked Hugo up and down.

"New captain," Webb said.

"Another one?"

Webb shrugged. "We're demanding."

"Demanding. Yeah. That's the word," the man said, still glaring.

"We come bearing gifts, Anton," Webb said with another disarming smile just as Rami and Bolt came round from the back of the Jeep, pushing the crate on it's lifter. Dolgorukov narrowed his eyes at Webb then pushed past the taller man to open it.

"Here, Anton," Rami said, handing over her panel which once again displayed the cargo manifest.

"Thank you, Anita," the short man said, taking it from her and glancing down it. "Still hanging out with these reprobates? You disappoint me, child."

"They're my reprobates, Anton," Rami replied with a small smile.

Dolgorukov chuckled. "Yes, I suppose they are. And good thing too. If it weren't for you and More the whole crew would have drifted themselves years ago." Bolt grunted and folded his arms, glaring. Dolgorukov looked up from the panel to the big man and his face suddenly cracked into a wide smile and he slapped Bolt on the shoulder, not something Hugo would have been prepared to do, even for a handsome amount of credit. "You know I'm only kidding, big guy. Webb, this load is almost enough to make me like you again."

"What did I tell you, Hugo?" Webb smiled "No one stays mad at us for long."

"Hugo?" Dolgorukov looked up, realisation slackening his face. "Kaleb Hugo?"

Hugo froze. He glanced around his crew but they were looking at him, faces suddenly still. "Yes," he said carefully.

Dolgorukov ran a hand over his balding pate and took a breath. "I... I thought I recognised you."

"Anton" Webb started, voice low.

"No," Dolgorukov said, holding up a hand. "No, it's fine. You want to hire ex-Service that's your choice. I'm not one for poking my nose where it don't belong." Webb snorted. "Not when it's not in my interest anyway. It's just..." He looked at Hugo again. If anything his skin was even paler. Hugo felt panic fluttering in the bottom of his stomach. "I know it didn't work out too well for you but...I knew some miners on that satellite...on X4-18. Whatever else happened, you saved a lot of lives that day."

Hugo let out a breath and managed a nod, his throat tight. Dolgorukov ducked his head, looked from him to Webb and his smile was back.

"And anyway," he continued, more brightly, "you know what they say. Better the sewer than the Service. And they don't come much more sewer than this lot." Hugo glared at Webb, expecting a sly remark but his commander wasn't looking at him. "I would stay mad at you, Zeek," Dolgorukov continued, "but you've saved my bacon. I've been out of burn connectors for weeks and I've got a dozen folk clamouring for gravgen units."

"I thought Harvey brought you stacks of those from Haven?" Webb asked.

"Haven't seen hide nor hair of that one for months," Dolgorukov replied, thumbing through the manifest.

"You haven't?" Webb asked, frowning.

Dolgorukov shrugged, handing Rami's panel back to her. "Don't ask me, Webb. That girl's a law unto herself."

"Where do you want this?" Bolt said, patting the crate.

"Over in the store, thanks," Dolgorukov said, pointing.

Bolt started to steer the lifter in the direction of the large metal structure on the other side of the yard, giving Webb a pointed look as he passed.

"Oh, Anton, alright if Bolt grabs some resistance straps? We need to replace the ones in *Father* and he's picky about these things."

"Help yourself," Dolgorukov said, tapping more commands into his own scratched panel. "There should be a couple in the store. Webb," he said, not looking up. "Can I have a word?"

Hugo didn't miss the quick glance the point threw at him. Webb seemed to catch it too.

"Yeah, sure..."

The two men wandered off a little distance, heads bent together and started muttering to each other in Hungarian.

"Should I be worried?" Hugo asked.

Rami came up beside him and shook her head. "I don't think so, Captain. We'll be on our way soon."

Hugo nodded, glancing around the cluttered yard and forcing himself not to shift on his feet. Bolt returned, straps in hand. Hugo saw Dolgorukov nod and pat Webb's shoulder.

"Now clear off," the point said in a louder voice, turning to pace away. "I need to get working on these gravgens."

"No rest for the wicked, Anton," Webb called after him. Hugo watched Webb as he watched the short man disappear into the store. Then he looked back. "Let's split."

They clambered back into the Jeep and Webb started the engine.

"What did he want to talk to you about, Commander?" Hugo said as they pulled back out onto the busy groundway.

Webb glanced up into the rear-view but whether it was to catch Rami's eye or to check the traffic Hugo couldn't tell. "He wanted to ask me whether having you as the captain was likely to screw up the deals we have with the Service reps that get us engine parts."

Hugo pondered for a moment. "Will it? For all they know I was dishonourably discharged."

Webb looked at him. "I'm willing to bet that most folk, Service or not, feel the same way that Anton does. They'd've done the same thing in your place. If they had the balls, that is."

Hugo grunted.

"It's those Analysts Hugo. They'll get you every time. You should never piss off the Analysts."

"Well I know that now," Hugo muttered.

Webb snorted. "Well done, Hugo. That was almost a joke."

"Captain," Hugo corrected.

Webb ducked his head. "Sorry. Captain."

"Zeek," Rami said.

Webb blinked. "Yeah, yeah. Hang on, I'll pull in."

"What's happening?"

"I'm just checking in on the moonframe, Captain. I need a grounded workstation for that."

"Rami likes to keep tabs on the set up of all local systems," Webb said as the Jeep pulled up onto a walkway. "It's a rather tedious hobby of hers."

"Commander," she said coolly. "If you want me to be able to get into and around every system I need to know if they upgrade. I'll see you back at the *Zero*."

"Bolt," Webb said over his shoulder. "You go with her."

"I don't need a bodyguard, Webb," Rami muttered.

"I know that better than most, Anita. But still. You're more likely to get a seat on the shuttle if Bolt is there, right?"

Rami sighed. "Very well. Try not to lose the new captain. Captain."

"Lieutenant. Crewman."

"Cap'n," Bolt mumbled and they climbed out the back of the Jeep and onto the brightly lit walkway before disappearing into the crowd.

"You hungry?"

Hugo blinked at his commander. He hadn't thought about it before, but suddenly his stomach clenched uncomfortably. All he had had that day was that cup of engine-oil coffee at the spaceport that morning, that morning that already seemed a million years ago. "Yes."

"Great. I know just the place."

Webb pulled them back into the traffic and lapsed into silence as he steered through the tangled groundways. Hugo had been trying his best to keep his bearings but now he just gave up. The hive of lights and metal that arched above them in a never-ending stream of neon and orange went on and on.

"Is this a first for you then, Captain?"

Hugo kept staring out the windsceen. "I've been to Tranquillity before. For conferences."

"Uh-huh," Webb said with understanding. "I'm guessing that was Southside?"

"Yes."

"Enclosed walkways? Air-conditioning?"

Hugo ignored him and clutched at the seat as the Jeep lurched under him and made its way up a ramp and through an entrance in the side of one of the megablocks. The sign over the entrance declared it to be Imbrium Block. Three of the letters were blacked out and the gate had been wedged open with an empty crate.

"Where are we going, Commander?"

"For lunch," Webb replied, pulling over into a parking bay. "Best goulash in town, trust me." Hugo mumbled under his breath as he climbed out of the Jeep and followed Webb across the parking pool to the wall of express lifts. "Level 102," Webb said when the lift doors closed behind them. There was a judder and a hiss and then they were zooming upwards. "Captain?" Webb said in a low voice, casting him a sideways glance from under the peak of his baseball cap.

"What?"

"Do you trust me yet?"

Hugo narrowed his eyes. "No."

Webb paused, then shrugged. "Too bad. Just take it on faith then that you want me to do the talking here."

The lift juddered to a halt and the doors hissed open. Hugo followed Webb as he strode out onto the broad walkway. "I thought you said we were going for lunch?"

"We are."

It was a wide and busy level, people rushing back and forth with panels and tools and grim expressions. One wall was a bank of windows looking out onto the blinking neon mess of Tranquillity. The ceiling was high above them and on the far left of the walkway were clustered a myriad of establishments: repair shops, tool merchants, computer supply outlets, transport rental and cubby-hole installations that proclaimed they could service ID badges. Whatever that meant. There were also various stalls and stands selling food from all corners of the Orbit. The smell of spices, cooking oil and herbs warred with the smell of too many people and oxygen that had been recycled too many times.

"Imbrium's a spacer block," Webb said as the ducked and weaved amongst the crowd.

"You don't say," Hugo mumbled, dodging around a harassed tech with trolley full of wiring.

Webb chuckled. "Good thing for you to learn early, Captain. The Service may set the rules, but the spacers play the game."

"And do you consider yourself Service or spacer?"

Webb grinned again. "Like you have to ask."

They turned off the main walkway and into a narrower passage. Most of the booth space was boarded up. There was one large unit right at the end of the passage with its large double doors open. A sign above the doors read *Sturm Hafen.*

"It means -"

"I know what it means," Hugo said.

Webb shrugged. "Sorry, Captain. Didn't think the Academy had any need to teach anything other than English and Japanese."

"How long is this going to take?" Hugo said as they got closer. "I have orders to report to Luscombe at Command."

"Not long," Webb said. "Besides, you said you were hungry."

As they drew closer he noticed a lifter pulled up at the entrance. It was loaded with chairs and tables broken into pieces and boxes full of shattered glass as well as a couple of smashed digiprint frames and other unidentifiable wreckage.

"Shit," Webb mumbled as he moved past it.

Hugo frowned then blinked as they moved into the dim interior of the windowless bar. When his eyes got used to the gloom he could make out a wide open space, cluttered with battered tables and chairs. There were booths along one wall and a pool table in one corner. A real one too, not a simulator. The bar took up the length of the room on the right. The mix of bottles on the shelves behind it was unlike anything Hugo had never seen. There were spirits he'd never heard of and some of the labels he couldn't even read. There were a few people in the booths with plates of food and jugs of drink, sitting alone or in groups of two or three, conversing in low voices or working on computers or the panels built into the table tops. No one looked up as they entered.

As they moved further in Hugo saw that the far end of the room was lacking in furniture. There was a girl sweeping and the sound of tinkling glass and men were piling up the remains of another broken table. There were scorch marks on the floor and wall, and one of the men had a bandaged arm. A very large man with his back to them was overseeing the proceedings, muttering in German.

"Jesus, Jaeger," Webb said. "What the hell happened?"

The large man turned round. He had very dark brows and hair and his frown was heavy. There was a cut with some livid bruising on his forehead and his lip was split. "Webb," he said. "What the fuck do you want?"

Webb shrugged and took a seat at the bar. He still moved easily but Hugo was sure he could detect a certain tension across his commander's shoulders. "Just here to eat, man. If there's any of your kitchen left?"

The big man sighed and rubbed his face. He barked something to the girl with the broom, who nodded, put the broom aside and scurried through some doors at the back. He then came round the other side of the bar. "Kitchens are open. What do you want?"

"Two of whatever. We ain't fussy."

The big man snorted, tapped some commands into a panel built into the bar. "That I know is true."

"What happened?" Webb said, looking around.

"What do you think happened? Upstart kids thinking they're rebels."

"Anyone hurt?"

"None of my lot. The snots won't be back in a hurry though," Jaeger said as he poured three glasses of something clear.

"Did this get reported?" Hugo said.

"Hugo," Webb warned.

Jaeger eyed Hugo keenly. "Who's this, then?"

Webb took a deep breath. "Jaeger, Meet the *Zero*'s new captain."

"Looks like Service scum to me."

Hugo riled and stood.

"Hugo, sit *down*," Webb barked.

Hugo held the big man's calm, dark gaze for a moment longer then sat himself down. Webb looked a bit pale.

"Look Jaeger. We didn't..."

Jaeger snorted again then held a glass out to both Webb and Hugo. "Relax, boy," he said. "I got a pounding headache. Don't feel like picking a fight with ex-Service types today. Now drink." He held up his glass. "*Prost*."

Hugo watched as Webb and Jaeger downed the clear liquid in one swallow. Hugo sniffed his and blinked as his eyes started to water. He felt Jaeger's gaze on him and followed suit. He coughed, fire burning down his throat.

"Atta boy," Jaeger said, refilling the glasses. "Oh, I forgot. Webb, some-one came by looking for you a while back."

Webb paused with his glass part way to his mouth. "Oh?"

"*Ja*," Jaeger said. He drained his glass, wiped his mouth on his sleeve and peered at Webb. "Short fucker. No hair. Odd-looking."

"Ain't ringing any bells," Webb said, just as the girl reappeared and put two bowls of a rich-smelling stew down in front of them.

"He didn't find you?"

Webb shrugged and turned his attention to his food. The thick scent was enough to make Hugo's stomach clench and he picked up his fork and began to eat. Hugo had to admit it was good, heavily seasoned, and had sizeable chunks of meat.

"Real beef?" Hugo asked, looking at Jaeger again who was pouring himself another glass from the bottle.

Jaeger smiled. "You wanting to see my license, Service-boy?"

"Listen, Jaeger," Webb cut in. "Have you seen Harvey lately?"

Jaeger held the glass against his forehead, frowning. "Harvey?"

"Yeah," Webb said, chewing. "Marilyn Harvey. Haven spacer. Pilots the *Phoenix*?"

Jaeger put the glass down, still frowning. "I remember. No, not for some time. I think I remember hearing she got herself in some shit."

Webb paused, fork halfway to his mouth. "Yeah?"

Jaeger shrugged, cleared away the glasses. "That's what I heard."

"Deep shit?"

"Is there any other kind?"

Webb blinked slowly. "What exactly did you hear?"

"It was a while ago. Something to do with the Splinters. I don't know what. If she's got any sense she's gone to ground."

Webb took another mouthful and frowned into his bowl.

"How'd you like it, Captain?" Jaeger said.

Hugo swallowed his mouthful. "It's good," he said.

Jaeger grinned. "That's what real meat does for you. Now, is that it? I know I owe you, Webb, but I've got rather a lot to get done."

"Nothing else, Jaeger," Webb said, scraping the last of his food from his bowl. "Just thought the new captain might want to see a true Tranquillity hotspot."

"You're a cheeky bastard," Jaeger said. Hugo didn't think it sounded like he was entirely joking. "You wanna be careful. One of these days your mouth's gonna get you a bullet in the back."

Webb held the large man's gaze whilst he swallowed the last of the stew. "You're one to talk," he said, face splitting into a nasty grin.

Jaeger tensed. Hugo stopped himself reaching for his gun with an effort. Webb just sat there, grinning, not breaking eye contact.

Finally Jaeger laughed, clapped Webb on the shoulder. "You little shit. Get the hell out of here. I've got a bar to rebuild."

"See you around, Jaeger," Webb said, standing.

"Not too bloody soon, I hope," Jaeger replied, turning and heading back toward the kitchens. "Oh," he said, turning. "What you want me to say to your bald friend if he comes back?"

Webb shrugged. "Some variation of fuck off?"

Jaeger smirked. "I'll think of something."

"Come on, Captain," Webb mumbled, suddenly not smiling. "Let's get out of here."

Ø

"What happened to his bar?" Hugo asked as they drove back through the groundways towards the harbour.

"Jaeger's got a long list of enemies," Webb said, frowning out of the windscreen.

"Why?"

"He fought on the other side."

"In what?"

Webb looked at him. "Governor McCullough's Revolution."

Hugo blinked. "He fought *against* an independent Lunar State?" Webb nodded. "Why?"

Webb shrugged. "He liked the moon the way it was. Lost him a lot of friends though."

"Why does he stay?"

"It's his home."

"And the bald man that was looking for you? What was that all about?"

"You know as much as me on that one, Captain."

There was silence as Webb steered them in and out of the traffic. It was coming up to the night cycle but the traffic on the groundways, walkways and flyways seemed as busy as ever.

"Which side did you fight on?"

"In the revolution?" Webb laughed. "Jesus, Hugo. I was still dodging youth unit officials and stealing food from dumpsters on Lunar 1 during that whole mess. Only difference to me was that there were slightly more bullets to dodge. What about you?"

"I was still an under-cadet in the Academy. My parents and one of my sisters fought against the rebels though."

"Did they make it?"

"My parents did. My sister didn't."

Webb didn't say anything. Hugo continued to watch the traffic.

"Who's Harvey?" He eventually asked.

"Just another point," Webb said, frowning out of the windscreen. He didn't offer anything else and Hugo didn't push. With the good food and strong drink swirling inside him and everything he had already seen and heard that day throbbing through his head, he was more than happy to leave it.

Ø

Webb hung back and let Hugo precede him onto the Zero's bridge. The new captain had done tolerably well, considering. At least he hadn't screwed up any connections or got them shot.

"Rami," Webb bent over her at her workstation, keeping his voice low. "I think Marilyn might be in some trouble."

"What else is new?" Rami said, not breaking in her typing.

"Think this might be real trouble. Splinter-type trouble," Webb murmured, glancing over to watch Hugo as he walked up to More and started issuing launch orders. "Can you dig around and see what you can find?"

Rami nodded, looking grave. "Although if she's gone to ground, I won't be able to find anything."

"I'll be more worried if you do find something. Just take a look, okay?"

"Okay, Zeek," Rami said, then she smiled at him. "I'm sure she's fine."

Webb nodded and straightened. "Find anything new on the moon-frame?"

Rami shook her head. "There's been a couple of upgrades since we were last here, but both routine."

"Good. Buckle up. I think the Captain's taking us back to Command."

"Command? Again?" Rami blinked.

"He has orders to report to Luscombe."

"It's not gonna look good, docking at Service Command twice in two days."

Webb shrugged. "We'll manage. Everything okay on the checks?"

"All clear," she said, closing down the reports on her workstation display.

"Commander?"

Webb turned. Kinjo was stood there, panel clutched in hand and eyes flicking between Webb and Hugo. Hugo was bent over More's control panel watching the sub-lieutenant run the rest of the pre-launch checks.

"All secure below?" Webb said, taking the panel from Kinjo.

"Yes, Commander," she said. "How'd it go with Dolgorukov?"

"Well," Webb said, checking a couple of reports and handing the panel back to the midshipman. "You stocked that cargo just right. He was pleased with the burn connectors."

He could see her fighting a smile. Then she sobered, glanced at Hugo and stepped closer. "How'd the captain do?"

Webb sighed. "Still early days, Kinjo. Get yourself strapped in below. Sub and Bolt ready to go?"

"Yes, sir," she said, saluting.

Webb laughed. "Good. Off you go."

"Commander?"

Webb turned towards Hugo. "Yes, sir?"

"We are ready to launch. Set in a course for Command."

"Yes, sir." Webb dropped himself back into the control chair next to More and strapped himself in. He tried to exchange glances with More to see if he could pick up what his sub-lieutenant was thinking. But More's face was its usual impassive mask.

Webb sighed again and let his hands run the start-up commands without really concentrating. More must have detected his distraction because he contacted harbour control and confirmed the launch. Webb just waited for the command and then engaged the engines. The *Zero* hummed and he felt her rock underneath him as she lifted off the ground. He glanced at the displays with half an eye to ensure they kept a plenty of distance between the ships berthed on either side and soon felt the ship pull itself free of the gravity. The sky outside the viewscreen melted from orange to black and then there was nothing but the candle-flames of stars amongst the vastness of space.

Webb programmed in the course and then took the ship round in an arc. Earth came into view, swirled blue and white like a marble. The Zero settled into her course and Hugo ordered full thrusters from his seat at the back of the bridge.

Webb smiled and looked over his shoulder. "You want to take her up to full, Captain?" Webb swore he almost saw a flicker of excitement in Hugo's dark eyes. The older man hesitated a fraction of a second then unbuckled his harness and came across the deck. Webb unstrapped himself and vacated the chair. Hugo sat down and for a moment just stared at the panel. Webb hovered, one hand on the back of the chair. He noticed both More and Rami sneaking glances.

Hugo reached out for the controls, glanced at the meter readings on the display and then took her in hand. Hugo took control with the fluidity of instinct, easing the *Zero* along her course without any wavering from the planned path mapped out on the display.

"She might look like she's held together with wire and gum, but her engine's top grade," Webb said. "More has her autopilot programmed like a dream, but manual is when she really shows her colours. Don't be afraid to push her."

Hugo appeared to be only half-listening. His hands were finding the commands easily enough and now he barely looked at the meter readings. Webb wondered whether Hugo even remembered the rest of them were there. He folded his arms and watched, keeping one eye on More but the sub-lieutenant wasn't having to correct anything Hugo was doing. He couldn't help but smile, and something eased inside him.

III

"Sorry to have kept you waiting, Captain."

"Not at all, Colonel," Hugo said, standing as the colonel moved across his office to the sideboard and poured a couple of glasses of blask.

"Here," Luscombe said holding one out. Hugo took it. "To future prospects."

Hugo lifted his glass. "To future prospects." The two men drank.

"Sit," the colonel said.

Hugo sat back down as Luscombe took his seat behind the desk. The colonel took another swallow of his drink and then gave Hugo an appraising glance. "So, you've completed a hand-off and are still in one piece. That can only be promising."

Hugo didn't reply, just took another sip of his drink. It was good and earthy, sliding a slow warmth through him. He remembered the clear stuff that Jaeger had given him and took another appreciative sip.

"Well, Captain? Report."

"We made contact with the point, Anton Dolgorukov. He appeared satisfied with the cargo supplied and Webb seems confident we can count on his co-operation in the future."

The colonel nodded, half an eye on the display on the wall that was displaying news and Service reports on a rolling feed. "Good. Not that I would expect any less. This was small potatoes. We would have given you something more worthy of your abilities but with the Zero timing is something that rules you, not the other way around."

"Did you authorise the giving away of those machine parts to this point then, sir?"

Luscombe shook his head. "Authorise? Hugo, you don't understand. I don't know all the ins and outs of the *Zero's* dealings. The crew maintain most of their relationships and business contacts independently. Webb knows his business better than I want to know. I only need a report after every mission directly assigned to you by me. And if anything significant is ever unearthed during the course of the Zero's regular business."

"Such as?"

"You'll know it when you come across it."

Hugo nodded, gritting his teeth.

"The Orbit has many levels of society, Hugo," Luscombe said with a sigh. "The Service has better control over most of them than any other force in history. But it seems the more united the upper echelons, the more fractured and disjointed the lower. We can't afford to be too careful. We can't fix all the problems, but we can monitor them. The *Zero* project ensures that nothing takes us by surprise."

Hugo swirled his drink around in his glass. "Sir..." he said slowly.

"Hugo," Luscombe said, draining his glass. "You are not being punished. I appreciate this has been hard.."

"I've been publicly denounced and dishonourably discharged."

The colonel leant back in his chair, regarding him levelly. "What you did was inspired by bravery and good motives. But it was also against orders."

"Orders from an Analyst. Not from my CO."

Luscombe shook his head. "I'm not about to have a debate about protocol. The Analysts advised full retreat. You ignored them. After that there was no way you would be given command of a Space Corps fighter unit again, no matter how successful the outcome. The Service cannot have heroes. We need to be united. We serve. We follow. We obey."

Hugo took another drink, looking at the wall. "Even if we know better?"

"Captain, I hope to have a long and profitable relationship with you but you are not going to win my admiration by arguing with me."

"My apologies, Colonel."

Luscombe looked at him a moment longer. For one minute Hugo wondered what would happen if he told the colonel to shove it. Shove it all. Shove the *Zero* and shove the Service. But the moment and the feeling passed, leaving in its wake a flush of shame.

"Against orders or not, however," Luscombe continued. "Your actions caught the eye of Admiral Pharos. She is deeply committed to the *Zero* project. She leaves the running of it to me, but this is her ethos. Her plan. You may not to be able to show it but you should be proud."

Hugo nodded. "Yes, sir."

"Good lad." Luscombe rose and went back to the sideboard, replacing the glasses. "We won't be able to meet in person often. Hudson will be able to come up with some sort of explanation for your presence here today but by and large, unless it's an emergency, it's best if you report via secure channel from the *Zero*. Lieutenant Rami knows how to program it."

"Yes, sir."

"Don't underestimate this task, Hugo," Luscombe said. "Others before you have. It did not end well for them."

Hugo rose, stiffly. "Just one question, sir..."

"Just one?" Luscombe's mouth twitched up at one corner.

"One main question, sir," Hugo said, forcing his hands not to clench. "Why not make Webb captain?"

Luscombe's smile widened. "You don't like him, do you?" Hugo didn't comment but felt his cheeks flush. Luscombe waved a hand. "It's okay, Hugo. Webb has a way of rubbing Service officers up the wrong way. But trust me on this. I have never known a better soldier or a more loyal commander. If you win him over, you will go far. But he'd be the first person to tell you he is not captain material."

"How so?"

Luscombe shrugged. "He can't handle being the middle man. He can't make the hard decisions. He will do anything and everything for his mission and his crew. But those are his first priorities. The *Zero* needs a captain that can implement the Service's agenda. It's not an easy task. You have to be of both worlds, Hugo. Under and overground. Official and unofficial. Service and..."

"Scum?"

Luscombe's gaze hardened. "Some might see it that way. You are more likely to succeed if you learn to broaden your thinking, however."

Hugo ducked his head. His face still felt hot. He ground his teeth to stop himself blurting the hundred angry things that rose to his lips and only raised his head again when he trusted his face to be blank and his tongue to be still.

"Are you ready for your first Red-Level assignment then, Captain?" Luscombe asked.

Hugo straightened his back and squared his shoulders. "Yes, sir."

"Good. Here." Luscombe handed over a disk. "Rami will be able to decode it. I'm curious about Albion Integrated's revenue stream of late. There appears to be...discrepancies. It's probably nothing, but I need to be sure."

"AI?" Hugo asked, taking the disk. "They're a very powerful organisation, sir."

"Indeed they are, Captain," Luscombe said. "All the more reason to make sure we know where their money's going. Now go. All the details are on the disk. I expect a report when you have the data. You have a week."

Ø

"The sort of data he's after will not be on any system I can get into remotely, Captain," Rami said.

"Then what are we supposed to do?"

"We have to get it from their grounded system," Webb said as he sat with his feet up on the galley table, cleaning his fingernails with his knife.

"In their command centre?" Hugo said.

Webb nodded. "Fun, huh?"

Hugo flicked again through the mission data on the galley wall display. There were official listings of AI's office, warehouse and factory locations, lists of its stock holdings and official credit standing, reports on inter-Orbit relations and the names of the CEOs. Hugo felt himself pale.

"They make weapons and equipment for the Service," he muttered. "How can Luscombe want us to spy on them?"

"Keep your enemies close and your friends closer, Captain," Webb said, dropping his feet down and leaning on the table. "Spinn?"

"Commander?"

"Rami's digging up official and unofficial schematics of AI's Earth-based command centre. Will you go through them with her and come back to us with some ideas?"

"Yes sir."

"Kinjo?"

The young girl perked up. "Yes, Commander?"

"You, Sub and Bolt put together what we need for a two-man infiltration mission. We'll need guns, high-memory wrist panels, bolt cutters, mobile spyware... Sub and Bolt will know what else."

"Yes, Commander," Kinjo said and then was up and scurrying out the galley towards the hold.

"This is impossible," Hugo murmured, still leafing through the data on the display.

"More and I will handle it, Captain," Webb said, standing. "You put your feet up. We'll be done before you know it."

"Commander," Hugo grated, turning to him as he moved to leave. "I have already explained that I do not intend to sit out missions."

"Sir," Webb said, visibly gathering his patience. "This isn't just finalising a deal with a low-security point. This is front-line, Red-Level infiltration and extraction. I'd strongly recommend you take a back seat for this one."

"Doctor. Lieutenant."

"Sir?" the two remaining crew responded.

"Could you give us a moment?"

Rami and Spinn looked at each other, then at Webb, before rising and leaving the galley. Webb stood with his arms crossed and his eyes narrowed.

"Captain, you're going to have to learn to trust my judgement."

"And you, Commander, are going to have to learn some respect. I am not a greengun. Neither am I stupid. I was made captain for a reason. You will listen to my input and you will formulate your plan involving me."

"You have no idea how to play this game yet, Captain," Webb said, infuriatingly cool. "You nearly made Jaeger into an enemy yesterday. By the time you learn how quickly short fuses burn out around here, you'll be too dead to appreciate it."

Hugo clenched his fists.

"You have your orders, Commander Webb," he ground out. "Consult with Rami and Spinn. Gather more data. We meet back here in two hours when we will formulate the plan. Under my supervision."

"Very well," Webb said eventually.

"'Very well, *sir*."

Hugo saw Webb grind his own teeth. There was a dangerous flicker in the commander's eyes.

"Very well, sir."

Hugo took himself off to the bridge and spent time going through the Albion Integrated data provided by Luscombe, memorising what there was. It wasn't nearly enough to plan anything. The Service would never launch an official campaign on so little. He gripped his hair in frustration and got up and paced over to the viewscreen.

The Zero was on a nowhere-course, drifting in a remote spaceway. More was at the controls but he just kept a cursory eye on their course, working mainly on a technical manifest for the mission. Hugo couldn't make much out of what he could read on the sub-lieutenant's display so he paced back along the bridge and dropped himself again into the new command chair. He fiddled with the controls on the arm display, then used it to go through the Zero's vitals and camera feeds.

Hugo couldn't quite ignore the slight chill that began to rise under his belly. Every member of the crew was bent to some task that was being executed with the ease of something done a thousand times. When he switched to the feed from the hold he saw that Sub and Bolt were actually laughing as they checked over the contents of the weapons locker. A bitterness underpinned by uncertainty bubbled up inside him and he had to grip the chair arms to restrain himself from once again running his hands nervously through his hair.

"It's alright sir," More's voice was quiet, but it still startled Hugo. The older man was looking at him. Hugo eased his scowl and More smiled. "You're not the first, is all sir. We've been told that the *Zero*'s learning curve is like jumping off a cliff."

"Is that how you found it?"

More frowned slightly. "It wasn't for me sir, but that's because I was trained especially for this."

"How long ago was that?"

More looked up at the ceiling, thinking. "Coming up on twenty years now, captain. Just after the revolution."

Hugo raised an eyebrow. "How old were you when you were recruited?"

"Twelve, sir. I was sent for training on the *Endeavour* then assigned to the *Zero*."

"You were recruited into undercover-ops training at twelve?"

More nodded. "Yes, sir."

"No schooling?"

More gave a small shrug as he went back to his work. "There wasn't much point, sir. Formal education is of little use in this game. The youth unit had taught me all I needed to know."

Hugo looked up. "You were recruited from a youth unit?"

"Yes, sir," he said. "We all were."

"All of you?"

More turned in his chair, scratching his stubble. "Well, we picked up Kinjo on Haven and Sub and Bolt were recruited older. But none of us have any family."

"No one has any ties to exploit, then? And nothing to divide their loyalty?"

"I think that was the admiral's thinking sir, yes," More replied. Hugo drummed his fingers on the command chair, watching his sub-lieutenant skim his way through fuel inventories and tech checks on the display. More tapped a couple more keys and the display went blank. He turned in his chair to face Hugo. "That's two hours, Captain," he said.

Hugo nodded, blinked up at the overhead bulkhead for a moment, then rose.

"Captain?"

"Yes?"

More just looked at him for a moment, eyes unreadable. "No matter how the commander acts...we all know that the Zero needs a Service-trained captain."

"You think so?"

"There's no medals, no credit. No thanks. But it's dark out there. And messy. We need someone to lead us, even if it means dragging us onto the right course by our teeth. Without that... we're just another rudderless pirate ship, scraping an existence off the underside of humanity."

Hugo held the other man's look for a moment, feeling that chill creep once again along the underside of his stomach. More stood, paused, then moved past him and off the bridge. Hugo stood for a moment longer, gazing out into the darkness beyond the viewscreen before following.

Ø

"Okay, what do we have?"

The whole crew were crowded into the galley, sat on the benches or leaning against the wall. Hugo did not miss the heavy look Webb was giving him, but he ignored it, turning first to Spinn and Rami who were stood either side of the wall display.

"Lieutenant? What do we have?"

"AI's central command centre is in this range of mountains in Old Europe," Rami began, queuing up visuals of the mountain range and the surrounding area. "There is nothing up there except some old battle-grounds, hiking trails and a couple of fuelling stations."

"That's a strange place for a base."

Rami nodded. "Officially, it's because it has cheaper labour and licence taxes."

"Any fallout?"

"Not here, sir," Rami said. "The histories say there were munitions-only land battles in this area during the Whole World War."

"Civilian habitation?"

Rami pulled the map out wider. "The nearest town is forty miles away. Not large, but big enough to have local monitoring systems. AI have a lot of remote monitoring of their own spread out all through the area as well." She keyed in a couple of commands, and a web of sensor-lines laid itself over the map.

"Christ, that's a lot of surveillance," Webb said.

Rami nodded. "This command centre houses their primary research labs, but even so. It doesn't look like they want anyone sneaking around. There's no harbour or docking port nearby, either."

"How close can the Zero get?" Webb asked.

Rami looked to Spinn. The doctor scratched his head with one hand and zoomed the map out further with the other. "There is a little less sur-veillance further west... in the foothills. There is a clearing in the woods not far from this groundway. Well, it's a road really. Old, but well main-tained according to the scans. It should be possible to manoeuvre the

Zero between the local long-range sensors long enough to drop a ground team, but we'd have to retreat to orbit immediately."

"How far is that from the command centre?" Hugo asked.

"About twenty miles, Captain," Spinn said. "The ground team will have to take land transports."

"Any chance we could bullshit our way in at the front gate?" Webb asked.

Rami shook her head. "It's a completely closed base. Shift rotas, worker profiles, maintenance schedules – everything is stored on their grounded system. We can't even hack you onto a shift, let alone set you up with fake swipe badges."

"Guess we wouldn't want it to be too easy," Webb mumbled. "Fine, in that case, we'll take the bikes. We can stay off-road and come up to the boundary wall under cover. Do we do this day or night?"

"Day," said Spinn. "They lock the data systems down at night. We cannot afford the extra time it would take to get in."

"How close can the bikes get to the base before being detected?" Hugo asked.

"Use your eyes, Captain," Webb said, keying in some commands into the panel laid into the galley table. A contour grid laid itself over the command centre map and sensor-read plan. "We come in from the north. There's a dip in the land, there." He pointed. "We can stash the bikes there."

"That's two miles north of the wall."

"So we'll hike."

"Unacceptable," Hugo shook his head, stepping up to the display. He zoomed the image back in and leaned in close. "That will take too much time and increase the chances of being detected."

"Captain, look at the scope on those sensors. They'd pick up the bike's heat signature when they got within a mile of the goddamned wall."

"Commander, I have put up with about all I will take from you," Hugo kept his face still as he looked as his commander. "Don't make me ground you."

"You -"

"Zeek," More said, laying a hand on the commander's shoulder. "Let's just hear him out, okay?"

Webb slouched back on the bench, arms folded. Hugo pointed at the readings on the display.

"Spinn, from this sight pattern I assume these are the same spec as Service ground sensors – sensitive to heat, light, movement?"

"Yes, sir," the researcher said. "AI make them for the Service."

Hugo nodded. "They are unbeatable across open ground, but the woodland will lessen their range and muddy their readings. Spinn, do you have a display marker?" The professor pulled a blunt length of plastic from his breast pocket. Hugo took the marker to the map, drawing two ragged lines from north to south, in and out of the trees and perfectly slipping between the read-lines of the sensors. "I assume you are capable of manoeuvring those bikes with some level of competency? Load the co-ordinates of these routes onto your wrist panels. If you can stick to them you can get yourselves to within twenty feet of the wall... here." Hugo circled the spot with the marker then looked back at his crew. He felt a flicker of satisfaction when Webb said nothing, just took a deep drink from his coffee mug. "Now," he continued, "since AI designed these sensors, I'm assuming they probably know their weaknesses in woodland?"

Rami nodded. "The satellite monitoring shows regular foot patrols, Captain."

"Bad day to be on patrol," Webb murmured into his mug.

"What's next?" Hugo said as he took his seat again.

"The security system is grounded like everything else," Spinn said. "Neither Rami or I will be able to get in to scramble any of the sensors or camera feeds. The first part of the mission will have to be disabling or getting interference into the security system. There is one place near that arrival point that should give you the access to the security systems...a motor pool security booth... here." Spinn used the display marker to ring a square on the display.

"That's *inside* the boundary wall..." Hugo frowned.

Spinn blinked his watery eyes at him. "Yes, Captain."

Hugo frowned. "What about the wall?"

"We climb the wall, Hugo," Webb said.

"How high is it?"

"Spinn?" Webb asked, sounding infuriatingly amused.

"About thirty feet, Commander."

"Piece of cake,"

Hugo glared at him. "You cannot be serious."

Webb grinned.

"Ignore him, Captain," Rami said, glowering at her commander. "He's winding you up. We have grips. The ground team can climb the wall."

"And the sensor web strung over the top?" Hugo asked, pointing at the red lines on the display.

"We jump," Webb said.

Hugo sighed, rubbed his temples. "We'll go through that later. What happens at the guard booth?"

"The ground team should be able to disable the alarms and misdirect the camera feeds from there," Spinn said.

"Don't suppose that booth is connected to the central data system?" Webb asked.

Spinn shook his head. "Only to the security net."

"Figures," Webb mumbled and drained his coffee.

"The central system that we're after is accessible throughout the main building," Spinn said. "But Rami and I have analysed the schematics and we think that you'll have the least trouble if you try and access the data we need from the smaller research lab. It's here..." Spinn used his marker to ring another part of the diagram. "It's on the third floor and looks to be a relatively quiet section."

Ø

Webb watched Hugo as Spinn and Rami went through the details of the command centre's third floor and the research labs. The captain sat stiffly in his chair with his arms folded, eyes fixed on the display, back and shoulders tense. Webb was sure he could see his jaw muscles working and he didn't appear to blink.

"I estimate the total time scale to be three hours, maximum," Spinn concluded, tucking his display marker back in his pocket. "The *Zero* should plan to be back at the drop point exactly three hours from mission start to collect the ground team. I estimate there will be a window of about ten minutes before the ship will have to retreat again."

"Ten minutes?" More said. "Anywhere else close by suitable for an emergency meet point, just in case?"

Everyone looked to the display. Spinn scrolled back and forth.

"What's that?" asked Webb, pointing.

Rami peered closer, zooming in. "It's not marked on the official map. Scans read concrete. As I said, this area featured pretty heavily in that last land war. It's probably a disused bunker."

"That'll do. You got those co-ordinates?" Webb said. More nodded.

"We may have a problem," Bolt mumbled.

"Oh?" Webb asked, looking at the crewman, who stood against the wall scowling at the display.

"That drop-off point," he said, pointing, "I don't much like my chance of piloting the *Zero* in and out of that shit-nest of sensors on my own."

Webb blinked back at the display. "Shit."

Hugo frowned. "Who can do it?"

"Me or More," Webb said, rubbing his chin. "Unless... Sub..."

Sub shook his head. "Not me, Commander. I could get a fighter through that mess, but not the *Zero*."

There was a moment of silence.

"So we'll have to re-think the ground team," Hugo said, turning in his chair.

"Webb has to go," Rami said. "He's the only one who can hack the data."

"Aren't you the systems expert, Lieutenant?" Hugo asked.

"Rami needs to stay on the Zero to help Spinn monitor the surveillance net," Webb said. "They have electronic scans as well as everything else so we'll have to maintain comm silence. The only sign that the ground team are in trouble will be if there's a change in the network activity."

"I'll go with you, Commander," Kinjo said, leaning forward, eyes wide. "You said I was ready for fieldwork."

Webb felt a smile tug at his mouth. "I was thinking fieldwork like making deals with points and reps, Kinjo. Not Red-Level infiltration."

"I can do it, Zeek," she said, voice rising. "I can. I can ride, I know systems, I can use the tech."

"No, midshipman," Webb said, laying a hand flat on the table. "Soon, I promise. But not this."

"I'll go."

Webb turned to look at Hugo, feeling his heart sink. "Captain, you're joking."

"I'm not sending anyone down alone and we seem to have run out of crew."

"Sub -"

Hugo stood. "No disrespect meant to Crewman Subune or Crewman Bolt, but this is a stealth mission, yes?"

Webb swallowed, looked over at the two hulking crewmen who were looking at each other. "Stealth's not our game, Webb."

Webb ran his hands through his hair. Hugo was right, of course. That just made it worse. "No. We'll just have to think again. Maybe there's another approach -"

"We've been here over an hour," Hugo said. "The plan is laid and we're on a deadline."

"This is not something you can just *do*, Captain," Webb said.

"I was taught infiltration techniques at the Academy, Commander."

"It's not the same," Webb said. "The Academy's tactics are for open warfare-"

"How would you know?"

Webb blinked up at him. Hugo's face was hard but there was a glint in his eye. Webb peered at him, trying to figure out if it was the argument or excitement that had put it there.

"Take me to the hold," Hugo continued. "Show me the tech you have lined up and we'll go over the details."

Webb covered his face with his hands. "Christ Almighty. Why me?"

"Commander. We are on a deadline."

"Very well, Captain," Webb said, standing. He didn't look round, though he felt all the crew's eyes on him. "Follow me. I hope to God you know what you're doing."

"A little faith wouldn't go amiss, Commander," Hugo said as they left the galley.

"I asked you about faith in Tranquillity, Captain," Webb muttered. "As I recall, you near as much told me to shove it up my ass."

"Just lead the way, Commander."

Webb shook his head and led the way down to the hold.

Ø

Webb sat on the darkened bridge hours later, gazing out into the inky vastness beyond the viewscreen. The arch of black nothing, only made more empty by the pricks of stars, rendered him infinitesimal. It soothed him. He sipped more of his bitter coffee, feeling it gnaw at his throat. It was next to silent, only the hum of life support to be heard, so he easily picked up the soft footfall behind the command chair.

"You're up late," he said.

"Just going over the last few bits," Rami murmured and Webb heard her slotting her computer panel into a port on the workstation behind him. "What are you doing up? I thought this was More's watch."

Webb swallowed the last mouthful of the coffee. "As Thomas seems able to sleep through Bolt's snoring, I thought it only fair to let him."

Rami came round into view. Her hair was tied back in a loose braid for the night cycle, strands of it hanging loose around her face. The light of the starlit nothing painted her face and its quiet smile in delicate highlights and soft shadow. "Did he not use the mouth spray I gave him?"

Webb shrugged. "You'd have to ask him."

She smiled, then leant in and kissed him, long and slow. He could smell her hair, clean and warm. She tasted of nightmint. He sighed into her mouth and felt her smile against him.

"I thought we weren't doing this any more?" he murmured when she broke away.

She settled herself in his lap, pushed his long hair back from his face. "You're worried."

"Let's run away, Anita," he whispered, quirking a grin. "You and me. We'll run away to Earth and find a house near water. River or sea, I don't give a shit. Just so long as we can swim. We'll swim every morning and eat real fish and food we've grown ourselves."

Even in the dim light he could see the sadness in her smile. She ran a thumb over his cheekbone. "Are you worried about Hugo?" she asked. "Or Marilyn?"

Webb sighed and wrapped his arms around her waist, pulled her closer to him and tucked his face into her neck. She put an arm round him, rested her cheek against his hair and just held him there. He let the warmth of her skin seep into his own and just breathed in her smell. For a while there was nothing but the sound of their breathing.

"You should get some sleep," she said eventually, seemingly realising he wouldn't answer her question. He nodded into her neck but didn't move. "Come on, Commander," she insisted, getting up and pulling on his hand. "We head to Earth in a few hours. Besides, I don't want to be around if the captain comes through and finds you in his chair."

Webb snorted. "Neither do I."

"Do you want me to get you something to help you sleep?"

Webb shook his head, letting her pull him to his feet. "No, I'll be fine," he said. He smiled and put a hand on her cheek. "Anita..."

"It's okay, Zeek," she said, taking his hand in hers. "I'll take this watch. Go."

He looked at her a moment longer, swallowing against the heat in his throat, then nodded and went back towards the crew cabin. Getting into his bunk, he lay in the dark, staring at the dark bulkhead and listening to his crewmates breathing.

He only knew he'd finally managed to fall asleep when the lights turned on and the computerised alarm woke him a few hours later. He heard Bolt curse and cough in the bunk above his and More and Sub stirring on the other side of the cabin. He quickly tucked his crucifix back inside his shirt and sat up, rubbing his sore eyes. He mumbled one last prayer as he rose and left the cabin to pad down to the galley for a breakfast he didn't want but knew he needed.

IV

The motorbike felt bulky and unfamiliar. Hugo gripped the handles tightly, imagining that his knuckles were white inside the gloves. Taking a deep breath, he tried to dispel the returning flicker of nerves twitching over his skin.

"You're gonna have to loosen up, Captain," Webb said, adjusting his goggles. "You stay that tense you'll floor yourself the minute we hit the dirt."

Hugo glowered. Webb straddled his huge black motorbike with an almost obscene ease. He was pulling on his own gloves as the *Zero* shuddered around them. Still gripping the bike's handles, Hugo shifted his balance again and stared ahead at the hatch. The display on the inside of the bike's windscreen was showing the map of the AI command centre and its surroundings – contour lines, surveillance web and all. Hugo went over their route yet again, mumbling co-ordinates to himself.

There was another almighty shudder and then a clank as the hatch opened. With a hiss, the hold filled with Earth air.

"Ready, Hugo?" Webb said, once again pulling on the battered black baseball cap.

"Go."

His face unreadable under the cap and the goggles, Webb cast him a single glance, then gunned his engine. The noise made Hugo tense but then Webb was moving out. Hugo took one more breath and followed. He blinked as he emerged into weak, winter sunshine, his goggles taking a moment to adjust to the light. The bike hit the earth with a jerk that knocked his breath from him. His heart was pounding already, but he kept his eyes ahead and felt the bike gather power and tear along the ground.

With a throb of air, a blast of heat and a belch of heaving metal the *Zero* lurched back towards the sky. Webb was already across the clearing and entering the trees. Hugo pushed the accelerator to try and catch up, forcing his breath to come calmly. The natural air of Earth made him giddy for a moment but he pushed himself past it, forcing himself to focus.

His goggles lightened again as he moved into the shadows beneath the trees. Webb was just ahead, twisting and turning between the trees like he'd done the route a thousand times. Hugo only dared cast a glance or two at the display and to make sure they were keeping on track. The sound of the engines was sickeningly loud to his ears, but there didn't seem to be another living being in sight.

Webb kept their speed up and soon the ground beneath them began to rise, and Hugo could see light up ahead. The mountain road was coming up, but Webb did not slow down. Hugo couldn't get the breath to shout at his commander. He looked at his display and saw the bike's sensors weren't picking up any nearby traffic but as Webb tore out onto the open road Hugo's heart lurched into his mouth.

He had no choice but to follow. The road went by in a blur and a moment of blissful smoothness and then they were off road again on the other side, still bearing north and weaving between the trees. Hugo gradually felt himself sink into the way the bike moved, leaning into its canter a little further and daring a bit more speed. Webb adjusted their route as they went, but kept to the edge of the sensor boundaries marked on the display. The ground rose steeper and steeper and Hugo saw they were making good time.

Still, he didn't allow himself to think about the next bit but just concentrated on keeping up with Webb and not crashing. Time became a jumbled and fractured thing made of nothing but the jerking movement of the bike over the uneven ground, the smell of leaf mould mingled with the bike's fumes, and the insistent hammering of his heart.

Eventually, after cresting a particularly steep rise, his goggles darkened again as they emerged into another clearing. Webb slowed and pulled his bike round to face south and cut the engine. Hugo pulled up beside him, slightly less skilfully. When he cut his bike's engine for a minute all he was aware of was the pounding of blood in his ears and the earthiness in the air that he tasted with every heaving breath.

"Still with me, Captain?"

Hugo nodded, feeling his breathing gradually calm. He studied the display on his screen and compared it to the readings on his wrist panel. "We're early."

Webb nodded, stretching. "Aye, Captain. We're out of range though. Just be ready."

Hugo looked again at the route marked on the display in front of him and the timer in the corner. This was the route he himself had scribbled on the display in the galley, the route that should get them right up to the boundary wall. Assuming they'd got the timing of the foot patrol right. And assuming their scans of the sensors' scope had been accurate. And that Hugo could keep on course.

"Christ," Webb murmured.

"What?" said Hugo, snapping his head up.

"It's just..." Webb pulled off his goggles and gestured out in front of them with a wide sweep of his arm.

"What?" Hugo repeated.

"It gets me every time," Webb said, shaking his head. Hugo peered out over the spread of the landscape in front of them. Dark pine rolled down in every direction. There was hardly a break in the thick green apart from the odd cratered clearing further downhill. The peak of the next mountain rose against the horizon, the trees at this distance looking like a deep, green carpet. The sky was an arch of clear grey above them. The breeze ruffled the trees and brought a fresh wave of pine and cold earth.

The chill made Hugo shiver, despite the boiler suit, long coat and gloves. "What gets you? Trees?"

Webb made an impatient noise. "Not just trees. Everything. The green. The life. Fuck, the smell of it. Of Earth. Do you mean to say you were actually *born* here?"

Hugo frowned. "Not *here*." He glanced about once more at the chilly, leafy clearing and then went back to studying his display. "Sydney."

"Service Headquarters, huh? Figures. Not a lot of forest there, I'm guessing?"

Hugo shook his head, checking his gun again in his shoulder holster. The countdown ticked lower and he felt his heartbeat starting to rise again.

"What about at the Academy?"

Hugo looked up again at the rolling view. "The Highlands are more like this. But we only went into the forests on training manoeuvres."

"Well," Webb said with a grin, pulling his goggles back on and adjusting his cap. "Guess we're about to find out if you got your credit's worth. Ready?"

Hugo swallowed. "Ready."

"Stay close, Captain," Webb said, then his engine was roaring again and he was off down the slope. Hugo pushed the starter button on his own bike. It roared to life and he followed.

The angles of their trajectory tightened. Struggling to control the bike, Hugo almost pulled it over twice. His teeth were hammering together as they sped over the bumpy terrain and his hands were starting to sweat inside their gloves. But he rode the wave of adrenaline and used it to anchor him. Webb managed to keep them on course to an alarming degree of accuracy, but he still expected gunshots to start exploding around him or alarms to sound any moment.

Between the gaps in the trees ahead he could see the gleam of metal. Their route got even more erratic. They got closer and closer until Webb finally slowed. They crept the bikes along the last few feet. Their route had brought them up to a dense thicket of younger pines, and they pulled up behind the shield of the trees and cut the engines.

For a while they just sat there and listened. Sounds of the base – voices, engines and the hum of electricity – filtered through to them, but nothing close by or out of the ordinary. Hugo let out a shuddering breath, feeling his shoulders relax.

"Don't let up yet, Captain," Webb whispered. "That was the easy bit."

Hugo followed Webb's example and pulled off his goggles, stowing them in one of the pouches on his utility belt. They dusted off their clothes – Kinjo had supplied them both with black boiler suits, the sort worn by generic maintenance and tech crews across the whole Orbit – double-checked the contents of their belts and pockets, triple-checked their weapons and then moved to the edge of the thicket. Hugo hung back as Webb peered around the side.

"Gotta hand it to you, Captain," he mumbled. "You got us pretty damned close. I can smell the fuckers."

"What's the situation, Commander?" Hugo said.

Webb scanned the scene a moment longer then ducked back behind cover. "Looks like we've just missed the patrol. Guess it's his lucky day."

"Can you see the sensor hubs?"

Webb peered round again. He checked his wrist display then nodded. "Our readings are right. We should be able to get down into a blind spot if we stick close to the trees and stay on a direct line." Webb leaned back and flashed another grin. "Guess it's our lucky day too. You ready?"

Hugo swallowed and nodded.

Webb took a breath of his own and stepped around the edge of the trees. Hugo followed so close he was almost stepping on his heels. He copied Webb when the Commander crouched, creeping up to the next tree bent almost double. He moved so lightly that his boots didn't even snap twigs. It seemed painfully slow going and yet all too soon they were at the last of the trees, the wall a mere five feet away. Hugo gazed up it, the cool grey merging with the sky over their heads. Squinting, he could see the red beams of the sensor web strung across the top.

Webb nudged him in the ribs. Hugo blinked at him and he gestured towards the wall.

Ready? He mouthed. Hugo nodded.

Hugo took a deep breath when Webb did and stepped out from behind the tree. The feeling of exposure was palpable, like dampness on his skin. Pulling out their grips, he and Webb strapped them on as they approached the wall. Webb exchanged one swift glance with him, then placed his right, followed by his left hand onto the smooth metal of the wall above his head. The grips took hold and with a strength that Hugo couldn't help but admire, the tall commander was then heaving himself up, twisting one grip off the wall, and reaching further up to re-attach it and repeat. He touched the toes of his boots to the metal, the magnets in them giving him some foothold, and he was soon setting a swift rhythm up the wall.

Hugo stood with his back pressed to the metal and watched him gain height whilst glancing about for any sign of movement. When Webb was above his head, Hugo touched his own grips to the wall, felt them take hold, then started to climb. He kept himself a foot below Webb's ankles, letting the commander pick the way and keep them in the narrow band of blindness between the two sensor hubs. Hugo kept his ears tuned for any change in the drone of activity beyond the wall. His arms began to ache but he kept moving, hand over hand, keeping his rhythm with Webb's.

Webb stopped. Craning his neck, Hugo he could see the commander was an arm's length from the top. He disengaged his right-hand grip and tucked it into his belt. Hugo held his breath. Webb's movements were smooth and controlled, but what he could see of the younger man's face was a rigid mask of concentration. Webb smoothed his right hand up the wall and slid it up over the top, took a firm hold then disengaged his left grip. His left hand joined his right then he lifted himself up, painfully slowly, until he was peering over the edge. His arms didn't even quiver as he held himself there, scanning. Hugo held himself perfectly still.

Webb ducked his head back below the level of the wall and Hugo saw his face was pale.

"Were you seen?" Hugo mouthed.

Webb shook his head, then his eyes widened. Hugo followed his look and saw the patrol man step out from beyond the far corner of the wall. They froze. Hugo felt his knuckles protest as his crushed the grips and his muscles burned with the effort of keeping motionless. But the guard turned his back in their direction and leant against a tree, pulling out a packet of cigarettes and lighting one.

Hugo let out a breath and looked up at Webb, but he was already moving. He pulled himself up until his arms were locked straight, head and torso above the top of the wall. Hugo swallowed but still no one shouted. He then watched as the commander brought up his right leg and got the toe of his boot under the sensor beams. Hugo glanced back, confirmed the guard was still smoking and looked back in time to see Webb hoist himself up. It happened so quick Hugo didn't catch exactly what the commander did but one minute he was straddling the sensor beams, balanced on the heels of his palms and the toes of his boots, then he'd dropped down out of sight. There was a soft clang as he dropped onto something metallic and then it was Hugo's turn.

He pulled himself up, disengaged his grips one at a time, just as Webb had. When he pulled himself up, for a split second he saw the base laid out below, a sprawling stretch of tarmac, metal and concrete and then he was letting his body take over. He got a foot up, clenched his teeth as he almost tripped the sensor beam, then heaved, got one arm over and shifted his feet. His spine protested at the angle as he cast one glance down to take in the corrugated iron roof of an outbuilding ten feet below. He allowed himself one breath and jumped.

It wasn't his best landing. His boots clanged onto the metal and he stumbled forward with a clatter onto his hands and knees. Ignoring the throbbing in his knees he shuffled over to the edge of the building and tumbled off. He hit the ground, rolled up and ducked behind a squat store house that shouldered up against the boundary wall. Webb was crouched in the narrow space. The ground was cracked and dusty and covered in cigarette butts. Webb was peering around the far corner but ducked back when Hugo came up behind him.

"I can see the security booth," he murmured. Hugo shifted himself and Webb made room for him to look around the corner. The concrete booth was about fifty feet away, antennas and cameras sprouting from the roof but no windows facing their way. There was nothing between it and their hiding place but a couple of gutted hulks of four-by-four land transports, some rusted cargo crates and a stack of dented lifters.

"So, this infiltration training you had, Captain," Webb said as Hugo ducked back behind cover. "Ever had to use it in the field?" Hugo shook his head. "Didn't think so," Webb shifted his crouch and looked Hugo directly in the eye. "Until we get into that booth, we're gonna show up on the video feeds. Walk easily. Don't hunch but don't walk like you've got a rod up your ass either. Anyone spots us, they need to think we're tech crew coming back from a sly cigarette, okay?" Hugo nodded. "You know you haven't snapped at me in like an hour? It's making me nervous."

"Get moving, Commander. We're on the clock."

"That's better," Webb said with a grin. Then he straightened, dusted off his knees and with an ease that Hugo couldn't quite believe, strode out from behind the store house, hands in pockets. Swallowing, Hugo followed, concentrating on keeping his face passive, his fists unclenched at his sides and his pace loose. It took a lot of effort not to look at the cameras.

Webb paused to let him catch up then fell into step beside him. They moved around the skeleton of one of the cars and stepped out onto the open space behind the booth. Beyond was the motor pool. There were civilian cars and flyers, but also a rather convincing bank of black four-by-fours, paint gleaming and with the AI logo emblazoned on the side. As they got closer he could also see a bank of fighter-class flyers beyond them. The main building of the command centre loomed up behind, ten stories high, all concrete and glass. People milled about the motor pool or came and went through the doors, most of them in clean white lab coats or crisp business suits. Lights were on on every level and he could see the silhouettes of workers moving about inside.

Glancing, Hugo took all this in and then they were coming up on the security booth. Webb confirmed the door was locked with a quick rattle of the handle. They glanced about but nobody was looking their way and Webb crouched down to pick the lock. Hugo moved to stand where he could shield him from anyone that may glance their way. He heard a chair shifting and a muffled voice from inside the booth just as the lock gave and Webb pushed the door open.

The guard was dead even before Hugo had shut the door behind them. Webb tucked his gun back inside his boiler suit and then sat himself at the controls. A bank of screens ran the length of the room, all showing different levels and corners of the command centre and motor pool as well as the area surrounding the boundary wall.

"You wanna shove him out of sight, Captain?" Webb mumbled as his fingers flew over the keypad. Hugo looked down at the guard sprawled across the floor tiles, blank eyes staring up and blood pooling under his head. Hugo dragged the body under the far corner of the work desk, leaving a trail of blood across the floor. "That'll do." Webb said with a glance. "Nearly there."

"Already?" Hugo said, coming up behind the chair, watching as the feeds on the cameras flickered or changed direction and screens displaying sensor arrays and alarm grids shuddered and re-aligned.

Webb shrugged. "Domestic system. Would have thought they'd have something more heavy-duty. Guess they rely on the fact that it's closed and grounded to protect it. That should do it. Come on."

They slipped out of the security booth and around the back then made their way towards the main building, keeping behind store houses and outbuildings where they could. They peeled away from the busier part of the grounds at the north west corner, and Hugo shivered as they passed into the shadow of the command building. The noise faded behind them. The rear of the building was separated from the boundary wall by a narrow strip of cracked tarmac. There were cameras on the wall but thanks to Webb's hack, they were all facing away. They paused when they reached a service door. There was no handle and no control panel.

"Are you sure this will work?" Hugo muttered.

"Trust me, Captain," Webb smiled, pulling thumb-sized charges from his utility belt.

Hugo glanced back up at the cameras one more time as Webb set the charges on the concrete jamb. Webb backed away and Hugo followed him until they were pressed against the wall. They crouched down and Webb covered his head with an arm then pressed the detonator. Hugo flung his own arms up just in time.

The was an odd sound, a sucking pop and a cracking, then the pattering of peppered concrete falling to the ground. Hugo looked up and saw the door, twisted and scorched, hanging off its hinges, blackened gouges in the jambs on either side.

"My own recipe," Webb said, clapping a hand on his shoulder. "Never fails."

The remains of the metal door were hot even through their gloves. They managed to shoulder it aside and slip into the darkened corridor beyond. Hugo took the lead this time, using his wrist display to confirm the way. The corridor gradually lightened and he saw a door with a window up ahead. Hugo approached slowly then peered out into the busy corridor.

"Everything looks normal," he said.

"Try not to sound so surprised, Captain," Webb whispered. "I have done this before, you know."

They stood there in the dark for what seemed like an eternity before there was a break in the foot traffic. They ducked out and across the corridor with Hugo's heart hammering hard enough to shake his skull, and through a door on the other side. It was another service corridor, windowless with closed doors on either side. Webb had off-lined the motion sensors so it remained as dark as the first passage. They pulled out lens-slights to make their way down to an even darker stairwell. Hugo craned his neck, sending the beam of his light between the flights of stairs. There was the steady hum and thunk of the bank of lifts on the other side of the wall, along with the general mumblings and footsteps of a workforce going about its business. Apart from that, all was deserted and quiet.

Hugo took the lead up the stairs. Every footfall echoed in the silence. They got to the third floor by counting the flights and pressed themselves to the wall either side of the exit. Hugo concentrated on the feeling of the cool wall pressed against his back, clenching his eyes shut and trying to ignore the sensation of his skin crawling.

"You get used to it," Webb murmured as he checked over his gun in the beam of his lenslight. "Undercover, I mean. Shooting people in the back. It gets easier."

"How do you know? You don't have anything to compare it to."

Webb's face darkened but then he switched off his lenslight and turned his back on Hugo. Hugo shifted back and shut off his own light as Webb braced himself and opened the exit door a crack. Hugo held his breath as the commander put his face to the gap.

"Come on," Webb said eventually and ducked out. Hugo followed. The corridor was empty, though the windows on one side overlooked the activity in the motor pool. He saw Webb pause and wrinkle his nose and a minute later it hit Hugo. An odd tang in the air...acidic, strong. For a minute it threatened to turn Hugo's stomach.

"What's that?" Webb mouthed but Hugo just gestured for him to move on.

They carried on creeping down the corridor. Even though he knew the cameras were off or misdirected, it still took an effort to move past them. They hugged the wall, as far from the windows as possible, and approached a bend in the corridor with ears straining for any kind of noise.

They were nearly at the corner when they heard voices from behind them. Hugo looked back the way they had come. The service door onto the stairwell was ajar and the voices were getting louder.

"Shit," Webb cursed, looking this way and that. "This would have been a good time to have fake ID."

"Quick," Hugo said, pointing to a door.

Webb crossed the corridor in two strides, dropped to his knees and began working on the lock of the store cupboard.

"Faster," Hugo growled, seeing the service door start to open.

Webb muttered another curse before the cupboard door swung inward and the two men tumbled inside.

"Lock it," Hugo ordered and Webb did so. They stood in the dark, breathing. Hugo was flat against the wall but Webb was looking out of the window in the door.

"Get away from the glass, Commander," Hugo hissed.

"Hold on," Webb said. "I want to see who's using the service stairs."

"Maintenance crews? Get back."

"Maintenance crews use the elevators like everyone else, Hugo...what the fuck?" Webb's face froze and he ducked back away from the window.

"What?"

Webb shook his head and pressed a finger to his lips. Hugo edged a little closer to the window. Three figures came into view. He recognised the tall, square-faced Gabor, the base commander, from Luscombe's files. He was accompanied by a woman in a security uniform holding a computer panel, and a much shorter man in a suit. They paused almost right outside the store cupboard and Hugo frowned. The shorter man had space-pale skin and no hair. His eyes were extremely light and looked out of his hairless face with a keenness that set Hugo's nerves jangling. The two men murmured to each other as they checked what the security woman was showing them on the panel, then moved on out of sight.

The second they were out of sight, Hugo's wrist panel started blinking. He looked at the display, saw Webb doing the same.

"What happened?" Hugo whispered.

Webb shook his head. "Someone logged into the security system and tripped my warning protocol. But they didn't do anything."

"They left the security scrambled?" Hugo said, frowning. "Was it them?" he asked, pointing out the window.

"I don't know," Webb said, shaking his head. In the wan light of his wrist display his face looked drawn. "There's something not right here, Captain," Webb whispered. "I think we should abort."

"No," Hugo said.

"Captain..."

Hugo looked at Webb, who stood rigid against the wall. "Commander, what's wrong?"

"I just got a bad feeling," Webb mumbled to himself, still looking out the window.

Hugo blinked. "The bald man with Gabor... you recognised him. He's the one Jaeger said was looking for you, isn't he? Who is he?"

"Captain, there's no time. We need to get out. Now."

Hugo shook his head. "You'll answer my question later, Commander. But for now we carry on."

"Sir -"

"That's an order," Hugo said. "Move. We're running out of time."

Webb took a breath and peered out the window. He then unlocked the door and crept out into the corridor, drawing his gun as he went. Hugo did the same, but they didn't meet anyone. All was silent. They passed several closed doors and paused at a junction with a sign to the labs.

"Are you ready?" Hugo said. Webb tugged at the peak of his cap and nodded. "Alright then. Lab 4. Go."

Hugo saw him take a breath and then move to cross the junction to the lab.

Hugo threw himself to the floor as the air was shattered by gunfire. The wall exploded in a rain of plaster and the ungodly noise tore everything apart. The firing was coming from somewhere out of sight down the left hand corridor. There was no sign of Webb, but then someone returned fire from around the next corner to the right. Hugo crouched down on one knee, edged himself to the corner, then leant round and started firing. The wall above his head exploded and dust almost blinded him. He ducked back out of range.

There was a lull and Hugo crouched, breathing hard, gun ready. He leaned as far as he dared but he couldn't see Webb or whoever was firing at them.

"Come out," someone barked. "You're out-gunned and there's no way out. Give yourselves up."

Hugo cursed under his breath. There was no sound from Webb's direction. He heard some muttering and movement. He steadied himself, and when the first guard came into sight, shot him down. His companion wheeled around and started firing, but blindly, angrily and Hugo managed to duck back around the corner. He leant around and fired again, drawing out two more guards, hoping Webb would use the opportunity to get away.

The security men fell back, took up a better position and worked on obliterating the corner of wall by his ear. Hugo continued to blindly return fire, and from the sound of a pained scream managed to take out one more, then turned and ran for the stairs.

The stairwell was still dark. He could hear approaching booted feet and angry shouts from below so went up, taking the stairs three at a time. Two floors up, the stairwell flooded with light and alarms started blaring.

He swore and shouldered open the next door he came across. He only had time for the briefest of glances at his wrist panel to determine the layout of the floor he was on before he hurtled around a corner, straight into a bank of armed men, guns drawn.

"Drop it," one of them snarled.

Hugo stood frozen in the sights of the half-dozen automatic rifles. He dropped his gun. One man put up his rifle and came forward. Hugo waited until he was at arm's length then grabbed the man by the collar, pulling him between himself and the guns. There was a confused moment of shouts and the man fighting against him that Hugo used to pull a flash charge from his belt and hurl it towards the bank of men.

There was a deafening bang and a flash of white and a hiss and the air was a confused mess of shouting, gunfire and foul-smelling fog. Hugo threw the startled guard away towards the rabble and flung himself through another door.

He was in a small room with a bank of workstations at one side and a wall of windows on the other. Three terrified people in lab coats scrambled away from the door as he came careening through. Hugo hauled a set of shelves over to block the door, spilling computer and machine parts onto the floor just as gunfire started to tear it apart. One of the women screamed.

Hugo didn't spare them a glance but ran to the window. He saw how high up he was and felt his stomach lurch but then came a sickening noise that shook the room, rattled the glass in its fittings and knocked him to the floor. More alarms started blaring and he could smell smoke.

He grabbed a chair from the nearest workstation and flung it through the window, glass flying everywhere. He clambered up onto the sill, feeling a chill ride up him as he looked down at the tarmac below. The breeze tugged at his hair. Forcing aside a sickness in the pit of his stomach, he climbed out, lowered himself until he was dangling from his gloved fingertips, took a deep breath and let go.

Ø

Webb blinked against the spots dancing in front of his eyes and shook his head to try and clear the ringing in his ears. He hauled himself to his feet, swearing as his limp arm tugged on his shoulder.

"Fuck," he swore again, wiping blood out of his eyes with his good hand. The corridor was a mess of debris, dust, flashing lights and pounding alarms. His charge had obliterated his pursuit as well as most of the third floor of the command centre, but he knew he didn't have long. He only prayed that Hugo had managed to make it back to the stairwell. He allowed himself one precious moment to lean against the scorched plaster. He tried to breathe past the pounding and flashing in his head, then gritted his teeth and slammed his dislocated shoulder against the wall.

There was a horrible crack that he felt more than heard. For a second everything went black but when he came back to himself he was running. The only people he encountered were workers picking themselves up from the floor, yelling and flinging themselves out of his way. He risked a glance at his wrist display and then changed direction, taking a corridor that led back towards the rear of the building.

He came up on another corner, more civilians scattering along the way and skidded to a halt when he heard angry shouts and the thunder of booted feet coming his way. He cast about, saw a grid in the ceiling and aimed. He fired and the grid swung down, hanging twisted from its fastenings. He shoved his gun inside his boiler suit, jumped and caught the edge of the opening, cursing as his shoulder took his weight. He scrambled up into the shaft just as more AI security came round the corner. It was narrow and dark but he crawled down it, pulling himself out of reach just as the shaft behind him exploded with gunfire.

He checked his display and turned a sharp left then right, shoulder, knees and back protesting with every move. The shaft narrowed as he turned again and he had to lie down to get himself through the gap into the next duct. His wrist panel blinked red as the *Zero* rendezvous time approached. He shook his head.

"Well that's that fucked," he muttered and kept crawling.

He felt a draught on his face and could smell the outside. There was light up ahead and he scrambled towards it. Between the slats of a ventilation grid he could make out the top of the boundary wall below and the forest beyond. The duct was too narrow to draw his gun so he had to lay on his back and pull a multitool from his belt to work on the screws. He gritted his teeth, willing his hands not to shake, but it still took far longer than it should before the grid fell away, landing with a crash on the concrete below. He shouldered himself round until he was able to get his feet out of the opening, then lowered himself out, catching his weight on his elbows, legs dangling into nothing. He craned his neck, trying to judge the distance between him and the top of the wall.

With a deep breath he twisted, gathered himself and jumped. For a sickening moment he thought he was going to fall short, then his ribs cracked into the top of the wall. He cursed again, clinging there for a precious moment, completely winded until stars stopped dancing in front of his eyes. More sirens sounded from the tripped wall alarms and lights along the top of the wall started flashing as he hauled himself over.

No time for grips, he reached for the branch of the closest tree, managed to grab it on the second swing and pulled himself across. He shimmied down the branch then scrambled down the trunk, hitting the forest floor with a roll then got to his feet and ran.

It only took him a moment to register that the captain's bike had gone from its hiding spot, then he scrambled onto *Sin*, gunned the engine, swung the bike south and hit the accelerator. Detritus and twigs flew up in his wake. The road was a paleness between the trees up ahead, then there was the smoothness of tarmac below him and he pulled the bike round and tore westwards. He counted out his luck second by second as he sped down the mountain road. Still no pursuit showed up on the bike's windscreen display or mirrors.

Even so, he waited until there were a few more miles behind him before he dared to take his eyes off the road long enough to glance at his wrist panel. The emergency meet point was coming up ahead. Taking a painful breath, he wrenched the handlebars over and heaved the bike back off-road, heading uphill and away from the little blinking cross on the display that marked the rendezvous. He spared a couple of glances back over his shoulder as best he could to be sure he left a clear trail through the undergrowth.

He came to a small clearing, braked and spun the bike in a tight arc. The trees were too dense to see the road but he was pleased to see the deep furrows in the leaf mould that marked his trail. He cut *Sin*'s engine and listened hard.

For some time all he could hear was his own laboured breathing. The stabbing pain down his ribs every time he inhaled shoved itself back into his awareness. He hung his head, forcing his breathing to steady and pushed past the pain, clearing his concentration to listen. A long way off, deadened by the intervening trees, were the unmistakable sounds of vehicles moving at speed. Another harried glance at the readings on his wrist panel confirmed the base's security had got themselves in gear and were heading his way.

With a wince and a curse he pushed down *Sin*'s kickstand and heaved himself off. He staggered on a protesting ankle but pulled himself up before he fell, gritting his teeth. When he had gained control over the pain, he reached out and ran a hand over *Sin*'s handlebar, a pang sweeping through him.

"Sorry, baby," he muttered and started pulling charges from his belt. When it came to actually attaching the charges to the chassis he cringed and almost, almost, considered abandoning the whole plan. But sense told him they would take longer examining wreckage, hopefully enough time to let them make a getaway. The proximity of the blinking lights on his display told him he had little choice.

Clenching his jaw, he set the charges along the body of the bike before turning and stumbling away. He didn't look back as he made his way down the incline, cursing, wanting to sprint but not managing more than an ungainly stagger. When he reached the road there was still nothing in sight. He was over and in the trees on the other side before he dared to breathe again. But he didn't slow his pace and kept heading vaguely south, casting about for anything that might look like a bunker. Looking around he caught the glint of metal further down the incline. As he limped closer he could make out the shape of the captain's bike stashed in some undergrowth.

"Commander."

Webb span in the direction of the voice. The captain's blood-smeared and scowling face was pale against the dark of the bunker's entrance sunk into the hillside. Webb scrambled over toward him and heaved himself over the log. He hit solid concrete with a bump and a stifled cry. The captain's hand fastened onto his collar and hauled him further back into the bunker. It was dark and dirty and only just big enough for the two men to sit side by side.

It seemed like no sooner had he been dragged away from the entrance than the sound of vehicles thundering past on the road above filled his ears. He felt the captain tense in the darkness beside him. The roaring was loud and fast but he estimated at least four vehicles, big ones, maybe even a couple of bikes too. He felt the captain ease as the sounds passed on.

Hugo moved to leave but Webb grabbed him, pressing a hand to his mouth for quiet. Sure enough, the growling of engines returned to the road above and then the screeching of brakes, banging of doors and shouts.

"They must have scanning equipment and have picked up the bike," Hugo mumbled as the sickening sound of men marching down off the road into the trees filtered through to them.

"We're not dead yet."

The captain raised an eyebrow as Webb produced a detonator. Clenching his eyes shut and muttering a quick prayer, he pressed the button.

Sin's explosion rumbled through the floor and rattled dust from the ceiling. There were shouts and the sounds of retreating feet and men being ordered back up to the road. Then silence. Webb leant back against the wall and rubbed a hand over his face, letting out a shuddering breath.

"Not too boring for you, I hope, Captain?"

Hugo just shot him a glare and attempted to sit up straight. For the first time Webb noticed the stiffness in the way he moved. He also cradled his left arm close to his chest.

"Captain?" Webb shifted closer.

"I'm fine," Hugo grunted, attempting to shift back toward the entrance.

Webb grabbed the captain's jacket to hold him still. "What happened?"

Hugo scowled for a second then looked away. "I jumped out of a window."

"No disrespect sir, but that was pretty stupid," Webb attempted a grin.

"I'm fine. Let's move."

"Sir, we are relying on each other to get out of here. I need to know what shape you're in."

Hugo's scowl deepened and he looked away. "Crack to the head," he muttered. "Broken forearm. Bangs and scrapes."

"Let me look," Webb said, but as he reached out his hand the captain recoiled. "Hugo, I need to see if you have concussion."

He cast Webb an unreadable look but suffered him to shine a lenslight in both his eyes.

"Maybe a little," Webb muttered, not happy, before turning his attention to the arm. Hugo held it protectively curled against his chest and it hurt too much for Webb to even touch it. Webb rifled through his utility belt for his medkit, aware that time was ticking by. "We'll have to bind it," Webb said, pulling out a length of bandage. Hugo's face darkened further but he allowed his commander to help him shoulder out of his coat, shift his wrist display from his bad to his good arm and bind the broken forearm against his chest. He winced as the bindings tightened over the break but made no noise. Webb took the opportunity to cast a glance over the rest of him as he helped him get the coat back on over the bindings. His skin was drawn and clammy and his breathing shallow and pained.

"Right," Webb said. "Hold fast. I'll get us some transport."

"What?"

"I don't much like your chances of holding on to me on the bike, Captain. Sit tight. I'll find something."

"No," Hugo growled. "We go together."

"I'll go faster alone."

"No, Commander. This whole mess is because we got split up. We can't let it happen again."

Webb bit his tongue on the automatic response, taking a breath. "It wasn't your fault, Hugo. Well, it was a little bit. If you'd listened to me when I said we should abort we'd be out and away right now." Webb saw him bristle and swiftly continued. "But it was messed up from the start, the whole thing. I should have guessed. It was all too easy."

All the captain did in response to this was raise one bloody eyebrow.

"Well, not the getting out," Webb conceded. "But the getting in."

The captain raised both eyebrows this time.

"Come on, Captain, think about it. Apart from our friend in the booth, did you even see a patrol before we got to the lab? And then they checked the security network and didn't fix it? And the minute we're out in the lab corridor lead is flying and I've got half of Albion Integrated's security force up my ass. If the bikes hadn't been so close we'd be dead by now. Or worse."

The captain grimaced and his glance slid away.

Webb was already pulling up a map of the immediate area on his wrist panel and shifting back to the bunker entrance before the captain grunted another order to wait. Webb ground his teeth but bit off the retort before it made it out his mouth.

"Commander," Hugo repeated, voice stronger. "What's your status?"

"Huh?"

"You heard me. I'm relying on you too and you don't look so good, either. What happened?"

Webb glanced away. "Urm...I blew myself up." It might have been the dark but Webb almost swore he saw a twist of humour in the captain's face when he looked back.

"That's even stupider than jumping out a window."

"Debatable," Webb countered and moved again to leave.

"Status, commander," the captain barked.

Webb exhaled and clenched his eyes shut, lowering his walls to allow the pain to seep back into his awareness. "Burns and scrapes. Superficial. Sprained ankle. Bruised ribs...probably cracked," he relented as another shoot of red pain rode up through him. "Oh, and dislocated shoulder," he flashed the captain a quick grin. "But I fixed that. Sit tight, captain. I'll be right back."

"Commander"

Webb hauled together his remaining patience and hunkered back down next to Hugo. "Here, look," he punched a couple of commands into the captain's and then his own wrist panel. A little green light started blinking in the corner of each. "You have my heartbeat and I have yours. You can monitor me, that will have to do. I'll be back." He clambered back over the log before the captain could protest further.

He moved west, parallel to but out of sight of the road. He clung to the hope that the security forces were too busy sifting through *Sin's* blast site to worry about extending the search but he also knew what he told the captain was the truth. Breaking in had been too easy, the escape too hard and the pursuit too desperate for Webb to believe that AI would just count their losses and let them slip away without hard proof that they were gone or dead.

It had clouded over, making night draw in quickly, making him feel a little easier about the impact his twisted ankle was having on his ability to move stealthily. When he reached his destination he halted out of sight of the road to allow his pained breathing to calm before he dared to approach the break in the trees.

There was no traffic, no sounds and nothing moving. The tourist car park across the road had four vehicles pulled up in it. It only took a few minutes to break into and hotwire one of the little civilian cars. The engine coughed to life and he offered up silent thanks to the unfortunate tourist and hoped they had comm units with a good range this far up the mountain.

He ignored the panic that rose in him at the sound the engine made as he roared back down the road. He turned a corner and slowed, swallowing as he saw the AI four-by-fours and a couple of motorbikes pulled up on the north side of the road. But there was no one around. He wasted no time in pulling up on the other side and hurrying back down the slope to the bunker.

The captain was slumped against the wall but his eyes snapped open as he scrambled back into the narrow space. "Come on, Hugo. Your ride awaits."

It took more effort than he cared to admit to help the captain back out of the bunker and up the slope to the waiting car. He outweighed Webb and, though he obviously tried hard to hide it, was struggling to hold himself upright. They paused at the tree line but it still looked as if none of the enemy had returned. Satisfied their luck was holding for now, Webb bundled Hugo into the passenger seat and limped back round to the driver's seat. He coaxed the engine back to life but didn't accelerate too hard until the AI vehicles had disappeared from the rear view. Then he ignored the protests of his ankle and floored it.

"Commander," Hugo's warning lost some of its power with the pain that cracked his voice.

"The town's this way," Webb said, flinging the car around a corner. "All I need is a system on the solarnet to get a secure connection to the *Zero* to arrange a new rendezvous. Think you can hang on?"

Hugo just grunted. "Who was that man with Gabor, Commander?"

Webb swallowed. "Herman Fitzroy."

"Aide to Lunar Governor Cho-Jin?" Hugo asked, eyes widening.

"Officially."

"And unofficially?"

Webb flung them around another corner, gritted his teeth. "He's Lunar Independence League. High up, too."

"What?" Hugo "He's *what*?"

"You heard me right."

"That's impossible."

"Is it?"

Hugo shook his head. "The revolutionaries were defeated...LIL was disbanded..."

"Not all that disbanded, apparently."

"How do you know this?" Hugo snapped.

"Well," Webb said, flinging them around another corner. "Fitzroy told me."

"He told you?"

Webb nodded, shooting him a narrow glance. "Sought me out. To recruit me." Hugo was silent. When Webb spared him a glance he was sat stiffly, glowering at him. "Don't worry, Captain. I'm not the revolutionary type. Not enough principles."

"Why didn't you tell me before?"

"The fact that I've been getting recruiting calls from underground insurgent movements is not something I thought would endear me to you on the first day."

Hugo clenched his good fist and stared out the windscreen again. "Does this mean that Governor Cho-Jin -?"

"I ain't touching that one with a ten-foot pole, Captain."

"The Lunar Strip won't survive another revolutionist governor...did you report this?"

"Hell no," Webb said, glancing again in the rear-view.

"Not even to the colonel?"

Webb could feel the frustration coming off Hugo in waves. "I got the hell away from Fitzroy before he told me too much. But the Service won't move against the moon without proof and if LIL found I'd ratted them out, I may as well have drifted myself."

"So the Lunar Governor's aide is LIL. And recruiting. And he's skulking around AI?"

"You ain't in Kansas no more, Captain."

"And there's nothing we can do?"

"Hell there's nothing," Webb said. "We can get the fuck out of here is what we can do."

There was silence for a moment, with only the sound of the car engine, Hugo's ragged breathing and his own blood pounding in his head.

Darkness drew in quickly and he turned on the car's lights, taking the bends fast enough for his stomach to protest. Hugo lapsed into silence punctuated only with hitches of pain and his laboured breathing.

Soon the road straightened out, the trees gave way to buildings and the road was lit by street lights. He forced himself to slow down, aware of the street cameras. It was apparently the local rush hour and the queues made him swear. He peered out the windows looking for quieter side-streets that wouldn't take them too far off course.

It felt like a long time before he spotted something suitable and pulled the car round with a jerk that had the captain grousing. He crept the car along and scanned the closed-up shops and businesses, ignoring the questioning stare he could feel coming from Hugo. The occasional civilian flyer zoomed overhead though thankfully nothing with flashing lights or sirens, and he allowed himself to breathe normally. Turning another corner he found another street of shut up shops that was even more deserted than the last and decided there wasn't much else for it but to chance it. He pulled over and cut the engine, trying to avoid the clearest angle on the nearest street camera.

"Where are we?"

"No idea. But I think I've found what we need. Sit tight."

"Wait," Hugo snapped as Webb opened the door.

"For fuck's sake, will you just trust me?"

"Wait, Webb. That's an order."

Webb had little choice since the captain had used his good hand to lock a death-grip on his sleeve. He swore again, painfully aware of the seconds ticking by, and turned back.

"You look like shit," Hugo muttered, scowling at him.

"Yes, I am aware, Captain, now let me go, we don't have time -"

"No," Hugo snapped. "I mean...just look."

Webb followed the captain's gesture and took a proper look at himself in the rear view mirror and grimaced. What little of his face that was not mired with dirt was covered in blood from a cut over his eyebrow. His hair was stiff with more of the same and his clothes were a scorched and bloody mess. Anyone even catching half a glance of him would call the emergency services, either before or after screaming bloody murder.

"Okay. I take your point," Webb muttered.

Hugo was already trying to work his way out of his coat which, though dusty and dirty, was long and more or less in one piece.

"Here," Webb said and leant in to help. Hugo threw him a look but didn't argue and Webb managed to untangle him from it with only the minimum of muttered curses. Webb pulled the coat on over his ripped boiler suit then pulled off his hat, scraped back and re-tied his hair then dusted off the cap as best he could before pulling it back on, tugging it low on his face, hoping it would hide most of the blood. Then he scrambled out of the car.

The night air had a bite of chill and he shivered. He pulled the coat tight around him and ducked his head, moving up the street as sedately as he could manage, all the while forcing himself not to limp. The drug store he had spotted was at a bad angle for the street camera but he still looked up and down the street twice before setting to work on the keypad by the door. It took him longer than it would have done normally to crack the code. The waves of nausea and dizziness washing through him were getting harder to push aside. He cursed as he struggled to focus but eventually the doors hissed open and he let out a shuddering breath, slipping inside. He found the control box to the alarm system near the door and disabled it with less trouble and moved down the rows of shelves to the shop counter.

He muttered another prayer of thanks when he saw that the store's till system was connected to the solarnet, even if it was old and took its time booting up. He resisted the urge to kick it, slumping in a chair and rubbing his eyes. There was a bit of stalling and static, partially his codes talking their way around the *Zero*'s security settings and partly the drug store's ancient connection, and then finally Rami's face flickered into focus.

"Commander?" Webb saw her trying to fight a smile. "It's good to see you."

"Likewise," Webb replied, feeling a smile spread across his own face.

"I know how you like to keep us on our toes, Zeek but..." she paused and her brow furrowed as as she took in his appearance. "What happened?"

"No time to explain," he sighed, "but please, God, tell me you're not still dirt-side?"

"No. When you weren't at the drop off point we retreated back to orbit."

"Thank fuck."

"What's going on?"

Webb shook his head. "Something's not right," he said. "Maintain comm silence until further notice. We can't get back to the drop off point, it's too close to the base. Is there anywhere else nearby you could come get us?"

She glanced off screen and tapped some keys. He felt his heart sink as her face darkened. "You're in a pretty sticky location. There's civilian monitoring stations everywhere."

"There must be something."

He saw her jaw tighten. "There's an abandoned air field to the north, about sixty miles. We may be able to slip through the monitoring there, if we're quick."

"Nothing closer?"

Rami shook her head. "Only if we risk getting picked up on the local scans."

"No," Webb said, rubbing his eyes. "AI will be monitoring them. Fuck it. We'll be at the airfield in an hour... have the medbay ready."

"The captain?"

Webb shook his head. "Not good. This whole thing stinks, Rami. I think they knew we were coming." She blanched. "Yeah," he said, grinding his teeth. "Right. Time to haul ass. Oh, Rami..."

"Don't worry," she gave a tight smile. "Already wiping the store's camera banks."

"And the street cameras too," he replied, smiling himself. "See you in an hour."

"Better had. Out."

The screen went blank. Webb glanced at his wrist panel, with the captain's heartbeat still flashing in the corner. He pulled up the local area map, worked out a route to the airfield, then hauled himself upright.

He loaded the pockets of the coat and boiler suit with pain killers, bottles of water and energy drinks. He opened and downed one of the bitter drinks as he hobbled back to the doors. The waves of pain coupled with exhaustion were threatening to pull him under. He blinked back the grey tickling at the corners of his vision. All they would need right now would be for him to fall asleep at the wheel.

The dark street was still deserted. Panic jolted him when he got back to the car and it appeared to be empty, but then saw the captain had laid himself out of sight across the front seats. He started as Webb pulled the door open, pulling himself upright with difficulty. In the thin street light his skin looked grey and he even forgot to scowl.

"Here," Webb said, dumping his supplies in the driver's seat and shouldering himself out of the coat. The captain's lack of protest as he wrapped the coat around his shoulders was more worrying than the colour of his skin. He opened a bottle of water and handed it over. Hugo took it without a word and dutifully sipped, eyes closed.

"Report," he croaked as Webb cleared and then clambered back into the driver's seat.

"We've got a rendezvous an hour to the north."

Hugo didn't reply but his gaze slid sideways as Webb swallowed some pain pills. "Status?"

"Damn site better than you, Captain," Webb muttered, blinking through the dizziness and opened another energy drink. The car growled to life and they pulled out. Webb concentrated on not going too fast though his pulse was pounding in his ears and his skin was itching with the sensation of being watched. Even when they pulled out onto better lit roads with more traffic and no one paid them any mind, he couldn't entirely shake the feeling.

He slid another glance at the captain's pale face and switched on the radio, fiddling until he found some loud music.

"Sorry sir," he said in response to Hugo's scowl. "But you need to try and stay awake."

Webb saw him grit his teeth but he didn't reply. Webb let the music fill him and anchor him, whilst he wove in and out of the traffic, bearing always north. He didn't breathe easily again until they pulled off onto another side street and the traffic diminished. He was just daring to think that maybe they were going to get out of the town unseen when sirens started blaring somewhere behind them and lights began flashing in the rear view. His hands tightened on the wheel and he threw a glance over his shoulder.

"Shit. Guess that's our luck all up. Buckle up, Captain."

The captain swore as the car leaped forward. The radio was lost in the roaring of the engine. Webb overtook the little traffic there was at a speed that jerked them about in their seats.

"Jeeps," the captain said.

Webb spared a glance from the road to see the captain had produced some binoculars and was craning to look out the rear windscreen.

"AI and not local enforcement, then," Webb gritted. He flung them around a bend in the road just as there was a roaring whine and blinding light as two flyers sped overhead. "Shit, shit, shit."

"If they were going to shoot us we'd be dead already," Hugo said.

Webb muttered darkly as they hurtled around another bend. The road inclined steadily as they climbed further up the mountain. It was worse than he'd thought from what he'd seen on the maps, twisting and dark. The captain used his binoculars to keep an eye out the back to start with, but Webb soon noticed the knuckles of his good hand were white and he locked his gaze ahead.

Eventually, even though Webb was the more reckless driver, the fact that the company men knew the roads and were in more powerful vehicles began to show. Their four-by-fours ate the road hungrily and it wasn't long before the headlights were flashing in his rear view again.

"How much further?"

"Not far. Hang on, captain," Webb warned and flung them off the main road and onto a dirt track that had been almost hidden in the trees. The little car jerked and bucked beneath them. The captain grunted and Webb felt a hiss of his own escape his teeth. He blinked past the pain and the tyres bit into the dirt, and they sped off in a cloud of dust and grinding wheels. The flyers did another pass overhead, their lights washing the gaps between the trees in white. Webb cursed again but managed to keep on track. When headlights didn't reappear behind he dared hope they hadn't noticed their change in direction.

"The flyers will have scanners," Hugo grunted.

"We just need to keep ahead a little longer... fuck."

"What?"

"We're early," Webb said, looking back from his wrist panel out the front.

"How early?"

"The *Zero*'s not due for another twenty minutes."

Webb didn't hear the captain's reply as the car pitched through a rough part of the track. When the headlight beams levelled out again he slammed on the brakes to stop them ploughing into a pair of metal gates. When the dust cleared he leant forward, seeing the solid iron loom up out of sight into the dark above them. There was wire fencing scattered with signs so old and rusted it was impossible to tell what they had once said.

"This is it."

"*What* is it?"

"Our rendezvous site. It's an abandoned airfield. Sit tight."

Webb didn't wait for the captain to answer but scrambled out. Above the rasping of his breathing there was nothing beside the low hum of the resting car engine. He strained his ears and picked up the distant, faint whine of flyer engines. He shook himself and limped over to the control panel for the gates. He shed the baseball cap, scraping his stiff hair back from his face and pulled the front off the rusted control box. His heart sank when he saw the state of the wiring underneath, all mildewed and cracked. He pulled off his gloves and wiped his hands on his trousers to try and get rid of the worst of the sweat.

It was just as he was reaching in to try and start rewiring that he heard the sound of tyres gritting on dirt and engines growling in the distance.

"Shit." His heart hammered in his ears and his fingers shook as he pulled and rearranged the wires. "Come on, for fuck's sake. Come *on*."

The wires sparked but nothing happened. He was spitting more curses when he felt a hand on his shoulder and jumped.

"You're shaking too much. Get ready to drive."

Webb let out a breath and obeyed without argument for once. The captain bent to the control panel as Webb scrambled back to the car. He was just shutting the car door and checking it was ready to go when, with a grinding of protesting metal, the gates began to swing inwards.

"Yes," Webb crowed, impressed despite himself. "Nice one, Captain. Now get your ass back here."

The captain dropped himself back into the passenger seat and Webb was motoring forward before he'd even shut the door. He could see flashes of headlights in the trees behind them. The gates had opened about half way and lumbered to a stop but the gap was just big enough for the civilian vehicle to squeeze through.

"Fingers crossed it's too narrow for the Jeeps," he mumbled. The captain grunted. One glance at his wrist panel told him there was no way it would delay them long enough.

The car sped through a maze of track and crumbled buildings before careening out onto an old runway. All they could see in the glow of the headlights was the ancient stretch of tarmac with grass growing high in clumps in the cracks and darkness beyond.

"How much longer?"

"Too damn long."

A derelict control tower appeared ahead and Webb made for it. He pulled outside the entrance and killed the car's engine before clambering from the car and moving round to the captain's door. Hugo was already struggling out of the seat. Ignoring the captain's protests and grunts of pain Webb grabbed his good arm and heaved it up over his shoulders. Once they were upright they staggered towards the doors.

Webb didn't know how they made it but they did. He kicked the door open and they stumbled inside. He attempted to lower the captain to the floor gently but ended up half falling and dumping Hugo onto the concrete. Resting on his knees, he hung his head and clutched his ribs. The sweat dripped from the ends of his hair and he spent a minute fighting the urge to vomit.

When he blinked himself back into a state where he could focus, he saw the captain had propped himself against the wall, good arm over his abdomen and face screwed up in agony. It wasn't long before the sounds of tyres in the distance filtered through to them and the flashing of approaching headlights appeared on the walls around them.

His wrist panel told him there was still twelve minutes to go before the *Zero* showed up.

"Captain. Captain Hugo?" He had to say it twice before the captain opened his eyes. "I'm gonna draw them off."

The captain made an inarticulate noise of protest.

"We don't have a choice, sir," Webb replied, gathering together the remnants of his strength to haul himself to his feet. "The *Zero* will be here in eleven minutes. If I can just keep them off that long -"

"No, Webb," the captain croaked. "That's an order."

"Sorry sir," he said and attempted to grin. "You'll have to throw me in the brig when I come back."

"Commander," the captain croaked as Webb half staggered, half fell back towards the door.

"I'll be back. Trust me."

"Webb! Come back, come back now! That's an order! Damn it, Webb!"

The door swung shut behind Webb, muffling Hugo's shouts. Headlights bobbed in the distance. He took a deep breath and dumped himself back behind the wheel of the car. The engine screamed as he tore it back to life and he threw the wheel round, powering back the way they'd come. He turned the headlights on full beam and was gratified to see the lights of the AI Jeeps turn his way. He actually laughed as he sped across the open space, the enemy gaining all the time but leaving the control tower behind.

A wire fence loomed ahead. He went at it head on, shutting his eyes at the last minute but not letting up on the accelerator. There was a sickening lurch and a crunch and blackness threatened to take him under, but when his vision returned he saw he was through the fence and powering along another dirt road. Heart in his mouth, he kept moving and felt the track smooth out under him as he hauled the car back out onto the main road and turned it uphill.

The one working headlight showed the incline steepening. On his right, the sheer cliff face arched up into darkness. On his left, a low iron barrier and then nothingness.

Even better, he thought. The company men were bound to take these corners more carefully than him. And sure enough, forcing his awareness above the hammering of his pulse that scoured pain through his limbs, he realised the pursuit was falling back. The flyers still made their passes overhead, trying to blind and confuse him with their sweeping lights, but he pressed on. He just needed a bit more ground.

He took the next corner so fast that two wheels left the road but then swore when the blinking lights of a road block came into sight up ahead.

"Fuck it all," he said and steeled himself. His sensible side made him slow before opening the driver's door and flinging himself out. There was a sickening moment of nothingness then everything was pain, heat, spinning, then it all went black.

V

Hugo cursed Webb in every language he knew. He had tried to scramble after him but his good hand had closed on nothing and the momentum tipped him forward onto his face. He landed on his broken arm and for a minute knew only white light. He came to a couple of seconds later, just in time to hear tyres screech and see the lights that had been flashing on the walls turn in another direction and fade away.

"Damn him, damn him to Hell." Hugo clung to his anger, fired it and fed it, not wanting to face what was underneath. When he stopped his cursing he realised how quiet it had become. The air was dark and tasted like dust. There was still five minutes until the Zero would arrive and he had to stay awake, had to get his crew scrambled and send them after Webb. He had to get him back safe so he could kick his insubordinate ass.

Everything swirled in and out of focus and he tried desperately to gather enough energy to watch the little green light still flashing away in the corner of his wrist panel. He breathed in and out, feeling his own pulse racing along with the fevered blinking. Then it went blank. Hugo shook the panel, tapped it with his finger. Still nothing.

"No," he ground out. "No...Webb, you bastard!"

The drone of ship engines filled the air and the lobby was flooded with light. The ground shuddered below him and more dust rained down from above. The door flung open and he didn't even try to deny the relief that flooded him when Sub and Bolt's hulking figures filled the doorway. He saw them cast a glance round, note that he was alone and move forward without a word.

"Webb," Hugo croaked, though the whiteness was closing across his vision. "Commander Webb..." But then he was being hauled up into someone's arms like he was no more than a rag doll and whiteness washed over and swamped him.

Ø

Pulling himself back took almost more than Hugo had. He could measure the length and breadth of his body with the aching. He felt the rise and fall of his breaths and there was a cool, minty taste in his mouth. One arm moved but one arm didn't. The one that didn't was throbbing. He took three deep breaths, using the pain to rope himself back into his flesh. At last, with an effort of will that almost had him sliding back under, he blinked his eyes open.

He grunted as the lights of the medbay flooded his brain. He felt his heart hammer and heard a beeping close by increase at the same rate. He forced himself to stay calm. Opening his eyes more slowly, he managed to focus on the bulkhead above him. The sounds of the ship started filtering through, the beep and whirr of equipment as well as the steady bleeping of his heart monitor. His breaths echoed. He raised his good hand and found a mask covering his mouth and nose and pulled it off. He took a deep breath of the metallic air of the Zero and his mind cleared.

Spinn's voice came from somewhere close by. "...they're too good to leave anything obvious."

"Well keep digging. Webb's never been wrong before."

There was a pause. "Any news?" the researcher asked, almost in a whisper.

Hugo turned his head to the side and could make out More's grim face on the screen of the doctor's medbay workstation. "Nothing yet. We'll let you know when there is." And the screen went blank.

Hugo dragged another breath in, held it and pulled himself up. The wires and tubes attached to him tightened and he growled, shutting his eyes against the flashing lights in his head.

"Captain!" When Hugo opened his eyes, Spinn was at his bedside, hands out as if he were thinking about pushing him him back down. "Captain, you need to lie down."

"Webb," Hugo croaked, his dry throat cracking. "Webb's in trouble..."

"Sir, Rami left strict orders -"

Hugo used his good hand to pull off the lead for the heart monitor and detach his IV line. He blinked against a wave of dizziness. When he came back to himself he screwed his eyes up, trying to bring the chrono display on the wall into focus with a sinking feeling. "How long have I been under?"

"Almost twenty four hours now, sir."

"*Twenty four hours?*" Hugo half-barked. "What's happened? Have we found him?"

"Sir..." Spinn managed. "You must rest."

Hugo flung off the thin blanket and hauled himself to his feet. Spinn looked like he might object again but Hugo silenced him with a look. He took a second to lean against the bulkhead and wait for his head to stop spinning and the gnawing pain in his abdomen to calm, then left, hurrying toward the bridge. He was clad only in a pair of thin med-issue bottoms and shivered in the corridor, but kept moving. His left arm in its brace he kept clutched against his stomach, right arm out to steady himself against the bulkhead. The drugs were wearing off and the pain flashed stronger with every step. He pushed it down and kept moving, heaving himself up the stairway to the bridge.

"Report," he barked as he set foot on the deck, causing Kinjo and More to jump and look up from where they were bent over the control panel. The viewscreen showed a wide stretch of stars and the cloudy curve of the Earth far below.

"Captain," Kinjo exclaimed in horror. "You shouldn't be up. Rami said -"

"Report. Now. Where the hell are we?"

"In orbit, sir," More responded, more calmly.

"Get back down to that airfield immediately, Sub-Lieutenant."

"Sir, procedure dictates -"

"Fuck procedure. We have a man down there." He deliberately refused to think about the green light on his wrist panel blinking to nothing. "Get moving. That's an order."

"Sir," More repeated, infuriatingly calm, raising a hand. "Let me explain. We received a transmission a few hours ago."

"What sort of transmission?" Hugo glowered, leaning against the command chair. Kinjo pursed her lips but didn't say anything.

"It was pretty scrambled," More said, turning and punching commands into the control panel. "But it looks like it was sent from a public comm booth, not far from the airfield where we found you."

"What did it say?"

"Not much," More said. "Took some decoding but it looks to be a set of co-ordinates."

Hugo blinked up at the display and saw More had pulled up a map of that twice-damned mountain range. "It's Webb. It's got to be. What's there?"

More shook his head. "Nothing, sir." A green cross flashed on the map. "There's nothing there. Older reports indicate there's a derelict church on the spot, but nothing else. It's miles from the main groundway."

"And miles from the local monitoring systems," Hugo mumbled. He straightened. "Get us a heading -"

More raised his hand again. "Rami and Bolt are already there, Captain."

"And?" Hugo asked, keeping his voice steady despite the coldness he felt welling up inside him.

"There was no one there. They decided to wait, but nothing so far."

More said.

"Well I bloody hope they've taken rations with them because they're staying there until he shows up," Hugo said.

More just nodded. "Yes, sir."

Hugo clutched the command chair as another wave of dizziness caused him to sway. He jumped when he felt warm hands steady him.

"Now sir, please. You must return to the medbay." Hugo attempted to glower as Kinjo tried to lead him away. She frowned and put her hands on her hips, determination in every inch of her small frame. "Now, sir, with all due respect, it seems Webb went through a hell of a lot to get you back to the ship in one piece. I don't think he'd be happy if you died right here on the bridge from ruptured suturing."

Hugo glared a second more but then sagged. He blinked down at himself for the first time and realised how heavily bandaged he was and how blackened and bruised the skin around the bandages was. Every beat of his heart brought a dull thud of pain from his innards, arm and head and he closed his eyes and nodded. He felt Kinjo's hands on him again, marvelled a moment at the strength in them, and let her lead him back towards the corridor.

"Don't worry sir," she said in a softer voice, though Hugo could hear the tightness in it. "It's not the first time the commander's disappeared on us."

By the time they were back in the medbay, everything was throbbing so badly he was grateful to clamber back onto the bunk. He let Kinjo re-attach his heart monitor but held up a hand when she brought the IV line round. "No," he mumbled. "I need to be able to wake up..."

She pursed for a moment but then softened. "Very well, Captain," she said, turning away. "On one condition." She rifled in a nearby cupboard and produced a protein drink and a bottle of tablets. She shook two onto her hand and held them out to him along with the drink.

Hugo eyed them suspiciously.

"They're just painkillers, sir," Kinjo insisted.

He took the pills and swallowed them with the protein drink. She stood with her arms folded until he'd finished the drink, then nodded, though her frown didn't ease.

"Rami's so gonna kill me," she muttered as she took away the empty bottle.

"Don't worry about the lieutenant, Midshipman," Hugo mumbled, ignoring the roiling in his stomach as it attempted to hold in the protein drink. "You were following orders. I will talk to her."

Kinjo sighed, though some of the tension left her face. She leaned over him to try and pull the mask back over his mouth. "It's just oxygen sir," she said, cutting off his protest before he could form it. "And something to encourage healing. Your body needs both right now."

He let her settle the mask back over his mouth and nose and the minty coolness sweetened his mouth and filled his lungs again. He felt himself relax and the pain ebbed back to a dull thing at the back of his awareness.

"Thank you," Hugo heard his own voice from far away, but drifted off before he heard whether Kinjo replied or not.

Ø

The part of Webb that was still capable of cognitive thought was glad that he could only measure time with the pulses of his heart that pushed the agony around his body. He thought that if he knew the actual amount of time it took to pull himself back to consciousness, blink open one working eye and haul himself to his feet, he would have probably given up on the whole thing and laid back down and died right there at the roadside. As it was, he took it one heartbeat at a time and concentrated on the memory of the captain's last order...

"*Webb! Come back, come back now, that's an order! Damn it, Webb!*"

He had to get back. He had to prove he knew what he was doing. He had survived worse. The other thought that kept him pulling his breath in and out was knowing that if he died, Rami would kill him.

The pull of the grin that this thought brought him caused pain to lance through his face and he gave up on the idea of facial expressions and cognitive thought for a moment in order to lean against the rock and concentrate on not passing out or throwing up. He was upright, at least. That was a good thing and frankly more than he expected of himself. Only one leg would take his weight. He didn't look down to see the state of the other one. It seemed every inch of skin was raw and sticky with blood. He quickly found out deep breaths were impossible, but was relieved to discover that the blood in his mouth had come from his split lip and smashed teeth and not from his lungs.

He spat the mess out and opened the one eye that would obey. The air was grey and chilled but whether it was early morning or late evening he couldn't tell. The road was deserted. There was scattered glass and scorch marks on the tarmac. Fluttering yellow tape roped off the gap in the barrier. He marvelled for a moment that the AI security force had failed to find him lying in the two-foot stretch of scrub and dirt between the side of the road and cliff, but then it probably never occurred to them that anyone would be stupid enough to fling themselves out of a vehicle going at that speed on a mountain road.

He was reminded again that he couldn't grin and instead attempted putting one foot in front of the other. He found if he was slow and careful, he could just about move. He made it over to the other side of the road and peered down the mountain. The wreckage of the car was gone. Not even a tyre or twist of metal left behind. He turned away, not having the energy to follow the thoughts to any sort of conclusion, to be faced with the ugly reality that he was going to have to decide what to do next. His wrist panel was a shattered, unresponsive mess. Guilt nagged at him as he realised his heartbeat feed would have blinked out on the captain's panel.

It had darkened since he'd come round which meant it was evening after all, which also meant he must have been lying by the road for a full day. He guessed he was still here because of one of the few Service statutes he agreed with: no crew member or vessel is to be risked for the retrieval of the dead. So in order to prove he knew what he was doing and had in fact survived, he needed to get another message to the *Zero*. Somehow.

Closing his eyes, he tried to bring the maps of the area into his mind's eye. They were stubborn and refused to complete themselves in any detail. All he could remember was that down the mountain led towards the airfield, the town and the AI Command Centre. So up the mountain it was.

It was easy when he looked at it that way. He shuffled back to the other side of the road so he had the cliff face to lean on and began following it uphill. Slowly. He stared straight ahead, concentrated on each breath, each step, each foot of progress gained. There was little traffic but he was glad that night was drawing in again, letting him see the headlights of any vehicle long before they came in sight. The sheer rock face on his right gave way to scrubby woodland and he was able to stumble into the shadows of the trees whenever anything passed.

He carried on, not knowing how long he moved for, just occasionally noticing the view around him changing and night setting in. The clouds hid the stars and he was grateful for the cover but couldn't ignore the pang of isolation he felt without them. He'd also hoped he might have been able to see one bright speck creeping across the sky and fancy it the *Zero*, drifting dutifully, waiting for his call.

He finally had to stop and lean against a tree, close his eye and will his lungs to keep breathing and his heart to keep beating. It would be so easy to just lie down in the soft leaf litter and let it all go. The world would carry on. The *Zero* would carry on. They could get another commander. It wouldn't be hard to find some other nameless colony orphan who knew how to sneak and steal and lie. Any one of them would put their necks on the line in exchange for regular meals. A couple of years training on the *Endeavour* training station and they could be shoved onto the Zero to pick up where Webb had left off. It would be like he'd never been.

But if he lay down and gave up, that would prove Hugo right.

"Well, we can't have that."

He wasn't sure if he'd said it out loud or just in his head, but the thought brought him swimming back to the surface and he pulled himself back up off the tree and kept moving. Almost as if he were being rewarded for his tenacity, light showed up ahead. Stationary light, not headlights. He moved off the road and approached from the shelter of the trees. His working eye screwed up as the light grew stronger and he felt his head begin to pound but he ignored it and stumbled on.

It was a fuelling station. An honest-to-God, open and working civilian fuelling station, complete with public comm booth. A single car was just pulling away and he stepped back into the shadows until it was out of sight. Peering back round he saw the clerk in the store had his back to the window and was watching sport on a wall display. He waited ten heartbeats to make sure the clerk was thoroughly engrossed and then stepped out onto the tarmac and dragged himself into the comm booth.

The blue screen flashed the minimum credit fee. He blinked a few times to try and stop his vision swimming and started typing in commands. Normally he could hack a civilian comm station blindfolded and it alarmed him how long it took him to get past its protocols. He was aware of the time with every beat of blood in his head and the fact that the comm booth was in full view of the public highway as well as the store.

Finally the machine let him in but he didn't let himself pause, willing his focus not to waver, and pulled up a map of the area. The civilian net maps didn't quite have the same amount of detail as his wrist panel would have, but he saw enough to satisfy him that he had made the right decision. There was nothing this far up the mountain apart from hiking tracks and some more battle-scarred landscape. It bugged him that he couldn't be sure, but from the looks of things he'd left most of the heavy-duty monitoring and scanning ranges behind. He cast about for somewhere suitable to select for a pick-up point that was within staggering distance of the fuelling station. His heart sank when he saw there was nowhere near that had the space to let the *Zero* come herself and none of it was as remote as he would have liked.

He settled for a spot further up the mountain and off the main road that would at least let a fighter land, took a note of the co-ordinates and then set about attempting to get them coded and sent to the ship. It wasn't his best encryption. Rami would have tutted and shook her head. But it was all he could manage. Even if he was capable of coding a secure visual link to the *Zero*, he was afraid how whoever answered might react when they saw the state of him.

With one last push he wiped the memory on the comm unit and pushed the doors back open, wincing at the smears of blood he left on the glass, then dragged himself over the forecourt. The sight of the goods in the store made him realise how thirsty and hungry he was. But he was way beyond any stealth or slight of hand so he shuffled back into the trees and kept moving, putting his hunger and thirst back in his mental box with the pain.

It could have been an hour later or it could have been ten minutes when it started to rain. He paused his uphill shuffle and laughed, tilting his head back. He revelled in the feel of the cool water rinsing the dried blood and muck from his face, revelled in the stinging feel of it getting into his wounds. He heaved a great sigh and took a moment just to feel it soak into his hair and the tatters of his clothes. The colonies' artificial weather never came close to that of the Earth and he knew as long as he lived he would never tire of the feel of being in amongst something so real and wild.

But it wasn't long before the pleasantness of the rain wore off and he began to shiver. His boiler suit was soaked and clung like dead skin. His legs seemed to be getting heavier. For a while he knew nothing except the cold making everything shudder and sting and the drag of his feet through the mud.

It took a long time to pull himself back together and when he did he realised with a start that he was no longer on the main road but shambling up an overgrown dirt track. The rain had stopped at some point and the sky was pinpricked with stars. The sight of them made his heart lift and he kept moving forward, hoping that his autopilot had taken him down the right track.

Some indefinable time later he saw a tall, dark shape blotting out some of the stars ahead. He ignored the pain in his jaw and lips and let himself grin when he saw it was a church spire. He had made it. Even if there was no one there, even if no one came, he had made it.

The concrete steps that led up to the front door seemed like a cruel obstacle after everything else but he delved down deep and found the last shreds of his strength. It took him a moment to realise that the door stood ajar and there was the sound of familiar voices arguing within. Even if he'd wanted to stop his tattered smile he couldn't. He shouldered the door open and staggered in. Two figures were hunched in the shadowy pews and they fell silent when he entered.

"Hey guys," he croaked in a voice he didn't recognise. "Good of you to come."

He let go the death-grip he had on his last threads of awareness and slipped into blessed darkness.

Ø

"Kinjo? Come in, Kinjo."

Hugo jerked, blinking through the fog. Rami's voice was tinny and distant and sounded strained.

"I'm here, Anita," Kinjo replied and Hugo heaved himself up onto his elbow, pulling off the oxygen mask and taking great gulps of real air in an attempt to heave himself back to reality. Rami's face on the wall display was pale and he felt his blood run cold.

"Get the surgical bay ready. Now," she barked. "I need all X-rays and scanners online. And get scrubbed up. I'm going to need you."

"Is he -?"

"Now, Kinjo. We're almost with you. Out."

Kinjo cast one pained look over her shoulder at Hugo before rushing into the surgical bay. He pulled himself up to sit on the edge of the bunk and watched her boot up all the scanners and screens. The next thing he was aware of was the ship shuddering under him as the cargo bay doors closed and pressurised.

He barely had time to gather his thoughts when Rami burst through the medbay doors, dishevelled and grimy, followed closely by Bolt who appeared to be carrying a vaguely human-shaped bundle of rags. Hugo only just had time to make out that it was Webb before Bolt was following Rami through the glass doors into the surgical bay.

He got to his feet and padded over like he was in a dream. Bolt laid the limp figure down on the table and retreated. If it hadn't been for the height of the frame and the boots, about the only bit of his clothing left intact, Hugo wouldn't have recognised his commander. Every bit of exposed skin was a ripped and bloody mess. One eye was completely obscured by blood and swelling and the rest of his face was just blood, cuts and burns. His mouth hung open in an alarming way and some teeth were missing. None of his limbs seemed to be lying at normal angles and he didn't seem to be breathing.

The sudden feel of a calloused but gentle hand on his bare shoulder made him jump.

"If he can be saved, sir," Bolt's voice was low. "Rami will save him."

Hugo leant against the bulkhead as Rami took a pair of shears to the remains of Webb's clothing. Kinjo was already starting the scanners and part of Hugo felt pride spark as he watched the women work. He stayed just long enough to see Rami peel away some of the boiler suit to reveal bone protruding from Webb's torso and then turned away.

He grabbed a white t-shirt from the stack of medbay supplies and left. He was relieved to realise that he didn't feel like was going to pass out with every step any more, though the sharper aches of healing tissue were now setting in. He paused as he pulled the shirt on, and took a minute to breathe in the quiet of the corridor. He'd seen injuries and worse before. But this was different. This was his fault.

He took himself onto the bridge. More was at the controls and Spinn was at one of the workstations. After a closer look Hugo saw that the researcher was bent over the shattered remains of Webb's wrist panel. He felt a stab of anger that the man could sit there and work when his commander lay below clinging to life. But it was mitigated by a wash of jealousy at not having any task of his own to distract him.

He lowered himself into the copilot seat and glanced over the control panel. There was no destination set but they were moving away from Earth.

"Any particular heading, Captain?" More asked.

Hugo blinked out at the vastness beyond the screen without really seeing anything. "Where's the nearest colony?" he found himself asking.

More tapped a few commands into the control panel. "Lunar 5, Captain."

"How are its medical facilities?"

"Service-grade. But, sir, I believe -"

"I know," Hugo cut him off. "He stands a better chance with Rami than with any overrun colony medic. Set a course, but keep the engines in economy mode. That'll buy us some time. Request docking but don't tell them anything and don't let anyone leave or enter the ship when we arrive."

More looked at him. His dark eyes were clear and Hugo thought he could read understanding in them.

"Doctor," Hugo called without turning round. "When will your reports on the mission be ready?"

"I can have them done in a couple of hours, Captain."

"Good. Do so. But don't send them to Luscombe. Not yet."

"Yes, sir."

Hugo thought he heard understanding in the doctor's voice too. "How long until Lunar 5?"

"Eight hours at present speed, Captain."

He scrubbed his good hand over his face, knew he was going to have to think long and hard about what to do next but his head, arm and muscles all pounded dully, making it impossible to focus. He wished he could ask Webb's opinion.

Ø

"Rami to bridge. Come in, bridge."

Hugo jerked awake, back and neck stiff from nodding off in the copilot chair.

"Hugo here, Lieutenant," he croaked, attempting to keep his voice steady. The chrono on the screen told him it had been several hours. Rami's face appeared on the viewscreen display. She was just pulling off her surgical mask. Her jaw muscles were tight and her dark hair was plastered to her forehead. "How is he?"

"Stable, captain. Just. I've cleaned and stitched everything up and set all the bones. He seems to have somehow managed to avoid any serious internal injury but the external trauma is extensive. We've done all we can. It's up to him now."

Hugo nodded, swallowing against a nasty taste in his mouth.

"What happened to him, can you tell?"

Rami shook her head. "Jumped off a cliff? Run over by a truck? It's impossible to tell, Captain. Something hit back hard, I'd say. But Webb never does anything by half. We'll know more in the next twenty-four hours."

"Thank you, Lieutenant. You and Kinjo..." His voice faltered. "Thank you. You should both get some rest now."

Rami nodded and the display went blank.

"You should rest too, Captain," More suggested.

Hugo rubbed his eyes again. Everything felt very heavy.

"I will be in my cabin," he said eventually, not able to face the idea of going back to the medbay. "Wake me if -"

"Any change in anything, Captain, I'll send for you."

Hugo gave the sub-lieutenant a grateful look but he wasn't looking. His attention was on the controls and Hugo saw the tension in the way the man sat. Guilt washed through him. Webb was their crewmate too. They had been nothing but calm and efficient through this whole episode whilst Hugo had shouted and snarled and thrown his weight about. As painful as it had been for him, he knew it must be ten-fold so for each one of them. And not once had their focus wavered.

He padded from the bridge with defeat sweeping through him. He could almost taste the shame and commanded his cabin door to lock behind him. He didn't turn on the light but just made sure his comm station was open and ready before collapsing on his bunk and turning his face to the wall.

He didn't manage to fall back asleep. He lay and stared into the dark, thoughts chasing themselves around his head until More came on the display to announce they were coming up on Lunar 5.

"Set in the docking course, then I want everyone to meet in the galley."

"Yes, sir."

More's feed went blank just as a beeping indicated another incoming message.

"On screen," Hugo said and Rami's face appeared. She looked better, not so pale.

"He's awake, Captain."

"I'll be right there." He paused long enough to pull on some proper clothes then made his way back down to the medbay.

Webb was still on the gurney, though it had been adjusted so he was sitting up. Half his face was obscured by bandaging. His torso was also bound, and his shoulder. All the blood had been cleaned away but his skin looked all the paler and the bruising all the more livid for it. His breathing seemed shallow too, but Hugo was damned if the man didn't attempt a grin when he came in.

"Managed to keep the *Zero* in one piece I see, Hugo," he croaked.

"More than you can say for yourself."

He gave a tiny shrug. "I've had worse."

"And frankly I'm getting a little tired of stitching you up, Ezekiel," Rami said as she scanned readings on a monitor.

"Wouldn't want you to get bored, Lieutenant."

"What's his status?"

Rami skimmed through a couple more read outs on the monitor. "Stable, Captain," he could hear the relief in her voice. "Hardier than a cockroach."

"Missed you too, Anita," Webb mumbled, though his smile looked grim with the broken lips and missing teeth.

"What happened?" Hugo snapped.

Webb's turned his head with an effort to focus his good eye on Hugo. "I shook them off."

"How?"

"Drove the car off a cliff."

Hugo crossed his arms. "I think that is stupider than jumping out of a window or blowing yourself up."

"In my defence, I wasn't in it at the time."

"Of course you weren't." Rami muttered, shining a lenslight in his good eye. "I'm guessing from the road rash you chose to eat tarmac instead."

"Better than eating cliff-bottom."

"Then what happened?" Hugo prodded.

"I don't know," Webb mumbled. "I was drooling at the side of the road from then until sunset. They took the car away though. Captain...that's not good news."

"I know. Lieutenant?"

Rami looked up. "Yes, sir?"

"What do you recommend for the commander?"

Rami made a disgusted noise. "I would want him to spend six weeks at least in re-coup. You'd have to drug him or lock him in the brig to keep him down that long though."

"Six weeks it is."

"Captain," Webb started to protest.

"We are approaching Lunar 5. We'll get you a boarding pod and you are to stay there and recover."

"Captain, no," Webb said, trying to sit up.

"Six weeks, Commander," he repeated, allowing frustration to come through in his voice. "And I trust you will spend it thinking on the consequences of disobeying my orders."

Webb fell silent, mouth open.

"Lieutenant," Hugo said, gesturing out the door. Rami followed him out. "Do you know anyone medical on Lunar 5 you trust?"

Rami contemplated him a moment then nodded. "Yes, sir."

"Contact them. In person, not on the comm. We'll get Webb to a boarding pod and get them to keep an eye on him."

Rami nodded. "Very well, sir."

"Now get to the galley. I've called a meeting."

Rami nodded and left, casting one glance over her shoulder as she did. Hugo looked up through the glass doors to where Webb lay, staring up at the bulkhead then turned and followed.

Ø

"Spinn. Anything you can tell me?"

Spinn scratched at his head. "There was very little I could get from either wrist panel, Captain, that would help explain anything. There is one thing though. They both seem to have picked up strong traces of phozone at some point while you were in the complex."

"Phozone?" Rami asked, frowning.

"What's phozone?" Hugo asked.

"It's a chemical agent, sir," Rami said. "A sort of preservative. It's used when working with biological samples. I have some in sickbay for preserving blood for testing."

Hugo frowned, remembering the smell on the third floor corridor. "AI make security systems and weapons," he said. "What are they doing with phozone?"

Spinn swallowed. "There's nothing on any official or public records that would explain it, sir."

"Can you check some unofficial ones?"

Spinn nodded. "I'll keep looking, sir."

Hugo sighed and rubbed at his forehead, trying to sort out his tangled thoughts. "Luscombe will be expecting a report," Hugo said.

The crew all sat around the galley looking stiff.

"Sir," Spinn started, twisting his fingers together. "I am inclined to respect Webb's judgement in this."

"You think it may have been a trap?"

"I do."

"Set by whom? And to what end?"

Spinn swallowed, looked to Rami and then back at Hugo. "If AI are in any way involved with potential Lunar independence sympathisers... you could potentially be quite a powerful playing piece in any political game."

"Me?"

There were nods around the room. Some gazes were darker than others.

"Service-trained," Spinn dogged on. "With a powerful family."

"Disgraced," Hugo put in.

"All the better, sir," More said. "More likely to make you sympathetic to their cause."

Hugo paused, crossing his arms and looking at the earnest faces all looking at him. "They've been trying to recruit Webb."

"They have?" Rami said.

"You didn't know?" A series of shaking heads around the room. "Fitzroy himself has talked to Webb and has been trying to track him down since. Don't you think it's more likely the trap was for him?"

"No," Kinjo said, firmly. "There's no reasoning."

"So he said," Hugo said. "But the fact remains that this Fitzroy himself has been after him."

"They may have tried to recruit him, Captain," Rami said, her voice a little tight. "But if they did, it is more likely because they were hoping to bring in the *Zero* and our network of connections. They don't know we're Service-commissioned. But we wouldn't be worth laying such a complex trap for."

"So, if they were after me like you think, why not just approach me in a bar like they did Webb?" Hugo carried on. "Why do I deserve such a complex trap?"

"You're a more valuable prize, sir," More put in. "And I imagine they thought you'd be... resistant."

"So we get to the next point," Hugo said, straightening his back and looking around his crew. "How did they know I was coming? Hell, how did they know *anyone* was coming?"

"I don't know, sir," Spinn said. "We've dug through everything we could. I've confirmed what tipped off Luscombe's fears – AI's revenue stream isn't entirely accounted for. But I can't find anything else untoward. Certainly no obvious link between AI and Fitzroy, let alone the Lunar Independence League or any way they could have known about Luscombe's assignment. Whoever's behind this... they're too good to leave a trail."

Hugo unfolded his arms and paced the length of the galley, then back. He ran his good hand through his hair. Everything was aching and he could not remember ever feeling more tired. "So what do I tell Luscombe?"

There was silence. Heavy glances were exchanged but no one looked at him.

"You're going to have to talk to me, crew," Hugo muttered. "Whatever mess we're in, I'm in it too. And I'm the one the Service is expecting to hear from, one way or another."

"Do you want my recommendation, sir?" Kinjo said in a very small voice.

"Yes," he said. "Yes I do."

"Play dumb. Don't play your hand until you at least have an idea of what the other guy is holding."

"You think Luscombe might be involved?" Hugo asked, trying to ignore the chill in his belly.

Kinjo shook her head. "We don't know, Captain. But it's best to play it safe until we do."

"I'll have to tell him something."

Kinjo lifted her chin and gazed at him levelly. "Tell him you failed. Tell him the mission went wrong. You tripped an alarm before you were able to find anything. It's partially true." Hugo looked at her, tension in her jaw but with her dark eyes burning.

"I should pretend we don't suspect a trap, but tell Luscombe that I screwed up?"

Kinjo didn't blink. "It was your first mission. He'll believe you."

Hugo looked around. "What does everyone else think?"

"I agree," Rami said. "Until we know more, best to appear we know nothing."

"Crewmen? You've been very quiet."

Bolt and Sub looked at each other. "I've lost enough poker against Kinjo to know to never second-guess her instincts," Sub eventually said.

Kinjo didn't react. Hugo drank her in, thinking how much the teenager reminded him of Webb, leant forward on her elbows, her eyes defiant as they held his. He cast a glance at the wall display scrolling through the little that Spinn had managed to retrieve from their wrist panels and unearth in public records on AI, Gabor and Fitzroy. He flicked through it all, stalling for time.

"Very well," Hugo said. "I'll say I made a mistake. The mission failed and we were unable to retrieve anything of significance."

"Don't tell him about Webb either," More put in. "If we're leaving him on Lunar 5 in the state he's in, best no one knows he's there."

Hugo nodded. "Fine. More, secure us a boarding pod for Webb and contact Lunar 5 control to confirm docking."

"Yes, sir."

"Lieutenant, you have your mission in hand?"

"Yes, sir," Rami said.

"Very well," Hugo said, turning back to look at his crew. "Eyes and ears open on all your channels, contacts, points, whatever. Anything, *anything* that gives us any clues as to what's going on, you inform me immediately."

A chorus of *yes sirs* went around the room and then chairs were being pushed back as the crew moved to leave.

Ø

"That is... unfortunate, Captain." Luscombe's face was hard on the cabin wall display.

"I'm sorry, sir," Hugo said, watching Luscombe's reaction closely.

"I suppose we should be just be grateful it wasn't worse," the colonel said, scratching his chin. He looked off to somewhere off-screen. "Very well, Hugo. We will have to leave this matter for now, return to it once the waters have calmed. We'll be lucky if AI don't triple the watch on their systems. But these things happen. You are certain you weren't recognised?"

"I'm certain, Colonel," Hugo lied.

"I think some more routine reconnaissance is in order for you until you find your feet."

Hugo ground his teeth together in his head. "Yes, sir."

"What does Webb have to say about the situation?"

"He agrees with you, Colonel. That it was too soon for me to engage in fieldwork."

The colonel nodded. "I will contact you when we have the next assignment, Hugo," he said. "Until then, work out how to get your head in the game, and quickly. I can play this one down to the admiral but if it happens again I won't have a choice but to let her know you are not fit for this position."

Hugo ducked his head, feeling heat flush his face. "Yes, sir."

"Right. Dismissed, Captain. You will hear from me in due course."

"Yes, Colonel," Hugo said, and his wall display went black. He sat down on his bunk and rubbed his face, willing the anger to subside. "Hugo to bridge," he muttered when he was a little calmer. More's face appeared on the screen.

"Yes, Captain?"

"How are we doing?"

More paused and turned to look over his shoulder. Hugo could make out the sound of cursing in the background. "I think Webb's almost ready to go, Captain."

"I'll be right out," Hugo said with a sigh then made his way to the ship's exit hatch where they were getting ready to help Webb leave.

"You're making a big mistake, Hugo," Webb mumbled. He held the leg with the ankle brace at an odd angle and one arm was strapped up to his chest inside his jacket. He had another baseball cap pulled down low over his bandaged face and he leaned heavily on Bolt.

"Commander, I'd rather manage without you for six weeks than let you stay and it take you ten weeks to get back on form."

Webb shook his head but then just hung it, swaying slightly. Bolt caught him by his jacket.

"You are to stay in your pod and recuperate. Rami has someone who can check on you."

"Come on, Zeek," Rami said, laying a hand on his shoulder. "Let's get you where you can lie down."

Bolt and Rami steadied Webb as he limped off the ship and down the ramp into the docking bay. Hugo watched them go and saw Webb attempt to straighten himself as they reached the exit into the colony.

"Orders, Captain?" More asked as Hugo stepped back onto the bridge. He resisted the urge to rub his temples. His arm and head were pounding. Every muscle burned and his eyes stung with exhaustion. He sensed Kinjo looking at him and straightened himself.

"We need to get away from the Lunar Strip as soon as we can. About the only advantage we have is that no one knows we saw Fitzroy with Gabor. Like Rami said, it's best we keep up the pretense that we know nothing about any potential LIL involvement. If they're not on guard they're more likely to let something slip."

"Where do we go?"

"Sir," Kinjo put in. "There are merchants around this area of Lunar 5 that have good connections with Haven."

Hugo blinked at her. "Are you trying to frighten me, Midshipman?"

"I mean they always have a good supply of high-quality, budget ship and machine parts. The sort that are hard to come by on the Sunside colonies."

"I didn't think anything was hard to come by in the Sunside Strip," Hugo muttered.

"You'd be surprised," Kinjo said.

"If we're to keep up appearances, Captain," More said. "Best we look to be heading away from the Lunar Strip for a reason."

Hugo peered from Kinjo to More and back again. "These parts and the people that buy them...are they legal?"

Kinjo shrugged. "More or less."

Hugo sighed. "Pick up a consignment of whatever you think would sell best in Sunside. Can you get enough to keep us in business for a few weeks?"

Kinjo nodded. "I think so, Captain."

"Do so. More, have everything ready to move out as soon as everyone's back on board." There were a series of acknowledgements and soon it was only Hugo and More left on the bridge. Hugo stared out the viewscreen at the interior of the dry dock, the ache from his own healing injuries a dull veneer over something much grimmer.

"Is there no-one on our side?" Hugo didn't realise he'd spoken out loud until More responded.

"In my experience, sir, there are no sides. Just things you know and things you don't. And people you trust and those you wouldn't lend a spanner to."

Hugo swallowed. "Do you think the crew trusts me?"

"Do you trust us?"

Hugo looked back at More, his dark eyes calm. "I suppose none of us have much of a choice," he murmured.

More gave a small shrug and turned back to the controls. "I suppose that will have to do for now."

Hugo watched More go through pre-launch checks and scans until Rami and Bolt returned.

"How was he?"

Rami shook her head. "Not happy. But I believe you've done the best thing, Captain."

Hugo nodded, ignoring the claw of guilt that hooked itself into his stomach. "Did you remind him to maintain comm silence?"

Rami nodded. "He's not daft enough to give his position away when he's this vulnerable. At least, not quite."

"Good work, Lieutenant. Be ready to move out. We're heading to Sun-side.."

VI

The incident at AI was reported on the inter-Orbit newsfeeds as an un-provoked terrorist attack. Gabor, face grave, urged the Service to do their utmost to find the culprits responsible and bring them to justice. Hugo always switched off before they reeled off the names of the dead.

There was no change that Rami or Spinn could find in the flow of credit or labour between AI and the Lunar Strip. Fitzroy's official sched-ule had him at Governor Cho-Jin's side on board the moon's flagship the Tide, en route to Sydney for a summit. There was nothing official about his impromptu trip to Old Europe and the AI base.

Rami used her fake profiles on underground and illegal message boards and rumour forums to track through all solarnet discussion of groups supporting the re-introduction of an independent Lunar State, but found nothing that she would describe as out of the ordinary.

"There are always troublemakers on these boards, Captain," she said, scrolling her way through a discussion that made the hairs on the back of his neck stand on end. "Disenfranchised sorts blowing off steam or craving the thrill of feeling powerful. But they're like surface rust on the hull: they're more often than not superficial. Only rarely does it go any deeper."

"Is there any mention of LIL?"

"Only in relation to McCullough's Revolution."

None of this however, comforted him.

Hugo accompanied the team on the first few ventures into the Sunside colonies, but quickly learnt he was still a long way off getting his head around the subtleties of underworld wrangling. He didn't let himself ponder too long on whether this was because he was slow to learn or just didn't want to.

He sometimes found himself useful just hanging by the Jeep with a dark look on his face, but this seemed to send things awry as often as it helped secure a deal. After the first few meetings he insisting on regular reports but resorted to staying aboard the *Zero* or pacing around whatev-er docking bay they were berthed in, overseeing routine maintenance on the ship.

They never stayed for long on any one colony. The *Zero* had points scattered all throughout Sunside and they checked in with virtually every one, parts in hand and ears open for gossip. Hugo looked up whenever anyone returned to the ship, only to be met with shaking heads. The mounting impatience and continued uncertainty made him itch.

"Give it up, Captain. You ain't gonna find anything."

Hugo looked up from the data he'd been skimming through on the arm display of his command chair to frown at Bolt, who was sprawled on the deck, shoulder-deep in an access panel.

"You carry on with your work, Crewman, and I'll attend to mine."

Bolt's sigh echoed in the cavity. He extricated himself and sat up, wiping his hands on an oily cloth. "If there was anything to find on this whole LIL thing, Rami would have found it, sir. Believe me, if there's trouble out there, you don't need to worry about tracking it down. It'll find us."

Hugo gave the crewman a heavy look for a moment longer before sighing and leaning back in his chair. Bolt lay back down and crawled back into the cavity, muttering. Hugo stood and went to his cabin to lie on his bunk and once again stare at the bulkhead.

Ø

The days slipped into weeks, one docking bay after another, until they were a blur. The burning frustration ebbed to a dull ache. It felt like it had been a year later when they reached Sunside 5 with the last of their supplies. Hugo had taken to sitting in Webb's seat, even though More was perfectly capable of piloting on his own, just so he felt more engaged. No one said anything as they approached the huge wheel-shaped colony, gleaming a burnished silver against the inky blackness of space. Sunside 5 harbour control assigned them a docking bay and Hugo went through the now familiar docking routine whilst watching Rami's face.

"Does it feel like coming home, Lieutenant?"

Rami didn't look. "It's not home, Captain. It's just where I was born."

He watched out the viewscreen as Sub, Bolt and Kinjo drove the Jeep across the bay and out the gate and onto the exitway into the colony.

"I'm going out," he said after standing and staring at the closed gate for the time it took for his frustration to reach a peak. "I'm on the comm. Rami, you have the bridge."

He retrieved his remaining gun and left, passing through the walk-through exitway gate with only a cursory glance from the customs guard. The Servicemen with automatic rifles didn't even glance at him. He blinked in the sudden light as he stepped out into the colony. The metal ceiling arched hundreds of feet above him, so distant and pale it was almost like a sky. Sunside 5 was, if anything, even warmer than the others.

It also smelt cleaner. It wasn't Earth but it was as close as he'd known a colony to get. He shed his coat before going any further.

He let the foot traffic on the walkways whisk him along, trying to ignore the ache from his arm and the tension of the inactivity that cramped up his neck and shoulders. He was concentrating so hard on not thinking about any of it that it took him a moment to realise what he was doing when he paused at a public comm booth and had to stop himself from dialling his parents' number at Service Headquarters. He stared at the list of inter-Orbit call prices on the screen, then made himself move away.

Pulling his head up, he looked around at another prosperous shopping quarter. Buildings were large and well maintained, paved walkways weaving between them. The traffic on the groundway was almost entirely hovercraft. A few shuttles hummed by on thin rails above his head but there were no skyways cluttering up the space between the buildings. Artificial trees were set at intervals and he thought he could glimpse the green of a park down one of the side streets. Almost as prevalent as the greenery were the security booths at every corner, armed Servicemen at each one.

He took himself across the groundway and into a café on the other side, ordered a coffee and sat himself in a corner by the window where he could watch the colony life roll by. The waitress brought him his coffee with a none-too-subtle glance at his scruffy spacer clothes and then left him alone. He sat there until the night cycle started to draw in and the café emptied out. Soon it was no one apart from himself and one woman sat a couple of tables down, also clad in a flightsuit, nursing a coffee cup and staring at nothing.

He drained his cup and the waitress shooed him out. Ignoring the heavy feeling in his shoulders, he turned back toward the docks. The walkways were empty. The quiet was only broken by the rattles of shop shutters being secured for the night. The Servicemen turned lights on in their security booths. Hugo eyed one as he passed, the familiar grey and black uniform jolting something inside him, then ducked his head and carried on.

As the light dimmed the streets emptied and the silence thickened. He was still some way from the docks when he became aware of a footfall behind him. He turned in time to see a shadow disappearing round a corner. He frowned and waited but no one appeared. He saw a Service officer across the way looking his way and moved on.

He passed a brightly lit entrance to an apartment block and heard it again. He made himself move a couple of paces further on then turned and caught a glimpse of the spacer from the café just before she melted into the shadows again. He peered at the spot where she disappeared, re-sisting putting his hand to his gun. The Service officer was still watching so he resumed pacing as casually as he could then stole down the space between the apartment building and the closed-up retail block next to it. The alley was clean, but dimly lit. He paused at the end but no one followed.

"Hey there." Hugo swore and spun, tried to pull his gun but found himself slammed against the wall with a hand pressed over his mouth. "Shut the fuck up, will you? Want to bring the trigger-jockeys down on our heads?"

Hugo blinked through the spots dancing in his vision into hard green eyes under a mop of mustard-coloured curls. The spacer grinned, glanced down the still-empty alley and let him go.

"Come on," she said, dragging him behind the building by a handful of his jacket.

"Let go," Hugo growled, still fumbling for his gun.

She loosed her hold when they were out of sight and looked him up and down, arms crossed and brow clouded. "Where's Webb?"

"Who are you?" Hugo said, finally managing to draw his gun and level it at the spacer's head.

She raised her eyebrows at him. "Come now, Hugo," she said. "Let's quit playing about. I need to speak to Webb. Where is he?"

"How do you know who I am?" Hugo said, gun held steady.

The woman rolled her eyes. "Honestly, Hugo. I thought you were sup-posed to be clever?"

"Who are you?" he repeated.

"Friend of Webb's. Where are you docked?"

Hugo kept the gun steady. "Name."

She sighed. "Harvey, if you're gonna be pissy about it. Marilyn Har-vey."

Hugo frowned as memories stirred. "From Haven?" She nodded. "How do you know who I am?"

She laughed. "Everyone with a newsfeed knows who you are, Kaleb Hugo. Now, are you going to take me to Webb or am I going to have to make you?"

Hugo sized up the spacer. She stood just about to his shoulder, in a red flightsuit and utility belt and heavy boots. He couldn't see any weapons but the way she held herself showed she wasn't afraid. He lowered his gun.

"That's better," she said. "Now. Where's the *Zero*?"

"Webb's not there."

"He's not?"

Hugo shook his head.

"Where is he?"

"What do you need to talk to him about?"

She eyed him narrowly. "I think that's probably my business."

"Must be something important for you to break cover," Hugo said, watching for any reaction but she kept her face still.

Harvey chewed on her lip for a moment, eyes narrowed at Hugo. "You really the *Zero*'s captain?"

"Yes."

She looked at him a moment longer then threw up her hands and sighed. "Fucking hell. Just my luck. Come on, Captain. Let's get out of sight. I've got something to tell you."

Ø

"Who is she?" Hugo hissed, not taking his eyes off Harvey who sat in the galley with her feet up on the table, chewing on a ration bar.

"She's a spacer, Captain," Rami said with a shrug. "One of our points."

"Smuggler?"

"When it suits her. She's given us good intel in the past and she's helped us on a few of our sticker runs. Plus she knows Haven inside out. You can't buy that kind of information."

"Do you trust her?"

Rami smiled, not entirely nicely. "About as far as I can throw her. But if she's broken cover to tell us something, I'd bet the *Zero* we're going to want to hear what it is."

"She knew I was the *Zero*'s captain."

"Disgraced Service officer turned pirate?" Rami smiled again. "Think every point in the Orbit knows your story, Captain."

Hugo peered again at her through the window in the door then moved on through into the galley.

"Anita," Harvey said, dropping her boots to the floor and rising. "Thank Christ. Where's Webb?"

"What's up, Marilyn? We heard you got into some trouble."

"You have no idea. It's more than my neck's worth to be running around Sunside, truth be told. But I can't sit on what I got any more. Webb needs to hear it."

"Webb's not here," Rami said, pouring herself a coffee.

"Well, I know that. Where the hell is he?"

"You can tell us, Marilyn," Rami said, sitting down and sipping her coffee. "We'll help if we can."

"I don't need *help*," Harvey said, dropping herself back on the bench. "I need to offload some serious shit. And you know me, I'm attached to my neck. But this..."

"Go on," Rami urged.

Harvey heaved a great sigh and shifted in her seat. She cast her eyes at the ceiling like she was looking for strength then brought her sharp, green gaze back to them and leant forward on her elbows, face intense. "I'm in over my head, in short. Mixed up with a bad sort."

"Splinters?" Rami ventured.

"Uh-huh," she said, eyes wide. "And before you say anything, you know I ain't normally that dumb. But they gave me no choice."

"How so?"

Harvey sighed, stared at her hands. "They found out about some shipping I did for... someone. Someone I shouldn't have shipped for."

"Who?" Hugo asked.

She shook her head. "I can't say. Someone dangerous. But I owed them. I ain't proud of it but if you owe someone, you pay 'em. If you know what's good for you, that is. So I did this run for them. I wasn't to hear from them again. Then all of a sudden this Splinter shit corners me in a bar. Says he knows. Says he'll talk to people who would be mighty interested to know who did that run, unless I agree to do the same run for him."

"What sort of run?" Rami said quietly.

Harvey bit her lip. "Weapons. Autos. Explosives. Serious shit."

"The Splinters are militarising?" Hugo felt his face drain of colour.

"I don't know," Harvey raised her hands. "I don't know, I didn't ask. I ran their weapons for them then I got the hell out of there."

"Where did you run them to?" Rami asked.

Harvey looked a bit pale herself. "Lunar 1."

Hugo looked at Rami. "They're rumoured to have a base there, aren't they?"

Rami nodded.

"Get Spinn," Hugo said and Rami left.

Harvey sat there, chewing on her fingernails. "I shouldn't have said anything. But I couldn't not, you know? You stumble on someone hiring out the Splinters... you can't let that stay quiet."

"You did right."

"Webb weren't lying, were he? You got Service connections, right?" Harvey went on. "Powerful guys who'll believe you?"

Hugo looked back at her. Her hands were steady on the table but there was a spark of fear in her eyes. "We know who to tell," he hedged.

Rami returned with Spinn who took in Harvey with a glance then looked back at Hugo. "Captain?"

"Well it's been fun," Harvey said, glancing at her wrist display and standing. "But I done my bit. You guys can tell the Service and they can make of this what the hell they want. I'm out."

"Sit down," Hugo said.

Harvey frowned. "I said, I'm *out*," she went on. "If the Splinters even get a sniff I've ratted them out they'll drift me if I'm lucky."

"Sit down," Hugo repeated. "You're not done."

"Don't take no Service-tone with me, Kaleb Hugo," she growled. "I ain't your crew. I only came to you to try and give the Orbit a fighting chance against whatever's brewing. I didn't have to."

"Hugo to bridge," Hugo said. There was a beep and More's face appeared on the galley wall display.

"More here, Captain."

"Are we all aboard?"

More glanced at something off-screen then back. "Yes, sir."

"Contact control. Prepare for launch."

"Hold on one fucking second," Harvey said. "Belay that, right now. I'm getting the hell off this ship."

"Marilyn," Hugo began.

"That's *Captain Harvey* to you, Service-boy."

"Harvey," he compromised. "You are right. You have put yourself in danger. Now you can either stay, help us and we'll protect you, or you can run and hide for the rest of your life. Which is it going to be?"

"Running and hiding," Harvey said. "No contest."

"Marilyn," Rami came forward. "You're surely safer with us. This'll be the last place they'll look for you."

Harvey chewed on her lip again.

"Where's the Phoenix?" Rami went on.

"She's safe," Harvey said, quietly. "Stowed her on Haven with folk I trust."

"Well then," Hugo said. "Welcome aboard, Captain Harvey. I suggest you find somewhere to buckle in. We're moving out. Spinn?"

"Sir?"

"Captain Harvey is going to fill you in on some details that I'm going to need you to cross check with whatever you have on the Splinters and Lunar 1. Then I want you and Rami to report to me with whatever you find."

"Yes, sir," Spinn said, eyeing Harvey warily.

Harvey had crossed her arms and set her jaw again. "This better work out worth my while, Hugo. And where the hell is Webb, anyway?"

"We're on our way to get him," Hugo said, nodded to the three of them and made his way to the bridge.

Ø

"I have to report this to Luscombe," Hugo said to the whole bridge. "Whatever's going on with AI and Fitzroy, this is bigger."

There was silence in reply.

"Spinn," Hugo said through clenched teeth. "Have you found anything?"

"Unsubstantiated rumours, Captain," Spinn said. "But coupled with movement of credit, ships and a few unexplained incidents on Lunar 1... I think Captain Harvey is right."

Hugo cursed. "How do these bastards still exist anyway?"

"Same way crews like we do, sir," More said, adjusting their course. "The Service can't hold everything in line, as much as they try. And if anything their hold over Lunar 1 has weakened since the revolution."

Hugo chewed the inside of his cheek. "I'm going to report to Luscombe,"

"Sir," Rami began but Hugo held up a hand.

"I won't tell him where I heard it," he said, glancing toward the galley where he'd left Harvey raiding cupboards. "But if someone really is militarising the Splinters, then I'm prepared to bet it's for a strike at the Service. I have to report it."

No one replied, but there were a series of tight nods.

Hugo stood from the co-pilot chair. "Hail Webb as soon as we're in comm distance of Lunar 5. Tell him to be ready. Lieutenant?"

"Captain?"

"Set me up a secure link to Colonel Luscombe from my cabin."

"Yes, sir. Captain?"

"Yes?"

Rami looked pale. "Be careful."

Hugo nodded and left the bridge and made his way to his cabin.

"Captain Hugo," Luscombe said when he came into view on the display screen. "This is a surprise. How have you been getting on?"

"Colonel," Hugo said. "I have something to report."

"Oh yes?"

Hugo took a deep breath. "Sir, evidence that someone may be arming the Splinters has come to my attention."

Luscombe made no reaction other than a slight flattening in his expression. "Really? Are you sure?"

"I am, sir."

"Where did you hear it?"

Hugo paused. "A source, sir. A confidential one."

"Ah," Luscombe said, eyes sliding off screen. "Do we have any details?"

"The source couldn't be specific," Hugo said. "Partially for their own safety and partially because they did not ask questions themselves."

"Probably wise, if frustrating. What do you have?"

"That the Splinters have been organising weapons and supply runs into Lunar 1. There's no credit trail to indicate who's paying, but the fact that they are organising ships and weapons is enough to worry about."

"That it is," Luscombe said. Hugo tried his best to read the sombre face but other than the gravity in it, the colonel's face remained unreadable. "Does Webb have any suppositions?"

Hugo paused, caught himself just in time. "Not yet sir," he managed. Luscombe held his gaze but Hugo couldn't be sure if there was anything significant in it. Hugo kept his face neutral.

"Well then," Luscombe said, straightening. "I guess we have your next assignment."

"Sir?"

"Stop them."

Hugo took a minute to find his voice. "Stop them?"

Luscombe smiled, not nicely. "The Splinters are thugs, Hugo, pure and simple. Terrorists for hire. No discipline, and loyalty up for the highest bidder. Whatever it is they're planning, you have smarts and training on your side."

"Yes, sir," Hugo said, keeping his face blank with an effort.

"About time we cleared out that rats' nest that is Lunar 1. Be careful, Captain," Luscombe said. "And I wouldn't screw up this time, if I were you."

"Yes, sir."

Hugo stared at the blank screen, feeling every beat of his heart clench in his chest. He moved out onto the bridge in a daze.

"Sir," Rami said as soon as he came in sight. "We can't get a response from Webb."

"What?"

"We're hailing his room. Nothing."

"He might have slipped out?" Kinjo put in.

"I told him specifically to stay put," Hugo growled. "How far are we from Lunar 5, Sub-Lieutenant?"

"We're still several hours away, Captain," More said.

"Get us there quicker. And try hailing him on his personal comm."

"We've tried, sir," Rami said, her voice tight. "It's off."

"If he's gotten himself killed or caught, I'll flay him alive," Hugo growled.

Ø

"You're overreacting, Hugo," Harvey muttered as she trotted to keep up with him. "I'm sure he's fine."

"He won't be when I get hold of him," Hugo mumbled as he wove through the crowds in the corridor. The air was heavy with the familiar Lunar Strip smell of oil and bodies.

Harvey shook her head. "He'll be there, you'll see."

"Who invited you along, anyway? You should be staying out of sight."

Under the wide brim of one of Webb's caps, she grinned, showing her teeth. "What, miss a showdown between Kaleb Hugo and Ezekiel Webb? You couldn't get tickets to that show for all the credit in Sunside."

Hugo snorted and ducked down another busy, low-ceilinged corridor towards the bank of express lifts to take them up to the residential levels of the spacescraper. He stood with his arms folded and scowled at the level counter as the lift zoomed up. He kept his anger stoked and hot so that he didn't have to acknowledge the fear that misted underneath.

Hugo was out and storming down the corridor before the lift doors had finished opening. He waved his ID badge to get them through another set of check points, checked the directions on his wrist panel then turned through some sliding double doors and onto a long, quiet corridor with numbered doors on either side. Hugo picked up his pace, glancing at pod numbers until they came up on the one he'd booked. The door was shut, the control panel dark. He took a breath and pressed the buzzer. He heard it trigger inside the room, and then there was silence. Harvey hovered at his side, looking entirely too expectant, and he pushed the buzzer again. Still nothing.

Hugo lifted his fist and banged on the door. "Commander, you had better be dead in there or I'll -"

The door slid open. A huge, balding man with spacer tattoos and a pair of cargo pants and nothing else stood in the doorway, blinking and glaring. His bleary eyes levelled on Hugo.

"What the fuck do you want? I'm on fucking night cycle."

Hugo blinked a moment. "Apologies, sir," he managed. "I...we thought

Zero Ø 109

someone else was here."

"Well they're fucking not. Piss off."

Hugo stood and stared at the closed door for a long time, unable to keep the anger burning hot enough to fight away the chill of fear. He turned and moved back down the corridor.

"Where are you going?" Harvey said catching up.

"Control. We need to see the camera feeds."

"They won't show you, Hugo" Harvey said. "If they haven't been paid off then they'll at least be smart enough to keep it zipped."

"I left him behind," he murmured. "Again. I shouldn't..." He paused as his wrist display began beeping. He clicked the answer command. "Hugo here."

"Captain?"

"Lieutenant," Hugo said, moving back out onto the busy corridors of the spacescraper. "He's not there. I'm heading to the building's control -"

"Captain," Rami interrupted again. "He's here."

Hugo froze and people cursed as they had to dodge round him. He shook himself and moved off to the side. "What?"

"Webb's here, Captain," Rami said, voice sounding a little sheepish. "He just showed up."

"Is he...?"

"He's fine, Captain. He -"

"Tell him not to move a single fucking muscle," Hugo growled. "I'm on my way."

"See, Hugo," Harvey said. "What I tell you? Nothing to worry about."

Ø

Hugo nearly knocked Spinn over in the *Zero*'s main corridor as he stormed through and took the stairs to the bridge two at a time. Rami was at her usual workstation and More was at the controls, the lean figure of Webb bent over his shoulder. The commander straightened and grinned.

"Captain Hugo," he said. "Miss me?"

Hugo clenched and unclenched his fists.

"Marilyn?" Webb exclaimed as he looked over Hugo's shoulder. "What are you doing here?"

"Everyone. Dismissed," Hugo said in a low voice. The crew paused, glanced between themselves, got up and left in silence.

Webb's grin took on a frozen look. "Done something wrong again, haven't I?"

"I gave you an order, Commander. You were to stay put in the boarding pod."

"Look, Hugo," he began, lifting his hands.

"*Captain.*"

Webb ducked his head. "Captain. Look. I just took myself down to the engineering levels. I know people down there. It was a better place to hide and I could keep my ears open."

"Commander Webb," Hugo ground out. "You have disobeyed me. Again. This cannot and will not be permitted to continue."

Webb crossed his arms and lifted his chin. The smile was gone. "You're going to have to starting coming round to the idea that sometimes I know better."

"I am your commanding officer," Hugo snapped, coming forward. "Whatever you think about me, I don't give a shit. You don't have to like me. But you better start respecting me."

"Or what?"

"Or I'll have you court-martialled, that's what," Hugo said.

Webb grinned again and Hugo wanted to hit him.

"You think you know everything, don't you?" he said. "With your medals and your training and your victories. Guess what, Hugo. You don't know shit."

"I've given you all the warnings I'm prepared to."

"Dammit, man," Webb said, voice raising. "You and your orders. Rules, the law? It's all *bullshit.*"

"I will have order, Commander. And rules. And the law. I make them and you will obey."

"Christ above! How can you be this fucking stupid?"

A lifetime's discipline crumbled away and Hugo found himself slamming his commander against the bulkhead. Webb blinked, dazed. Close up, Hugo could see the scarring along Webb's jaw, twisting his lip up slightly at one corner and the notches missing from his ear and eyebrow. There was fading bruising along his neck and temple and two of his teeth were whiter than the rest.

Hugo let go and staggered back and Webb caught himself on the control chair.

"You don't understand..." Hugo said, quietly, tasting disgust at himself at the back of his mouth. "You've got it all wrong."

Webb's face was still as he looked up at Hugo through his hair, breathing shallow. "Have I?"

Hugo glared at his hands. "You don't... I can't..." He made a wordless noise and slammed a fist on the control panel. "Stop acting like you're fucking *dispensable.*"

Webb's eyes widened. Hugo turned his back on him and strode away. He locked his cabin door behind him and pulled open his locker, scrabbled around until he found his box of blask sachets. He rinsed out a glass in his basin and emptied a sachet into it. He downed the measure of black liquid in one go and pressed the glass against his forehead, closing his eyes and swearing under his breath. The door buzzer went but he ignored it whilst emptying another sachet into his glass.

"Captain," came Webb's muffled voice. "You know I know the code to get in, right?"

Hugo glared into his drink for a moment then paced back across the cabin and unlocked the door. It slid open and Webb was stood there, leaning on the doorjamb. Hugo turned away, propped himself against the bulkhead, sipped his drink and stared at nothing.

"I shouldn't have said that," Webb said as he came into the cabin. "You're stubborn and you're cranky and that rod up your ass has got to be ten foot long. But you're not stupid."

"That's your idea of an apology, is it?" Hugo said, but his voice sounded more tired than reproachful, even to himself. Webb shrugged. Hugo sighed, swirling his drink round his glass. "Well I'm sorry too. Are you hurt?"

"Nah," Webb waved dismissively. "Don't worry about it. You're not the first captain to threaten me with bodily harm." The grin was back. "Tell you what, though. You're the first one that's managed to ground me."

Hugo eyed him narrowly. "Is that a joke?"

Webb shrugged again. "I stayed on the same colony, at least. It's an achievement, Captain. I'm serious. Ask Rami about Captain Akmar trying to get Bolt to weld me into the brig. True story."

Hugo shook his head. "How do you do it, Webb?"

"Do what?"

"Fight on both sides," Hugo looked up. "Be everyone's enemy and no one's ally. How can you keep your head together?"

Webb rubbed his jaw. "As you've pointed out, Captain... I've never known different. The *Zero* is all I've ever had. It's who I am."

Hugo sighed again and went back to his locker to find more blask and another glass.

"It's why you should believe me when I say you need to loosen up your thinking. Your head is still Service. It's dangerous."

Hugo took a moment to weigh up his commander, new scars overlaying old and a darkness in his eyes that he hadn't seen even in battle-weary generals twice his age.

"I will not have anyone in my crew acting like their life is cheap, Commander. Especially you."

"Why, Captain. I didn't know you cared."

Hugo glowered. "The crew look to you. You are their leader. And I can live with that, if you obey my orders. But you don't." Webb opened his mouth but Hugo raised a hand. "You were reckless when you went off on your own on Earth. You were reckless when you left your boarding pod. I may still have a lot to learn, Commander, but I've known soldiers like you before." He paused, holding his commander's heavy gaze. "You head into anything bent on destruction, that's all you achieve." They stood and looked at each other for a moment longer before Hugo said, "Do you understand?"

Webb looked away. "I understand. Though I'm not sure you do."

"It's a start," said Hugo and he held out a glass to Webb. Webb accepted, frowning at it. "Sit."

Webb lowered himself onto the bunk, stretching his stiff leg out in front of him and Hugo sat himself in the chair. He lifted his glass. "To the Zero."

"May it have a future," Webb said, lifting his own glass and they both drank. Webb coughed. "Jesus, Hugo. Is this blask?"

Hugo nodded, enjoying the way it warmed his throat.

"Where did you get it?"

"Kinjo found a supplier on Sunside 4."

Webb raised his eyebrows, looked at the remnants in his glass. "Tastes old, too. Bet you grew up drinking this, huh?"

"My father drinks it, if that's what you mean."

"I need a payrise," Webb muttered. Hugo took his glass from him and poured them both another. "So are you going to tell me where Marilyn sprung up from?"

"That brings me to why we've come to get you early. She tracked us down on Sunside 5. She was after you."

"That can't be good," Webb mumbled, watching the blask swill in his glass.

"It's not. The Splinters are running weapons into Lunar 1."

Webb froze with his glass to his mouth, stared at Hugo over the rim. "What?"

Hugo nodded. "It's true. They cornered Harvey into doing a run for them."

Webb lowered his glass. "Fuck."

"Yeah," Hugo said. "She felt she couldn't sit on it."

"Aye," Webb said. "Jesus. If they know she's come out with this, they'll be after her skin."

"What do you think it could be?"

"Well, someone's got a nasty score to settle, that's for sure."

"Do you think it could be LIL?"

Webb's eyes widened for a moment but then he shook his head and drained his glass. "No. They're not that stupid."

"Just because you're revolutionary doesn't necessarily mean you're smart."

"Fitzroy's smart," Webb said. "Two generations in the Lunar Strip have lost parents and friends to revolution and chemical plague. They may still want to kick the Service out, but they won't fight another war for it."

"The timing is not reassuring."

"If anyone's going to try and re-establish a Lunar State, it's going to be done through politics. For that LIL needs power, influence. And not the sort bought with fear. Hence cosying up to bigwigs like Gabor. Fitzroy's got something up his sleeve, that's for sure. But no one in the Lunar Independence League would hire the Splinters. This is something else."

Hugo took one last mouthful of his drink and put the glass aside. "I don't know if that makes it better or worse."

"Tell me about it."

Hugo folded his arms. "We're to stop them."

Webb coughed on his drink. "Come again?"

Hugo crossed his arms. "Luscombe wants us to go to Lunar 1 and stop whatever it is the Splinters are planning."

"Can't he just use us as target practice for the Resolution? It would be quicker."

"It was a direct order."

"Jesus," Webb said, rubbing his eyes. "This'll be fun."

"We're launching tonight. Once we're on course to Lunar 1 I want us all to meet in the galley to work on a strategy."

"Aye aye Captain. And if you have any more of this," he said, draining his glass. "I'd bring it."

Ø

"You're space crazy, the whole fucking lot of you."

"Marilyn -"

"I ain't joking. I don't care what contract you found on them, it ain't worth it. And I ain't gonna be dragged down with you. Let me off at Lunar 3."

"We'll drop you if you want," Webb said. "But I'll bet the *Zero* and the

Phoenix that the Splinters will be on you the minute you try and catch a run out of there."

"So we march up and knock on their door instead?" Harvey shook her head. "You're morons. Suicidal morons."

"Captain Harvey," Spinn put in, not loudly, but Harvey still jumped. "I feel it is in your best interests to help."

"Do you, professor?" she said. "Well you can feel whatever you want. I like my head where it is."

"Marilyn," Webb said. "If we win... they won't come after you again."

"Big fucking 'if' there, Ezekiel."

"It would be smaller if you helped."

She glowered a moment longer then shook her head with a wordless noise. "I'll talk to some people for you. That's all I'm doing, mind. And only because this'll give the Splinters someone else to want to murder other than me."

"Your faith is touching."

"Yours is useless."

Harvey and Webb exchanged glares for a moment longer then looked back to Hugo. Hugo took a breath to make sure his voice was steady. "Harvey, where did you run your cargo into?"

"Docking bays on the Earth-side rim," she said.

"That's as good a place to start as any. Is there any business we could convincingly be conducting whilst we're there?"

Webb laughed. "Nothing you'd like. But, yeah. Sure we can find something to keep us busy."

"Kinjo, Sub, Bolt," Hugo said and they looked up. "You can sort that?" They nodded.

"A new bike would be good..." Webb said with a smile.

"We'll see what trading we can find," Sub said.

"Make it good," Hugo urged "In the meantime, Rami, Harvey and I -"

"Hang on one cotton-picking -"

"Captain," Hugo cut Harvey off. "You're in or you're not. And if you're in, this is my ship and you're following my orders." Hugo thought she was about to burst a blood vessel, green eyes hot and jaw bulging. "Rami, Harvey and I will set out to ask questions. Commander, what points do you know that would be worth starting with?"

"I've got several points who might know something," Webb said, eyes narrow. "But am I going to have to be the one to point out the obvious flaw in this plan?"

"You are not accompanying us, Commander," Hugo said.

Webb's face darkened. "Hugo, I was born on this colony."

"I'm aware of that."

Webb kneaded his temples. "You came and got me from Lunar 5 specifically because of it."

"You are not physically up to fieldwork."

"Captain-"

"No arguments, Commander. You are to help us plan and give us details of your contacts. We will keep in touch by comm. But you are to remain on the *Zero* with More and oversee everyone's movements."

"Hugo, please, just listen a second..." Webb said, shifting in his seat and holding his hands up. "It's just... this isn't Earth. Some of the points here are as likely to shoot you on sight as tell you anything."

"Then you had better choose who we speak to wisely," Hugo said firmly. Webb didn't say anything more, though Hugo could tell he wanted to. "We don't know how much time we have so we will set out immediately. I want everyone ready." Everyone nodded and acknowledged the orders, apart from Webb and Harvey who were both still glowering. "I want a complete check-over of our weapons and tech stock completed before we dock. How long to Lunar 1, Sub-Lieutenant?"

More looked at his wrist display. "Four hours, Captain."

"Get us docked in the grimiest rim harbour you can find. The sort that aren't interested in having accurate records."

"You're getting good at this, Captain," Webb said, though he didn't smile.

"You have your orders. We have four hours to prepare. Be ready."

VII

Webb swallowed a couple of pills with a dry throat. Exhaustion rolled through him in waves, but it wasn't enough to overwhelm the sneaking finger of doubt that worked its way up his spine. He'd tried distracting himself with the tech check, but he was still tiring quickly and Kinjo had eventually shooed him off. He stared at the bottle of pills for a moment, trying to untangle his thoughts.

"Are you okay?"

He looked up to see Rami stood in the medbay door, a penetrating look on her face.

"I'm fine," he said, turning to replace the bottle. "Just a headache."

"Is that so?" she said. "Strip."

"Right here in the medbay, Lieutenant? After last time?" Webb smirked.

"I assume you want to keep those new teeth, Commander? Do as you're told."

Webb chuckled as he unzipped his flight suit and shouldered himself out of it. "I'm fine, honestly. You'd be proud. I barely moved off my ass for the whole five weeks."

"A likely story. Sit."

Webb smiled and lowered himself into a chair and allowed Rami to shine a lenslight in his eyes. Her hands on his skin were warm. He felt himself relax despite himself, even when she fingered the tender areas on his jaw.

"So," she said. "Do you think it can be done?"

"Scuppering the Splinters?"

She nodded.

He sighed then, flinching slightly as she lifted his arm and examined his shoulder. "You know..." he said, quietly. "It might just be possible, yeah. We'll need some luck and some smarts. But... yeah. Maybe."

"If we do," Rami said as she lifted up his other arm and started feeling her way down the healing skin on his ribs. "It means we'll have made Lunar 1 a better place."

"We'd be swatting a fly on a dying horse," he muttered while Rami knelt and unfastened his ankle brace. "But I guess it's something. Listen, Anita - you will be careful, won't you?"

"You know me, Zeek," she said whilst she prodded at the bones in his ankle. She muttered to herself, replaced the brace and stood. She was about to move away but Webb caught her hand. She looked at him, dark eyes steady and he pulled her down and kissed her, then just held her there, pressing her forehead to his. "Promise."

She paused a moment and he felt her sigh. "I promise."

He nodded and let her go. She retrieved a syringe from the cupboard and filled it from a vial.

"So," he said, rubbing at his shoulder. "What's the verdict?"

"Well," she said. "I think some of your tattoos are a write-off."

"You never liked them anyway," he said, and was pleased to see her smile slightly. She bent and gave him the shot and he watched her face as she did so but it was calm and unreadable. She helped him shoulder back into his flight suit and he stood.

"Oh. Here," Rami said and pulled something out of her pocket. He held out his hand and she dropped his crucifix onto his palm. The gold was warm. He felt a genuine smile spread across his face.

"Commander?" came More's voice from the wall display.

"Webb here," he said, fastening the chain back around his neck.

"We're approaching Lunar 1. Do you want to handle control?"

"What's wrong, More? Not scared, are you?"

There was a pause, though More's face on the screen didn't change. "No."

"Relax, Thomas. I'll be right up."

The screen went blank and Webb turned to go but felt Rami's hand on his shoulder. He looked back at her. "You be careful too, okay?"

He grinned. "When am I ever not?"

She shook her head and let him go.

He cursed as he shambled up the stairway to the bridge. He could feel Hugo's eyes on him as he limped to the controls and felt frustration flame again. But he didn't look back and dropped himself into the seat.

"Ah," he sighed, running his hand over the panel. "I missed you girl. What's More done to you, eh?"

"Approaching now, Zeek," More said, adjusting the course slightly. The Earth-facing rim of the disk-shaped colony already took up most of the viewscreen. A couple more breaches had been patched up since he was last here, though no one had bothered clearing up the carbon burns that blackened the hull around them. He adjusted their course, pulling them into an emptier spaceway to dodge the heavier traffic heading towards the hub. When they dropped in line he keyed in a couple of commands to start hailing Docking Control.

"Section 4 Control here," a bored-sounding voice eventually crackled through the channel.

"Hey, Control," Webb said, ratcheting up his accent a notch. "Gotta drydock for a class 2?"

"Might have. Purpose of visit?"

"Well it ain't gonna be leisure, is it, Control?"

"Your manifest is thin, *Zero*," the voice returned.

"We're buying. You'll get us for a few weeks at least, if you'll take rolling payment."

"Got any collateral?"

Webb sighed loudly. "Come on, Control. You want credit coming into your colony or not?"

"No collateral, no dock, *Zero*."

"Commander," Hugo put in. "We've got credit for an up-front payment."

Webb held up his hand. "Stow it one second, Captain," he flicked the comm back on. "Control, if you insist on being such hard-assess...we've got some fighters aboard. Service-class."

"Fighters?"

"Three. In good shape. Transmitting details."

There was another pause. Webb peered out the screen as they got closer and could start picking out the patterns of lights from viewports and the honeycomb entrance to the docks. "They'll do, *Zero*. Logging them as guarantee. Head on bearing 5-6-1 to bay 3694. Welcome to Lunar 1."

"Our humble thanks, Control. Out." He flicked off the comm and slumped back in his chair. "Fuck. Don't it just feel great to be home?"

"You put up the fighters...?"

"Relax, Captain. Having credit for front payment on weeks' worth of docking is more likely to get you noticed than having a few modified fighters aboard."

"Is it too late to turn back?"

Webb looked to Harvey where she stood in the hatchway, glowering out the viewscreen at the approaching docking bay doors.

"Relax, Marilyn," he said. "What could possibly go wrong?"

"You had to say it, didn't you?" Harvey retorted and Webb thought for a moment that she looked a little paler than usual.

He looked away and concentrated on bringing the Zero into dock. 3694 glowed in red over the hatchway and they steered her in. It was a class 2 craft bay, but only just. Webb muttered as they brought her in and had to ease her down to avoid scraping her stern on the hatchway. They landed and the hatch closed behind them with a clang. A tinny voice announced depressurisation would be complete in one minute. Everyone left the bridge except Hugo, who stayed in his chair and gazed out the viewscreen at the oil-streaked metal of the docking bay. For a second Webb thought he saw a flicker of something like doubt in his eyes, but it was gone again when the captain looked his way.

"Don't you have work to do, Commander?" he said then left before Webb could reply.

Ø

Hugo strapped on both his holsters before pulling his jacket over the top. He double-checked the knife sheath in his boot and triple-checked his wrist panel for connection to the *Zero*'s systems and Lunar 1's mainframe and the solarnet. All was as it should be. He gazed at the man that stared back from the mirror over the sink. His hair was scruffy and his jaw had three days' growth. There were grey smudges under his eyes and he wondered what his mother would think if she saw him now. Then he shook his head and made himself leave the cabin.

The crew were gathered in the hold. Kinjo, Sub and Bolt were just clambering into the Jeep. Rami and More were checking something on a handheld computer panel and Harvey was leaning against one of the fighters. She had pulled her unruly yellow hair back into a tight tail and was wearing one of Webb's caps again as well as a large light-visor. It obscured her eyes but he could still see she was scowling. Webb was a step back from everyone, watching with an unreadable expression.

"Captain?"

Hugo looked up and More presented him with another handgun, identical to the one he lost at AI. Hugo loaded it into his empty holster, reassured by its weight.

"Everyone has checked the connectivity on their comms?" There were nods and affirmations and Hugo nodded. "Right. Move out."

More opened the cargo bay doors. As the ramp lowered, the bitter smell of oily, recycled air filled the room. Sub started the Jeep's engine and it rolled out and down the ramp and across the narrow bay. The docking bay exit opened and the Jeep drove out, the doors hissing closed again behind it.

"Are we ready?" Hugo asked. Rami nodded whilst checking her own weapons and tech, and Harvey's scowl deepened.

"Captain," Webb said, face grave.

"Yes?"

Webb chewed his lip for a moment then shook his head. "Just...follow

Rami's lead, okay?"

Hugo felt heat flush his face but he stopped the retort that came to his mouth and made himself nod. Rami stood straight but her glance flicked back and forth between them.

"Are we ready, Lieutenant?"

"Yes sir," she said and moved to leave.

"Stay in communication, Commander," Hugo said as he fell into step behind her. "Are you coming, Harvey?"

"I think it's important you know, Hugo," Harvey said whilst pacing over. "I'm already regretting this."

"We'll make it worth your while, Captain," Hugo said.

"You'd better," she said and sauntered out and down the ramp.

Hugo paused to look back at Webb. He stood stiffly, and his eyes didn't have the smile Hugo was used to. "It's for the best, Commander. Stay on the comm."

Webb nodded but didn't answer. Hugo turned and followed Harvey. The bay doors opened onto a wide space that was heaving with machinery, crates, cargo and spacers. The metal hull of the colony curved up above them to where the day-cycle lights rendered it the dull grey of a winter day. The noise was tumultuous. They skirted the edge of the harbour, trying to stay out of the way of the hover craft, cranes, tugs pulling industrial-sized lifters and spacers haggling over import fees until they reached the gate. After a cursory scan by a greasy customs agent who didn't even check when the scanner bleeped over their guns, they stepped into the streets of Lunar 1.

"For fuck's sake, Hugo," Harvey muttered as she paced along beside him. "Will you slouch a bit, already? People are looking."

Hugo glanced about, saw indeed that a few faces were turned his way and attempted to stoop his shoulders and keep his gaze on the walkway, as Rami was doing.

"Where are we going?" he asked as they turned down a side-street, dodging the throng of people coming and going from the dockside bars and warehouses.

"Shuttle station," Rami said. "We'll head hubwards where most of the business is. We need to start putting word about that we're down on our luck and in need of a quick-profit run."

"And the Splinters will come to us like they did Harvey?"

"With any luck."

"We get through this with our necks, Anita," Harvey muttered, "remind me to have a word with you about your definition of the word 'luck'."

"We'll start low and build our way up," Hugo said, glancing at his wrist panel. "Webb's given us the names of some scrap dealers - "

"You'd save yourselves a hell of a lot of time if you just talk to Evangeline Webb."

"Who?"

"She's the one that told that Splinter-scum about me and that damned run."

"Are you sure?" Rami asked.

"She was the only that knew about it, since she brokered the damn deal for me. Bitch set me up. Twice. Trust me, go talk to Evangeline. If she's helping them set up runs, I'd bet my boots she knows what they're up to."

"Where are you going?" Hugo halted as Harvey stopped at a cross-section.

"I got my own points that might know something."

"You're safer with us," Rami said.

"Not if you're going to see that bitch," Harvey grunted. "Give her a kick in the teeth from me." And then Harvey melted away into the crowd.

"Do you think she'll come back?"

Rami shrugged. "I don't know. I think she'd like to see an end to the Splinters as much as anyone. Whether she is truly willing to risk her skin though... I suppose time will tell. Come on Captain. Shuttle port's just down here. Evangeline Webb's got a lounge on this line."

"You know her?"

Rami shook her head as she lead the way. "Zeek's had some dealings with her. I've never met her."

"Are they related?"

Rami frowned at him. "No, sir. The name Webb is for Horatio Webb."

Hugo had to think for a moment. "Lunar 1's founder?"

She nodded. "It's the name the youth units give kids that don't have or know their own. Zeek thinks it's the Nova nuns' way of making sure the Orbit never forgets just how Horatio's grand vision turned out."

They went down some stairs into the underground shuttle station. They passed a man sprawled on the bottom step, naked apart from a wrap of filthy blankets. He clutched a sheet of scrap metal that had words daubed on it in what looked like engine fuel. As Hugo got closer he could read *strengthen what remains and is about to die, for I have not found your deeds complete in the sight of my God.*

People rushed past without looking. Hugo could smell him as they moved onto the shuttle platform.

A shuttle was just rattling in and Rami ducked and dodged the crowds and got aboard. Hugo scrambled to follow and got on just as the doors were closing. There were seats free but Rami didn't move to sit so Hugo took a handhold next to her and attempted to glance around without making it obvious. There was a large spacer leant up against the wall further down, scowling at a computer panel and a couple of women in medic tunics sat with their heads bent together, whispering. There was also a child curled up across two of the seats, face turned into the cushion. He peered at her to make out she was, in fact, breathing but then looked away when Rami prodded him in the ribs and shook her head.

"When we get off, Captain," she said, voice so low her lips barely moved, "we should put in a call to Commander Webb. See what he can tell us about Evangeline."

"Why not now?"

Rami shook her head again. "Best get somewhere a bit quieter. Or a lot noisier."

Hugo blinked as the shuttle emerged into the wan light of the colony's day-cycle. The shuttle rattled its way between the tops of megastructures, the bottoms of which were lost in shadow. He watched the shelves of the rim-levels and docks disappear behind them as the shuttle lumbered towards the interior of the colony. Crafts zoomed by on skyways and he couldn't stop himself clutching the handhold tighter as the shuttle rattled over the joints in the rail. It slowed down and coughed itself to a halt at a platform at the top of one of the spacescrapers. The medics got off and a couple more people got on and then they were off again.

Rami nudged him as they pulled into the next stop and Hugo took the lead and stepped off the shuttle. He was pleased to have solid concrete under his feet again. He followed Rami into the spacescraper and as she wove her way amongst the crowds to a food court. Most of the plastic tables were empty and Rami picked one near the edge, furthest away from the nearest diners but not too close to the foot-traffic heading through the level.

She hunched over the table and tapped a few commands into her wrist panel. "*Zero*, this is Rami. Come in, *Zero*."

"Webb here," came the tinny voice. "How's it going?"

"We might have something," Rami said. "Harvey said we should check out Evangeline Webb."

"She did?"

"Yeah," Rami said. "It sounds like she might be on to something. Any suggestions?"

"Is the captain with you?"

"I'm here, Commander," Hugo said. "Tell us what you know about this point."

He heard Webb sigh. "She's a typical fence. All business. She sets up contacts, brokers deals, that sort of thing. It wouldn't surprise me if she took the chance to make credit on what the Splinters have got cooking. Just... be careful. She can't know you're out to mess up one of her revenue streams."

"Do you think she'll talk to us?"

"Make her think you're desperate and watch her eyes light up," Webb replied. "We just better make sure we're done and off this colony before she figures it out."

"Very well, Commander," Hugo said. "We will report back once we're done."

"Watch your backs."

"We will. Out." Rami pulled her sleeve back over her wrist panel. "You ready, Captain?"

"As I'll ever be," he said. He paused, chewing on the inside of his cheek for a moment. "What should I do, Lieutenant?"

"I'll do the talking, Captain," she said with a polite glance away. "Just get in the headspace of someone whose luck's all drawn out and you won't go far wrong."

"Shouldn't be hard," Hugo said as they stood.

Rami made her way back out into the foot traffic and towards a bank of express lifts. Hugo remembered Tranquillity and Sturm Hafen and mentally schooled himself to be calm. The lift opened on a much quieter level. There was an open space before the lifts with a fountain in the middle. There was graffiti all over the marble and the benches around it were battered, but a stream of water still glittered from the top. All around the space were bar fronts and cafés, neon signs flashing their names and offers. The chorno display on the wall confirmed that it was before midday, Lunar 1 time, but there was still a few people milling about. Not enough people to hide amongst, however, which made Hugo's skin itch.

He lengthened his stride to keep pace with Rami as she checked the bar and club names until they turned a corner and she paused outside one called *The Seven Sisters*. The doors were open and there was faint music coming from inside.

"Okay, Captain," Rami said. "Here we go. Just follow my lead."

Hugo nodded and followed her as she paced into the club. It was dim and virtually empty with only a few people clustered around a couple of card tables in the corner. There was thick carpet underfoot and all the tables were black marble with white strings of stars lasered around their edges. The man behind the bar wore a white shirt and a black tie. He was polishing glasses and watching them. After a glance around, Rami turned and made for one of the booths. She sat down and Hugo watched as she hunched her shoulders and bent over the table, starting to leaf through the information in the table-top display. Hugo sat beside her, making himself focus on the show and drink listings that Rami was flicking through and attempting to adopt the same sort of nervous posture.

A waitress in a smart white shirt and black tie like the barman appeared with a notepanel. "Are you guys after a drink?"

Rami looked up. She paused, blinking with wide eyes, swallowed then said, "Is Mistress Webb around?"

The waitress eyed them a moment. "She's unavailable. I can help you though, I'm sure. What would you like? We are well known for our stock of Old Europe wines. Perhaps you'd like to try one with some lunch? We have some great specials today."

Rami didn't twitch. "We'd like to speak to Evangeline. We're a crew."

The waitress's eyes flicked from Rami to Hugo and back again. "Pretty small crew."

Rami made a good show of gathering patience. "We represent a crew."

"You the captain?"

"I am," Hugo said and the waitress's eyes locked on him. "Evangeline has been... recommended to us. We hoped we might get a minute of her time."

The girl weighed them up a moment longer. "Wait here," she said and then strode across the lounge to a door behind the bar and vanished through it. Rami let out a breath when she was out of sight and exchanged a glance with him. She gave a tiny nod then went back to looking through the table display. The barman kept polishing his glasses and watching them. Hugo watched the door.

The waitress returned after what seemed like a very long time. Hugo's palms had started to sweat.

"Follow me," she said and turned and strode away without looking back.

Rami and Hugo stood and followed. The waitress led them through the bar door and then they were heading down a long, white corridor to an express lift. The plexiglass doors slid shut and they were humming upwards. The lift halted and the doors slid open on a room crammed with workstations, display screens showing camera feeds, news reels, stock lists and people. Comms were bleeping and people were passing panels back and forth, but no one looked up. An older man in a smart suit stepped onto the lift and turned his back on them, frowning at a panel in his hand. Hugo could make out at least three holsters under his coat that he didn't seem bothered about concealing.

The doors opened again on a wide, carpeted hallway lit by ornamental sconces. The man turned left and paced away without a glance. They followed the waitress in the other direction. The air was still and quiet and had a sweet tang to it. Hugo felt a wash of disorientation coming on, such was the quiet and luxury after the hubbub of the rest of the block. The walls were painted black with a border of stars. The waitress went past closed doors to a large double-leafed set at the end of the hall. She opened one and ushered them in without a word.

The room had a high ceiling and was open and airy. Tall windows looked out on the grey and blinking spread of the colony. The carpet and furniture were all black and the walls washed white, and a twisting chandelier flooded the room with soft light. Hugo had barely time to take all this in before a man a head taller than him was stepping up to him, vast chest blocking his view.

"Arms up," he said. Hugo obeyed and the man patted down his jacket and shirt, pulling his guns from their holsters. He opened his mouth to protest but Rami, being patted down and relieved of weapons by another equally sizeable bodyguard, caught his eye and shook her head. The two men laid all their guns and knives down on a table beside the door in a neat row and then stood back to stand either side of the door.

Beyond a seating area of low, black couches was a large desk. There was nothing on the smooth surface apart from a couple of paused newsfeeds. Behind it sat a woman a little older than himself, Hugo guessed, but with hair so black it couldn't be natural. It set off her space-pale skin in a way that was striking but unsettling. Her eyes were so light he felt like they were looking right through him but the pale, unpainted lips held an easy smile.

She stood up in one smooth motion and Hugo saw a silver cross glint at her neck above the collar of a tailored dress.

"Do come sit," she said, voice too smooth to be welcoming. He waited for Rami to move forward towards the straight-backed chairs in front of the desk before he followed. "Is there something I can help you with?"

"Mistress Webb," Rami began.

"Evangeline, please," the woman said, seating herself back in her chair.

"Evangeline," Rami said, with a smile. "My name is Anita Rami. I'm the lieutenant aboard the Zero."

"*Zero, Zero*," Evangeline murmured, tapping a manicured fingernail against her lips. "I know that ship, I'm sure. Though I have not met you before, my dear."

"No, Ma'am," Rami said. "I think you may have had dealings with our commander. Ezekiel Webb?"

"Ah," Evangeline said, smile broadening. "Yes, of course. I remember that young heartbreaker. And how is he?" she said, pale gaze sliding from Rami to Hugo. "Still kicking, I hope?"

"Yes, Ma'am," Rami continued. "He was the one who suggested you would be worth talking to."

"He did, did he?"

"Yes, Ma'am."

"Darling," Evangeline said, placing her long-finger hands flat on the desk and leaning forward. "Please do not call me Ma'am. It does make me feel ever so old. Now, does either you or Silent Samuel over here want to get to the point? I am sure you appreciate I am a busy woman."

Hugo kept his face still and was impressed when Rami didn't flinch. "Of course," she said, glancing once over her shoulder at the security men by the door. "Can I speak freely?"

"I don't know, Anita, can you?" Evangeline smiled again, leaning back in her chair and regarding the lieutenant through her lashes.

Rami shifted slightly, but lifted her head and did not break the fence's gaze. "We were hoping for a run."

"Is that so?"

"Yes," Rami said. "There doesn't seem to be much business around the Lunar Strip at the moment. We..." Rami paused and Hugo kept his eyes locked on Evangeline. "We run well. And fast."

"I am well aware, Lieutenant. But, darling, I'm afraid you're hitching on entirely the wrong skyway here. I don't know what you heard," her eyes narrowed ever so slightly and Hugo didn't miss the slight hardening of her posture. "But my line of work no longer encompasses anything small-time. No offence intended, Anita."

"None taken," Rami replied. "But you must still...know people? Is there anyone that needs any business doing? And fast? We'll give you more than your standard cut if you can get it set up soon."

Evangeline's eyebrows raised and she steepled her fingers. "My usual cut is already rather steep, Lieutenant."

"You can have a half over again. If you can get us something within the week."

Evangeline pursed her lips then pushed herself out from the chair and paced across to the window. She folded her arms and gazed out the glass, one finger tapping against the sleeve of her dress. The artificial light washing in made her look bloodless. When she looked back in their direction Hugo felt himself go cold at the smile on her face.

"You know, darlings," she said. "I would never want anyone to say I don't come through for those in need. And you are in luck. If you'd come to me in a week it would be too late but as it stands, I may just have something for you. It's not a run and it's high risk but quick profit and right up your street." She raised her head and looked down at them. "You know all about high risk, yes?" Rami nodded. Evangeline's icy eyes slipped from Rami to Hugo. "And what about your tall, dark and handsome stranger here, Anita? Does he understand?"

"He does."

"And who is he, Anita? Does the *Zero* just collect heartbreakers out of habit?" she purred, eyes locked on him.

"Captain Hugo, Mistress," Hugo said, standing and bowing to her.

"Such old fashioned manners," she said as she sat back down. "Ex-Service, I'm assuming?"

"Yes, Mistress," Hugo said, remaining stood until she gestured for him to sit again.

"Well it can't hurt to have an Academy-trained strategist aboard, I'm sure," Evangeline said, starting to tap commands into the display on the surface of her desk. "Though I'd be careful who you tell around here, Hugo. The Service aren't exactly going to win any popularity contests on this colony. Anyway. Lieutenant. Captain. As I'm sure you'll understand, I deal with verbal contracts only. But I have two guarantors at the door who make sure it's binding." She lifted her head and smiled again, showing straight white teeth. "So. The deal. I have a client that could do with some high-grade munitions. I seem to remember young Ezekiel had a hand for them?"

"Yes, Mistress," Rami said, her manner staying cool.

"Excellent. A double standard cargo at least, I would say. Get it through import and get it here..." Evangeline tapped at a spot on the colony map being displayed on her desktop. "They will pay you once they are satisfied."

"What sort of thing do they want?" Rami said, eyes locked on the map until Evangeline cleared it with a sweep of her fingers.

"Does young Webb make red cement?"

Hugo wasn't entirely sure that Rami's flinch was acted. "He knows how."

Evangeline nodded. "You get a double cargo of red cement to my client's storehouse at midnight tomorrow, it will be worth all our while."

"By tomorrow?" Hugo stumbled.

Evangeline's smile thinned. "Darling, if it were easy it wouldn't be worth my time. Do we have a deal?" She held out her hand. Hugo wanted to run out the door. Instead he watched Rami move in slow motion and shake her hand before it swung round toward him. "Captain?"

Hugo hesitated one heartbeat. He saw the woman's eyes harden but then he leant forward and took her hand. "Deal."

"Welcome to the big boys' club, Captain," Evangeline smiled. "You pull this off I'll be happy to talk future business. But now, if you'll excuse me. I have to place a few calls."

Rami and Hugo stood. Hugo bowed then turned and followed Rami back to the door where the security men, faces like stone, returned their weapons. There was no one to show them out. They moved down the corridor, boots muffled on the fine carpet and Hugo felt every beat of his heart in his head. They climbed back aboard the lift which took them back down to the club without being commanded. They wasted no time getting across the lounge and out the door.

"Lieutenant," Hugo began but Rami lifted a hand and kept moving.

"Not yet, Captain."

Rami increased her pace back across the fountain square and to the block of lifts. They were inside and zooming back down and Hugo once again opened his mouth but Rami shook her head, glancing above their heads. Hugo looked up and saw a camera in the corner and dropped his gaze again.

They came out on a different level and Rami led them on a twisting path amongst banks of boarding pods and budget residences. They came out on another shuttle platform just as one came heaving up. Rami stepped on and Hugo followed. This time Rami took a seat and Hugo sat beside her, watching her hard face.

"Do you think her client is the Splinters?"

"I'd say so, Captain," she said. "And we'll have to move fast. It sounds like they've nearly finished preparing."

VIII

"Christ Almighty, Captain," Webb said. "We let you out to broker one deal and you end up having me make red cement for the Splinters?"

"We'll just have to make sure we bring them down before they get a chance to use it."

"Fucking right we will," Webb muttered, adjusting his crouch to get a better angle on the bike's wheel. "What does Rami think?"

"She and Spinn are trying to dig up all they can about the area the storehouse is located, seeing if they can find any contracts or names."

"There won't be any," Webb said, tossing the spanner back into the toolbox.

"Nevertheless," Hugo said. "We can at least find out what names they're using on credit accounts. We may be able to find out more from there. Can you get this done?"

Webb sighed and levered himself upright on his stiff ankle. "Yes. I can do it. But we should send someone to the storehouse tonight, see what's what. We might get lucky and not have to hand over anything."

Hugo nodded, jaw looking tight. "Has Harvey come back?"

"She's not with you?"

Hugo shook his head. "She went to talk to some contacts."

"Fuck," Webb said. "She better not have got herself caught."

"What were we saying about faith, Ezekiel?" Harvey's voice echoed through the hold from the top of the ladder. She grinned as she clambered down and moved to join them, pulling off her visor and cap.

"Find anything?" Webb asked.

Harvey frowned and pulled the tie from her hair, shaking out the curls. "There's shit going down alright. Half my folk are running scared."

"Your folk?" Hugo asked.

"Haven folk, Kaleb," Harvey said, patting his shoulder. "I know this is all new but try to keep up."

"What's happening, Marilyn?" Webb said, frowning.

"I had to make sure I didn't sound too interested, but what I could gather from the few Haven types there are left is that everyone's keeping their heads low. Those that are still in business are sticking to the legitimate kind."

"Not wanting to tread on Splinter toes?"

"Aye," Harvey said, face grave. "They've spread their net pretty far from the sounds of it. Stamping out or scaring off competition. If I were to go with my instincts I'd say they're gonna try and seize the colony."

"For whom?" Webb asked, going cold.

"I don't know. That's all I got and I was lucky to get that."

Webb felt a chill rise up from his belly and threaten to choke him. "We have to stop them." Hugo looked grave and even Harvey didn't argue. Webb looked away, rubbing at his forehead to try and stop the spinning. He felt the captain's eyes on him.

"How are you feeling?"

Webb blinked back to him. "Okay, Captain. It's just... we *have* to stop them."

Ø

Webb managed to persuade Hugo to make More and Rami the ground team for going to size up the storehouse that night, with Bolt along for backup.

"This is better done quick, Captain," he said. "And they know what they're looking for. Besides, I'm going to be elbow-deep in explosives. Someone's going to have to stay on the comm."

Hugo agreed, though he didn't look pleased. If Webb didn't know better he would say the captain was developing a taste for the work. Either that or, more likely, Hugo chafed at taking a back seat whilst sending his crew into danger. Webb could sympathise. He watched Rami, More and Bolt leave the docking bay in dark clothes, guns at hips and night goggles round their necks, then made himself go down to the cargo bay to start on his own work.

He sat himself at a workbench, closed his eyes and took a few breaths. He willed every muscle to relax, even the ones still tight and aching from healing. When his hands were steady he pulled on a pair of heavy gloves and some goggles, re-tied his hair so it wasn't in his eyes and set to work. He sunk himself into it, the smell of the solder and bloodgrease burning in his throat, the weight of the tools. The cement darkened from pink to red in the crucible and he took the heat away just at the right moment and set about wiring up detonator cages.

"Guess this sort of thing never leaves you, huh?"

Webb swore and glowered at Harvey over his shoulder. "It's really not a good idea to sneak up on me when I'm playing with this shit."

Harvey chuckled before coming and perching on a stool next to him. "Couldn't you knock up fake stuff, just in case?"

"They're bound to have a dip-test at the hand-off," Webb murmured.

Harvey leant in to watch as Webb threaded the wires through the cage, making sure nothing touched. "Decent folk don't touch stuff like this."

"Ain't many of them round here."

"Hey, Zeek?"

"Hmm?"

"What's the deal with Hugo?"

"What do you mean?"

"After that Akmar character, I didn't think you'd ever let an ex-Serviceman near your helm again."

Webb pulled another connector through the grid, clipped it off and tied to the cage. "What can I say? There aren't exactly swathes of spacers lining up for the position."

"Bullshit," she said. "I'd take it in a heartbeat."

"What and leave the *Phoenix*?"

She exhaled through her nose. "You *know* what I mean."

Webb loaded the completed cage into the frame and started another. He didn't reply.

"Whatever," Harvey said. "It's your ship. I just hope he's up to it is all."

"Time will tell, I guess."

"The next twenty-four hours will tell," she mumbled.

Webb sighed and looked at her, pushing aside creepers of doubt. "Marilyn, I'm kinda busy here..."

"Fine," she said throwing her hands in the air. "Just don't come running to me if you blow the whole sector into drift."

"We won't be able to," Webb said, smiling.

Harvey shook her head and pushed herself up off the stool. "Space-crazy," she repeated. "I always suspected. Now I know."

Ø

Hugo paced between the bridge and his cabin, checking his wrist panel and the bridge's display for messages every few minutes. He tried to tell himself that no news was good news but the tension from waiting was re-awakening all the aches in his shoulders and head. He took Kinjo's repeated advice and went down to the medbay for some painkillers but then returned to the bridge to once again check the message banks.

The night-cycle was easing into day when the three crew members returned. Hugo had them report in the galley where Kinjo had hot tea and some of their fresher rations ready. They all looked tired, faces drawn and clothes dusty.

"What did you find?" Hugo asked the minute they'd all sat themselves down and started in on the rations.

"The warehouse is a Splinter stronghold, Captain," More said, after swallowing a mouthful. "I'd bet the *Zero* on it."

"Can you be sure?"

"They have a night patrol," More said.

"Lots of industrial units do."

"Not armed with AG19s, they don't. Haven-made too, I'd say."

Harvey stiffened.

"They have three patrols on at any one time," Rami said, setting down her flask of tea, "split into four hour shifts. Our scans didn't show any electronic sensors so they're not scanning comms, but there are cameras and motion-sensors around the entries and exits. As well as the patrols, there was foot traffic between it and the apartment block next door, none of it civilian."

"Doctor? How does this tie in with what you've found?"

Spinn was twiddling his board marker and squinting at schematics on the wall display. "It would appear that they have some of that apartment block under their control also."

"Just some?"

Spinn nodded. "The top few floors still look to be civilian residences."

"Bastards. They'll be counting on that to protect them from assault," Webb ground out. He hunched forward on his elbows. "What's the warehouse for?"

More rubbed his chin. "Stockpile, I'd say."

"How integral do we reckon it is?"

"It's difficult to tell without knowing what they've got in there," More said. "But given how heavily they're guarding it... and the size of the place..."

Bolt swallowed his mouthful. "I'd say there's a fuck-tonne of munitions in there, cap'n. I could smell the gun grease."

"Do we think it's their command base?"

Webb shook his head. "No way they'd put all their eggs in one basket."

"I'd say the commander's right, Captain," Spinn continued, leafing through pages of colony layout on the screen. "Taking the names and credit codes used to secure the warehouse and apartments, I can tell you there are a dozen other areas where they have control of buildings and depots. And that's only the ones they aren't worried about being found."

"This cache is big though," Rami said, finishing off her tea. "And it's where they're storing the cement. I think if we destroy this building we could scupper whatever it is they're planning for the colony."

"Maybe is not good enough. We have one strike before they're after our blood," Hugo said. "I'm assuming you've tried scanning and hacking into their camera feeds?"

Rami nodded. "Spinn and I both tried. As far as we can tell there are no cameras inside the building. Or, if there is, they're on a closed system. And I don't know what they've put in the walls but our scanners were not getting through." Rami paused, tapping her finger on the side of her empty flask. "If we want to find out what's inside we're going to have to make the hand-off."

"She's right, Captain," Webb said. "Don't let this go to your head or anything Hugo, but I agree with you. We need to be sure our move is going to count before we make it."

"And what is our move?" Hugo said.

"I can engineer an isolated blast that'll take out the whole building," Webb said, levering himself to his feet and limping closer to look at the plans. "If we plant some low-level foundation charges here, here and... here," he drew some circles on the plan with Spinn's display marker, "that'll get it going. Whatever they've got stashed in there should take care of the rest. Hopefully it'll take some of the fuckers along with it. But, either way, if they're not scanning comms, the ground team should keep their wrist panels locked to transmit," Webb said. "We can monitor vitals and communication without them having to check in."

"What are the chances of damage to the surrounding area?" Hugo said.

Webb shrugged. "Minimal. If it's done right. But we'll have to get the cement back out of there and far away first."

"How?"

"We break in and grab it and get it out of there before setting off the charges," Webb said. "Spinn, is that a drain there? How big is it?"

"It would be too narrow for crates of cement," Spinn said, shaking his head.

"We can program our crate lifters to life right up and over the wall, Rami put in. "But it would take time."

"Sir... I really think you should let me do this," Webb said, after a pause.

Hugo weighed him up. "What's your status?"

"I'm fine."

"Lieutenant?" Hugo said. "What do you think?"

Rami finished chewing a mouthful of fruit without looking at either of them. "I don't think the commander is fit for fieldwork yet, Captain."

Webb stared at Rami but she took a deliberate bite of apple and didn't look up.

"Very well. Lieutenant, Crewman Bolt. We will make the hand-off and establish what's inside. Then we will report in and move from there."

"Won't this be fun," Harvey grated.

"You're not involved with this, Captain," Hugo said. "You might be recognised."

"Thank fuck," she said, leaning back on her bench. "Some sense at last."

"You are to stay on the *Zero* and help Spinn monitor the local systems for anything that might hamper the ground team."

"Hey, I'm flattered and all Hugo but I ain't exactly a systems whizz," she protested.

"Then you can make him coffee," Hugo said. "And help Kinjo and Sub in the hold. Anything they need, you make sure they get."

"Sir," Kinjo said in a small voice. "Sub and I could cover the apartment block... we could give the ground team warning if anything starts stirring."

Hugo eyed her, hands clasped together, unblinking. He considered it for a moment but shook his head. "I think the fewer people we've got in the field for this one, Midshipman, the better. If all goes to plan we should be out of there before they even know what's happened."

"I wish I had a tenth of credit for every 'if' that gets used on this ship," Harvey muttered.

"Commander?" Hugo said, looking at Webb where he leant against the wall by the display, still looking at Rami who wouldn't look back. "No protests?"

"Thousands," Webb muttered. "But you won't listen so I won't bother."

"Good. First thing's first. Everyone needs to get some rest. Flag goes up tomorrow before midnight"

Ø

"Are you sure you've got all that, Captain?" Webb said.

"Commander if you ask me that again you're grounded. I'll deploy the welding torch if I have to."

"It's just..." Webb scrubbed a hand over his face. "Fuck it. Whatever. Just, *Jesus*, make sure this shit is well, *well* away before you ignite any charges."

"I've seen this cement in action, Commander. You don't have to tell me again," Hugo said, checking over his weapons. He didn't look up to see Webb's face, knowing the tightness in it would only fan the cold flames that were dancing along his nerves.

"Sir," Rami leant out the Jeep. "We have to go."

Hugo climbed into the passenger seat. The ramp went down and Bolt started the engine. The commander's face was pale in the rear-view mirror as they pulled away.

Even on the night cycle the harbour was a hive of activity. Cranes still moaned, scanners beeped, lifters hummed and spacers swore. Floodlights washed everything a sickly sort of yellow and Bolt steered the Jeep down the exitway between loading bays towards the gate. Another customs agent with a computer panel came out of the booth at the gate and shone her lenslight on the reg panel and then in the back on the cargo. She came round to the driver's window.

"*Zero?*" she said around a mouthful of gum. Bolt nodded. She peered at her computer panel. "Your record says you're here buying."

"We're taking parts back," Bolt grumbled.

"At this time?"

"I'm on a deadline."

The woman stood there chewing for a second longer, shining her light first at Hugo then Rami and again on the crates in the back. "Open it up."

Bolt sighed and got out the Jeep. Hugo concentrated on sitting still. He watched in the rear-view as Bolt opened the back door and the woman swapped her lenslight for a scanner.

"Won't work," Bolt grunted, reaching in and keying in code into the topmost box. "Old crates."

The crate popped open. The woman leaned in with her light, wrinkling her nose. "I smell bloodgrease."

"Cheapskate used it to oil the connectors," Bolt growled. "Captain told me to get them off the ship. The dealer might like playing it fast and loose but we'd prefer our engines didn't blow in drift."

"Too right," the woman said, leaning back. "You got a purchase record for these?"

Rami handed the woman a panel and she peered at it. "There's no seller details."

"The shit didn't give us his name. But we know where he is," Bolt said.

"Fine. Get this crap away from my dock. And report that dealer to the Sector Enforcers."

"Yes Ma'am."

Hugo let out a shuddering breath as the gate disappeared from the rear-view. No one talked as Bolt wove the Jeep through the dim groundways. The traffic thinned as they left the docks behind. They steered around the clusters of bars and clubs and kept to darkened side-streets. Factories, maintenance yards and warehouses, all locked and closed down for the night-cycle, loomed in the dark around them behind tall fences.

He closed his eyes and reached inside for the part of himself that knew how to wear fear like armour, but all he found was a bleak emptiness. He opened his eyes and clenched his fists until his fingernails dug into his palms and sunk himself into the pain instead, using it to anchor himself.

A barred gate with a blinking control lock and two cameras appeared in the headlights. Bolt drew up alongside them and stopped the Jeep and waited, engine humming.

"Everyone's panels locked to transmit?" Hugo mumbled.

"Aye, Captain."

"Good. Here we go."

Two men clothed head-to-toe in black with assault rifles stepped into the Jeep's headlights whilst the gate continued to creak open behind them. They looked like skeletons in the bald light, heads shaved and faces obscured by goggles and dust-scarves pulled up over their noses. They waved them forward. The headlight beams bobbed off a wall of concrete. A finger of light appeared in the solid surface as they edged closer, widening as doors in the side of the structure opened. More silent, faceless figures appeared in the opening, gesturing them through. The interior of the building was brightly lit. There were empty crates and piles of scrap piled on one side, empty workstations on the other. More Splinters with guns were arriving through interior doors, all with scarves and goggles. They took up positions around the Jeep and one tapped the barrel of her rifle on the driver's door. They climbed out in silence.

Hugo peered over the shoulders of the nearest Splinters, trying to make out more of what lay in the room beyond. He made out ranks of crates, racks of guns and a row of armoured flyers before the doors clicked shut.

"Hey, spacer-boy," someone snapped. "Eyes front."

Hugo looked away and stepped up beside Bolt. The man who'd spoken, who was so thin his temples looked hollowed-out, kept his face turned toward Hugo a moment longer. Everyone was silent and Hugo felt his palms dampen. Then the first man turned away and gestured to someone further back to come forward. He wasn't in a suit any more but Hugo recognised the man who had relieved him of his weapons in Evangeline's office. The man looked from him to Rami then back to the Splinter and nodded. The thin Splinter turned back to them.

"Bring it out."

Bolt and Hugo moved towards the back of the Jeep.

"Just you," the Splinter snapped, pointing at Bolt.

Hugo stayed put as Bolt moved out of sight around the back of the

Jeep. He didn't dare look at Rami but kept his eyes focussed on the thin man. Bolt brought round first one then the other crate and lowered the lifters to the ground.

"Open them."

Bolt popped the tops and lifted off the false top-trays of engine parts to reveal the neat cubes of red cement stacked underneath. The leader leaned in to see before nodding to another Splinter at his side. The nominated man slung his rifle over his shoulder and came forward, pulling a device with a long probe from his belt. Hugo counted his heartbeats in an attempt to calm them down. The Splinter knelt by one of the boxes, pulling his goggles off as he leaned in. Hugo was aware of heavy scrutiny locked on him as the man dipped the probe into the cement. There was a series of beeps. The Splinters and Evangeline's man all watched in silence. Hugo watched the leader who watched him right back.

The tester straightened then nodded at the leader before resuming his place.

"Over there," came the leader's muffled instructions as he pointed to a spot against the wall. "You got your accounts?"

Rami took a step towards him with her computer panel held out. Hugo looked away when he felt Bolt's elbow in the ribs and turned to fire up the second crate's lifter and follow Bolt with the first to the spot indicated. It made his skin crawl to turn his back on the guns but he forced his pace to be easy and his movements smooth as he stacked the crate in the corner. They returned just as the leader was handing computer panels back to both Rami and Evangeline's man.

"Open the exterior doors," someone barked and the exit started grinding open again. The ring of men began to break up, some disappearing back into the building, some towards the cement crates. Evangeline's man was talking in the leader's ear but the thin man's blanked-out face was turned toward Hugo still. He didn't look away as Bolt backed the Jeep out of the warehouse.

"Take us a few miles away, Crewman," Hugo said as the gates of the compound closed in the rear-view mirror, amazed his voice was steady. He swallowed over and over with a dry throat as they put distance between themselves and the stronghold. He instructed Bolt to pull over once there was more light in the puddles on the groundway.

"Zero?"

"Webb here."

"Did you get all that?"

"Affirmative." Webb's voice sounded a little too cool, even over the wrist panel's speakers. "Sound like a merry bunch. Did you get inside?"

"Yes."

"And?"

Hugo looked at Bolt who nodded. "We're going to take out that building. Tonight."

"Tonight?"

"Affirmative," Hugo said. "Before they get a chance to use the cement."

"You think they plan to move that soon?"

"The building is crammed," Hugo murmured. "Whatever they're going to do they're ready to do it."

There was a pause. "Good luck then, Captain. We'll be listening."

"Get Spinn misdirecting the external cameras and sensors where he can. We'll leave it an hour then we move in."

"Affirmative. Out."

"Take us further away where we can hide the Jeep and get ready," Hugo said zipping up his jacket and fishing gloves out of his utility belt.

"Yes, sir," the crewman said and started the engine. He couldn't read either of their faces and hoped this was only a sign that they were focussed.

It was the slowest hour Hugo could ever recall experiencing. He tried to make himself not watch the chrono but every time he came back to himself he was staring at the red numbers, ticking from one minute to the next with aching sluggishness. Rami and Bolt murmured to one another as they checked over their tech and the charges in the compartment under the driver's seat, but on the whole it was a silent waiting game. That night cycle seemed darker than the ones he'd spent suited in drift during orientation.

When the hour was up Bolt edged the Jeep as close to the complex as they dared, parking behind a boarded-up meltworks. They pulled on their goggles and slipped into the dark, keeping to the shadows as they stole over a low wall into the next yard. The bulk of the Splinter warehouse showed up black against blinking track-lines and the distant orange of the colony's night-cycle ceiling. Hugo took up the rear, keeping his ears tuned for any movement.

It seemed like an age later and yet far too soon when he had his back pressed against the compound wall. A glance at his wrist display confirmed they still had four hours left until the day-cycle began. All was silent apart from the dull hum of life-support somewhere overhead.

He turned to Bolt and Rami, waiting for his order, and nodded. In the green haze of the night-vision he saw them return his nod, strap on grips and start climbing.

There was no precise ascent through a sensor blind spot this time. This was a scramble with time a beast at their heels. They crested the wall right next to a camera. When they hoisted themselves over and started the climb back down the other side and no shots were fired, he assured himself Spinn had managed to get a hold on the camera feeds at least.

His boots hit tarmac just after Rami's. They crept through the shadows to the back wall of the warehouse. Nothing moved.

"Ten minutes," Hugo whispered after they'd confirmed the coast was clear. "And I don't care what happens, you get in trouble you get on the comm."

Bolt and Rami nodded then disappeared into the dark. Hugo watched them go, gathered himself and turned and skirted the warehouse wall in the other direction. He kept close to the concrete, controlling his breathing with an effort. When he reached the corner and peered round, he saw a Splinter patrolling the length of the building, rifle held ready. Hugo ducked back out of sight and pulled out his gun. He held himself still until the man came into view then there was the pop of his silenced weapon and the man lay crumpled on the ground. Hugo stared at him for a moment, the blood showing a dark green in the night vision, then bent, grabbed a handful of his stab-proof jacket and pulled the body around the corner. He shoved it into the deepest shadows and hurried back to the corner.

After having confirmed there was no other patrol in sight, he knelt and pulled a charge from his pack, nestled it into the juncture between the ground and the wall and pressed a code into the keypad. There was a bleep and a small red light flashed twice and then went black. Hugo got up and ran the length of the building to the next corner. Once again he flattened himself against the concrete and peered around. He could see the barred gate, sentries on either side, but they were both facing away. Hugo knelt and laid the second charge, activated it and then sprinted back the way he had come.

Rami turned the opposite corner just as he came back round the rear of the building and waved for him to follow her. He kept close to her heels as they hurried to join Bolt waiting at a side door. They took up positions on either side and Rami glanced at her wrist panel and held up her hand, splaying the fingers.

Five minutes, she mouthed. Hugo checked his gun then stared ahead into the faint haze of the night vision feeling blood pulse through his hands.

Five minutes ticked by and then three more before the next patrol opened the door. A man and a woman stepped out, pulling their dust-scarves up over their faces as they did. Hugo's and Rami's shots hit the first one in the head and chest and then a shot from Bolt brought down the other. There was barely even a sigh from them as they crumpled to the ground. They dragged the bodies out of sight from the door then ducked in, clicking it shut behind them.

He pulled down his goggles, blinking in the brightness and followed Rami and Bolt at a run down the bare corridor. They ducked through the first open door and found themselves in the dark and echoing hangar. In the light from the corridor he made out stacks upon stacks of munition crates, racks of guns and the gleam of yards and yards of bullet belts as well as the row of armoured fighters hulking in the shadows like insects. All three of them stood frozen and stared around at the stockpile for a moment before Rami brought them back with a click of her fingers. They let the door close behind them, plunging them back into darkness, and used a lenslight to start searching.

"You think getting the cement back through the gate is the best option?" Hugo whispered as he helped Bolt check over the nearest stack of crates.

"It's the quickest way," Bolt muttered.

Hugo didn't ask any more and just focussed on the search, aware of time ticking by.

"Captain," Rami's hiss came from another dark corner of the hanger. "Over here."

Bolt and Hugo trotted in the direction of Rami's voice. She had found the doors that lead through to the entryway they had brought the Jeep into earlier. After a quick scan around with their lenslights they saw their crates still in the corner where they'd left them.

"Zero?" Hugo whispered into his panel.

"Webb here. How's it going, Captain?"

"We have laid charges and located the cement. Moving to re-take it now."

"Roger."

"Captain," Rami breathed, shining her light into one of the crates. "There's some missing."

"What?" Hugo said, leaning in. Sure enough, two cubes had been removed from one of the crates. "Find them. We can't leave without -" He blinked and cursed as light flooded the room.

"Freeze," came a hiss from behind them. Hugo froze, bottom dropping out of his belly. Rami and Bolt looked over his shoulder, faces hard and pale. "Turn around. Good and slow."

Hugo turned, holding his hands away from his sides. Two men stood there, rifles trained on them and nasty smiles over their dust scarves that melted away as Hugo turned. One glanced at the other, though the guns never wavered. One nodded and the other's face screwed up and he pushed at something on his throat. "Armin. Armin, come in."

"What?" came a crackly voice from the speaker on his throat comm.

"The *Zero* fucks are back."

"Who?"

"That spacer lot from today. Bastards are only trying to steal back their sale."

"What the hell are you telling me for? Take care of it."

IX

"Webb, *wait*," Kinjo pleaded. "You can't. Rami said -"

"Screw what Rami said," Webb said hitting the hatch control. "Get back up to the bridge and monitor their transmission. Let me know if anything more goes wrong. You ready, Marilyn?"

"As I'll ever be," Harvey grumbled as she pulled on gloves, but Webb couldn't miss the tight smile under her goggles.

"Just keep up," Webb said, getting on his bike and firing the engine. "Kinjo, *go.*"

He watched over his shoulder just long enough to make sure the midshipman was heading back up the ladder then was riding down the hold ramp before it had finished lowering. He tore out of the docking bay and onto the docks, weaving between stacks of cargo. People jumped out the way, angry shouts drowned in the engine noise. The gates were ahead, the customs officer staggering out of her booth to see what the noise was. He pulled the bike in the other direction towards a loading ramp. He sped up the ramp, across an industrial lifter, pulled up the handlebars and revved. The bike jumped the distance between the lifter and an outbuilding. He was vaguely aware of the customs officer shouting but then the bike juddered to the edge of the outbuilding roof and he accelerated off the edge.

The bike cleared the dock wall and hit the tarmac of the groundway on the other side with a bone-juddering impact that sent waves of pain riding up from his ribs, but he just gritted his teeth, and then he was tearing away from the docks. He spared a single glance over his shoulder to make sure Harvey was following then turned back and increased his speed, heart hammering in his ears, cursing Hugo with every breath.

Ø

"Okay you lot," the Splinter said, the leer back. "Against the wall." Hugo didn't move away from the cement. The man who had spoken scowled and hoisted his gun to aim. "You wanna take this whole sector with you? See if I care."

"Wait... " Hugo held up a hand.

"I thought so. Step over there."

Hugo managed to throw a look at Rami and Bolt. They were stiff but their faces were calm. Rami flicked her eyes his way and nodded almost imperceptibly then looked back toward the Splinters.

"Move," the second man growled.

Hugo raised his hands and took a slow step away from the crates. Bolt did the same. The second they passed between Rami and the men there was a flash of movement, a thunk and a gurgling sound and the first man was stumbling back, hand clutched at his throat. The second the other man took to gape at his dying cohort was all that was needed for Bolt to put him out with a shot to the head.

"Quick," Hugo said, rushing forward and grabbing one of the fallen men's rifles. "Grab the lifters."

"Captain," Rami began as she retrieved her knife from the first man's throat.

"There's no time," Hugo snapped. "Grab one each and move now. *Now.*"

Rami and Bolt looked at each other then ran for the crates. Hugo rushed over to the door control, pulling on his goggles. "As soon as I've cleared the gate," Hugo said, reaching for the light switch as Rami and Bolt drew level with the crates on lifters, "you move. Get that shit as far away as you can as quick as you can. I'll retrieve the missing cubes."

"Captain -"

"Are you ready?"

He saw Rami swallow, then she nodded and pulled on her goggles. Hugo shut down the lights then hit the control for the door. With a screech it started to open. In the night vision he saw the two sentries by the gate turn in the direction of the noise. Hugo dropped to one knee and fired. The night split apart, the rifle hammering into his shoulder. Sparks flew on the metal of the gate and the two men went down. "*Go.*"

Rami and Bolt dashed to the gates. Hugo watched long enough to see Rami hack the controls and the gates start to open then he dropped the rifle, drew his hand gun and turned back into the building. He glanced at his wrist panel, saw there was twenty minutes left, cursed and ran back across the warehouse floor. Just as he was passing the two dead men he heard a crackle then a tinny voice.

"Mario? What was that noise? Is it done?"

Hugo pushed sweaty hair back from his face and knelt next to the first body, fingers sliding in the blood for the throat comm. "It's done," he grunted.

"Good. Dump the waste then relieve Arvo and Nam on the gates. No more fuck ups."

Hugo took another steadying breath, pressed the throat comm. "Acknowledged," he said, then held his breath. No reply came and he let the breath go and scrambled to his feet and ran for the storage hanger.

The stores loomed up on all sides in the dark. It would take weeks to look through it all, but he couldn't see the Splinters being stupid enough to throw a couple of red cement charges loose in with all their supplies. He hesitated one moment then went with his gut and made his way back to the door into the corridor. He flattened himself against the wall and opened it a crack.

His night vision blurred and flashed in the light and he pulled off his goggles, squinting. There was no sound or movement. He waited ten more heart beats then stepped into the passage and ran, keeping his steps light and gun ready. He glanced in the windows of the doors he passed but just found darkened store rooms and supply lockers.

There was a flight of stairs at the end of the corridor. He strained his ears, glanced at the time on the wrist panel, swore and raced up. The next level was another brightly lit corridor with doors on either side. Still there was no one around and he dared to hope most of the Splinter force was in the apartment block for the night-cycle.

He peered in the window of the first door he came to and saw a room with banks of displays and workstations. Lights flashed and reports and newsfeeds scrolled on the screens but no one was sat at any of the keyboards. He spotted a long workbench with tools, scanners and other equipment scattered along it, including the probe the Splinters had used to test the cement. With one more glance along the corridor to confirm he was still alone, he ducked inside. He caught the telltale smell of blood-grease in the air and felt his heart beat rise and started rifling through the piled junk on the workbench.

He muttered curses as he kept searching and found no cubes then jerked as someone grabbed his collar. The shock caught him off balance and they slammed his face into the worktable. He tasted blood, saw stars and then there was the cold muzzle of a gun pressing into the back of his neck.

"Drop it, asshole."

Hugo recognised Armin's voice from the throat comm. He dropped his gun and it clattered to the floor. Then he was being hauled up off the workbench and bundled out of the room. He tried to pull away but the hands that had him were strong and the tightened hold on his collar cut off his air. He scrabbled at his throat as he was manhandled down the corridor and then the world exploded in a shower of white stars.

Somewhere beyond the pounding in his skull he was aware of being hauled through another door and flung on the floor.

"Hold him."

Hands pulled him into a kneeling position and the hardness of a gun was pressed against the back of his head. He blinked until his vision swam back and saw he was in a bare room with blank walls, a few chairs and wall displays and Splinters stood all around, all in black, all armed. Armin stood before him, wiping Hugo's blood off the butt of his gun. Hugo recognised his tall and whip-like frame as that of the Splinter who had done the talking when they made the hand-off. Without his dust-scarf or goggles Hugo saw that his face was sharp and pinched, his cheek-bones severe angles in the thin face with black eyes like holes drilled into his head. He holstered his gun then crossed his arms, his face unsettlingly composed. He was just opening his mouth to speak when another man, face and shaved head beaded with sweat, came barrelling into the room.

"Armin," he began before focusing on Hugo. "You got him...?"

"Did you catch the others?"

The sweaty arrival shook his head. "They killed Arvo and Nam and got away."

Armin regarded the man for a moment the turned his attention back to Hugo.

"So. You stole back your cement. That alone is enough to make me want to skin you from the feet up, but first you're going to tell me why you stayed behind?" Armin's thin brows drew together in a frown. Hugo attempted to pull against the hands holding him but they shook him and he saw stars again. "Now, come, Zero. You're dead anyway. So are your crew. Buy yourself some dignity and a quick end for your crew and tell me why you are still here?"

"Armin..." Someone, a woman, from behind him pulled off Hugo's wrist panel. She brought it round and handed it to the thin Splinter. "Set to transmit," she said, glaring at Hugo.

"I see," Armin said, turning the panel over in his hands. "A set up. We shall have to have words with Mistress Evangeline."

Hugo squinted, trying to see the countdown on the panel but Armin held it facing away. He locked his black eyes with Hugo's then brought the panel close to his face. "Do come play," he said into it. "We're wait-ing." Then he threw it on the floor and smashed it with his boot. "Tie him up and throw him in a holding cell. We'll wait for his friends. Get a dozen troops over from the block and get them round the walls and doors. I want these *Zero* fucks dead before day-cycle."

There were a series of mumbled assents and then Hugo was hit on the head again and the world went black.

He came round just as he was dumped in a holding cell. Every pulse was like a hammer in his skull. He cursed and forced himself to lie still and just breathe until the dizziness and nausea lessened. He fumbled himself into a sitting position and just had time to take in the white walls, bare floor and locked, windowless door when the room was plunged into darkness. For a few precious minutes he just sat there and breathed in the darkness, then he tried the binders securing his wrists, pulling and twisting until the metal bit into his flesh, feeling the skin split and blood pool in his palms.

He laid his head back against the wall and again forced himself just to breathe. He tried to bring up his internal clock and figure out how much time there was left but the whack to the head had skewed his count. He slumped back down, pressing his cheek against the cool floor and closed his eyes. He tried to pull back the veils of pain and uncertainty and find the bit of himself that used to take over in a crisis. Time slipped by and nothing came. He scowled in the darkness, the movement awakening fresh pain in his head and resorted to counting down the seconds.

A time later, that his internal clock told him was only a few minutes, even if it felt like he had lived through the destruction of Lunar 1 a hundred times, a series of bangs, shouts and the rattle of gunfire filtered through the walls. He lifted his head and strained his ears, hope warring with despair in the pit of his belly. Then there was a shout and the thunder of rifle fire outside the cell. He sat himself up then swore when the door banged open, flooding the room with light that clawed at the inside of his aching head.

"Need a hand there, Captain?"

"Webb?" Hugo spat, trying to get to his feet. "How the hell did you get in here?"

"It's amazing where an unguarded drain and enough stun charges can get you," Webb said, holstering his gun and pulling off a Splinter face-scarf.

"You *idiot*, there's not enough time. You should have left me -"

"Don't flatter yourself, Hugo. We came for the missing cement. Figured I had just enough time to save your ass."

He pulled out his lock pick and knelt behind Hugo. He cursed softly and Hugo wondered just how badly he'd damaged his wrists but then there was a click and his hands were free. He hissed as his shoulders were freed of the pressure.

"We need to move."

Webb didn't wait for a reply but helped him to his feet then they were out in the corridor.

"Webb!"

They turned and Harvey, cap, goggles and scarf obscuring most of her face came trotting down the corridor, slinging a pack on her back as she came. "Got the missing cement. It was in their lab, like you said."

"Nice work, now... shit. They've found us." All three of them looked back and forth as the sound of shouts and feet came from the stairwells at either end of the corridor. "Get back," Webb said then drew his gun and shot out the glass in the strip of windows running below the juncture of the wall and the ceiling. "Quick," he said gesturing to Harvey.

Harvey came forward and Hugo, ignoring his strained shoulders, helped Webb give her a leg up then she was scrambling out and onto the roof. Hugo jumped and pulled himself up. The night air was cold on his sweaty skin. He turned himself, got his elbows up onto the flat roof and scrambled up, Harvey helping with a grip on his elbow. As soon as he was clear Webb was up behind them and then they were running across the roof, feet pounding on the metal. There were shouts and the sound of people moving about on the ground but it quietened as they crossed edge furthest from the gates. Hugo squinted in the dark and could make the top of an outbuilding in the gloom below. Without a word Webb took a run up and jumped, landing with a roll on the corrugated iron.

"You next, Harvey."

Harvey shook her head. "No, you get over there and be ready to catch the pack," she said. "I don't much fancy rolling over on the cement."

Hugo nodded, took a breath and jumped. His roll made his head spin but he was up again just as Harvey was stepping to the edge.

"What is she doing...oh crap -" Webb said then took position next to Hugo, arms outstretched as she swung the pack back and flung it. Hugo managed to catch the straps and then Harvey jumped, tumbling onto hands and knees beside them. Webb was just helping her up when Hugo felt the lightness of the pack and the bottom drop out of his stomach. He unzipped it and looked inside.

"Hugo, we've got, like, four minutes -"

"Wait," Hugo said, voice tight. "There's only one cube in here."

The two spacers froze.

"How many were missing?" Webb murmured.

"Two..."

They spent a second rooted to the spot staring at each other but then the air around them was torn apart by gunfire. They threw themselves flat on the roof as the metal shook under them with the impact of the shots. Hugo cursed and started to shimmy back towards the edge closest to the warehouse but Webb grabbed his jacket.

"There's no time," he said, voice tight and face strained. Hugo looked at the warehouse then the countdown on Webb's wrist panel and slammed his fist on the iron with a wordless snarl.

"We gotta move, *now*," Harvey hissed as the guns stopped and orders were bellowed out below.

Hugo took one last look at the warehouse, saw Webb doing the same, then turned and followed Harvey as she crawled to the back of the out-building and dropped off the edge into the darkness. Once they were down, they edged to the corner, paused for a painful second then ran across the open space, firing into the dark as they went before throwing themselves behind a stack of empty crates. Harvey knelt and continued to return fire over the barrier even as the metal crates and wall behind them burst in showers of dust and shards. Hugo took the gun Webb offered and joined Harvey as the commander knelt at their feet. There was the sound of metal scraping on tarmac as he hauled back a grid from a drain.

"Move," he snapped, then dropped himself into the opening.

"Harvey, go," Hugo said and she fired off a few more rounds before lowering herself into the hole. Hugo kept firing until he heard a scream then shoved the gun into his belt and dropped through the opening. His boots splashed ankle-deep into water and then Webb was shoving him out the way and reaching to pull the grid back into place.

"Run," he called, splashing off into the darkness, Harvey close behind.

Hugo was aware of a ceiling just over his head and walls close on either side but it was black as space. He made himself trust his ears and Harvey and her night goggles ahead to lead the way. His heart and head pounded and his breath heaved. Just when he thought his lungs or legs would give out they were careening out into the gloom of the night cycle.

Webb was up ahead, vaulting over a low wall, Harvey scrambling up after him. Hugo got to the wall just as Harvey disappeared over the top. He pulled himself over and then they were dodging around heaps of scrap scattered around a shadowy yard. Webb and Harvey didn't slow their pace, but climbed up a pile of twisted metal stacked against another wall and dropped over the other side. Part of Hugo wondered how Webb was doing all this on his injured ankle but then pushed the thought aside and concentrated on following as fast as he could.

He was down and running on the other side when the air was shredded with a blast of heat, light and noise that rattled the teeth in his head and seared the skin on the back of his neck. He was flung to the floor and had just enough time to cover his head when debris pelted down on him. The bruising rain seemed to go on forever and then there was a horrible, black moment when all he knew was the ringing in his ears, the burning of his breath, the taste of smoke on his tongue and stillness so complete it was unnatural.

He twitched, testing his limbs. When he found they worked, he got to his hands and knees, chunks of brick and metal shifting and falling away as he did.

"Webb? Harvey?" he croaked, peering around. Everything was lit in flickering orange. His heart seemed to stop for a moment before two shapes shifted in the mess and Webb and Harvey levered themselves up out of the debris and onto their knees.

Webb shook his head, dust scattering from his hair then looked up and stilled. Harvey followed his gaze, slowly getting to her feet, face grim. Hugo swallowed, got to his feet and turned.

Scrap from the yard was scattered all around them. Everything beyond the wall of the yard was blown away. The skeleton of the obliterated warehouse finished falling in on itself in a rain of sparks as they watched. The remains of the apartment block beyond heaved, groaned and keeled over with a thunderous clamour of collapsing concrete that shook the ground under their feet.

When the smoke reached the detectors, rain started to fall. They could hear the hissing of its pitiful attempt to douse the flames. Even when the sound of screeching tyres and the shafts of headlights slicing holes in the orange darkness on the roads nearby filtered through to him, he couldn't make himself move. It took Webb shaking him and shouting in his ear to make his legs work.

He followed Harvey and Webb across an abandoned lot, over a wire fence then around the corner of a boarded up-building. Two bikes were parked in the shadows. Hugo got on behind Webb without even having to be told, put an arm around his waist and then just hung on. The bike roared and they tore away. Webb's cargo jacket smelt like engines and bloodgrease. He sunk himself into the feeling of the artificial rain trickling through his hair and down his neck, trying to bury himself away from the throbbing in his head, the buzzing in his ears and the stinging of burnt skin.

Webb twisted the bike around corners at a speed that some part of Hugo baulked at. Spray drenched his back and the air howled in his ears, but he didn't look up. He kept his head pressed into the commander's back and his eyes shut. Even when there was the sound of vehicles behind him and gun fire whining past his ears and Webb yelling at him to return fire, he didn't move.

There was more gut-wrenching speed, spray running down his collar and a spreading ache from his limbs clamouring for attention. Just as the arm holding him on started to pulse with fatigue, they slowed. He only straightened when Webb pulled away and the bike tilted under him. He stumbled off, came up against a wall, bent over and vomited.

When there was nothing left to heave and the world had stopped spinning, he looked up to see they were in a narrow alley, concrete towering up into the dark above them. A large set of doors were rumbling open in the wall opposite. Harvey was stood by the bikes and Webb was at the control panel for the doors but they were both looking at him. He straightened, wiping his mouth on his sleeve.

"Get in," Webb muttered, wheeling his bike into the dark opening, Harvey following behind with hers. Hugo put one foot in front of the other and followed. He found another wall to lean against as the doors ground shut behind him. As soon as the lock clicked, they heard tyres screeching nearby. He held his breath but they faded away and all was silence.

An ancient strip light fizzed to life above his head and lit up a cluttered space, all shelves of dusty parts. The floorspace was almost completely taken up by the bikes and the *Zero*'s Jeep.

"Captain?" Rami clambered out of the Jeep and came forward. "Are you okay?"

Hugo didn't reply and stepped back when she reached out.

"Anita," Webb warned, shaking his head.

Rami threw Hugo another concerned glance but fell back.

"Come on," Webb continued, squeezing his way past the Jeep to a door in the wall behind it.

"Will it all be safe here?" Rami said, moving to follow.

"Safer than on the *Zero*. Captain?"

Hugo gritted his teeth then pushed himself up off the wall and followed the crew out. He felt Webb's eyes on him as he passed but didn't look up.

"Follow me," Webb said, pulling on one of his baseball caps then trotting down the narrow, dingy corridor. All the doors to the other storage lockers were locked and the controls rusty. Webb ran the length of the hallway and when they reached the end, drew his gun and peered out into the street for a long time before slinking out.

The streets, alleys, walls and fences they dodged around, under, and over, went by in a blur. The rain had stopped but the taste of wet metal and tarmac was heavy in the air. Twice Webb had to redirect them to avoid people in the streets heading to morning shifts. He stood and scanned a wide stretch of groundway for several minutes before apparently being satisfied it was clear and heading to a maintenance hatch in the middle, kneeling and levering it open.

"Quick," he hissed. Bolt dropped down first, then Rami and Harvey. Hugo lowered himself down after them and then Webb clambered in and was securing the hatch behind them. He pushed through them again and led the way down the maintenance passage, lit so well that it made Hugo's eyes ache and showed up the filth and blood on the crew's clothes and faces. They trotted single-file, turning corner after corner, descended and climbed ladders, twisted and turned until part of Hugo began to wonder if Webb actually knew where he was going or whether he was just trying to get them as lost as possible.

The steady light and unwavering pace of their pounding feet on the metal grid flooring dulled his senses. It was only by skidding that he stopped himself barrelling into Rami when Webb finally stopped under another hatch. He stretched to fiddle with the control panel, cursing, and Hugo could see his hands were shaking. The commander pulled off his gloves, tried again and the hatch hissed and opened. He waved them all up the ladder.

Everything was lit with the dull grey of the activating day-cycle. Hugo blinked around yet another deserted lot with cracks in the tarmac, surrounded by a high metal fence. Brick and concrete structures, some derelict, reared up beyond, all darkened windows, iron fire escapes and gurgling gutters.

Webb secured the hatch back into its place and waved at them to follow him across the yard. Hugo squinted up at the colony 'sky' far above, trying to make out a sector number, but they were too close to the hub, and the roof was too high to make out. Webb peered out a gate in the metal fence then dashed out, across another alley and down a set of steps to a door below ground level. The rest followed. Even though they were miles from where they'd been, all the crew still peered around and fidgeted as Webb pressed the buzzer.

"Where are we?" Rami mumbled. No one answered her. Webb pressed the buzzer again.

"What?" a voice barked from the intercom.

"Doll? It's Webb."

"Wanna narrow if down a bit for me, pal?"

"Ezekiel."

There was a pause and the door was pulled open by a stocky woman, hair cut close about her head, clad in a welder's tunic and heavy cargo pants.

"Ezekiel? What the...?" she started then her eyes took in the rest of them and her face fell. "Get in."

Everyone filed in and the woman closed and locked the door behind them. They trudged down a dark corridor and through another heavy door into a room with only one frosted window high up in one wall. The floor was bare but the walls were full of shelves crowded with all sorts of junk from machine parts and fragments of stone to hard-copy pictures in gilt frames. There was a solitary table with a single chair pulled up to it and another three in a stack in the corner next to a low bench scattered with threadbare cushions. In the other corner there was an ancient workstation and a fan overhead moved the stuffy air around.

"I'm sorry, Doll," Webb said as they all filed in. "We just need somewhere to lay low a while."

"What happened?" she asked, but suddenly stiffened and her eyes flicked to a muted wall display under the window. It was tuned to a newsfeed showing footage of the burning and collapsing apartment building. Hugo's throat tightened. The woman moved across the room and shut it off. "Never mind. Look, I'm sorry to do this, lad, but I'm just on my way to a shift."

"No worries, Doll. Go. And thanks. I owe you."

She looked round them all, lips a thin line, then nodded. "You remember how to get into the bolthole?" Webb nodded. "Good. I'll be back at noon. And, Lord God, get washed up, the lot of you. You look like death."

Then she left, locking the doors behind her.

"Rami," Webb said. "Get a message to More. We need the *Zero* ready to launch..."

"Belay that."

"Captain," Webb began.

"We're not leaving," Hugo ground out. Rami, Bolt and Harvey exchanged glances. Webb's clear eyes remained on him. "The job's not finished."

"Sir -"

"I'm going to annihilate them."

He glowered at the floor a moment longer then stumbled across the room and through another door. Lights flickered on as he stumbled down some stairs. He didn't know where he was going and he didn't care. He just had to be alone. His feet hit flat concrete and he found himself in a windowless corridor with bare brick walls that smelt of underground. He fumbled at the first door he came to, and found a bathroom and locked himself in.

He leant on the metal sink, staring into his eyes in the mirror, trying to see if he was still in them anywhere. Growling, he shrugged off his jacket then ran the cold water and washed off the caked dirt and blood from his face and hands. The water ran black down the plughole.

He kept splashing his face over and over, willing his spirit to rally and his flesh to steady but couldn't stop the trembling and couldn't stop the flames burning his skin or the metal and brick groaning and crashing in his ears. When he looked back in the mirror the dirt and blood had gone but his skin was pale, empty eyes rimmed in red, hair a wild tangle and one temple purpled with bruising. He'd seen faces like this before on defeated enemies. He remembered the pity and scorn that had risen in him at the sight and hung his head and breathed deep until the returning urge to vomit passed.

He scooped another handful of water and drank, more because he knew he needed it than because he felt any need. When he felt he could control himself he unlocked the door. Webb was leant against the wall outside, arms crossed and eyes narrow.

"Alright, Hugo," he said. "Let's do it. Let's destroy the Splinters."

Hugo swallowed. Webb held his gaze and he could see resolve in them and something else, something like determination, but colder. Webb glanced down at Hugo's sliced and bruised wrists and nodded down the corridor. Hugo followed him through another door. The lights turned on as they entered, revealing a clean but cluttered kitchen unit, with a sink and cupboards on one side and the work surface on the other entirely given over to a gutted engine of some kind.

"Where are we?"

"Somewhere safe," Webb said as he started rifling through cupboards. "Sit."

Hugo perched himself on a stool as Webb pulled out a medkit. He drifted in a daze as Webb, surprisingly gentle, took one hand and then the other and cleaned the cuts on his wrists.

"You know what happened today would be a stroll in the park compared to what would have happened if the Splinters had been let loose on the entire colony with that cache, right?"

Hugo stiffened. A bitter mist of hot and cold was roiling inside him but none of it formed itself into thoughts or words. It tasted familiar at the back of his throat and he hated it.

Webb threw the bloody sterilising pads in the disposal and pulled out a length of binding. The silence stretched on as his commander bound his wrists and finally he found something to say: "So what do we do?"

Webb paused and looked up. His eyes searched Hugo's for a moment, then he looked away. "First thing we do is get the cement, the *Zero* and the crew the hell away from Lunar 1."

"The whole crew?"

"They need to think we've bolted. And I trust the *Zero*'s chances more if she's got everyone aboard."

"What about tech? Weapons?"

A ghost of Webb's grin passed over his face as he finished binding Hugo's wrists. "Lunar 1 is a paradise for all the worst sorts of dealers. We can pick up anything we need."

"We should let Luscombe know..."

"If I may suggest, Captain," Webb said, not breaking his look. "This is the sort of mission the colonel would prefer learning the results of rather than having to approve or know of beforehand."

Hugo nodded, uneasiness flickering inside him as he rubbed the bindings. "So we send the *Zero* away. Then what?"

"I haven't the faintest fucking idea," Webb said. "But we better think of something."

X

"I'm staying."

"Now who's space-crazy?"

"This whole poxy mess is your fault, Ezekiel," Harvey countered, prodding him in the chest. "If you hadn't said I should come to you with this kind of thing, I'd be buried in some hole on Haven, waiting for the Splinters to blow themselves up or get themselves drifted by the Service. Now you've got me in this deep the hell am I gonna let you have all the fun. I'm staying and I'm going to *obliterate* the bastards."

Webb felt a smile quirk a corner of his mouth. "Fine. I can't make you go. But a whole lot of shit's gonna go down before we're through with this."

"Don't I just know it."

"Glad to have you on team, Captain," Webb moved towards the door of Doll's apartment. "Your first mission is to keep an eye on Hugo whilst I get Rami and Bolt back to the Jeep." Harvey's eyes widened and Hugo's face darkened but Webb continued before either of them could protest. "I'll be back. Stay put. And don't answer the door."

Webb paced down the corridor, trying to ignore the stiffening in his ankle and the demanding ache spreading along his ribs.

"Shouldn't we wait until the night-cycle?" Rami asked as they came up to the front door.

"They could find the *Zero* any second now," Webb said, unlocking the door and peering up and down the alley for a good three minutes before scurrying across. They ducked back into the abandoned lot then dropped one after another back into the maintenance ways. Webb moved along without thinking, trusting his feet to find the way, feeling Rami's eyes in the back of his head the whole way. It took a lot longer to get back to the storage unit than it had taken them to get away. Not only did he now pause to listen at every corner to make sure the way was clear of day-cycle maintenance crew, but his legs were getting heavier with every step and his breathing shallower over the pain gathering force in his ribs.

It took him two goes to get the code right to open the door to his storage unit again. "Stick to the back groundways and alleys where you can," he said as he moved out the way of Jeep towards the door controls. "And stay on the comm. Let us know the minute you're away."

"Aye, Commander," Bolt said, clambering into the driver's seat.

"Zeek?" Rami said.

"Go, Lieutenant."

"Zeek, please..." her face was calm but her eyes flickered with pain. "I..." she fumbled, glanced at Bolt who was deliberately looking away. "I'm sorry... for saying you shouldn't be on the ground team. I just wanted -"

"It's okay," he said. And then, again, in a softer voice, seeing her lips thin. "Really. Now go, get yourself safe. That's all I need from you right now."

She nodded, jaw set and climbed into the Jeep and shut the door. Webb activated the door, checked the alley and then waved them out. He watched until the Jeep was out of sight, feeling something tighten inside him, then locked everything back up. He made his way even more slowly back to Doll's, pausing in the maintenance ways to smell the exhaust and the oil and to repeat to himself why he stayed.

Ø

"This Armin sounds like the key to the whole thing," Webb was saying, staring into a mug of tea Harvey had made with stuff she'd found in Doll's cupboards.

"I'd say so," Harvey growled as she spun an ancient yo-yo up and down. "He's the scum that cornered me in that bar. He's gotta be high up the chain."

"If he survived," Webb said, "we need to find him and watch him. He'll lead us to the ringleaders."

"Do they even have leaders?" Harvey muttered.

"If they've been hired, there'll be some nasties running the show."

"So, we identify the ringleaders. Then what?" Hugo said.

"Depends on who they are," Webb said. "And if we find them."

"There's that lovely word again," Harvey muttered, catching the yo-yo.

"We need to know more... " Webb muttered.

"Reconnaissance starts tomorrow," Hugo started but then they all looked up as the door opened. Hugo went for a gun that wasn't there just as Doll came through the door, oil smudged on one cheek and red goggle-marks around her eyes. "Still here, then?"

Webb stood. "We'll be moving on soon," he said.

She looked around. "Weren't there more of you?"

"They've left with the ship."

Doll glanced between them. "And you stayed behind?"

Hugo saw Webb swallow. "We've still got some business to take care of..."

The older woman's shoulders slumped a little and she shook her head.

"The job is never done, is it?" she said, moving through the room towards the stairs. "I'm going to wash up and fix some lunch. You all look like you're about to keel over."

"No, please," Webb said. "Don't go to any trouble. We'll be moving on as soon as it's dark."

"Whatever mess you're in, Ezekiel," she said turning at the door, "I will sleep better knowing you've at least got somewhere safe to come back to." She smiled at Webb and Hugo thought he saw his commander pale. He opened his mouth but Hugo cut him off.

"Thank you, Ma'am," he said, standing.

"No," Webb said, stepping closer to here. "I'm not having you mixed up in this, Doll."

"Dear boy. Don't you think I'm old enough to make my own decisions?" She patted Webb on the cheek. "Just don't tell me what's going on. Everyone's safer that way. Sit down and I'll get us some food. You always were a terrible eater, Ezekiel. It doesn't surprise me you're still so thin. I'll be right back."

Webb stared after her and Hugo saw Harvey stifle a giggle behind her hand. Her face quickly fell though when Webb turned and they saw the look on his face.

"I won't have her put in danger, Hugo," he said.

"Commander, we need a base," Hugo said. "If this place is as safe as you say it is, it's our best option." Webb chewed his thumbnail, glowering at the table. "Webb," Hugo said. "I promise we'll keep her safe."

Webb sighed, pulled off his cap and dropped himself into a chair as the smell of cooking started drifting up from downstairs. Hunger raked claws through Hugo's insides. Webb sat and frowned at the table top and Harvey glanced between them for a moment as the thick silence stretched on.

"I'll go help," she said, replacing the yo-yo on a shelf and disappearing downstairs.

Hugo watched her go then turned back to Webb. He was still staring off at nothing and Hugo was suddenly far too tired to try and bring up the planning conversation again. He hauled himself to his feet and turned on the wall display. The channel was still showing footage of the burning apartments along with reports on suspects and terrorist involvement and calls from the local Enforcers for Service intervention. He made himself watch, feeling the cold anger flicker. Webb didn't look.

When Doll and Harvey returned with steaming bowls, their eyes flicked to the silent wall display and then away.

"Grub's up," Doll said, placing the bowls on the table.

Hugo's stomach clenched at the savoury smell of noodles and herbs. "Thank you," he said, pulling a bowl towards him. "Mistress...?"

"Captain Hugo," Webb said, already shovelling noodles into his mouth. "Donatella."

"Donatella...?"

"McCullough," she said with a smile, handing Hugo some chopsticks.

Hugo stared as the woman pulled her own bowl towards her and began eating. "*McCullough?*"

"Indeed," she said, smiling again. "A long story for another time. Doll is fine... Kaleb, isn't it?"

Hugo nodded after an elbow in the ribs from Webb.

Doll nodded, looking down at her food. "And how are you finding your new position?"

Hugo chewed and swallowed his mouthful, still watching the woman as he did so, trying to figure out if her face was familiar. "Ask me when this is over."

Doll looked up with a wan smile then looked to Harvey. "And you, my dear?"

"This is Captain Harvey," Webb said, seemingly relieved to redirect the conversation.

"Marilyn," Harvey said around a mouthful of noodles, holding out her hand.

"Two captains," Doll said, shaking Harvey's hand. "I am privileged."

"Not that privileged," Harvey muttered.

"The *Phoenix*, yes?"

Harvey froze, noodles dangling from her mouth. Hugo would have thought it funny if it wasn't for the very real fear in Harvey's eyes.

"I'd be careful around here, my dear," Doll continued. "Contracts were out for you even before whatever happened with the apartment block."

Harvey swallowed her mouthful, eyes locked on Doll. "I am always careful."

"Glad to hear it," Doll said, watching the wall display over Harvey's shoulder.

The rest of the meal was consumed in silence. Hugo tried to catch Webb's eye but the commander kept focussed on his food.

"All done?" Doll said and started collecting bowls. "Now, I assume if you are anything like Ezekiel you all sleep about as often as you eat properly. Come, my dear," she said, gesturing to Harvey. "There's a couch in my room. The boys can get settled in up here."

Doll took Harvey downstairs and then reappeared with her arms full of blankets.

"This is more than we deserve," Webb said and Hugo couldn't quite miss the catch in his voice.

"I know," Doll said as she piled the blankets on the bench. "I've got to get to my afternoon shift now. Get some sleep. And keep this door locked."

"Thank you," Hugo said again. Her appraising eyes turned on him momentarily before she nodded then left.

Webb stood rubbing the back of his neck. Then he shook himself and moved across the room to shut off the wall display.

"McCullough?" Hugo said, folding his arms.

"She'll tell you herself if she wants to, Hugo," Webb muttered.

"I can't plan this mission if you keep information from me, Commander."

"She's not part of the mission," Webb said, reaching to close the shutter on the window.

"She's providing us with a base. She's involved, even if she doesn't know what in."

"It's not my story to tell."

Hugo ground his teeth. "Is she a fence?"

"No."

"She knows who we are."

"I've known her a long time. And she works in a meltworks. She hears things, knows things," Webb said, hauling the table into a corner to clear the floor. "You have to on this damn colony so you know whether to bolt down the nearest alley when you see someone coming."

"She could be useful."

"We're not using her," Webb said, face hard. "She's risked herself enough by hiding us."

"Commander, I fear you may be letting your personal feelings cloud your judgement."

"Too right I am," Webb said, closing the distance between them. "Doll is out of this. Out of it all. She offers us a base, that's fine. But that's it. Get those ideas out your head right now or I'm walking and you can do this on your own."

Hugo raised his head, held the commander's troubled gaze a moment then sighed and looked away. "Is there anyone we can use?"

"No," Webb said, grabbing a blanket from the bundle on the bench. "We're on our own. Get used to it."

Ø

Hugo drifted awake, wondering what had woken him but then just lay there, marvelling at the fact that he had fallen asleep at all. He tried to stay in the drowsy safe place where he felt he could turn over and go back to sleep but after the tea that afternoon, nature had other plans. He sighed in the dark as he drifted fully awake and his head filled with the realities of the last few weeks like a fire gaining air.

Shaking away what he could, he rose off the bench and was just moving to step over Webb when he noticed that the commander was not in his blankets. There was light coming under the door from the stairway.

Padding over to the door, he pushed it open and saw there was a light on in the kitchen unit. The door was ajar and he heard the soft murmuring of voices. Without wanting to think about why he did, he moved down the stairs slowly enough so as not to activate the motion-sensitive lights and edged up to the kitchen. He peered through the gap.

Webb was knelt on the linoleum, head bowed and eyes tight shut, clutching something at his throat. Doll stood over him, one hand on his head, the other hand raised in the air. She was mumbling soft words over him with her eyes closed. Hugo felt like a bucket of cold water had been dumped over his head but was unable to look away. When Webb finally rose, wiping his eyes, the spell was broken and Hugo padded away, used the bathroom and crept back up the stairs.

He heard Webb return to his blankets sometime later and listened as his breathing levelled out but couldn't be sure if the commander ever actually fell asleep. Hugo felt the thoughts chew themselves out inside his head, staring at the dark wall, tasting guilt on his tongue.

Ø

He woke with a start. He had managed to fall back asleep but this time it had not been dreamless. He stared at the wall until he only saw the brickwork and not flames and smoke. Rubbing his eyes, he sat up, groaning as every muscle protested and the back of his head throbbed. The shutter had been opened and dust danced in the weak light. The room was empty. The chrono on the wall display confirmed it as a little after six in the morning.

Once he had stood up he became aware of returning hunger and of voices and a low buzzing noise coming from the stairwell. He picked up the filthy remains of his t-shirt, scowled as he pulled it on and then reached for his dusty trousers then went downstairs in bare feet. It wasn't until he got to the bottom that the image of Doll praying over Webb from the previous night rose again in his mind. He paused in the corridor to school his face then moved on through to the kitchen.

"Morning, Captain," Webb said. "Have some of this coffee. Don't know where Doll gets it from but it's dynamite."

"It's sometimes good to have connections," Doll said.

Hugo blinked. Harvey was sat on one of the kitchen stools, head bowed as Doll ran a pair of clippers over her head. Hugo felt something shift inside him as the last of Harvey's yellow curls fell to the floor. She looked up, shook her head and ran her hands over the shaved locks, brushing away the last stray strands. Hugo felt his breath catch when she looked up and smiled, the missing hair making her face look rounder, younger, her eyes standing out as a more brilliant green than before. Her smile faltered and Hugo realised he was staring and looked away, feeling his cheeks flush.

Webb was grinning at him, still holding out the coffee. "Suits her, huh, Hugo?"

Hugo took the mug, glowering.

"Should save you from everything but a close look," Doll said, brushing hair form Harvey's shoulders. "I have an old welding tunic I don't fit into any more. You wear that too, you're just another solder-monkey."

"Thanks, Doll," Harvey said, running her hand over her head. "You got a scarf too?"

She nodded. "Somewhere. Hold on."

Harvey got to her feet and dusted herself off. "Right, I'm ready."

Hugo swallowed his mouthful of coffee. "Ready for what?"

"We need supplies," Harvey said. "Unless you're planning on glowering the Splinters into submission?"

"You're not going on your own, Harvey," Hugo said.

Harvey frowned, hands on hips. "I'm more likely to be recognised if I get spotted with either of you two trigger-happy morons. Unless you want me to take the clippers to that lot, Webb?"

"Hands off," Webb growled as he poured another coffee.

"Kaleb?" Harvey said with a half-grin, waving the clippers. Hugo ran a hand through his hair. He'd never worn it so long.

"Not so fast," Webb warned. "He still walks too much like a soldier. You give him a trooper haircut he'll stick out a mile."

Harvey put the clippers down and Hugo swore she actually pouted. "Pity. I think it would look good."

"It did," Webb said, smiling around his coffee mug.

Hugo frowned at the pair of them as Doll returned.

"Here you go." She handed Harvey a dust-scarf and grey welding tunic.

Harvey zipped the tunic on over her flight suit, turning up the collar and wrapped the scarf around her face.

"That'll do," she said. "Don't wait up."

"Stay on the comm," Webb shouted after as she left.

"I've got to go too," Doll said, zipping up her own tunic and grabbing a pair of goggles off the side. "Spare keycards are in the lockbox. And get some food in you, the pair of you."

Webb watched her leave and as soon as there was the sound of the door closing above, he drained his coffee.

"Right, come on Hugo."

"Come on where?" Hugo said, downing his own.

"You wanted to get started right away."

"Shouldn't we wait for weapons?"

"Here," Webb pulled a gun out of his waistband and handed it over. "Now come on."

Ø

Webb seemed to be moving better today. He was barely limping and his back was straight, his movements more fluid. He didn't take them back through the maintenance decks but through a maze of alleys and out onto a main groundway to a shuttle stop.

"Keep your head down, Hugo," he muttered, though Hugo didn't need to be told again. He took a handhold and didn't make eye contact with any of the people crowded into the shuttle. He made out lots more welding tunics and some med tunics, boiler suits and lots and lots of cargo boots. The view out the window as the shuttle climbed above building-level showed mile after mile of factories, warehouses and meltworks with only the occasional and ill-maintained spacescraper breaking up the metal-and-concrete landscape. The shuttle stopped at each of the megastructures and people shuffled on and off in near-silence.

"Where are we going?" Hugo murmured.

"Sector 2," Webb replied. "Spinn said the Splinters had some other buildings around there. And there's a bar owned by someone who has fenced for them before. We may be able to catch some news of Armin."

"Why does everything we do start in a bar?" Hugo grumbled.

Webb raised his eyes to Hugo's long enough to smirk. "Welcome to the underworld, Captain."

"Do you not have any trustworthy points that could give us some solid information?"

"Most points I wouldn't trust enough to dare start poking for leads on the Splinters," Webb said. "And those I would trust, well, they're too valuable to get caught up in this mess."

"So what in the hell use are any of them?"

Webb frowned. "Ask me that when we're not attempting to bring down a terrorist ring that has designs on their whole fucking colony, Hugo."

Hugo shut his mouth but ground his teeth, frustration and just a little fear mounting in his insides as the shuttle lumbered on. Webb finally had them get off at a ground-level stop on another busy groundway. The walkway was teeming with workers, a lot of them pushing or pulling lifters. Most of the vehicles that moved along the groundway had cargo of some kind.

"Trading sector," Webb mumbled as they moved down a narrower street into the shadows of some taller buildings. There was less foot-traffic on these streets but several of the buildings had openings in the walls at every level with lifters and forklifts being used to load and unload boxes and crates of cargo. Webb wove amongst the machinery and people in overalls with panels shouting orders. Hugo kept to his heels. No one gave them a second glance.

"There," Webb said at last.

On the other side of the street was a three-story building with a sheet-iron roof and dark windows. There was no sign but the door stood open and Hugo watched as people in overalls came and went through the entrance.

"Okay, Hugo. Head down. Here we go."

Webb crossed the street and walked in through the door, Hugo close behind. He peered into the gloom, making out benches and tables and booths along one wall, some gaming equipment in the corner and an unmanned bar with cracked panels laid in its top. Despite the hour there were already clusters of people at the tables with bottles of drink and bowls of food, some of whom looked like they might still be there from the night before. Only the people closest to the door looked up as they came in and their glances slid away, uninterested. He scanned the faces he could see and didn't know whether to be frustrated or relieved when he didn't recognise any Splinters amongst them.

Hugo started to move toward the booth in the furthest corner with the thickest shadows when Webb took a hold of his elbow and steered him to one closer to the bar.

"You take that booth it looks like you're trying to hide," Webb murmured as he gestured for Hugo to take a seat. "Stay here."

Hugo tried to look around without making it obvious whilst Webb went to the bar and tapped into one of the panels. He saw his commander crane his neck and glance around as two bottles of beer rose out of a sliding section of the bar. He returned with the bottles, shaking his head.

"No one here I recognise," he said, still scanning the crowd. "But that's doesn't necessarily mean anything."

"Who's the owner you mentioned?"

"Name's Callum Hannah," Webb said. "He's more of a rat than a proper fence. Buys and sells info but that's about it. Small potatoes really. But he's not above doing deals with the likes of the Splinters -"

"Shit..." Hugo said, fingers tightening around his beer bottle.

"What?" Webb said, following Hugo's gaze to a door behind the bar through which three figures had just emerged.

"It's Armin," Hugo said, shifting round so his back was to them.

"You sure?"

Hugo nodded.

"Keep looking at me," Webb hissed, though his own eyes were watching over Hugo's shoulder. "Don't turn round. Drink."

Hugo took a swig of the sour beer, trying not to grimace as it roiled in his empty stomach.

"He's with Hannah," Webb mumbled, beer in front of his face. "I can't decide if this if good luck or really, really bad luck. Shit. Keep still, they're looking this way."

Hugo turned his face to the wall, leaning back in his seat in what he hoped was a casual way and took another mouthful of beer. Webb did the same, idly mapping out patterns on the scarred table top with his fingers and gazing into the middle distance. Then his fingers paused and he glanced back toward the front door.

"They've gone."

Hugo let out a breath and put the beer down. "That was too close."

"No shit. Maybe this wasn't such a good idea."

"Follow him."

Webb put his own beer down with a clank. "What?"

"It might take us days to track him down again and we need more information about him. I can't come, he'll recognise me."

Webb rubbed his mouth, glancing from Hugo to the door and back again. Then he nodded and fished a set of keycards from his pocket "You remember the way back to Doll's?" Hugo nodded, taking the cards. "Get yourself there and lock yourself in."

"Have you got a comm?" Hugo asked as Webb rose.

"I do, but you don't so it's not much use."

Hugo grunted, rubbing his bandaged wrist where his wrist panel usually was.

"Don't sweat it, Hugo. I'll be back. Harvey'll be back at Doll's soon and she's got a comm."

After a nod from Hugo, Webb strolled across the dingy room and out the front door and was gone. The prickle of guilt was back but he swamped it with resolve and another mouthful of beer, counted to a hundred then left.

Ø

For a while after getting back to Doll's, all Hugo could do was sprawl on the bench and glare at the wall. He went over the warehouse mission again and again, attempting to pick apart any details that might be useful for formulating a plan, but his head was throbbing again and all he could remember in any detail was the hollow face of Armin with his drilled-out eyes.

With a growl of frustration he pulled himself up off the bench and booted up the workstation. It turned on quickly despite its battered appearance, and was connected to the Lunar 1 mainframe and the solarnet. Hugo felt his spirits lift a little and started searching through everything he could find recorded on the Splinters. He searched the local records and news reports, the public property listings and even some of the gossip and rumour boards that weren't coded, but tracked down next to nothing.

Grunting in frustration, he logged onto the solarnet and searched Orbit-wide news networks and records but still came up with little besides historical reports and a little Analyst data that classified them as inactive. He leant back in his chair, rubbing his face, wishing he could put Rami and Spinn on the case. He closed down all his dead-end searches and then after the slightest hesitation typed *Donatella McCullough* into a new one. He swallowed, clicked *search* and began to read.

"You know I would have told you if you'd asked."

Hugo spun around to see Doll closing and locking the door behind her.

"I'm sorry," he said. "I needed to know -"

"That you could trust me?" Her smile was soft and a little sad.

"Can we?" Hugo said.

"I may not be Service-mad, my boy, but don't worry. I do not have the leanings of my late husband. I didn't then. I don't now."

"You kept his name."

She shrugged. "I loved Duran. Still do. The part of him I knew anyway. He wasn't a bad man. He just had strong beliefs about a future for his people."

"He was willing to sacrifice a hell of a lot of those people for those beliefs."

Doll regarded him coolly. "If I were mean-spirited I would mention the amount the Service was willing to and did sacrifice in retaliation. But that's not something I like to think about much. Come. I bet you ignored me earlier when I told you to eat."

Hugo followed her down into the kitchen where she shrugged herself out of her tunic and set about boiling water and opening tins.

"Did you know what he was going to do? Governor McCullough?" Hugo asked quietly.

"No. I watched him watch his people trying to scrape lives out of vacuum and saw the anger build. But I didn't realise where he was going until it was too late," she said, pouring the contents of a can into a pan. "I tried anyway. For the sake of peace, I told myself. But his drives were always more powerful than his desire for personal happiness. I left when I saw he wouldn't come back from the edge. I came here to attempt to do my bit to ease the fallout."

"A youth unit?"

"St Augustine's," she said, turning round and leaning against the counter. "That shows up in my records, does it? Interesting."

"That's where you met Webb?" Hugo guessed.

"It was the only unit that managed to hold on to him long enough to name him. He was happy there, I think. For a while. Then the Service came for him."

Hugo felt the blood drain from his face. "You know?"

"Oh, yes, I know," Doll said, turning and getting mugs out from a cupboard. "The *Endeavour*, the *Zero*, everything. I was there when Spinn made the deal."

"Spinn?"

"He was the recruiting agent. He brokered the deal with St. Augustine's for a young, nameless orphan with intelligence and potential."

"What was the deal?"

She shrugged, not looking at him. "An offer the unit couldn't refuse, apparently. Then they took him away in the night. And I let them."

Silence stretched between them for a while as Doll stirred the mixture on the electric stove and made up mugs of sweet-smelling tea.

"They gave him a life," Hugo said into the quiet.

"They bought his life. Like you would buy a flyer or a shipwright contract. They bought him, programmed him and now they own him. Just like the rest of that crew."

"The Service saved all that crew from youth units and backwaters," Hugo said, willing anger to flare. "Without the Zero they'd be lost."

"They'd be free," she said mildly as she placed a plate and a mug in front of him.

"They'd probably be dead. Or worse."

"At least they would have made their own paths."

Hugo shook his head, glaring at the food.

"Here," she said, handing him a fork. "Eat."

He looked up at her, took in her shorn head and the shrapnel scars on her face. She had a heaviness in her eyes. Then he took the fork and started on the stew. It was synthetic meat but the sauce was rich and savoury and he dug in, unable to deny how hungry he was.

"Webb has a purpose," Hugo lumbered on, not looking up as Doll sat and started on her own lunch. "And St. Augustine's benefited."

"After they took Ezekiel, the Service paid off the managers and shut the unit down. It was about the same time their hold on Lunar 1 slackened all round. I tried to keep track of what happened to him, but that's not so easy with the *Zero*. Next time I saw him he was the man you know and it was too late to save him. I have since faced up to the fact that it was too late the minute I let them take him away. Maybe even before then." Her face took on a far away look for a moment before she took another mouthful.

"So the youth unit closed down and you buried yourself away in the meltworks?"

"It's a living. And I hear things. It helps me keep track of the bigger picture and not forget who I am or what I've done." She looked up at him. "You think I'm full of shit, don't you?" Hugo swallowed his mouthful but didn't answer. "That's okay. I hope you never have to come to understand what it's like to fail someone who depended on you. Finish your tea."

Hugo scraped his plate clean and swallowed the last mouthful of his tea and Doll took the dishes to the washer.

"I met your parents once, you know," she said. "Many years ago, in Sydney, when Duran was still using words to try and win his battles. They were fine people, I remember. Stood tall and talked well. Every inch of both of them said they belonged to something they believed in. But what about you, Hugo?"

"What about me?"

"Do you believe the Service is worth your life?"

"I believe in peace," Hugo said. "The Service fights for peace. So I fight for the Service."

"Fighting for peace," Doll shook her head. "I never understood that notion."

"Peace has to be won," Hugo said, wishing his palms would stop sweating.

"You saved a lot of lives with that decision you were publicly disgraced for," Doll said as she straightened and closed up the washer. "Do you think the Service shares your idea of what peace actually is?"

"Whatever the outcome of my actions," Hugo said. "I disobeyed orders."

"To do what you thought was right."

"If everyone thought they knew better, the system would crumble. The Orbit would fall into anarchy."

"Is that what your parents taught you?"

"It's what life has taught me. Look what happened on this colony. And on Haven."

"You ever been to Haven, Hugo?" Doll asked.

Her change in tack caused him to frown. He shook his head, wiping his damp hands on his trousers.

"You should. It would be educational." She pulled her tunic back on and then stood looking at him for a while. "Tread carefully Hugo. And I don't just mean on Lunar 1."

He sat and glowered around the kitchen for a while after she left the apartment again, waiting for the whirling uncertainty to settle into anything: determination, indignation, anger. But his mind kept flowing between everything like rainwater down rocks and couldn't catch a hold. He growled and got up and went back up the stairs, thinking he'd go back to the workstation, when the door buzzer went. He paused on the stairs and it buzzed again. He climbed the rest of the stairs and stood staring at the intercom, heart thumping.

A crack on the glass of the window had him pulling his weapon and spinning before he realised what it was.

"Hey, Kaleb. It's me. Let me in, already."

Hugo let out a breath in a rush and holstered his weapon. Even through the frosted glass he could tell Harvey was grinning at him. He fished out the keycards then went and pulled open the door. Harvey bundled past him, laden with packs that clinked and jangled.

"I know it's a hole but you gotta love the industrial markets on this colony," Harvey said, dumping her loads on the table. "You don't need a licence for anything." She looked around. "Where's Webb?"

"We found Armin."

She paused and looked up. "And?"

Hugo opened his mouth to reply when the door buzzer went again. He looked at Harvey who was staring at the intercom looking uncertain, then her wrist panel beeped.

"It's Webb," she said, looking at the display. "Hey," she said, pushing the control.

"Wanna let me in?"

Harvey went to let him in whilst Hugo started unzipping packs and unloading boxes of ammunition.

Webb came in, pulling off his cap and wiping his forehead on his sleeve.

"What happened?"

Webb shook his head, dropped himself into a chair. "Hannah took Armin and his pal to another fence's joint. They were in there for the best part of an hour."

"And then?"

"Then they moved on to another. They went all over the sector calling in on info wranglers, fences and a couple of places owned by other underground-ring types. If I didn't know any better, I'd say they were trying to drum up business."

"You mean we did it?" Harvey said, pausing from laying out goggles and climbing wire. "We stopped them?"

Webb nodded, a tired smile on his face. "From whatever they were planning with that shit at the warehouse...yeah, I think we did."

"We need to take them down for good before they get another contract," Hugo said.

"Sooner than that even," Webb said, face sombre.

"Why?"

Webb looked between them. "They went to the *Seven Sisters*."

Hugo paused. "To get Evangeline?"

Webb shook his head. "They walked in through the bar. If they wanted to kill her, they'd've waited for her to leave and shot her in the back. No. They went to talk."

"Crap," Harvey said.

"What?" said Hugo. "What am I missing?"

Webb sat forward in his seat. "She's a fence with some reach. And because of the mess with us, they've got her over a barrel. I followed them to her office -"

"You did *what?*"

"Relax, Captain, I used the back way."

"There's a back way?"

Webb smirked. "There's always a back way."

Hugo sighed and sat down. "And?"

Webb's face fell. "They got what they wanted."

"Which was?"

"Us."

"What?"

"They contracted Evangeline to track us down and bring us in."

"Fuck," Harvey said, flinging herself on the bench. "We're screwed."

"We're not screwed yet," Webb said. "This is good news."

"What is?" Hugo ground out.

Webb grinned. "Evangeline was told to go after the *Zero*."

Hugo paused. "They think we're all on it?"

"Uh-huh."

"You're sure?"

"Heard it with my own ears."

Hugo frowned. "Where exactly were you?"

"Air ducts are wonderful things, Captain. But either way, that's the good bit. The bad bit is Evangeline is out for our blood and her reach is considerably wider than the Splinters'."

"We need to get a message to the ship," Hugo said.

"Doll's workstation is capable of a secure link. I'll get something to them tonight. Don't worry, Captain," Webb said, looking keenly at him. "More and Rami can handle themselves. It isn't the first time."

"We need to get this thing done," Hugo said, leaning forward. "And quickly."

"We will," Webb said, grinning. "I've got us a starting point."

"Do I dare ask?"

"I followed Armin all the way home," Webb's grin widened. "I know where the son of a bitch lives."

"Nice one," Harvey said, grinning.

Hugo swallowed, not liking either of their smiles. "After the mess at the warehouse," he said, "the ringleaders will be getting together to re-group. And soon."

Hugo jumped when Webb slapped him on the shoulder.

"You're getting good at this, Hugo."

"Did you see if Armin had a comm unit in his apartment?"

Webb raised his eyebrows then nodded. "Yeah, I saw it."

"Can you get into it to monitor incoming calls?"

Webb chewed his thumbnail. "Rami could, piece of cake."

"The lieutenant's not here, Commander," Hugo said. "Can *you* get into it?"

Webb's face darkened slightly but he paused and nodded. "Yeah, I reckon so. I'll have to get into the system relays under the building with a half-decent panel..."

"Ta-da," Harvey sang, pulling a scratched but serviceable computer-panel from one of the packs. Webb took it and booted it up, skimmed through some of its systems.

"Aye, this should do."

"Good. We move out at 0400. Harvey and I will take up position at a surveillance point whilst you get under the building and get that thing hooked in. Then we wait."

"You got it, Captain," Harvey said, still smiling.

XI

"Will you just relax, Kaleb? You're making me nervous."

"It's been nearly an hour."

"He'll be back," Harvey insisted again, checking the magazine on her gun.

Hugo growled and peered through the binoculars at the window of Armin's apartment, but it was still shuttered and dark. "When was it alright for you to start calling me that?"

"Maybe I'm starting to like you."

Hugo looked down and saw a narrow smile playing on her face as she holstered her gun. Hugo sighed and slumped onto the floor next to her to check through his own supplies again. Harvey was just opening her mouth to say something else when they heard footsteps. They both froze, hands on guns but then Webb came through the storeroom door, locking it behind him.

"Did you get in?"

"Yeah," Webb said, pulling a glove off with his teeth. "But we have a problem."

"What?"

"The fire-system door sensors clocked the bastard leaving ten minutes before we got here."

"Shit," Harvey muttered. "Do we wait for him to come back?"

"It might be too late by then," Hugo said. "Can you access his comm unit's history?"

Webb slumped cross-legged on the floor, pulled off his other glove and fished the panel out of his pack. His face lit up with the light from the display as he flicked through the data and scowled. "The bastard's wiped it."

"Can you get it back?"

Webb frowned. "I can try."

"Do it. See if he had any transmissions before he left."

Webb muttered, shifted and then balanced the panel on his knee and began searching through the system. Hugo craned his neck to try and see the readings on the display but it was in an old code that Hugo couldn't make head nor tail of. He made himself not drum his fingers on the floor and instead went through his utility belt and checked his boot knives for the fifth time.

"Ah," Webb said, sitting up. "Got something."

"What?"

"Hang on, hang on. It got scrambled when it got trashed. It came in at 0420 though, four minutes before he left. Hang on...I'll see if I can dredge up the video."

Harvey scooted over and looked over his shoulder. Hugo moved closer too, watching Webb's fingers tapping commands. The screen was fuzzy but gradually came into focus to show the face of a man with dark features, heavy eyebrows and beard and thick, black hair.

"He was with Armin at Hannah's yesterday," Hugo said.

Webb nodded. "They went to see all the points together. I think we have the number two in our little ring."

"Where's the sound?" Hugo said as the man shook his head and his lips moved.

"Just hang on, will you?" Webb growled, rewinding the feed and tapping in a few more commands. "Anita normally does this...wait...I think... there."

The feed started over again. "It's no good," the man said, shaking his head. "It's over." There was a pause, but the recorder had either lost Armin's mic feed or never recorded it. "Tough shit," the dark man continued. "He wants us there in two hours. You'd better be there." Then it fuzzed to a blank.

"That sounds like somewhere we should be..." Harvey mumbled. "Is there anyway to tell where they're meeting?"

"Even if they mentioned it, the rest of it is too scrambled."

"Well than, can you trace where this transmission came from?" Hugo asked.

"I think so..."

"Do it. If we can get to this man before he leaves, he can lead us to the meeting point."

Webb sighed and shifted on the floor and bent back over the panel. Hugo had to stop himself from pestering Webb as the minutes slipped by. He got up and walked back to the window and stared at the shuttered blinds until Webb announced he'd traced the location.

"Can we get there in time?"

"If we move like shit off a shovel. Come on."

Ø

A bike ride later, the speed of which had left Hugo's lips chapped in the wind, and they were kneeling on a flat roof in the shadow of a lift shaft, scanning the windows of a building over the way. He shifted from one knee to another in a puddle to try and keep the feeling in his legs.

"How long has it been?"

"It's under an hour until the meeting time..." Webb mumbled.

Hugo cursed. "Can you hack into the fire system to see if he's still in there?" Hugo asked.

Webb shook his head. "This dump won't have one. You're lucky if you even get a fire *escape* around here...wait..."

Hugo brought his binoculars back up just as someone emerged from the front door. The dark man paused to light a cigarette, scowling up and down the street as he did so.

"That's him," Hugo whispered.

"If he heads for a flyer we're screwed," Harvey muttered.

"Didn't you bring the tracker?" Webb said.

"The launcher's bust."

"What?"

"What do you want? It was cheap -"

"Quiet," Hugo snapped, watching the Splinter. He took another long drag of his cigarette then turned right down the walkway towards the parking pool next door.

"Shit," Hugo cursed. "He's going for a vehicle. Give me the tracker."

"Hugo -"

"I said give it to me. Now."

Harvey dug in her pack and pulled out the launcher gun and detached the tracking device. Hugo grabbed it then snatched Webb's cap off his head. He ran across the flat roof, ignoring the commander's protests, and clambered down the fire escape. He paused at the edge of the groundway, hanging in the shadows of some trash skips until there was a break in the traffic. He dashed across the groundway and around the side of the smoking man's apartment building to the parking pool. He got to the gate just as the Splinter was stamping out his cigarette and climbing into a battered flyer.

Feeling his heart hammer against his ribs, he wove between the parked up flyers and cars, hands in pockets, slumping his shoulders and keeping his head down. He heard the engine hum to life but kept his gaze on his feet. He passed behind the Splinter's flyer close enough to touch the tracker to its rear bumper just as heat blasted from its exhaust and it pulled out of its berth.

Hugo didn't break his stride or look back until he reached a gate at the back of the lot. Releasing a breath he hadn't realised he'd been holding, he hurried back round the groundway, just in time to see the Splinter's flyer join the queue of craft heading up the nearest guidance strip towards a skyway.

"Have we got a feed?" Hugo asked as he jogged back across the roof to where Webb and Harvey were bent over the panel.

"We got it, Captain," Webb said. "Looks like he's heading hubwards."

"Let's go."

They hurried back to the yard where they'd hidden the bikes. Hugo started his engine even before Harvey had got a decent grip round his waist and then they were off. Webb kept them on back ways and alleys again. It made Hugo dizzy trying to keep orientated so he gave up and just stuck as close behind the commander as he could. He felt every minute slip by like stones dropping into water. The buildings around them got bigger and the ways busier. Eventually Webb pulled them up in behind a complex of storage units that was swamped in the shadow of a spacescraper. Craning his neck Hugo saw skyways coming and going from different levels and shuttles rattling back and forth on rails towards a dozen platforms branching from its sides. Huge letters across the side read *Houston Block*. Hugo got off his bike and went to peer over Webb's shoulder at the blinking light on Webb's windscreen display.

"He's parked up in a pool on level 179."

"We need to hurry," Hugo said. "And avoid cameras."

"Follow me," Webb said, swinging off the bike. They skirted around the storage units and followed close behind as Webb scrambled up a wire fence onto the roof of *Houston Block*'s ground-level entrance lobby. Hugo felt his heart go into his mouth when Webb jumped the gap between the roof and an industrial lifter parked up behind the lobby, then began scrambling up the cab until he could reach the bottom of a maintenance ladder on the side of the building.

Hugo had paused at the edge of the roof, but when he saw Webb start climbing, he gestured for Harvey to follow, jumped the gap with his heart in his mouth and scrambled to the ladder. The sweat broke all over him as he hauled himself up, rung after rung, until they were so high he didn't dare look down. Eventually Webb checked his wrist panel and stopped them at a maintenance hatch. He shimmied onto the narrow platform and bent close to the control panel. Hugo felt his arms and shoulders start to burn with hanging on but Webb soon had the hatch open and was helping Harvey down off the ladder and into the maintenance duct. When all three of them were in Webb started hurrying along the duct, bent almost double.

"Do you have any idea where you're going?" Hugo growled.

"Not a clue," Webb said. "But I know what I'm looking for."

They came to a junction and Hugo looked at his wrist panel. Only ten minutes until the time the Splinters were supposed to meet. Webb turned left and straightened as they emerged into a maintenance passage with a higher ceiling. He peered down every tunnel that branched off the one they were on, until stopping and ducking down one that went left and bent over a workstation sunk into the wall.

"Keep watch," Webb said as the workstation display flickered to life. Hugo took up a position at the junction and Harvey at the next one down, and then there was the sound of Webb's fingers on the keys, his breathing, and nothing else. The air was hot and close and the lights dim. He looked back over his shoulder at Webb's face, a mask of concentration, then made himself look back down the corridor. He heard footsteps and voices approaching and drew his gun but they faded away again around the next bend.

"I'm in," Webb muttered at last.

"In what?"

"The camera feed from the parking pool. Hang on... he took a lift to level... 198..."

"Can you get into the feed from that level?"

"Give me a freakin' second," Webb growled, fingers tapping. "Wouldn't hurt you to pick up some system skills of your own, you know."

"We're running out -"

"I *know*," Webb snapped again. "I can't... hang on, got the bastard..." Webb stared at the screen then shut the booth down. "Got it. This way," he said and started heading down towards Harvey.

He led them on a twisting route until they saw a door up ahead. Loud banging and humming filtered through from the other side. Webb peered through the small window in the door, holstering his weapon.

"You two ready?"

"For what?"

"We've got to get across this bay to the elevators. There are engineers. And cameras. Act natural."

With no further warning Webb palmed the door control and was strolling out onto a metal walkway. Hugo took a breath and followed. The walkway spanned a vast, echoing shaft. Air rushed upwards in a constant hot stream and as far up and below as he could see was a towering, empty space criss-crossed with walkways. People moved about in engineer coveralls, hauling lifters, speaking into wrist panels or running with packs of tools. The clunk and whirr of machinery and electricity thrummed in the air.

Hugo stopped himself from gaping down the multitude of floors into nothingness and made himself walk swiftly but easily. When they were over the chasm Webb led the way, weaving between maintenance workers with his head down until they reached a bank of express lifts. Webb chose one in the quietest corner and keyed in level 198.

The door hummed shut and the lift shuddered as it took off upwards. They came out onto a virtually identical walkway on level 198 then Webb led them down another corridor. They twisted and turned at a jog before Webb skidded to a halt, checked his wrist panel, then reached up and pulled at a grill in the wall.

"You're kidding me," Harvey muttered. "An air duct?"

"We don't have to go far," Webb said. "But don't even sneeze, seriously. We'll be right over them."

Webb looked back down the corridor and Hugo checked too, then Webb was pulling goggles on and hauling himself up into the duct. Harvey muttered under her breath as she pulled on her own goggles and accepted Hugo's leg up and crawled in after him.

"Captain," Webb's hiss filtered back through to him as he clambered up. "Pull the grill shut."

Hugo managed to grab the edge of the grill and pull it back up behind him. Magnets clicked and held it in place, then they were crawling down a narrow, metal space with the stale air gusting in their faces. The green wash from the goggles revealed only the unbroken metal of the duct and Harvey's shuffling figure up ahead. Progress was painfully slow but he made himself stick to the speed that Webb set, keeping their progress almost silent.

They turned two tight junctions and then his vision greyed as light came in from somewhere. He reached and pulled the goggles off just as Harvey clambered out of sight. He reached the grey square ahead and saw that it was an opening onto a small space with a fan whirring away under a metal grill. Webb and Harvey were crouching on the grill, hair and clothes wafting about in the turbulence, with their faces pressed against a grid through which light was streaming. Hugo shuffled himself into the space, letting his boots touch down on the grill as softly as possible, then crawled up next to Webb and looked through the grid.

He was looking down on a small, windowless room with unpainted walls and nothing in it apart from a couple of mismatched couches, a table with a broken leg shoved in a corner and a blank wall display. There were no cameras that he could see and a rather complex lock panel on the door. The lean figure of Armin was propped against the wall, arms crossed and face set, black eyes fixed on the bearded man they had followed who was pacing the length of the room, smoking. Webb leant back away from the grill as he came directly under them before turning and pacing back again.

The sweat on Hugo's skin had cooled and then chilled in the draught by the time the door opened to admit someone else. His patched jacket was open over a stained shirt that was pulled taut over the swollen belly and his hair was strung in a greasy rope over one shoulder. He was stubbled and chewing as he strolled in then dropped himself onto one of the couches.

"Well this is a right fucking state of things, isn't it?" he growled as he glared back and forth between Armin and the other man.

"And where were you?" The smoking man glowered. "Where was your credit-stacked surveillance net when those bastards were climbing in over the wall?"

"Don't put this on me, Breonan," the fat man said. "If you'd let me have a station in the compound like I'd said at the beginning they wouldn't have got close enough to screw you right in the ass."

"I hope Marlowe spills your fat guts," Breonan growled.

The fat man laughed, pulling a narrow panel out of a pocket inside his jacket. "I'm not that one who can't even hold onto a poxy storehouse without getting it blown up. Perhaps Marlowe will finally see sense and put me in charge of this thing."

"Suppose you're gonna claim you can pull a weapon cache out of your ass?"

The fat man grunted, scrolling through text on the computer panel. "Even I can't salvage this job," he said. "It'll be ten years before we see another contract like that one. But I've found a way to make it right." His doughy face split into a nasty grin and Breonan started across the room.

"Enough," Armin's voice wasn't loud but it still stopped Breonan in his tracks. "Get yourselves together, for fuck's sake. He'll be here in a minute.."

Breonan stood over the fat man, clenching and unclenching his fists then flung himself down on the other couch. "You better have something good, Ankle."

The fat man scowled. "Better than anything you've managed to dredge up from the fences, I'm willing to bet."

Armin looked like he might say something more but then the door opened again. Ankle and Breonan both got to their feet and Armin straightened up from the wall. The man that had entered was taller than all three of the other men, clean shaven and clad in a tailored suit. His shirt was black and his tie a dark green and his steel-grey hair was combed back from his high forehead. He had deep, dark eyes and didn't fit in this grotty room with these men, but the way the other three Splinters kept silent and still as stone as he closed the door behind him made Hugo's skin crawl.

It took him a moment to realise that Webb had gone stiff beside him. He glanced at his commander, and saw his face in the slatted light from the grill was a frozen mask with eyes blazing and muscles bulging in his neck and jaw.

Hugo poked him to get his attention. *You know him?* Hugo mouthed. Webb managed a tight nod but didn't look away from the suited man as he glanced between the three Splinters, eyes like shards of glass.

"We fucked up," the suited man said after a long silence. "Do we agree?"

"We fucked up, Marlowe," Armin said, holding himself straight, sharp eyes unwavering. His fists were clenched.

"They were professionals," Breonan said. "They had to be. There's no way-"

"That sounds an awful lot like an excuse, Breonan," Marlowe said, eyes sharp. Breonan fell silent. "We lost the cache, the storehouse, fifty men and the contract all in one night. Thanks to Ankle, there's no way the Service or the Enforcers are going to be able to trace it back to us but not for one moment are we to think this was acceptable."

Heads shook and there were contrite mumbles from the three men. Marlowe stood there for a moment longer, letting his cut-glass glance slide from one man to another.

"So..." he said. "Has anyone managed to find a way to placate our disappointed client?"

Ankle swallowed then shuffled forward and handed over his panel. Marlowe took it and started scrolling through.

"Well, this looks like a happy coincidence," he said, handing the panel back. "Put the word out to whoever we've got left. Call in points from the Lunar Strip and anyone we've got on Earth. And inform Evangeline Webb, as she's halfway there already. We make this happen, maybe our client won't pull the colony apart and string us all from yard arms."

Ankle nodded and started keying commands into his panel. "You got it, boss. It's as good as done."

"Very good. Try not to fuck up. Again."

Glances were exchanged then all the men were heading for the door. Hugo rocked back on his heels.

"Harvey, you and Webb follow the fat one. I'll follow the suit."

The fact that Webb didn't even argue unsettled him. They crawled back down the duct and then hurried out of the maintenance ways into a trading lobby just as the four Splinters emerged from a door virtually hidden behind a stall opposite.

Harvey and Webb melted into the crowd after Ankle whilst Hugo skirted around the edge of the square towards Marlowe. He met up with two Splinters at the corner of the square, all dressed in black with shaved heads and weapons at their hips that they didn't even bother concealing. They fell into step behind Marlowe without a word.

Hugo hung back as far as he could whilst keeping them in sight, keeping to the edges of the corridors, keeping plenty of crowd between them and him. They led him on a wandering path amongst the passages and dealerships until they reached a wide open space with a bank of public express lifts.

Marlowe turned and muttered something to one of his companions as they waited for the lift. Hugo hung in the entrance of a drug stockist after they'd boarded, keeping the lift's number panel in view and saw that it stopped on level 350. He waited ten more heartbeats then made his way into a lift to follow but there was no option for level 350 on the controls. He cursed then became aware of people watching him glowering at the control panel and chose the ground level.

He waited until he was outside in the alley again before putting in a call through to Webb's comm.

"Webb here, Captain."

"Where are you?"

"Still trailing Ankle. You won't be surprised to learn he's stopped for something to eat."

"I couldn't follow Marlowe. He went up to a secure level in the block."

There was a pause. "We'll check it out when we get back to Doll's. Head back there now, Captain. We will meet you there."

Ø

Hugo used Doll's workstation to scour the public records and registered schematics of Houston Block. The 349 public floors included business levels, entertainment levels, residential levels and a few levels that were vaguely classified as 'storage'. The ownership of everything seemed to be a jigsaw of nonsense but 350 was privately owned with no record of who owned it.

Searching for anything significant linked to the name Marlowe, however, turned up a public profile as well as many articles and records. The suited man was Councillor Vincent Marlowe, an associate of the rag-tag mess that went for local government on Lunar 1 with strong links to the local Enforcers who'd attempted to fill the gap the Service had left after McCullough's Revolution. There was nothing linking him to the Splinters, but that didn't surprise Hugo. He was just checking again that there was indeed still nothing on the rumour boards when the intercom buzzed three times.

"Where's Webb?" Hugo asked when he opened the door to only Harvey.

"He won't be long."

"What happened?"

Harvey scowled as she pulled her jacket off. "That Ankle's a nasty piece of work. We followed him all over the sector. Webb only recognised some of the points he dropped in on but none of it was good news."

"What sort of points?"

Harvey ran a hand over her shaved head. "Drugs. Weapons. Even dropped in on someone that Webb is sure is a blade."

Hugo shuddered. "And then?"

Harvey turned a chair round and sat in it, rubbing her eyes. "We followed him back to his place. A hole it was too, under some barhouse in Sector 3."

"We need to stop them before they execute this new contract. Their client wanted all of Lunar 1 brought to its knees. God knows what they want now that that's not happened."

"But how?" Harvey asked. "This shit called in on ten points at least today. Their connections are like a poxy great net over the entire colony. We can't wipe it all out."

"We have to think of something."

Just then the buzzer went again and Hugo let in a harried-looking Webb.

"Well...?"

"I have a plan," he said as he moved across the room and shuttered the window.

"What?"

Webb turned to face them, held their gazes a moment, jaw tight, then came forward whilst fishing something out of his pocket and put it on the table. Harvey looked at it and paled.

"Boot black?" Hugo asked, confused.

"Jesus, I don't know Webb," Harvey murmured. "If you're suggesting what I think you're suggesting…"

"Does someone want to fill me in?"

"The black cross," Webb said.

"What?"

Harvey shook her head. "It ain't good. Some Lunar 1 folk sent some of that shit Haven way a few years ago. It wasn't pretty."

"What is it?" Hugo asked, getting impatient but the set look on Webb's face sent uncertainty creeping through him.

"The black cross is a symbol. For revenge. For retribution. For the punishment of a grievous and personal sin," the commander said, voice flat.

"Boot black?" Hugo repeated, though quieter this time.

"You wear it on your face," Harvey ran a finger down the middle of her face then across her eyes. "Anyone sees you wearing a black cross…well… let's just say it ain't something you want to be seeing."

Webb pulled a can of spray paint from another pocket of his cargo trousers and set it on the table next to the polish with a toothy rattle.

"We take them out in their homes," he said, "where they think they're safe. All four ringleaders. And we leave the mark."

"Well if you're after shitting people up…" Harvey said, eyeing the spray can like it might bite.

Hugo gathered himself. "And then what?"

"The whole network will fall apart. No one on this colony will want to be associated with anyone who's died under a black cross."

Hugo looked the commander in the eye. "How do you know Marlowe?"

"From a long time ago. It's not relevant."

Seeing the grim set of Webb's face, Hugo didn't push. "Marilyn, do you think it'll work?"

She tore her eyes from the spray paint. "Yeah. If we can get all four of them without being caught or recognised… I think it'll send whoever's left into holes they won't be in a hurry to climb out of."

"Then we do it," Hugo said, the words feeling heavy in his mouth.

A nasty smile spread across Webb's face but the sound of Doll returning for lunch had him slipping the boot black and spray paint back into his pockets before she came into the room.

Ø

Hugo's head ached and his skin crawled as they spent that afternoon with hard-copy schematics of the different sectors spread over Doll's table, planning their first move. Webb played with his knife the entire time, flipping it over in the air or twizzling it with the point making notches in the table top.

Breonan, in his dilapidated apartment block without even an alarm system, didn't stand a chance. Someone had left a window open on the ground floor so they didn't even have to break in. They didn't bother checking for cameras. Webb said that if they got picked up on any feeds in their incongruous black gear, peaked caps and black crosses daubed on their faces, more the better.

The man had counted on his lock system to keep his enemies out but hadn't counted on Webb and his multi-tool. All three entered the darkened apartment in their goggles. Webb found him in the bedroom and put a bullet in his head before he'd even drawn breath to yell. He sprayed a cross on the wall over the dead man's bed before turning and pushing back past Harvey and Hugo and out of the apartment.

They were back at Doll's in under two hours. Webb made them scrub their faces clean before she came back from her night shift.

Harvey went with Doll down to her room once she returned but neither Hugo nor Webb made a move to turn in after they had gone. They both sat at the table, staring at a card game they had stopped playing half an hour ago.

"Do your parents know the truth, Captain?" Webb murmured into the silence.

Hugo jolted then frowned. "What?"

Webb met his eyes. He looked tired. "Do they know the truth? You know, that you weren't really discharged? That you're still bleeding for the Service, but you'll not be getting any more medals for it?"

Hugo tossed his cards on the table, trying to stoke up anger but then sighed, defeated. "No."

Webb shrugged, gaze sliding away. "Figures."

"Why?"

Webb blinked slowly at nothing. "Nothing, Captain. Just... nothing."

They scoured the news reports and rumour boards again the next day but found nothing to do with Breonan.

"Doesn't mean anything," Webb muttered. "Either they've not found him yet or they're not telling if they have. It doesn't matter. The ball is rolling."

"Who's next?" Harvey asked.

"Ankle's next," Hugo said, going back to the table to where his weapons were laid out to be checked and cleaned.

"When?"

"Tonight," Webb said. "Then we lay low for a couple of days and let the rumours gather some steam."

Ø

"There are no windows at all," Harvey said as she clambered back up on the burnt-out flyer hulk next to Hugo. "It's all below ground level."

Hugo frowned and looked back through his binoculars at Ankle's door. It was down a flight of steps at the back of a noisy bar.

"Can you hack the lock, Commander?"

"Seems our fat friend is a little more prepared than his pal," Webb replied, frowning around his binoculars. "There's a camera over the door. The minute someone starts trying anything with the control, he'll know and he'll be sounding the alarm."

"How are we going to get in, then?"

"He's going to have to let us in."

Hugo lowered his binoculars and scowled. "And how are we to persuade him to do that?"

"Have faith, Captain," Webb grinned. "We will be shown the way." Hugo glared but then Webb's grin widened. "See?"

Hugo looked back through his binoculars just as a moped pulled up at the end of the alley. A girl in a bright blue cap and high-viz jacket clambered off then pulled a pizza box out the basket on the back.

"You can't be serious..." Hugo said.

"Harvey, *go*," Webb said and Harvey was over the wall they were leaning on and moving in the shadows toward the girl, drawing her gun.

Webb followed and Hugo scrambled after, hissing protests. They caught up just as the girl, eyes wide and mouth opening and closing, was dropping the pizza at Harvey's feet and scurrying back to her moped. The little engine hiccoughed and then she was tearing away.

Harvey scooped up the pizza and Webb was gesturing at the door with his gun. Hugo pulled out his own weapon and took up position on one side of the stairwell just as Webb did so on the other. Harvey made sure the peak of her cap was obscuring her painted face and tucked her gun in the back of her waistband, then made her way down the stairs and pushed the buzzer.

"What?" snapped a voice from the intercom.

"Pizza," Harvey said in a bored voice.

There was a whirr as the camera adjusted its angle. Hugo pressed himself against the wall. Harvey didn't flinch, just shifted the pizza so it was more obvious. There was a pause in which Hugo felt every beat of his heart and every muscle tighten, then the door opened. Harvey looked up and Ankle cursed and tried to slam it shut but Harvey got her boot in the gap. Hugo dropped down into the stairwell and shouldered at the door. Sputtering came from the other side then Webb jumped down next to them and leant his weight to the ramming and the door gave way.

The pinging of their silenced gunfire filled the air but the fat man scrambled into another room. They followed but he was through another door before Hugo and Webb had clambered around the jumbled furniture. They both slammed into the door but it didn't budge.

"Get back," Webb snapped and took out the handle and lock with a couple of shots. They shouldered the door and it cracked against the wall inside. Ankle backed up into a corner, gibbering and dropped his panel on the concrete floor.

"Listen... whoever you are... just wait one second," he stammered as he held his hands up, staring at their faces. Webb moved across the room in two strides and pulled the spray can out of his belt. He stood shaking the can and staring at Ankle as Hugo came forward, keeping his gun trained on the Splinter.

"No, please, I..." Ankle's chins wobbled as his mouth fell open. He glanced from Hugo to Webb and back and his eyes widened. "*You?*" Webb turned his back and started spraying a black line across the papers and posters pinned to the wall. "No. Stop. I can help," Ankle came forward, hands up. "I can help you guys. I can. I can get the contract erased, like it was never there. Just let me..." He stooped to retrieve his panel.

"Don't move," Hugo growled, taking a step closer.

The can hissed as Webb sprayed the second line of the black cross on the wall. Ankle whimpered.

"Who's your client?" Hugo snarled. Ankle opened and closed his mouth a few times, eyes fixed on the gun, but no sound came out. "*Who is it?*"

"It's all -" Ankle squeaked, coughed, wiped his mouth on his sleeve then tried again. "It's all on there..." he sputtered, waving at the panel on the floor.

Hugo stared at him a moment longer then bent to retrieve it.

"Hugo, look out!"

There was movement, a bang and flash of heat across his arm. When the world stopped spinning, he blinked up at the ceiling for a moment that stretched on forever before Harvey was grabbing the shoulders of his jacket and hauling him back and onto his feet. His senses came back to him with a rush and there was a sharp, throbbing pain in his bicep and liquid heat soaking into his sleeve.

Ankle was sprawled on the floor, Webb stood over him with his gun drawn. The Splinter had a hand clutched at his chest where blood was pumping through his fingers as his breath came in great bubbling heaves. Blood and spittle trickled through the stubble on his chin as Webb kicked a gun away from Ankle's other hand. The commander muttered something in what sounded like Latin, then fired again. Ankle jerked, then was still.

"You okay, Kaleb?" Harvey said.

Hugo shook himself, holstered his gun and clutched at his arm to slow the bleeding. "We need to get out of here."

There were nods from Webb and Harvey and they moved back to the door. Hugo paused, averted his eyes from the dead man's stare and grabbed the panel from the floor, tucked it into his jacket then followed the others back out of the apartment. They shut the door behind them and Webb shot out the door camera as they passed.

Ø

Harvey helped him wash and bind his wound when they got back to Doll's. Hugo watched the bloody water swirl down the sink and felt clouded. He wanted to be angry, hurting, guilty... anything. But it was all just numb. He barely felt it when Harvey tightened the bandage over his injury. They washed the black crosses off their faces in silence.

They rejoined Webb in the lounge just as he threw Ankle's panel back on the table with a disgusted noise. "It's completely fried," he muttered. "Slimy bastard must have installed a suicide protocol."

"What, you didn't think we'd caught a break, did you?" Harvey grumbled.

Hugo rubbed his head but then paused as they heard Doll coming back from her evening shift. He pulled on a t-shirt to hide the bandaging but she didn't glance up when she came through the room. Webb watched her go, face blank.

"Two down, two to go," he muttered, but only after they'd heard Doll's bedroom door close.

XII

That night, Hugo turned this way and that on the bench for a long time until he gave up and just lay on his back and stared into the darkness. He wasn't convinced Webb was asleep either but couldn't think of anything he wanted to say. He got up before the day-cycle began and went into the bathroom to splash his face.

Webb was up and scrolling though channels on the wall display when he returned. He leant against the wall and watched over the commander's shoulder, arm throbbing. Doll left for her shift without a word or a look at either of them. He saw Webb tense as the door shut but he didn't speak.

The morning wore on and light crept in through the frosted window. Harvey brought them breakfast and coffee and made them eat but all three had their attention on the newsfeeds. Hugo was just pushing the last of a packet of eggs around his plate when Sector 3 and the name of the barhouse Ankle lived under was mentioned. Harvey put down her mug and Webb turned up the volume.

"The victim," a reporter said over an image of Ankle's front door, roped off with yellow tape, "is believed to be a resident of the apartment. Enforcers are releasing no details at this stage but locals believe it to be gang related."

The report lasted under a minute then the feed moved on to a piece on a drug bust in Sector 2. There was no mention of Breonan.

Harvey went out after breakfast for more supplies. Hugo hadn't wanted her to go on her own but was too tired to argue and felt that, because he was so highly strung, he was not going to blend in with the stooped and shuffling crowds in the markets anyway.

Webb didn't even seem to hear her leave, so fixed was he on the newsfeed. Hugo got up and started going through their weapons, unable to keep still. Webb didn't speak, just kept watching the display and spinning his knife on its point on the table.

"How long do we wait?"

"A couple of days," Webb said. "Let them sweat."

"How much do you think Doll knows?"

Webb stilled his knife. "She'll have put two and two together by now."

"We should ask her. She could tell us exactly what people are saying."

"No."

"Commander..."

"I said no. Leave her be."

Harvey arrived back with more supplies and food to restock Doll's cupboards and Webb went to help her pack it away. Hugo was left to stare around the cluttered little room with the bare concrete walls and the newsfeed that reported nothing useful.

Doll came back earlier than usual and Harvey prepared a meal. She thanked them for the food but dinner was a distant affair and Hugo was glad when it was over. Doll left them, indicating that she was retiring early and Harvey, scrubbing her face, went with her. Hugo knew he wouldn't sleep so didn't even bother with the pretense of getting into bed. Webb didn't either and continued tapping keys at the workstation. He would occasionally report on something he found to do with stock or credit transfers between points that may or not be the Splinters making new deals, but Hugo suspected it was just a way for him to distract himself and Hugo bitterly wished he had a way to do the same. He had cleaned and serviced all the guns, knives and tech twice over. His nerves felt like strung wire.

When his mind began wandering to what Gamma Company might be up to, he got to his feet and grabbed the deck of playing cards and started to lay out a game of Dead Man's Candle.

"And... *now*."

Hugo looked up from his game, frowning. "What?"

Webb turned in his seat. His smile was a bit frayed. "You've done it, Captain."

"Done what?"

Webb held up his wrist display and pointed at the chrono on it. "You've now officially been captain longer than any other schmuck."

Hugo blinked. "It feels like I've been captain since the day I was born."

"Don't it just?" Webb said, stretching. "Whatever you think of this work... it gets under your skin. One way or another."

Hugo stared at his cards, not seeing them. Webb sighed and strolled over to drop himself in a chair at the table. He leaned over and picked up the Ace of Clubs and moved it over onto the King, completing the group. "I don't pretend to know what it's like," Webb murmured. "I just know lasting this long has to say something."

"What does it say?"

Webb shrugged, moved a Ten of Hearts onto its Jack. "You tell me."

Hugo sighed and propped his elbows on the table and rested his head on his fists. "Something's got me this far...but whether it's good luck or bad I can't decide."

Webb didn't say anything but he heard him move across the room and then there was the clink of glass. "Here."

Hugo looked up as Webb placed a small bottle of blask and two glasses on the table between them. "Where in the hell did that come from?"

Webb smiled and poured some out. "I told Harvey to watch out for it. You'd be amazed what you can find towards the hub."

"How much was it?"

"Christ Almighty, Hugo. Try not thinking, just for like ten minutes, okay?"

Webb held out a glass to him. Hugo took it and drank. It was certainly not the best but it was familiar and it warmed him. He made himself just enjoy the taste and the way it helped him slump a little easier in his chair.

"Armin's next," he eventually said.

"Couldn't happen to a nicer guy," Webb muttered.

"Do you think we're doing the right thing?" Hugo asked after a pause.

"Don't you?"

He took another mouthful instead of answering.

Ø

They were just gathering plates from another quiet dinner with Doll the following evening when the buzzer went. Hugo froze, as did the others. Doll glanced between them all, face serious.

Bolthole, she mouthed and Webb scrambled to the bench. He started hauling it away from the wall and Hugo bent to help as Doll gestured to Harvey to help her gather up the remains of their dinner and the tech that was scattered about the room.

"Hurry," Webb hissed as he hauled up a trap door under the bench. Harvey clambered down, arms full of packs and Hugo jumped down after her. Doll and Webb handed down the blankets and the rest of their supplies and then Webb dropped down beside them and lowered the door. They were plunged into utter darkness and then there was a scraping as the bench was pushed back into place.

Hugo could hear Harvey and Webb breathing but couldn't even see his hand in front of his face. Touch revealed they were in little more than a concrete hole, so shallow that he had to stoop. He heard Harvey and Webb shuffle themselves to the floor and followed suit, trying to stay quiet.

"What?" Doll's muffled voice filtered through the metal and concrete.

"Doll? It's Phoebe. Open up."

There was a pause and the sound of bolts and hinges then Doll's voice, distant, reached them again. "I thought you had the evening shift?"

"I did," came the woman's voice again and there was the sound of the door closing. "Foreman's shut us down. Came to tell you to keep your door locked and to not bother coming in tomorrow."

"What happened?"

There was the sound of scraping chairs and the newcomer heaving a sigh. "It's these killings. The foreman's spooked."

"Which killings?" Doll said after the slightest hesitation.

"Come on, Doll. Which do you think? I don't mind telling you it's a relief to be able to scurry away and lay low. You know that Ankle guy was at the meltworks just the other day?"

"I didn't see him."

"Slunk in the back way, didn't he?" Phoebe continued. "I was having a smoke behind the slag shed. Foreman let him in himself. Well, now he's been crossed too, it's got the foreman scared shitless. Someone's after Splinters, but no one knows why, or where they'll stop. The foreman's shutting down operation and about time too."

"Until when?"

"Until they're caught," Phoebe said. "Or until they're done."

"Thanks, Phoebe," Doll said after another pause. "Are you going home now?"

"I've got someone coming to pick me up. I ain't risking the shuttles."

"Good. Stay safe."

Again there was the sound of chair legs on concrete and muffled good-byes and then a solid silence in which Hugo blinked into the darkness. For one unreal but unsettling moment Hugo was sure that Doll wasn't going to let them out again but after another long second, there was a juddering from above and light fell in around the edges of the trapdoor.

They emerged just as Doll left the room. Webb's face tightened and he followed her. Hugo hesitated, looking after them.

"Don't," Harvey said quietly.

"Get everything packed up," Hugo replied, then went through the door and down towards the kitchen.

"...don't justify anything to me," Hugo heard Doll say as he approached the kitchen door.

"Just let me explain," Webb replied, voice brittle.

"There's no point, Ezekiel," Doll said. "I can't understand. And I'm better off not knowing."

"She's right, Commander," Hugo said, stepping through the door. "Donatella, we're leaving. If Ankle truly was involved with your meltworks there may be more people around with questions. We've put you in enough danger already."

Doll looked like she was wrestling with something but eventually nodded and turned her back, busying herself in a cupboard. Webb's face was set and pale as he watched her.

"Commander," Hugo said, startling the commander out of his thoughts. "Go and help Harvey pack."

Webb swallowed and for a moment Hugo thought he was looking at him without really seeing him. Then he nodded and moved to leave.

"Ezekiel," Doll said, not turning round but hands stilling on the counter. "What I said still stands. You will always find sanctuary here. Remember that."

Webb stood in the doorway, face drawn. Then he nodded again, though she wasn't looking at him, and left.

"Thank you," Hugo said, taking a step closer to her. "I won't forget what you've done for us."

She did turn around then. Her face was calm but there was a brightness of tears in her eyes. "You seem like a good man, Hugo. A grade above others of your kind I've encountered, at any rate. I am actually daring to have hope for that crew for the first time." Hugo held his tongue and just let her carry on drinking him in for a moment. "Just... promise me something?"

"What?"

Her eyes drifted towards the door. "Watch over him. I didn't and now it's too late for me. But you might still get the chance to save him."

Hugo swallowed, something unidentifiable creeping up his spine. She looked back at him, tears gone but face expectant.

"I will," he said.

Ø

"This is going to be fun," Harvey muttered as she shifted on her knees at the storeroom window, peering across the familiar street with her binoculars. Armin's blinds were open and all the lights were on in his apartment but this just revealed to them that they were, indeed, out-gunned and outnumbered.

"Just be grateful he's still here and hasn't scurried off into some hole," Webb mumbled.

The figures in the apartment all stood around with heavy expressions, their guns ready. Armin came in and out of view as he paced amongst the men and the rooms, talking into his wrist panel or into the wall-mounted comm unit. Even at this distance Hugo could make out the mask of cold fury that was his face. He never got close to the window.

"What's the plan?" Harvey said, scanning the street and roof. Hugo followed her gaze and saw more figures in black strolling on every level. These Splinters had their weapons hidden but they all wore night goggles and stood with the readiness of the hunted, scanning their surroundings and hands repeatedly going to hips and inside jackets.

Webb grinned. "Wreak havoc."

"We'll go in from the roof," Hugo said. "Harvey, you take the room on the right. Webb and I will go take the main room. Stay quick and keep firing. Our only advantage is surprise."

"Aye, Captain," Webb said with a salute which wasn't entirely mocking. Then Hugo followed Webb and Harvey up the stairs where Webb broke into a workroom that was level with the other building's roof. He stood back with Harvey as Webb opened a window and lined up the long-range rifle.

The first figure patrolling the roof jerked and then went down and the second followed soon after. Webb shifted onto his other knee and brought the gun round just as the third Splinter noticed his companions were down. He was just running towards shelter, bringing a wrist panel up when he, too, fell. Webb shouldered the rifle then pulled a wire launcher from his belt. The grappling hook flew through the air and tangled round the metal railings that fenced in the roof space of Armin's building. Hugo scanned the alley and street below as Webb secured the line. The Splinter in the alley didn't look up.

"Go," Hugo said as the figure below wandered away. Webb clambered onto the sill, got one leg hooked over the wire then swung underneath and started pulling himself across. Harvey took a breath then clambered up and followed.

Hugo leaned out and checked the coast was still clear. He made sure his gloves were fastened tight about his wrists then climbed onto the sill. Despite seeing the line support both his companions, he still gave it a tug before trusting his weight to it. He hooked his knee over, then there was a sickening feeling, like launching without artificial gravity, as his body swung into space. Then he was dangling from the wire and he had his other leg hooked over and he was pulling himself along.

Sweat broke out all over his body and his shoulders strained. Darkness arched up above him, broken only by the pinpricks of the sector's track lights, like regimented stars across the sprawl of the colony's hull. He suppressed a whirl of disorientation and kept moving until he was at the other side and Harvey and Webb were helping him over the railing. They took a moment to lean over and scan the ground again as Hugo drew his gun and double checked the roof was clear.

"Should we take them out?" Harvey whispered as they leant over to see two Splinters meet in the alley and whisper to each other.

"They're patrolling too regularly," Hugo muttered. "See?"

Another figure came round the end of the alley and passed the first two who split up and went in opposite directions, the newcomer pausing where they'd been to look up and down the alley before carrying on.

"Alarm will be sounded either way soon enough," Webb muttered.

"Remember," Hugo said, "No survivors. Ready? Move."

Hugo felt his heart start hammering as they checked their weapons then set about securing more climbing wire to the railing. It increased as they climbed over the railing and dangled out over nothing.

"One," Hugo said, looking once up into the lines of track lights above him. "Two," then he looked back down at his gloves clasping the wire. "Three. Go."

Hugo shifted his boots with an effort and they started abseiling down the building. He was vaguely aware of Webb on one side and Harvey on the other but concentrated on keeping up the pace. They stepped over one set of darkened windows and then another. He waited for bullets to start flying from below but nothing came.

One last scramble and his feet connected with the glass of Armin's apartment. He fired and the glass shattered and gave way and they swung inwards, the air reduced to a confused mess of flying glass and gunfire. He landed on his knees, disconnecting the wire and rolled. More shouts and shots rang out. He came up shooting then threw himself behind a couch where Webb was already kneeling and returning fire.

Hugo got to his knees and began firing as the last of the glass from the windows shattered behind them. There was already a figure slumped over the table near the door and another sprawled on the floor, a bloody mess where one eye had been. There was another Splinter propped against the wall, clutching at his neck and sliding to the floor.

Someone was shooting from behind a downed book case and someone else from around the corner of a hallway. A light was flashing over the door and a buzzer sounded. Webb shot out out the lights and the control panel. The door jerked open an inch then shuddered shut again.

A light fixture overhead crashed down next to them, shot down by one of the Splinters, sparks and dust belching into the air. The whole apartment became a swaying jumble of light and dark, dust, blood and shouts. They dropped back down behind the couch to reload, Webb cursing as he did so.

"There's more of them than we thought," he muttered.

"Keep firing," Hugo said. "We can't let anyone walk away."

He leant around the remains of the couch, concentrating his fire on the bookshelf. The Splinter behind it threw herself to the ground and it was a minute before Hugo registered that the firing from both the bookshelf and the hallway had stopped. He climbed back on to his knees beside Webb to peer through the smoke filling the room when there was a movement from the corner and something was flying through the air. He heard Webb swear then the wind was knocked clean out of him as Webb flattened him into the floor.

"Cover -"

Webb's warning was swept away by a gut-wrenching boom that Hugo felt more than heard. It rattled his teeth and ballooned in his innards and was accompanied by a blinding flash. His blood thundered in his head and all he could hear was a warped ringing and his vision swam in and out of focus. He was vaguely aware of Webb's weight being hauled up off him and then rough hands dragging him out from behind the sofa. His body wouldn't obey and the gun fell out of his hands.

He blinked, trying to claw back his senses and as he was propped up on his knees. His vision returned and he looked up into the skull-like face of Armin as he pulled out earplugs. Muscles like chords stood out in his neck and his eyes looked more than ever like they had been bored out of his head. His mouth was moving but it was a moment before the blaring in Hugo's ears subsided enough for him to make anything out.

"...I will make you understand."

"Bite me," snapped Webb. His commander was knelt next to him, hands behind his head with a Splinter rifle levelled at his back. There was cold metal pressed against the back of his own neck too. As the last effects of the stun charge wore off, anger began to burn in his gut. He opened his mouth but then Armin pressed the muzzles of his guns against their foreheads, redness rising on the paper-white cheeks.

"This ends here."

"Armin, wait..." Another Splinter came up, eyes wary but jaw set. "The contract said we were to take him alive if we could."

Armin's guns never wavered. "They will get the body and be grateful. These black cross fucks are not leaving this building breathing."

"Armin, no," the second Splinter tried to pull him back but Armin span with a wordless cry of fury and stuck him. The gun at Hugo's neck twitched. Realising it was now or never, he reached up and grabbed the

Splinter behind him whilst he was distracted, hauling him over his shoulder. The man landed heavily on the floor. As he lay winded, Hugo pulled the rifle from his grasp and came up firing.

He took out the Splinter still dazed from Armin's blow and then the one behind Webb. Webb rolled out the way of the crumpling body, grabbing a weapon as he did so, coming to his knees and the air was reduced once again to thundering chaos. He was aware on some level of streaks of fire lancing over his shoulder and calf, but he didn't let himself think about it and kept firing.

When he finally stopped and let the smoke clear there were only bodies around them and a heavy silence that clamoured around the ringing in his ears. Armin was against the wall, hands clutched over his abdomen and both legs a mangled mess. Hugo stepped over the dead and the dying, grabbed a handful of shirt front and hauled the Splinter up against the wall.

"Who wanted Lunar 1?" Hugo snarled. Armin spat blood in his face. Hugo slammed him against the wall. "*Who?*"

A smile that was all blood and teeth split the skull-like face. "Get fucked."

"Tell him," said Harvey who had appeared at his side, pressing her gun to the Splinter's temple.

Armin's smiled widened. "See you in hell, Service-boy," he whispered, shuddered and then the grin slid off his face and he went limp. Hugo let him go and he slumped to the floor.

Harvey scowled, face a tight mask under the dirt and boot black. "What's going on that we don't know about?"

Hugo didn't have time to answer. Shots started to tear the front door apart.

"Quick," Webb shouted, gesturing back towards the window. Hugo grabbed Harvey's wrist then clambered back over the debris as Webb sprayed a black cross on the wall over Armin.

Hugo threw one more glance back at the mess that was all that was left of Armin, then all three of them were grabbing their climbing wires and clambering up the side of the building. Hugo's pulse thundered, his shoulders burned and his wounds throbbing. His ears still buzzed and his breath came in short bursts but he kept climbing.

The lights were now on in the next apartment up but the terrified couple shrank back from the windows as they climbed past. He just had time to register the man tapping something into a comm unit then they were past the window and making for the roof.

They were just reaching the railings when there were shouts and firing from below and a bullet went right past his ear. With one last push that he thought would burst his chest right open, he hoisted himself up over the railing and rolled onto the roof. Harvey and Webb were already running.

The roof sloped upwards and they skidded and scrambled about on the corrugated metal. Webb sat down on the edge up ahead, swung his legs over then cast a glance over his shoulder. As soon as he saw Harvey and Hugo were close behind he pushed himself off and disappeared. There was a clang and Hugo reached the edge and saw Webb had dropped himself onto a metal fire escape a storey below.

"Come on," he shouted then he was clambering down the ladder. The rusty structure rattled and squeaked.

Hugo's knees jarred as his boots made contact with the metal then he was holding his arms up for Harvey. The short spacer muttered a string of curses as she lowered herself until she was dangling from her fingertips. Hugo reached and took a grip of her waist and helped her down and then they were both scrambling down after Webb.

There were flashing lights, sirens and more shots starting to ring out from somewhere back the way they'd come and when they reached the pavement at the bottom of the escape, they saw that the main street ahead was a riot of flashing lights and people running. Flyers whined by overhead and the street was flooded with light.

"This way," Webb hissed and ran away from the activity. They dodged round mounds of rubbish, boots splashing through puddles until they reached a wire fence. Webb was already scrambling over the razor wire curled round the top. Hugo felt it rip through his clothes and into his skin as he followed.

Once all three of them were back on the ground, they fell into the all-too-familiar routine of following Webb on a mad scramble through the dark, over walls and under fences, down back streets and behind buildings, a twisting trail that never took them to anywhere with light or traffic, until they made their way back to where they'd hidden the bikes.

The day-cycle was breaking when they cut the engines of their bikes in the dusty space of an abandoned workshop. They hauled themselves off the saddles with a collective groan, staggered and slumped onto the floor.

The water from their canteen was the sweetest thing Hugo had ever tasted. He swallowed mouthful after mouthful. When he thought he couldn't swallow any more he passed it on to Webb who tipped his head back and drank deeply. Hugo forced himself to ignore the trembling of the adrenaline crash that was setting into his limbs and made himself take in his crew's condition.

Webb was sat a bit awkwardly but the only stiffness he could see was from exhaustion and not from any injury. Harvey had clambered to her feet and was splashing her face from a basin on the side without a sign of any wounds, though she was leaning heavily on the workbench.

As his breathing slowed, he became aware of the wet stickiness on his face and the burning in his shoulder and leg. He staggered over to the workbench and the basin. Harvey blinked up at him through the water and smudged boot black. Her eyes darted about his face then she was tipping the dirty water down a drain and refilling the basin from a groaning tap in the wall. Hugo reached for the water but Harvey smacked his hands away before shrugging herself out of her jacket and picking up a rag. She soaked the rag in the water and reached up and started wiping down his face. Hugo closed his eyes and let her clean away the spit, dirt and blood.

Ø

Webb winced as he pulled his jacket off. Every breath sent fire through his ribs, his ankle was pulsing and every movement seemed to reawaken the stun charge headache. He shifted his leg out in front of him to try and ease his ankle then pulled their stashed pack out from under a workbench and fished out the computer panel. He encouraged it to boot up with a couple of swearwords and taps on the floor, trying to push back the waves of trembling that were attempting to bring him down.

He looked up as Harvey helped Hugo out of his jacket then started to pull his shirt off. Even if he hadn't had been too exhausted to make a joke, the stiffness in both their movements and the blood smeared across Hugo's skin would have swamped his humour.

"You okay, Captain?"

Hugo looked up blearily, blinked slowly then nodded.

"Sit," Harvey ordered and helped Hugo up onto the workbench where she started washing out the gouge on his shoulder.

The panel finally booted up. Webb activated the motion-sensor hubs they'd placed at the doors and windows of the old workshop. He was just about to try and stream some newsfeeds when he noticed a blinking light in the corner. Heart climbing into his throat he opened up the coded messaging program.

"What is it, Commander?"

Webb looked up. The captain's eyes were on him and his scowl was back. "Message from Rami, Captain," Webb said, skimming the code.

"They had a near miss with some bounty hunters on Lunar 5 by the sounds of it."

"Anyone hurt?"

Webb shook his head as he reached the end. "No. But they had to high-tail it out of there pretty quick. Evangeline doesn't mess around."

"They need to get out of the Lunar Strip," Hugo muttered, reaching down and attempting to pull off one of his boots.

"Sunside?"

Hugo shook his head. "They need to get out of space. Tell them to go to Earth, Tokyo or somewhere else neutral and lay low until this is over."

Webb nodded, rubbing his eyes and setting about typing in a coded reply. He paused as he reached the end, trying to think of something personal to say to Rami, but couldn't. He sent it, then went back to scrolling through news sites. "Well folks...we made the headlines at last," he mumbled.

"About fucking time," Harvey said, throwing the bloody rag back in the basin.

"Are we still on track?" Hugo asked pulling off his other boot.

Webb checked a few more forums and reels. "Looks like it. No one knows who's doing it. We must have taken out everyone before they could get word out."

"Good," Hugo said, rolling up his trouser leg to reveal another gash in his calf. He reached for the basin but Harvey pulled it out of his reach.

"Let me change the water," she muttered then took the basin back to the tap. She dumped out the bloody water but then just stood leaning against the bench with her head bowed. Her shoulders started to shake.

"Marilyn?" Webb hauled himself to his feet and limped over to her.

"I'm fine," she growled, scrubbing a sleeve over her eyes and turning on the tap. Webb exchanged a glance with Hugo.

"This isn't your fight, Marilyn," he said quietly. "We got Armin. Your score is settled. You don't have to stay."

"Stow it," she spat, turning off the tap and not looking at him. "Don't patronise me." Webb blinked and took a step back. She brought the basin out of the sink and dumped it on the bench beside Hugo, water sloshing out onto the dusty surface. "It's not over," she said. She looked at him, eyes sharp, without a flicker of fear. She glanced from him to Hugo, who returned her look with a heavy one of his own, then stalked across the workshop to where their blankets were bundled in the corner, curled up in one and turned her face to the wall.

"You need any help?" Webb said, seeing Hugo bending to clean his leg.

Hugo shook his head. "Get some sleep, Commander," he said in a low voice. Webb sighed then nodded. He dug out a medkit from one of the packs and took it to Hugo who nodded his thanks then he went to go to his own blankets, though he doubted very much that he would manage to sleep.

"Webb..."

Webb turned back to the captain. He had paused with binding in one hand and a sterilising pad in the other and was gazing off into the distance. "Yes, Captain?"

"Marlowe's next."

Webb felt a shiver run across his skin and stopped himself from showing anything on his face. He managed a nod. Hugo carried on appraising him and Webb wondered what he was seeing. Then he looked away and the moment was gone.

"You were right about Doll," Hugo murmured so quietly that Webb barely heard it. "We were right to keep her out of it."

Webb didn't know what to say so he didn't say anything. Hugo finished binding his leg then got down from the workbench. "Are you going to wash that off?"

Webb frowned, then remembered the boot black. He moved over to the sink and turned on the tap. The water spluttered out in fits and starts but he pulled off his gloves and scooped handfuls of it to scrub at his face. When he was done both Harvey and Hugo were curled on the floor in their blankets. Webb checked the motion-sensors' stream one more time then shut the panel down, pulled off his boots and wrapped himself up in his own blanket and lay on the concrete. The workshop was a fractured spread of shadow and scrubbed highlight from the night-cycle track lights bleeding in through the dusty windows. He stared into the shadows for a long time, purposely not thinking about Marlowe.

Stiffness from sleeping on concrete and the exertion of the night before awoke him just as the day-cycle started to grey outside. The others were still asleep and he crept from his blankets and padded away with the computer panel. Every tendon seemed to be on fire and the shooting across his ribs had faded to a dull but insistent ache. He got himself to the other side of the workshop and worked his way through some stretches in an attempt to loosen himself up then he sat cross-legged on the floor, booted up the panel and started work.

He wasn't sure if it was the increased volume of his cursing or the brightening day-cycle that woke Hugo, but the captain joined him before long, slumping onto the floor next to him and peering at the panel.

"What have you found?"

"There's only two ways we're going to bring down Marlowe," Webb muttered, leafing through the schematics of Houston Block for the hundredth time. "And you're not going to like either of them."

"What are they?"

"Option one: we wait for him to leave and take him down in the street."

Hugo shook his head. "Not an option. We can't break pattern now. It needs to be in his home."

"Well that's Houston Block," Webb growled. "Fucker has the whole top floor as his own private playground by the looks of it. Half the businesses in the block are his. The other half answer to him, I'd wager."

"I couldn't find anything conclusive when I looked."

"You didn't know where to look, Captain," Webb replied dourly. "I wish I didn't. Houston is his domain and he'll have that place tied up tighter than a ship hull, with enough armed personnel to take us down ten times over. Each."

"What's the second option?"

Webb looked up. "We take out the power."

Hugo blinked. Once. Slowly. "Take out the power?"

Webb nodded. "We plunge the whole of Houston Block into the fourteenth century. Only then do we stand a chance of getting past the alarms, locks and men with guns and into level 350."

"And what happens after that?"

"I haven't got that far."

Hugo carried on looking at him, but didn't scowl. Webb wondered when it was that Hugo had started listening to him. Then he wondered if that was a good thing.

"Can it be done?"

Webb rubbed the back of his neck. "We'd need to disconnect it from the mains *and* disable the back up generator. And either way I reckon it would only buy us ten or twenty minutes before they re-route the connection. But it's possible...I think."

Hugo chewed on that for a moment. "And there's no other way?"

"Not that I can think of."

"Why do I get the feeling I don't want to know what you're talking about?" asked Harvey as she strolled towards the tap with a canteen.

Webb allowed a mischievous grin to spread over his face, lightened by Harvey's return of character. "You think we've had fun so far?"

XIII

The hardest part was splitting up from the others and trusting them to do their bit. But he had to. And, though he didn't say as much, when he looked in himself he didn't find any doubt. Hugo would get it done.

Still, it was easy enough to trust him to do his duty, he thought. Not as easy to trust him to not get himself killed in the process. But Webb shook the thought away and carried on down yet another maintenance way, flattening himself against the wall as a couple of technicians wandered past at a junction.

He scrambled up and out of the next exit hatch and took a moment to stare up into the murk and listen to the sound of traffic and machinery permeating the chill air around him. He reassured himself that, one way or another, he wouldn't have to come back to this godforsaken colony again after tonight.

He pushed the tangled feelings aside and started to run. Houston Block reared up ahead, a towering spread of orange and white lights, shuttle platforms and skyway junctions, so huge that no matter his pace he never seemed to get any further towards it. He skidded to a halt in the shadows behind one of the relay blocks, held his breath then pushed a button on his wrist panel. A burst of red and orange reared up above the buildings behind Houston and the ground trembled.

"Back up generator destroyed, Captain," Webb mumbled into his wrist panel. "How are you two doing?"

"Nearly there," came Hugo's clipped reply.

Webb fished his night goggles out ready and craned his neck up to look at the megastructure, counting down under his breath. He had just started to panic that something had gone wrong when all the light from the block went in one go and he was plunged into darkness. He let out a sigh of relief, feeling his heart start to pound and pulled on his goggles and set about pulling a tarpaulin off their stolen flyer. The chaos of the suddenly blind skyways filtered down in a series of crashes and beeps as well as the whining of thrusters reversed in a hurry. Closer by there was the screeching of tyres as the groundway entrance choked with confused traffic and then, slowly, shouts started to build in volume.

Webb clambered into the flyer's pilot seat then started to count, fingers tapping on the wheel. "Hurry, Hugo," he hissed, then heard booted footsteps sound in the darkness nearby. Harvey and Hugo clambered into the flyer, both shouting for him to go.

He gunned the thrusters before Hugo was seated and jerked the stick up. They climbed until they were zooming up parallel with the darkened levels of the block. He dodged amongst the confused skyway traffic and pulled them round a shuttle parked at a blackened platform that rang with panicked shouts, and then he could see the top of the structure approaching. With every breath he felt a suffocating heat build inside him. He clenched his teeth and pulled on the air brake. The flyer jerked and shuddered then smoothed over the edge and levelled over the sprawling roofspace.

"Go," Hugo barked even before they'd stopped.

Webb felt every pound of his boots meeting the metal roof as though it were from far away. With an effort, he pushed away the heat and sank into the darkness that lurked behind it, feeling it fill and calm him like a vacuum. He found an emergency hatch and knelt beside it to lay charges. He hadn't had the materials or the time to knock up any of his implode charges so he shooed the others back a good distance before hitting the detonator. There was a flash and a creaking bang and a groan and then they ran back.

The silence that surrounded them when they dropped into the pitch-black maintenance way was eerie. He set off at a run, skidded around a corner, not caring what noise his boots made on the grill floor. There was confused shouting and the tinny reply of a comm up ahead. Webb didn't break pace but hurtled round the next corner.

They left the two Splinters bleeding on the floor and forced open the checkpoint they'd been guarding and pelted down the corridor beyond until skidding to a halt at a signal from Webb. He stood staring at the door for a moment, breath heavy in his chest.

"Commander," Hugo hissed next to him.

Webb shook himself and placed more charges. They backed away as far as they could and Webb pressed the button. The heat and sound blasted them back, but they recovered quickly and ducked through the ruined door and squeezed into the tiny maintenance space beyond. Another door, wooden this time, barred their way but the charges had taken out the hinges and they shouldered it open and staggered into the room beyond.

A large bedroom showed up in the dull green of the night vision. Shelves and shelves of hard-copy books lined the walls and there was a huge wall display mounted over a dark fireplace. Webb took all this in in a second and went toward the door when he was frozen to the spot by the sound of a stifled sob. He turned and saw a small figure hunched in the corner, arms clutched over his head, shaking. The heat inside Webb blazed white and for a moment he was blinded, choked with anger, fighting back memories threatening to swamp him. Another sob came from the boy. Webb made himself move over to him.

"Hey," he said, holding out a hand. "Hey, buddy. It's okay. We're not gonna hurt you."

"What's a child doing in his bedroom?" Harvey asked but no one answered. The silence that followed was thick.

The boy didn't move until Webb tried to take a hold of his wrist. Then he flung himself away and shouted at the top of his lungs.

"*Vince*," he screamed. "In here! Vince!"

Webb swore and grabbed after the boy but Hugo was already there, seizing the boy and clamping a hand over his mouth. He bucked and struggled and kept screaming Marlowe's name against Hugo's glove.

All the lights came on. All three of them swore and pulled off their goggles, blinking. Alarms began blaring and there was more noise from deeper in the building. The boy had gone quiet and Webb looked over and saw he was slumped in Hugo's arms, eyes closed, wetness on his cheeks.

"He's okay," Hugo growled at the look on his face. "He fainted. Quick, Harvey. Take him."

"What?"

"Take him and get him out of here."

"You can't go on without me," Harvey said.

"We've got no choice," Hugo said, heaving the slight body up in his arms and passing him to Harvey. "Take the flyer. Get him to the nearest youth unit."

Harvey shook her head, muttering under her breath, threw one unreadable look at Webb then left the way they'd come with the boy in her arms.

"Move," Hugo said. "Now."

Webb nodded, drew his gun then moved to the bedroom door. He took a moment to press his ear against it. There were footsteps coming their way.

"Stand back," he hissed at Hugo then flattened himself against the wall beside the door just as it came crashing open. The men that had entered didn't have time to take in that they weren't alone before Hugo and Webb had taken them down. Peering back out the door he saw the corridor beyond was clear.

"This can't be it," Hugo said, eyeing the bodies on the floor.

"It won't be," Webb replied. "Come on."

They jogged down the corridor. There was a thick white carpet under their feet that muffled the sound of their boots. When they reached the end they took a moment to breathe and then peered around the corner.

A huge space opened up in front of them, a display at one end that took up an entire wall. A long plexi-glass table dominated the centre of the room, scattered with hastily abandoned hand-panels, papers and comm units. There were at least twenty Splinters milling about it, all dressed in black and all with automatic rifles. Marlowe stood at the end of the table, his face still but his eyes blazing. Webb felt his stomach flip inside him. The man stood tall and calm as he issued orders to his men over the blaring alarms.

Webb and Hugo both pulled back around the corner when Marlowe's glance slid in their direction. Hugo was grinding his teeth and glaring at the opposite wall. Then, after a pause, he holstered his gun and pulled a grenade out of his utility belt.

"I like your thinking," Webb said.

"This all ends tonight, Commander," Hugo said. "One way or another."

"Yes, sir."

Hugo searched his face for a moment longer but Webb kept his expression blank. Then the captain pulled the pin and hurled the grenade round the corner. Webb braced himself but the blast still made him stagger. He didn't give himself time to think but ran out, firing blindly into the smoke and flames. They flung themselves behind the remains of the table and continued firing. More cries confirmed that they'd taken down another couple of Splinters but then the air around them was exploding with shots.

As the smoke from the grenade began to clear, he could see that all that was left of the ceiling and walls was a scorched and flaming mess. A number of mangled bodies were strewn about. At least a dozen Splinters had taken up position behind a downed section of wall and from the shouts that filtered through over the sound of the gunfire more were on their way.

"I have one charge left, Captain," Webb shouted.

"Do it."

Webb ducked back behind the table, wincing as plaster and glass rained down on him. He pulled out the last charge, activated the timer, then hurled it towards the Splinters.

This blast was smaller but still shook the room. There was the groaning of protesting metal and the floor heaved and tilted. He flung himself flat on the carpet and tried to dig his fingers in. The table slid with them and a series of crashes and screams before the floor stopped tilting.

Webb got back to his knees to peer round their barricade. Half the room had caved into the level below. The section of wall and the Splinters behind it had gone and all was smoke and shouts and noise.

Gunfire broke out again as new arrivals took up position across the room. The remains of their table bucked and splintered. Webb cursed and ducked down to reload then noticed a tall, suited figure slipping away in the confusion.

"He's getting away," Webb shouted, firing and managing to take out one of the men covering Marlowe's escape. The second one got up and ran after Marlowe. "Hugo, cover me."

He didn't give the captain time to protest but came up shooting. He sprinted through the smoke and leapt over the tear in the floor. He landed, staggering, tore round the corner and pelted down the corridor after Marlowe. Bullets flew in the air all around him.

He turned another corner in time to see the tall man and his Splinter guard keying open a heavy door. Webb increased his speed and got there just as the door of the panic room was sliding shut. He skidded the last few feet, shoving his boot in the gap. The heavy door cracked on his foot and he grunted in pain but shot out the control panel and shouldered it open.

He staggered inside the small room, bringing up his gun, but was knocked to the ground from behind. He scrambled up onto his hands and knees but the Splinter kicked him onto his back, bearing him down into the floor. The world span back into place just as the man on top of him leant his whole weight onto the rifle pressed over his neck. Webb coughed and choked, trying to hold off the weight, his vision blurring and blood pounding in his ears. Just before it all went grey, he caught sight of Marlowe, watching with his arms folded and a soft smile on his face, and a surge went through him.

With an effort that had his shoulders screaming, he heaved the Splinter off and delivered a kick to his head whilst the big man was still trying to regain his balance. There was a crack of bone and he went down like a sack of parts. Webb scrambled for his gun but Marlowe lunged, grabbed hold of his collar and slammed him against the wall. The breath was knocked from him and his head span. He tried to fight it, but the strength of the broader and taller man brought the memory screaming back and it swamped the fire inside him. Feeling the fight go from him, Marlowe tightened his grip on his throat, lifting until his heels left the floor.

"I know you, don't I?" Marlowe said, face so close Webb could smell the cigars and rum on his breath. "I wasn't sure before… but now I've seen you from this angle -" he leaned in closer, choke-hold tightening and leaning his full weight into Webb's body. "- yes, I remember." There was a horrible moment when a smile that was all teeth and eyes that were grey as iron filled his entire vision. "You've grown."

Heat flared from somewhere desperate and Webb gathered it to him, snarled and shoved. Marlowe staggered and Webb stuck out, landing a blow that cracked into his jaw. Marlowe spat and struck back but Webb managed to duck and land a kick on the older man's kneecap. He swore and bent away but then threw himself forward.

Webb ducked again and went for a blow to the ribs but Marlowe had recovered and dodged. Webb's momentum carried him too far and Marlowe grabbed his arm and twisted it up behind him, forcing him to his knees. He cursed and struggled but Marlowe got a grip of his hair and pulled his head back so he was looking right up into the cut-glass gaze.

"Seriously though, kid. The black cross? Really?" he said, leering down at him. "What, did I not pay you enough? I'm normally generous with the ones good enough to remember."

Webb snarled, got his legs under him and pushed up. His head connected with the Splinter's nose with a satisfying crunch. There was bubbling and cursing and Webb knocked him to the ground with another kick. He was on him in a moment, heaving him up by a fistful of his suit and raining blows on his face. The other man tried to bring up his hands but Webb just pounded through them.

Eventually he stopped for breath. Marlowe lay limp in his grip. Then, through the blood and the matted hair, Marlowe smiled.

"You son of a bitch," Webb hissed, pulling out his knife and pushing it hard enough against Marlowe's throat to split the skin. "This ends. It all ends. Tonight."

"Oh no," the man croaked, dribbling blood. "Oh no, my little gutter-shit." He coughed before it warped into a sickening laugh. "Kill me, if you've got the guts. I dare you. But if I'm in there -" He tapped Webb in the centre of his forehead. "- I'm there to stay, pretty one." The mess of his face shifted as the grin widened.

Webb hauled Marlowe up into a sitting position and leaned in to hiss in his ear. "I'm gonna hunt you down in hell just so I can kill you again. And again. And again."

Blackness rose in a wave and closed over his head. All he felt was an ache in his knuckles from the tightness of his grip on Marlowe's suit and the knife. He was distantly aware of the thick stickiness that coated his face and clothes and the hot, coppery taste in his mouth. Then there was a voice nearby calling his name.

"Webb," Hugo repeated. "What the...?"

Webb blinked and wiped a sleeve over his face to clear the blood out of his eyes and mouth. Hugo stood in the door with a face like stone. Webb shook himself and got up, re-sheathing his knife and dropping Marlowe's body to the floor. His limbs felt like they were made of iron. He closed his eyes for a precious second and waited to feel something, but nothing came.

"What's going on?" he mumbled as he became aware of the cacophony filtering down the corridor.

"The Enforcers have arrived," Hugo said. "Looks like his connections weren't enough to protect him from them finding out about his involvement with the Splinters. But we need to move. Now."

"Go," Webb said, pulling out the spray paint. "I'll catch up." Hugo didn't move though as Webb turned his back and sprayed a cross on the wall that reached from ceiling to floor. Underneath he scrawled *God has found thee lacking*. He threw the can at Marlowe's body, spat on it and shoved past Hugo into the corridor.

"Reinforcements came from this way," Hugo said, jogging away from the chaos of the conference room. "There must be another way out."

Webb followed, forcing his body to obey though it felt like he was wading against over-tuned gravity. They ducked and turned until Hugo managed to find a hatch back into the maintenance ways. Alarms blared and they had to shoot their way through several checkpoints that the alarm system had locked down. The few people they encountered were all maintenance personnel who threw themselves out of the way or ran in the opposite direction when they saw them coming.

They burst out of the maintenance ways onto a retail level. The square in front of the closed-up businesses was virtually deserted apart from a few confused people blinking up at the flashing lights and alarms. They jumped out the way as Webb and Hugo came pounding over the square. When they skidded into a parking pool they ducked low to avoid being seen by a troop of Lunar 1 Enforcers shooing civilians towards the express lifts. They ran, stooped double, behind a row of flyers and broke into the first one that looked fast.

The Enforcers were so engrossed in getting the civilians off the level that they didn't notice Webb and Hugo until the engines fired and the flyer rose from its berth. Shouts and a few shots rang out but they were out of the building and pulling the flyer off the skyway before anyone had a chance to understand what was happening.

Webb managed to piece together enough rationale to steer the flyer on a non-direct route back to the workshop, where they dumped it a couple of streets over and ran the rest of the way. By the time they were heaving open the rusted door and staggering inside, Webb's urge to vomit was winning the war against his desire to lie down and pass out.

He ignored Harvey who rushed forward to them as they came in and concentrated on putting one foot in front of the other until he reached a foreman's office in the corner. He pulled the door shut behind him then leant against the wall in the dark, breathing in the smell of dust and old metal. His control snapped like string and he sank to the floor, pressed his forehead onto the ground, covered his head with his arms and lost himself in the blackness.

Ø

Hugo watched the water in the basin darken as he scrubbed off the boot black. He couldn't deny the rising feeling of relief that washed through him at the thought of never having to smell the stuff again.

"We're done then?"

Hugo blinked at Harvey through the dripping ends of his hair. "Yes. We're done. Did you get that kid somewhere safe?"

Harvey nodded. "They took him in at St. Michael's. Though by the time I got him there he was calling for Marlowe again."

Hugo swallowed as a chill rode up his spine. Harvey rubbed her face as she sat in the corner with their blankets. She looked small and tired, but when she let her hand drop her face was clear and she sat straighter.

Hugo finished washing his face then pulled off his jacket. He checked over, cleaned and replaced the dressings on all his injuries. Neither of them said anything, though they both stole glances at the door of the foreman's office.

When Hugo was done he leant against the workbench, letting his body be still. Exhaustion was pumping through him like lead in his veins but he couldn't bring himself to move toward the blankets. He took a breath, ran a hand through his hair, then paced over to the foreman's door, ignoring Harvey's mumbled warning.

He paused with his hand on the handle, feeling uncertainty flicker in the fog of weariness, then pushed it aside and opened the door. It was silent and dark inside. There was a single dirty window high in the wall that only let in enough night-cycle light to produce deep shadows around the piled-up furniture, broken workstation and unidentifiable mounds of junk. As his eyes got used to the gloom he discovered a hunched shape in the corner wasn't another mound of clutter. Hugo clicked the door shut behind him, blocking out Harvey's concerned face, then lowered himself to the floor next to Webb.

After a few heartbeats of deep silence Webb shifted and pulled himself upright. His movements were sluggish, like those of a sleepwalker. Even in the poor light Hugo could see the blood from his attack on Marlowe had darkened to a grisly mask about his mouth and jaw. The boot black was smudged down his face. The eyes that peered out of the mess were dull.

"I don't feel anything," he mumbled after just staring at Hugo for several loaded seconds. "I thought, when he was dead... after I killed him... I thought I'd feel different. But I don't."

Hugo let the silence stretch for a minute whilst Webb blinked into the darkness.

"How old were you?"

Webb lifted his shoulders in a weak shrug, a sad and defeated gesture. "Old enough to know what I was agreeing to. Young enough that I thought anything was worth not having to face another day hungry." He tilted his head back so that it rested against the wall and closed his eyes, hands fumbling for something at his throat. The was a glint of gold in the darkness then his fist closed over the pendant. His breathing calmed. "It happened a lot, even before the plagues had left the colony swarming with kids with nowhere to go. And I was luckier than most. At least I got away breathing. But..." He paused and for a second Hugo didn't think he was going to continue. But he kept his mouth shut and waited. Webb eventually sighed and rubbed his face. "It never went away. It's like... I don't know. It's like you've swallowed cement. The weight of it... it stays."

"It's right that he's gone," Hugo said a few heartbeats later. "He can't hurt anyone any more. But you didn't need to kill him to change anything. You defeated Marlowe long ago."

There was a snort in the darkness, a soft one with no real power behind it. "How'd you figure that one?"

Hugo leaned in, making his commander meet his eye. "The man I met aboard Service Command... the man who is the commander of the *Zero*... he is not a broken man. He's someone who has taken something that might have destroyed him and turned it into a strength. Into a reason not to be defeated."

Webb didn't answer but Hugo could feel his eyes still on him.

"We can't choose what happens to us," he continued in an even lower voice, glancing off into the shadows. "What we can do is choose what we do with it."

"You're a good man, Hugo," Webb said softly after another few moments. "Too good for this shit."

Hugo looked into the shifting shadows of his commander's face for a moment longer. When the silence threatened to spiral into a darker place, he made his voice work. "You gonna wash?"

Webb laughed, though it was a little hollow, and scrubbed his sleeve over his eyes. "Aye. I guess I should."

They both got to their feet and Hugo went for the door.

"Hugo," Webb said before he could open it. "Anita doesn't know. No one knows."

"They won't hear it from me."

Webb stared up at the grey window. Then he took a breath and nodded. "Thank you," he said.

Hugo ducked his head then opened the door and stepped back into the workshop.

Ø

The three hours rest Hugo made himself take whilst waiting for the signal from the *Zero* only served to make everything that had been trembling with fatigue dissolve into a stiff, sore, creaking mess. The others didn't appear to be much better off. They all groaned and muttered as they packed their remaining supplies. The greyness of the returning day-cycle was rising outside the dirt on the windows and Hugo took a moment to rub his eyes. If he ever thought he knew exhaustion before, he was wrong. This went right to the bone. Right to the soul.

"The Zero will be docking within the hour," he said when he checked his wrist panel.

"Good," Webb muttered. He stood straighter than he had been the previous evening, but there was still strain in his face. "Let's get the fuck off this colony."

XIV

Hugo didn't entirely know how to process the fact that he felt a palpable relief to be stepping back on board the *Zero*. The only thing he could be certain of was that he couldn't deny it. Kinjo and Rami met them in the cargo hold where they all but dragged them from the bikes and ushered all three straight to medbay. He staggered in the corridor when the deck tilted as they launched and was grateful to finally slump into a chair.

Hugo allowed Kinjo to strip him down to his skivvies and check him over, muttering answers to her questions, tiredness lapping at him in great sucking waves. She tutted and fussed over the healing gunshot wounds in his shoulder, arm and calf and then finally dismissed him to go and get washed, under strict orders to come back and get his wounds dressed once he was done.

He left, throwing one look towards Rami whose face was tight as she checked over the unresponsive Webb.

He turned the shower to its hottest setting, sinking himself in the blissful feeling of the water scouring away the layers of dirt and blood. He closed his eyes and pressed his forehead against the cubicle, visualising his skin peeling off in great chunks. He willed the bleakness to crumble away with it.

Telling himself he would get his wounds dressed later, he went back to his cabin. His narrow bunk had never looked so tempting. Every muscle and bone begged to be laid down but he couldn't bring himself to give in until he'd unloaded some of what was in his head. Leaning heavily on his table he turned on the wall display then started keying in commands to get a comm link to Colonel Luscombe. He almost nodded off standing up as the word '*Connecting*' flashed on the screen, but then a window opened up and a young woman in Service uniform was blinking at him.

"Captain Hugo? Is that you?"

"Commander Hudson," Hugo blinked. "Yes it's me. I need to report to the colonel. Urgently."

She hesitated then said, "Hold, please."

The feed went blank with the hold sign flashing in the corner. Hugo frowned, trying to put his finger on what was making him uneasy but the window opened back up and a much older woman appeared on the screen, storm cloud coloured hair scraped back from her face, eyes sharp.

Eight silver pips glinted on the shoulders of her uniform.

"Captain Hugo." Her voice wasn't loud but it was heavy, like tempered steel.

"Admiral Pharos," Hugo managed, pulling himself up from the table and attempting to stand straight. He saluted and tried not to think about the fact that he was only in a pair of utility trousers and hadn't shaved in days.

"Well? Report."

"Ma'am," he said. "I was given strict instructions only to report to Colonel Luscombe..."

"You answer to the colonel, but he answers to me, Hugo."

"Yes, Ma'am."

"Report. Now. What the hell happened on Lunar 1?"

Hugo swallowed. "Ma'am. We successfully carried out Luscombe's orders-"

"This was one of Luscombe's initiatives?" she asked, brow clouding.

"Yes, Ma'am," Hugo said. "As a result of some information we received."

She looked off screen for a moment, frown heavy on her brow, then turned back. "Well then? What happened?"

Hugo stared at a point just above the screen as he reported. He went through their plan, their attack on the storehouse and what followed, skirting around the issue that attacking the Splinter ringleaders had been his idea and leaving Harvey and Doll out completely.

When he was done, he stood there trying not to sway. Pharos looked at him for a long time, hands clasped together on her desk and face still and completely unreadable. "Very well, Captain. We shall continue to monitor Lunar 1 and see if your strike has been conclusive. I would like to confirm that at no point did anyone know who it was?"

Hugo shook his head. "I don't believe so, Ma'am. Everyone who saw us was destroyed."

"Any losses on your side?"

"No, Ma'am."

"What about Webb?"

Hugo frowned. "Ma'am?"

"Where is he?"

"Medbay, ma'am."

"Was he injured?"

"Scrapes and bruises only as far as I know," Hugo said, trying to read her eyes.

She nodded once, then leaned forward and started typing into a keypad out of site. "Very well, Hugo. I will pass this onto Luscombe. But, as I have you here, I have your next mission."

Hugo swallowed, and blinked back the fuzziness creeping at the corners of his vision. "Already, Ma'am?"

"Is there a problem?" she said, without looking up. "Perhaps you'd like a vacation?"

"Of course not, Admiral," he said. "Apologies."

"Your little attack on the storehouse triggered an official investigation," she continued. "During the course of their enquires, the Analysts have identified a source of the majority of the credit sent to the Splinters."

"They have? Who was it?"

"We don't know who. Only what. It was revenue generated from a mining satellite."

"A registered one?" he pushed. Her eyes narrowed. "Ma'am?" he added.

"The operation is being run by a dummy corporation wrapped up in false accounts, licensed to fake profiles. The Analysts haven't been able to pull it all apart. But that's beside the point. You're to destroy it."

"Ma'am?"

She tapped another series of keys and a blinking light appeared on his display that indicated waiting information. "That's your mission, Captain Hugo. Destroy satellite X6-119."

"Ma'am," he repeated, ignoring the heaviness that was gathering in her expression. "Forgive me, but I don't understand."

"You don't have to understand, Hugo."

"No, Ma'am," Hugo said, mind blundering about trying to find the right words. "But -"

"Captain, I hope you have not become lost in the woods?"

"No, Ma'am."

"I see no other explanation for you starting to outwardly question orders."

"No, Admiral," he said. "Please, my apologies. Destroy the satellite. Very well, Ma'am. Acknowledged. It's just -"

"I am amazed at what you managed on Lunar 1, Hugo," Pharos cut him off. "And I haven't forgotten the fortitude and initiative you displayed on the day of the Black Dawn uprising. It is why I chose you for this. Now prove to me I wasn't wrong."

His back stiffened but he managed to keep his face straight. "Yes Ma'am," he managed, bowing his head. "I'm sorry I questioned -"

"You have your orders. Report in to Luscombe as soon as it's done."

The feed cut off before he could reply. Hugo let his shoulders sag. He blinked at the blank display for a few moments before keying up the data she had transmitted, not able to completely push aside the feathering of uncertainty in his belly.

"Hugo to bridge."

"More here, Captain," More's face, gaze focussed off screen as he steered the ship, appeared on his display.

"Where are we?"

"Just heading out of Lunar space now, Captain. Any heading?"

"No," Hugo said, rubbing his forehead. "Not yet. Take her out somewhere she can drift for a while. Where's Webb?"

"Rami sent him to the crew cabin I think, Captain."

"Very well. Keep at top speed until we're well clear of the Lunar Strip."

"Yes, sir."

There was no buzzer on the crew cabin door and the room was dark inside. "Webb?" Hugo asked, stepping in.

"Captain," Webb said and the lights flickered on. Webb was hauling himself up from his bunk.

"Don't get up," Hugo said, easing himself down on the bunk opposite and spreading out his sore leg with a grunt. "Did I wake you?"

"No," Webb snorted, as though this were a silly suggestion.

"Are you alright?" Hugo said, gesturing toward the bandages wrapped around the commander's chest.

"It's nothing. Rami likes to fuss. What about you?" Webb said, eyes flicking from wounded shoulder to stiff leg.

"I'm fine."

"I wouldn't want to be in your shoes when Kinjo finds out you've ignored her."

"I'm fine," Hugo repeated.

Webb shrugged. "Was there something you wanted, Captain?"

Hugo chewed on the inside of his cheek for a moment. "I've just been reporting to Pharos."

Webb raised his eyebrows. "What did she want?"

"Well, first of all she was concerned about you."

"Me?" Webb said, frowning.

Hugo nodded.

"Didn't think she even knew my name."

"Apparently she does. And she seemed worried that you might have been injured."

Webb rubbed the back of his neck. "I got nothing, Captain. I guess I represent something of an investment... though I've been nearly blown up more times than I haven't, so why she should give a shit now, your guess is as good as mine."

Hugo eyed his commander a moment more but there was nothing in his face apart from the tightness of fatigue. "She also gave us our next mission."

"No rest for the wicked, huh?" Webb said, rubbing his face.

"We're to destroy a mining satellite that appears to be the source of the Splinters' credit."

"Okay," Webb said, shifting on the bunk and wincing. "Should be simple enough."

Hugo frowned. "That's it?"

"What?"

Hugo folded his arms. "Are you being deliberately obtuse, Webb?"

Bewilderment crossed the commander's face. "Huh?"

"She doesn't want us to break into it, hack into it or anything that would get more data for the Analysts. She wants it destroyed."

"So we destroy it," Webb said, shrugging. "If those are the orders."

"You were quick enough to exceed orders when there was a chance to destroy Marlowe."

Webb's face darkened and his jaw clenched. Hugo felt shame swamp him. He swallowed, throat tight and got up to leave.

"Sit down, Hugo, for fuck's sake. Fine. *Tell* me what the problem is."

"I don't know," Hugo snapped, balling his fists and pacing back across the cabin. "I don't know," he said again, calmer. "It's just... she's more concerned with destroying it than with finding out who owns it."

"After all this, how is your head still in Service-mode, Hugo?"

"What?"

"Ours is not to reason why," Webb mumbled, propping his chin up on his hand. There was a haunted look about his eyes for a moment but then it was gone so quick Hugo wasn't sure he'd seen it. "Besides, the amount of time it would take the Analysts to track down the trails, assuming that's even possible, whoever it is will have stripped the asteroid bare and have enough cash for Christ knows how many more nasty little plans."

Hugo paused. "I hadn't thought of that."

A ghost of Webb's former grin crossed over his tired face. "There you go then. Besides, if this happens now, anyone looking into it will think it's part of the black cross vendetta and file it under 'the fuck am I getting involved'."

Hugo sighed and leant against the bulkhead, kneading his sore shoulder. "God you irritate me when you're right."

Webb gave a weak laugh and laid back down on his bunk. "You just wait until I'm wrong. That'll shit you up six ways from Sunday. But if your instincts are bugging you, get Rami and Spinn to see what they can find. At least that way we'll know a little more about what we're blowing up."

Ø

After relaying his orders to Rami and Spinn Hugo relented and let Kinjo drag him to the medbay to treat and bind his gunshot wounds. He just grunted in response to her questions until she gave an irritated little snort and filled a syringe from a vial.

"What's that?" Hugo said, attempting to glower.

"You need to sleep."

"I'm fine, Midshipman," he said, standing stiffly.

She set her jaw. "Sir, if our lives are in your hands I think we'd all be happier if you were well rested."

He opened his mouth to protest again but found he was just too tired and allowed her to administer the shot. She had to help him back to his cabin and he'd slipped away before she'd even turned the lights out.

He'd only started dreaming when a bleeping sounded somewhere close by. Whilst he tried to claw back from oblivion the bleeping became sirens, lights flashed and he could taste smoke and blood. He snapped his eyes open and blinked at the bulkhead until he pulled himself back together. He was breathing like he'd run up the stairs of a megablock and sweat was cooling on his skin.

Bleep, bleep, bleep.

He rubbed his face and sat up. There was a blinking light on his wall display. Kinjo must have set it to sleeping mode.

"On screen," Hugo grunted and Webb's face appeared.

"Hugo? Rami might have found something..."

"Report," Hugo said as he came up onto the bridge.

"I don't know that it's anything, sir," Rami said, clicking keys on her workstation, her eyes scanning the data on screen. "It's just..."

"What?"

Rami turned in her chair, frowning. "I managed to dig up the satellite's equipment manifest..."

"And?"

Rami exchanged a glance with Webb who was leant against the co-pilot chair with his arms crossed and a deliberately blank expression, and then with Kinjo, who was hovering nearby, nodding encouragement. Rami sighed. "All the mining and processing equipment is Albion Integrated."

Something jumped inside him. "AI?"

"Yes sir," Rami said, raising her hands "Now, it might not be of any significance. AI are one of the biggest suppliers of this sort of tech."

"But, Captain," Kinjo interrupted the lieutenant. "It's not that simple..."

"Go on," Hugo said, trying to keep the impatience out of his voice.

"Some of the tech on this list, sir," Kinjo said. "It's highly advanced. I know for a fact some of it is still registered at prototype status. I don't see how this little satellite could put together a rig like this unless -"

"Unless AI are involved with more than just selling them their equipment..."

Kinjo nodded.

"We need to get this information to the Analysts," Hugo said.

"Sir, the Analysts probably already have it," Rami said. "It wasn't hard to find. It's only significant to us because of what happened on Earth."

"Luscombe got the orders for our AI mission from somewhere. Kinjo needs to tell him just what she's told me."

"It's not enough," Rami said. "The Analysts can't move on hunches."

"Damn it, I'm not letting whatever's happening here get buried," Hugo said. "If the Analysts need more evidence, we'll get them more evidence."

"Pharos is expecting the whole thing, evidence and all, to be drifting dust by tomorrow, Hugo," Webb said.

"Rami, Spinn," he said. "Find a way for us to get a ground team into that satellite. Webb, follow me."

Hugo paced off the bridge towards the galley. He heard Webb sigh and follow. He was just trying to untangle where to start when he was brought up short by the sight of Harvey with her feet propped up on a galley table, chewing on a ration bar and watching a newsfeed on the wall display.

"Is now a good time to discuss you getting me home?" she said, not looking up.

Hugo swallowed. "I'm sorry, Captain," he said, hating the formal tone his voice took on. "I'm afraid we have something to take care of first."

She frowned at him. "You've taken on another contract already?"

Hugo resisted looking at Webb for guidance. "Something along those lines."

Harvey shook her head and stood. "I'll never get my head around this ship. Look, Hugo, not to be a pain in the ass but I'm done. Officially out. I've done more than I said I would."

"We're grateful -"

"Stow it," she said. "I wanted a chance at Armin and I got it. And I think the Splinters will have more things to worry about now than tracking me down. So I thank you, but that's my lot. Take me to the nearest colony."

"We can't."

Harvey scowled. "This isn't a negotiation, Kaleb."

"There's a deadline, Marilyn," Webb said, coming forward. "We will be finished by this time tomorrow," Webb threw a significant glance at Hugo. "We'll take you all the way to Haven after that, okay?"

Harvey scowled at one of them then the other. Then she sighed and shrugged. "Fuck it. Fine. But you owe me. Big time. And I'm staying in the crew cabin until Haven. I'm done getting messed up in any more *Zero*-grade shit."

"Of course," Hugo said. "Marilyn?" She paused at the door. Hugo tried to untangle his tongue from his teeth. "Thank you," he managed.

She hesitated, seemed about to speak. Then she glanced at Webb and just nodded and left.

"You know that whole thing where sometimes I know better, Captain?" Webb said, slouching down on the couch and rubbing at his bruised jaw.

Hugo turned to face him and straightened his back. "There's something going on here, Webb. Don't tell me you don't see it."

"I can see it," Webb said, propping his chin up on his hands and tracing a finger through the crumbs on the table. "I just think you're borrowing trouble is all."

"Webb," Hugo said. "Whoever or whatever owns that satellite are the ones responsible for trying to stage a coup on your home colony. How can you follow orders that you know will result in destroying evidence that could bring them to justice?"

Webb looked up at him for the longest time. He wasn't grinning but he wasn't angry either. "This is bigger than us, Hugo. I've said before we're not meant for stirring up Orbit-wide politics. We follow orders. Our orders on Lunar 1 were to stop the Splinters. That's what we did."

"And Earth?" Hugo said. "That whole shit storm that nearly got us both killed? And now it looks like it might all be linked, and you just want to stick your head in the ground and follow orders?"

"You've been doing this for ten weeks, Hugo," Webb said. "I've been doing it for fifteen years. This is the deal. You risk your life, you get screwed over but you take your pay and you thank the Service and pray you will still be useful in the morning."

"They made me captain for a reason," Hugo insisted, stabbing his finger on the table top. "And I say we can do more than just blow it up."

"If you're so sure," Webb said quietly. "Then why are you justifying yourself to me?"

Hugo blinked. Webb looked up at him, eyes clear. "Because I want you on my side," Hugo said eventually.

"I am on your side."

Hugo tried to read his pale eyes but couldn't. He felt something go out of him and he slumped on the bench, staring at a motorbike poster on the bulkhead without seeing it.

"I can see why you were made captain," Webb said eventually, looking at his hands. "And I will follow your orders. Just..." he sighed then looked him in the eye. "Just be aware even if we find something, the Service may not want to know."

Hugo remembered Pharos and her clipped words and steely gaze. Then he remembered Doll and her sombre, defeated air. But he shook both memories away and stood. "We will see what we can find," he said. "Then we'll know at least we've tried. Whatever the Service do with it is up to them. And the consequences will be on their heads and not mine."

"Okay, Captain," Webb said after a pause. He stood and something like his old grin spread over his face. "That's an attitude I can get on board with."

Ø

"Are you sure you're ready, Midshipman?"

Kinjo nodded, eyes bright and hands compulsively checking over her vacuum suit. "I am, Captain."

"And you know what you're looking for?"

"I do. I won't let you down, sir."

"Hugo," Webb leaned out *Father*'s cockpit.. "We'll be showing up on their sensors any second."

"Get aboard, Midshipman," Hugo said and Kinjo nodded again and clambered up, taking Webb's hand and cramming in with him behind Bolt's pilot seat. Hugo took *Son*'s ladder two rungs at a time and slipped into the squat-space behind More just as he hit the hatch control.

"Helmet on, Captain?"

Hugo pulled his helmet up over his face and zipped it up. "Sealed and ready."

"Hold on."

The fighter hummed as the engine fired up and there was a lurch and clang as the hold depressurised. The ramp lowered and Hugo tried to shift so his knees weren't protesting and found a handle just as More engaged the thrusters and *Son* was zooming out into space. Craning his neck, he could see the rocky bulk of the mining satellite up ahead, its surface pocked with shadows. There were already fighters streaking towards them.

"Are they on an attack vector?"

"Looks like it, Captain," More said, pulling the fighter over.

"How many?"

"Twelve, sir."

Hugo cursed and braced himself as the first hammer of fire rammed into the fighter's shields. More ducked and swerved to avoid the next burst.

"What happened there?"

"I don't know, sir. They're aiming for non-vital systems."

Father and *Ghost* arced by on either side and the enemy fighters split to follow them. More brought *Son* back round just as a flurry of cannon fire burst through the space they were in. They got closer and closer to the asteroid until Hugo could make out the blinking lights of the mining installation on its surface

"Are you ready, Captain?" More said.

"Move in."

"Aye, sir," he replied, opening fire on the surface of the asteroid. *Father* came in above and concentrated its cannon fire on the same spot. There was a burst of suckered flame and a cloud of debris, then More was pulling up and spinning round to twist the fighter's course around the satellite. Enemy fighters swerved to follow and More managed to take out one and wing another as he arced around the asteroid. *Ghost* was a white streak across the viewscreen and then it was gone again, three enemy fighters in pursuit.

As *Son* came full circle the *Zero* came into view, moving fast and firing on the fighters in pursuit of *Ghost*. Hugo caught himself gaping. He'd never seen her in action before. She went by as a streak of light just as another enemy fighter exploded in a ball of flame that was sucked into nothing. She sped around the satellite in a blur, cannon fire crashing into the rock, then passed out of sight as More slowed *Son*'s course.

Hugo felt every heartbeat like a hammer in his temples as More manoeuvred *Son* onto the rocky surface, still firing as the cockpit hissed and the hatch opened.

"Go, Captain, move, move!"

Hugo didn't let himself think but clambered up from the squat-space and fired his wire launcher before he could even aim properly then pulled the recoil trigger. With a jerk that nearly pulled his arm from his socket he was hauled from the fighter and hurtled towards the surface of the satellite. The darkness of the crater caused by *Son*'s cannon fire loomed ahead, wreathed in drifting debris. Rock and metal pinged off his visor and then there was a flash of light as *Son* took off again. His heart clambered into his throat and every breath echoed in his helmet but then his boots were connecting with the solid surface. He clutched the wire to keep him anchored then moved over the surface in uneven bounds that his zero-g instructors at the Academy would have been ashamed of. But they got him to the hole quicker than approved, controlled jumps would have have done. He got a grip on the broken edge and peered in, seeing the remains of some sort of store room. Craning his neck he watched the fighters and the *Zero* chase each other across the silent span of space. "Webb, I'm on the surface. Where are you?"

"Bolt's bringing us round now, Captain. Get away from the entrance."

Before Webb had finished talking *Father* hove into view, light bursting from its balance thrusters as Bolt manoeuvred the fighter through the gap in the rock. A blast of fire hammered into the rock just behind him. Hugo clutched onto the rock as the surface shuddered beneath him, hearing his breath echoes quicken in the dead space of his helmet.

As soon as *Father*'s thrusters went dark, Hugo detached his wire from the rock and re-launched it into the fissure. He drifted into the room then felt his stomach lurch and he was bumping onto the floor as the gravity got hold. He scrambled to his feet just as Webb, Bolt and Kinjo were clambering out of *Father*. They ran towards a light shining through a door on the other side of the room, scrambling over crates and bundles of stores scattered by the blast.

Webb bent to the door controls as Hugo peered through the window into a corridor beyond. Red lights were flashing but it was empty of people.

"Spinn. Come in Spinn," he said "Do you have us?"

"Aye, Captain," the researcher's voice came through on his helmet speaker. "The nearest quarry is down the corridor on your right. There's a flyer pool on the same level."

"Copy that. What's everyone's status?"

"The *Zero* took a hit on the aft vector burner, but Rami's compensated. Other than that everyone's functional, Captain. They seem to be aiming for non-vital systems. But it won't be long before they get enough hits."

"Just keep them busy and be ready to blow the satellite's thruster bank as soon as we're clear."

"Aye, Captain. Out."

"How much longer, Commander?"

"Just getting past the breach controls," Webb muttered. "You might wanna activate your grips."

Hugo pressed the control on his suit and felt his feet fuse to the floor.

"We've got company," Bolt said.

Hugo peered back out the window and saw three armed men coming up the corridor towards them.

"Get back," Webb barked.

Hugo scrambled aside as the door slid open. The force of the corridor depressurising blasted at him. He got his gloves onto the bulkhead and felt the magnets take but his body still bent with the force of it. One of the men managed to grab the door jamb as he hurtled past but his fingers peeled away one by one and he followed his companions out into drift, face twisted and gaping. Hugo watched all this happen in eerie silence, and then Webb was clamouring in his ear piece to move through.

Pulling against his magnets, he stomped through the door. Bolt followed, pulling Kinjo with him. Webb staggered through after and slammed his palm against the control. The door shuddered closed and they stood leaning against the wall and panting. The blaring of alarms filled his ears as the air pressure stabilised.

"Clear," Webb said, checking his wrist display and unsealing his helmet. "Let's go."

Hugo could smell smoke and iron as they moved down the corridor, stumbling into Bolt when the ground shook underneath him. He gathered his balance and they picked up speed. Empty corridors branched off on both sides but up ahead was a set of double doors plastered in neon safety signs.

"There," Hugo said, pointing towards the doors, but then there was a shout and four armed guards ran from a side corridor. There was a confused moment where they skidded to a halt, yelling and pointing, then the floor in front of Hugo exploded in rifle fire.

Hugo swore and threw himself down another corridor, his crew scrambling after him. He was just pulling out his own weapon when the firing stopped.

"Throw your weapons down and come out," someone shouted. "Now."

"What the fuck is a mining satellite doing with this much security?" Bolt growled, checking his weapon.

"I said get out here, now, spacer fucks," the voice raised up another notch. "We ain't kidding. Throw out your guns and come out with your hands on your heads."

"Webb," Hugo muttered. "Throw a charge."

"Christ, Hugo," he hissed. "This corridor's too narrow -"

A barrage of gunfire tore the ceiling apart. "Running out of patience, spacer scum."

"Do it," Hugo snapped.

Webb swallowed then unzipped his vacuum suit and pulled out a charge. He paused but then activated it and threw it around the corner, flinging himself to the floor. Hugo crouched and covered his head just as the air was blasted apart. Debris rained down on him and the lights flickered off then on again.

Once the clatter of falling detritus had quietened, Hugo got to his feet, blinking, shaking dust and chunks of metal and rock from his hair. Bolt helped Kinjo to her feet and then Webb was scrambling back towards the corridor.

"Well, that did the trick. Come on," he said and started climbing. The blast had torn the bulkheads open and chunks of rock had caved in. There was no sign of the security men. Dust hung heavy in the air and it tasted like iron. Hugo clambered after Webb. The ground shook again and Hugo heard a groaning noise.

"Webb," was all he had time to shout. He caught the back of Webb's suit and stumbled backwards. More rock crashed down from the hole in the roof, and the air again was full of dust and stone. When it stilled, Hugo coughed and clambered off Webb who sat up groaning and clutching his ribs.

"Are you alright?" Kinjo said, clambering up next to them.

Webb nodded and scrambled to his feet. "Damn site better than I might have been. Thanks, Captain. Though a little more warning -"

They all froze when the sounds of more shouts and running feet echoed down a corridor behind them.

"Is that *more* security?" Bolt said.

"I'll draw them off," Webb said. "Get to the quarry."

"Commander -" Hugo was cut off by a rumble and the corridor rocking around them.

"There's no time, Captain," Webb said, already moving back down the corridor. "The *Zero's* fire is taking this place apart. Move, move."

"Bolt, go with him," Hugo ordered. "Kinjo, this way."

They scrambled the rest of the way over the fall of rock and sprinted towards the quarry doors. He heard gunfire and shouts somewhere behind them but didn't look back. "Spinn," he said into his wrist panel as they approached the doors. "Spinn, come in."

"Remind me to *never get fucking involved* with you lot *ever* again."

"Harvey? What are you doing there?"

"She's helping me pilot, Captain," Rami replied in his ear piece, voice tight. "What do you need?"

"Concentrate fire on the satellite, Lieutenant."

"Captain?"

"We need as much confusion in here as possible."

"The structure is already destabilising, sir."

"Just do, it Lieutenant. And be ready for our signal."

"Aye, Captain," Rami said, then there was a thundering noise and the corridor shook again. They reached the doors and Hugo palmed the control but they didn't move.

"Breach protocol, Captain," Kinjo said.

Hugo swore and bent to the panel. He wiped dust and sweat from his eyes and started tapping keys, trying to dredge up his eleventh-grade systems knowledge and what he'd seen of Webb and Rami's tricks for getting round them. The sound of shots in the distance caused panic to spark which shifted the blankness in his brain. His fingers flew and the door hissed open just as the floor bucked violently enough to make them stagger against the wall. There was a sickening moment when the gravity weakened and he started drifting from the floor but there was another slam and it was back. They picked themselves up and ran into the quarry, pulling their guns out as they went.

Their boots rattled on a metal balcony that bordered the perimeter of the hollow. The rock ceiling arched into darkness above them. The ground level was lit by scattered flood lights. There were piles of rock strewn about, some still clouded with dust from a fresh fall which had taken out some of the lights, leaving great chunks of the space below in shadow. Between mined stacks of rock were the angular arms, lifters and belts of mining equipment. The heavy smells of iron and cold stone were thick in the air.

"There," Kinjo shouted and pointed towards a large machine against the wall on the level below. "That's a new model, Captain."

"Are you sure?"

"Positive, Captain. Those drills aren't even licensed yet."

"Go, then, go," Hugo said, gesturing and they were both running towards the nearest ladder.

The warning lights flashing over the doors scattered the shadows around them as they clambered down the ladder. Their boots hit rock and then they were running towards the machine. Kinjo climbed up the side of it like a cat until she reached the control systems near the top of its arm and pulled out a multitool. Hugo kept his gun ready, scanning the quarry, but everything was eerily still.

"Got it," Kinjo said, pulling out a circuit board from the machine and tucking it inside her vacuum suit.

"You sure, Midshipman?"

"Yes, Captain," she said, starting to climb back down. "This will have all its electronic signatures. We'll be able to prove it's not been cleared for public use -"

"There they are!"

Hugo swore and fired at two men running from a door on the other side of the quarry. They fired back but then there was an ear-splitting crash and Hugo was flung off his feet. He shook his head, dazed, then felt his heart jump into his throat when the rock near his ear exploded with shots. He rolled away and threw himself behind the nearest rockfall. He came up to return fire when he froze at the sound of a high-pitched cry.

"*Kinjo.*"

"Don't even think it," growled one of the men. He had an unkempt beard and a knife at Kinjo's throat.

The other man, pale and with cruel eyes, stood with a gun pressed to her temple and a nasty smile on his face. "Come out, *Zero* scum. Now."

"Captain?"

Hugo jumped as Bolt crawled up beside him, face pale, staring out over the top of the rocks. Hugo swallowed, panic fluttering. "Crewman, can you take them out?"

Bolt raised his weapon and aimed. "I don't know, Captain."

"You're playing a dangerous game there," the bearded man called, as Kinjo continued to struggle. "Come out now. We know he's with you."

"Who?" Hugo called, trying to keep his voice steady and his gun from shaking as he kept it aimed.

"Ezekiel Webb," called the gun man. "Send him out."

Hugo's breath tightened in his chest.

"Do it now," the pale man continued, "and we'll let all the rest of you go. It's the best deal you're gonna see. Trust me."

Bolt looked to Hugo, eyes wide. All Hugo could do was kneel there with his mouth open, desperate thoughts chasing themselves in circles around his head.

"You've got ten seconds, Captain Hugo," the gun man called again, and Kinjo gave another choked cry as the knife wielder tightened his grip. "And I'm a fast counter. Ten... nine..."

There was another thunder of distant cannon fire and the floor shook and dust rained from the ceiling, but the man didn't pause in his counting, pressing the gun to Kinjo's temple even harder as he did.

"Bolt, take him out," Hugo hissed. "My hands are shaking too much."

"Even if I do, Captain, the guy with the knife will have her."

"Six... five... you're killing her, Captain..."

"*Stop*," came a shout from the shadows.

"Webb, *no*," Hugo cried, scrambling to his feet as a gun skidded across the floor and Webb stepped into the light with his hands up. The gunman fired at Hugo and he threw himself back behind the rocks. "Webb you fucking idiot!" he shouted.

"Let her go," Webb growled, face dark. Kinjo gave a strangled sob, trying to shake her head.

"That's him," the knifeman mumbled.

"Alright, Webb," the gunman said, beckoning with his pistol. "Come with us now, nice and quiet, like."

"Let her go first," he replied, still hanging back.

The ground shook again and all the floodlights went. The gravity pulsed off then on again then the lights returned and in the confusion the men pushed Kinjo towards Hugo. She stumbled to her knees then scrambled away just as Webb dove for his gun. But the knifeman was too quick and grabbed him by the vacuum suit. Hugo and Bolt ran out, guns aimed but he had Webb on his knees and a grip on his hair, knife at his throat.

The gunman was panting and aiming at the commander's head. "*Stay back.*"

"Christ Almighty, Hugo," Webb growled. "Fucking *run* already."

Hugo just stood there, panting, gun levelled. Another crash and a groan heaved through the rock around them and more boulders crashed down, crushing machinery and another floodlight. Masses of dust swirled in the air and the gravity warped and shifted and they all slid to the side, scrambling to keep balance.

"Fuck this. We're not going to get him away. Do it," the gunman shouted. "Just *do* it."

"*No*," Hugo yelled, scrambling upright but the knifeman had already yanked Webb's head back. There was a confused moment when the ground shook and more rock fell but then Webb was falling forward and the knife man was stood there, clutching a handful of Webb's hair.

"What the *fuck*?" Webb growled, getting to his knees when the knifeman nodded to the other and ran. The gunman aimed and fired and

Webb went down.

Kinjo screamed. Bolt yelled and ran after both the men, firing wildly. Hugo stood frozen. His chest was banded with hot metal and his gut was filling with ice. He swayed with the shifting gravity and shaking floor and it took him three blinks before he processed the sight of Kinjo knelt next to a sprawled Webb, blood on her hands and her body shaking with sobs.

He stumbled to the floor and pushed her away, turning Webb over. His eyes were open but his face was still. He looked odd, Hugo thought, with his hair cut ragged by the knife. Hugo's heart thumped against his ribs and he leant in to listen for breath but there was none. There was warmth between his fingers where his fists clutched the bloody vacuum suit. For a moment nothing existed except blackness threatening to drown him.

"Captain." Hugo felt Bolt's hand on his shoulder. The floor bucked and more rock fell as his awareness slammed back to reality. "We need to move. Now."

"Go," Hugo said, throat aching. "Move. *Go.*"

Bolt nodded and got Kinjo to her feet and they stumbled away. Hugo bent and got his arms under Webb and lumbered upright. The commander was lighter than Hugo expected but he was still panting and his shoulders were burning when he got to the door where Bolt was waiting.

"Sir," Bolt said, face drawn. "Sir, it's against protocol. We need to move fast-"

"Move, Crewman," Hugo snarled.

"Sir-"

"I said fucking *move.*"

Bolt looked from his face to Webb and he saw him swallow. The crewman holstered his gun and leant and took Webb's body from him, hoisting him up like he were a doll. "Let's go, sir."

Hugo felt his throat close up but he nodded, pulled out his gun and jogged ahead. Kinjo took up the rear, pulling her own gun but not looking like she would be able to use it.

The lights in the corridor were flickering and the air was full of smoke and rock dust. There was a shout once and someone turned the corner but careened across and down another corridor before they could fire a shot. There was heat and sweat and grit grinding between his teeth and the taste of iron heavy in his throat.

Bolt took *Father* and, somehow, though Hugo never quite remembered how, he and Kinjo found the flyer pool, hotwired one and zoomed out of the satellite. Bolt must have signalled the *Zero* because the flyer's cockpit was washed white by the fireball of the imploding satellite. All he could hear though was Kinjo's thick breathing and his own pulse in his ears.

Ø

"He gets *nothing*?" Hugo's hands hunted for something to throw. "He gave everything, *everything* to this ship. And now he's dead. And he gets *nothing*?"

Luscombe's face on the display was like granite. "Webb knew the risks, Hugo. This is unfortunate, but this is the game. And if you had followed orders, this wouldn't have happened."

Hugo felt his fingers burn with the grip he had on the table. He still had the taste of smoke in his throat mingling with the burn of alcohol. Every breath that raked in and out was like fire.

"They knew we were coming," he spat. "They were riddled with security. And our fighters are barely scratched. They were trying to bring us in alive."

"This is all supposition, Hugo," Luscombe said. "I don't know where the hell this idea came from but it's culminated in you risking your crew on a hunch. And look what happened."

Hugo opened his mouth but none of the curses he could think of were foul enough.

"It's a bloody good thing you still destroyed the thing," Luscombe continued, "or I'd be heaving your arrogant ass into the Command Centre brig to rot. You could have messed up the entire operation, Captain Hugo. Be glad we got out of it with as little losses as we did."

Hugo's glass shattered against the wall display. The liquid trickled down and the screen flashed and warped but Luscombe was still there, face like thunder.

"Drift the body, Hugo" the colonel said, voice dangerously low. "And then take yourself off to some hole, a dark one, and stay there. I don't want to so much as hear the word *Zero* until I send for you."

Ø

"Rami, find us somewhere in North America, outside the fallout but away from any civilian habitation. I'll be damned before I see him drifted."

Rami swallowed and looked at him. Her eyes were dry but her face was pale. It was a moment before she managed to speak. "Somewhere remote, sir?"

"Yes."

"Somewhere near water, perhaps..."

Hugo swallowed, seeing something flash in her eyes then die. "Where can we find a priest?"

"A Nova Catholica priest, sir?" More asked. "We'll struggle on Earth.

We'll have to stop by Lunar 1."

"Set a course."

"Sir," More said, not looking up, already obeying. "I feel I should point out-"

"I don't give a shit. Lay in the course for Lunar 1. Rami?"

"Yes sir," she replied, not looking up from her workstation as information and maps flickered across her screen. "I'll find somewhere suitable."

Hugo nodded, though no one was looking at him. The bridge was still filled with the beeps and whirs of the computers and the clicking of Rami and More's fingers on the controls, but it all seemed fuzzy and far away, like all his senses had been wrapped in cotton.

He swallowed a foul taste in his mouth and returned to his cabin, shut off the lights and lay on his bunk glaring into the dark.

Ø

Doll murmured everything in Latin, but Hugo didn't need to understand the words to know what she was saying. It was written on her face. Her skin was pale and there were dark circles under her eyes. She looked older. Immeasurably older. She sprinkled some soil onto the fresh patch of turned earth and Hugo thought she had started to cry but then he felt a wetness on his own face. The patter of rain on the leaves of the surrounding trees rose to a hiss as the rain got heavier, churning the surface of the lake into a pitted stretch of bubbles and ripples.

The earthy smell of wet soil rose from the ground and the chill felt good. He willed it to numb the burning under his skin. He turned his face up and blinked through the water, up to the steel-grey sky. A real sky. One that stretched to a horizon and was a muddled mass of clouds and rain and wild things and not made of metal. The rain stung his eyes but he didn't look away.

It was a moment before he realised Doll had finished. She was looking at him. He didn't say anything but just stood and blinked rain water from his eyelashes. She inclined her head, then wandered away towards the trees, an arm around Kinjo's shoulders. Sub held his pack over Bolt to try and shelter him as he used the lasertool to cut an E then a W and the year into the boulder they'd rolled down from the tree line to mark the grave.

When it was done the crewmen straightened, shook rain out of their eyes and both saluted. They then followed Doll and Kinjo back towards the *Zero*. More followed shortly after without a word or a look at Hugo, then it was just him and Rami. Spinn hadn't come down.

For once, the lieutenant's face was open, a mask of pain, eyes haunted and angry, though even now it didn't look like she was crying. Part of Hugo felt he should leave her alone. There was more going on in her face than he could understand. She deserved to say her goodbyes in private. But he couldn't move.

He stared out at the rain-pocked lake, feeling fat drops trickle down inside his collar and his clothes cling to every inch of his skin. Eventually Rami left. He sat down in the mud beside the grave marker, letting the rain stream over him until night rolled in.

XV

"You're doing it again."

Hugo blinked until the darkness faded to the edges of his awareness and he was back in the room with the orange stripes of street light across the ceiling and the smell of old sheets and damp skin.

"Here's a novel idea," Harvey said raising herself up on her elbows to look down into his face. "Talk to me."

Hugo looked at her, green eyes appearing black in the meagre light, then pulled her in for a kiss, only partially to change the subject.

"Fine," she said, pulling away. "Have it your way. I gotta go. I've been away from Haven too long already."

She clambered out of bed and padded around the grimy boarding room, picking up her clothes. Hugo watched her, trying to untangle what it was he was feeling. She stuffed the last of her possessions into a pack and slung it on her shoulders. She paused, sighed and sat on the bed, tilting his chin up so he looked right into her eyes.

"Just promise me you'll look after yourself, okay?"

He still couldn't make his voice work. She shook her head again, leant in for a last, lingering kiss, then she was gone. He lay and stared at the ceiling for a while, part of himself insisting yet again that he needed sleep. After half an hour, as usual, he gave up, dressed and went downstairs.

The barman nodded to him as he came in and poured him a blask without a word. Hugo nodded his thanks, keying his credit code into the panel in the bar, then shouldered in over his drink to prepare for another evening. The bar was virtually empty. That was why he came here. Not even the barman tried to converse with him. He swirled the black liquid in his glass, savouring the bite. It wasn't good, but it was cheap. It was everywhere in Sydney, good and bad. After his third mouthful he realised he'd left his wrist panel in his room again. He scowled into his drink. If Luscombe called, he could bloody well leave a message.

He didn't look up when a large man took a seat on the stool next to him, despite there being many empty ones. He ordered his drink and sat in silence for a moment. Hugo glared at his glass.

"Master Kaleb," the large man said after taking a sip of his drink. Hugo finally looked up. The man's hair and beard were a lot greyer than Hugo remembered. He looked tired too, but otherwise as stoic as ever. "I'm glad

I found you."

Hugo glared back at the bar. "Go away, Colwyn."

"Your mother would very much like to see you."

Hugo didn't move but he didn't leave, draining his drink instead. The man finished his own, unhurried, then laid a hand on Hugo's shoulder. The familiar weight of it made something shift inside him. Without even entirely registering what he was doing, brain murky and vision blurry, he got up and followed Colwyn out of the bar.

The flyer ride was silent, for which Hugo was grateful. Colwyn took the main skyways right over the city. The lights from the harbour bridge swirled on the choppy waters of the bay and Memorial Music Hall towered up beside it, all lit up in blues and whites. There was a queue of expensive flyers for the top-level parking pool and as they passed by he saw elegant people with drinks and fine clothes on the balconies. He watched the hall fade away in the rear view mirror, unable to define what he was feeling.

His heart hammered more than it did before a mission as he stepped into the apartment. The wide hall was empty. The lounge area to his left with its sunken couches and shelves of books was dark.

"Special Commander and Major Hugo will see you in the den when you are ready, sir. There are supplies in the guest bathroom, should you wish to use them." Colwyn inclined his head slightly, gave Hugo a meaningful up-and-down glance and left.

For a long moment Hugo just stood in the hall, breathing. The apartment still smelt of fresh linen, with the hint of lemon from the carpet cleaner his sister had always bought. It had once meant home. His boots sunk into the white carpet without a sound. For one horrific moment he was back in the corridors of Marlowe's complex. But he shook his head and the illusion was gone. These carpets were familiar and more trodden and the walls were blue, not white. There were digiprints and vases on the tables, shapes, colours and patterns he had known for years.

In the guest bathroom he ran the water so hot it steamed. Razor, soap, comb and toothbrush had all been laid out on the marble side. When he was done some of the fog in his brain had cleared and he looked more like the man he remembered last seeing in this mirror, though with the longer hair combed back and the growth of beard gone, the bleakness in his eyes and the narrow press of his mouth were more noticeable.

He paced through the halls towards the den, becoming more certain he'd made a mistake with every step he took. He didn't know if he wanted to tear the place apart or sink to the carpet and sob. When he reached the den, he paused to try and make out the muffled voices through the door, but they were talking too low. Biting the inside of his cheek, he pushed the door open and went in.

His mother, father and eldest brother looked up as he came in. Every back was straight and every face was tight. The only clear emotion that Hugo could pin down was relief that they weren't in uniform.

"Kale," Giles eventually broke the silence that had been ballooning out of control, frown heavy. "Is that really you?"

"Yes, it's me," he said, coughed and tried again for a less defeated tone. "What do you want?"

"What do we want?" his father said. "After everything that's happened, that's what you have to say?"

"You summoned me," Hugo mumbled. "So I'm here. What do you want?"

"What the hell's happened to you, son?" His father's face was stormy.

"Nothing you want to hear about."

Giles and his father exchanged glances. His mother hung back, face blank. She hadn't moved a muscle since he came in.

"Are you going to tell me what you want? Or are you just going to stand here staring at me?"

"This attitude is not helping, Kaleb," his father said,. "And don't try and tell me you didn't want to see us. Why else would you be here?"

"My crew are trading with some reps at Service Headquarters."

"Are they now?"

"I shouldn't be here..." Hugo began, shaking his head and turning away.

"No, wait," Giles said. "Kale, listen a moment."

Hugo swallowed but kept his face blank. His father shook his head but Giles just stood there, mouth working.

"We have good news, Kaleb," his mother said once the silence had blundered on a few more seconds. She didn't look him in the eye but rather somewhere over his head. "Your brother and I have found a unit, Earth-based, that will take you on. It will do until you have a chance to regain some of Command's trust."

"What rank?"

His mother looked him in the eye now and it was like someone had dumped cold water down his neck. "Private."

"You want me to step down to be a dirtside private?"

"Step *down*?" his mother replied after a pause.

His father heaved a great sigh and rubbed his forehead. "Kaleb, you'll never pilot in the Space Corps again. Running your career aground with Black Dawn was bad enough. But then to... to turn to..."

"I didn't believe it," his mother cut in, words like pebbles dropped on marble. "I said my son would never, *never* countenance throwing away his life like that. Everything he'd earned and trained for and believed in, discarded like trash. Never. Not Kaleb Hugo. But it's true, isn't it?" Hugo swallowed his response with an effort. "You could have come to us," she continued. "We could have stemmed this months ago – had you reassigned, re-trained. But what did you do?"

He nearly told them everything. The words formed on his tongue. "I am a captain," is all he eventually said, however.

"Captain?" his father grunted. "Captain of a crew that's not only got a Service record as long as the central skyway but also seems to be on the wrong side of Lunar Strip fences and terrorists."

"I'm not going back to the Service," Hugo said, raising his head and suddenly feeling calmer. "I don't belong there any more."

"Kaleb Hugo," his mother said, voice low and lips pale. "If you do not report to your unit in Siberia for duty within a week and humbly accept this chance we have pulled out of the mire for you... then you are on your own. Totally."

"I already am."

"Son," his father said, face softening. "It's not too late."

"Yes it is."

"Kaleb," his mother said again, high spots of colour appearing on her cheeks. "We cannot be associated with criminals and insurgents. If you make this move... you are no longer my son."

"Erica," his father said, but she raised her hand.

"This is bigger than us. Bigger than you, Kaleb. We belong to the Service. We serve the Orbit and protect it from the likes of your so-called crew."

"You don't even know my crew."

His mother raised an eyebrow. "I know enough. Make your choice, Kaleb. And make it now. But remember you won't get another."

"Kale," Giles said, watching his face. "Don't be a fool..."

"I am not a fool," Hugo said slowly. "And I am not Service. Not any more."

For the briefest of moments he was sure he saw despair sweep through his mother's face. But then it was stone again and she turned and left the den without another word.

"You're better than this, Kaleb," his father said. "I hope you realise that before it truly is too late. But even if you do, you'll have to make your way back on your own."

He held his father's gaze for a moment. What he could read in the major's face was everything he knew and yet everything he could no longer understand. The older man drained the drink he'd been holding and looked away. He set his glass on the side and the door clicked closed behind him.

Hugo stood staring after him. The anger was still hot but there was also confusion, guilt and a chilled finger of fear. But, underneath, there was something else... something stalwart. Something he thought he'd lost.

"Here," Giles was at his elbow holding out a glass. "You look like you need it."

His brother's face was more open than their parents' and all it wore was concern with a twist of confusion. He took the glass of blask and sipped it. It was the taste of the brand he had missed, earthy and sharp with the clean warmth of a quality blend, but he didn't enjoy it.

"What the hell do you think you're doing Kale?" Giles implored. "You were always one to push at boundaries... but this? You've gone a little far just to make a point."

"I'm not making a point."

"Then what are you doing?"

"This was the hand I was dealt, Giles," he said, finding his voice calm. "I have to find my way on the path I'm on."

"What, smuggling and gun-running?"

Hugo levelled his gaze at his brother. "You don't know the *Zero*."

Giles blinked at the heaviness of his tone. "Maybe I don't. But I know what people say. And that's enough to drift any remains of a future you might have left."

"Future is something Mother thinks about. And Father and you, Andrew and all the others. But it's not real. All I have now is who I trust and who I don't. It's honest. It's real. And it means I have the chance to choose to do the right thing, not be told what the right thing is."

"You're romanticising."

"I'm not *romanticising*," Hugo growled. "It's ugly out there. Fucking ugly."

"I know," his brother replied coolly. "That's why I fight for the chance to make it better."

"You don't understand."

"I'm *trying* to understand, Kale. Explain it to me. Make me understand what you're doing."

"You can't. You're on this side of it," he waved his arm around the den with the deep carpets, strategy books, maps and trophies. "You are told what it's like, but now I've *seen* it. I've been there. It's made me bleed and it's in my skin. I can't go back now and pretend I don't know. Even if I could... I wouldn't. I'm... free."

Giles shook his head. "Not in a million years would I expect you to see law-dodging, hacking and stealing as freedom."

"It is."

"Well," Giles said, looking him up and down. "Forgive me, Kale, but this bright, bohemian freedom of yours doesn't exactly seem to be treating you well."

Hugo felt his shoulders slump. He drained his glass and slumped onto the edge of a sofa, staring at the carpet. "Something happened. I..." His throat closed up. He shook his head and clutched his hair. "Something happened."

"You lose someone?"

Hugo swallowed. Giles had always been able to read him. "Yes."

"Who?"

"My commander."

Giles was quiet for a moment then came and sat next to him. "I assume this was a good commander?"

"Yes. He was."

"It's a dangerous Orbit, Kale. Even without going looking for trouble. And you've jumped in the pit."

"I know," Hugo growled. "Don't you think I know? It's just -"

"It's fine," Giles said, putting a hand on his shoulder. "Don't explain. I'm sorry." Hugo stared straight ahead as Giles pulled his glass from his numb fingers and set it aside. "Is that why you came here?"

He looked up, blinking until the room wasn't blurry any more. "I don't know. After... after that... I wasn't sure about anything. But now I'm back... " He looked around the room again. "I know I don't belong here any more."

"You got lost in the woods, huh?"

Hugo looked at his brother. He was smiling, but it was sad.

"Goodbye, Giles," he said, standing.

"Kale," Giles called just as Hugo reached the door. He sighed, rubbed his chin. "I know Mother likes to be dramatic. And, who knows, maybe she's right. Maybe the Special Commander of the Service can't afford to accept a son that's strayed so far. But if you ever need help... if you are ever really lost. Or hurt..." Giles blinked and Hugo waited. "You can count on me."

Even if Hugo could think of anything to say his throat was too tight to speak. He managed a nod. His brother smiled and then he left, knowing he would never make use of the offer.

Ø

It reminded him of something... this... feeling. He'd felt something like it before...

He tried to make sense of the stirring sensations. It was like being underwater. No. It was like being in zero-g. It was dark and empty and there was nothingness around him. He wasn't scared though. He knew of fear... he was vaguely aware of it ghosting around the edges of his perception. But he left it where it was.

It was warm, here. And quiet.

But as soon as he'd identified this thought, bits of himself began to find their way back. He was gathering more and more of himself together, like matter being sucked towards a star. The more that accumulated, the harder it was to stay lost. Mists of memory began to solidify. Feelings became more tangible. Reality started to gain substance.

He had a name... it filtered through the fog, formed and became real and then he remembered the person that gave it to him.

Suddenly, it was like gravity had been turned on and he felt himself fall. With a jerk he slammed into his flesh. Somewhere far away he felt himself gasp and cough. The burning sensation pulled the last remnants of his drifting self together. He dragged his breath in and out. Slowly, like a ship's systems powering up, he became aware of his head, shoulders, his back, arms, hands then torso and legs. Now he was scared. He was scared that it took him a moment to figure out what to do with them.

After a couple more calming breaths, Webb opened his eyes. He tried to cry out as the white light stabbed into his skull but it came out dry and choked. Something clattered nearby and there was a confused noise that he couldn't figure out.

He blinked again, more slowly. His head pounded and for an immeasurable time, there was only the thick pulsing of pain and sensations warring for attention. He kept blinking until his eyes did their job and a tiled ceiling came into focus. A steady sound nearby consolidated itself into the beeping of a heart monitor. He took a couple more breaths and the fevered bleeps slowed down.

Now that his hearing seemed to have untangled itself from his sight and touch he lay there listening, but all there was was the monitor. He tried clenching his hands and wiggling his toes. Waves of tingling broke over every inch of his skin. He kept still until it subsided, pulling dry breaths in and out and blinking at the white ceiling. He became aware of a sharp acidic smell. It nagged at him. He'd smelt it somewhere before but the memory slipped through his fingers like sand.

When the pins and needles had eased he pulled together his strength and got himself up on his elbows, paused whilst everything tingled and pulsed and his head span and then, finally, he sat up.

It took another few moments for his vision to focus again but when it did he saw he was in a completely nondescript white room. A hospital, he guessed. White walls, white bed clothes and a view of some tall trees out of the window. Earth, then? The door was ajar and there was a computer panel on the floor next to an array of blinking equipment by his bed. There were wires and tubes attached to his arms, chest and head.

As the feeling came back to him, everything started to itch furiously. His arm felt like it weighed a hundred pounds but he lifted it up and pulled out the oxygen tube from his nose and a couple of the pads from his temples and rubbed at his skin.

As he did so his hands brushed against his short hair and he froze. He swallowed then ran both hands through the cropped length. His heart monitor increased its beeping as it all came flooding back... the satellite, the death-grip the man had on his hair that loosed as he cut it off and then...

He put a hand to his chest. He remembered the searing explosion that had cracked him open and then blackness and then... nothing. There wasn't even an ache there now. He frowned and pulled up the white medical-issue t-shirt. There was no scar, not even a mark on the skin. He stared. All his other scars were gone too. And his tattoos. He checked his arms and shoulders. All his skin was unblemished, unscarred, blank. He felt for the familiar nicks in his ears and eyebrows but they were smooth.

What the hell...?

The door was pushed open and a woman in a medical tunic and a man in a white coat rushed in. They stood for a moment and stared at him.

"See, Dr. Yoshida?" the woman said. "I told you. He's awake."

"It's not possible," the man said, stepping up to his bedside and shining a lenslight in his eyes. This sent a fresh pulse of agony through his head and he cursed, but the dryness in his throat turned it into a hacking cough.

"Where am I?" he croaked, when he had his breathing back under control. The two medics were staring at him like he'd started spitting snakes. "Hello?" he rasped. "Can you tell me where I am?"

"It's not possible," the man repeated, shaking his head.

"Sorry fella," Webb said, raising a hand. "It's not an unreasonable question. Can you tell me what the hell's going on? Is this a Service hospital?"

"Service?" the man repeated, eyes widening further.

"Well? Is it or isn't it?"

The medic glanced at the woman who was picking her computer panel up from the floor, never taking her eyes off him. "Do you... know who you are?" he said.

This started tendrils of uncertainty uncoiling under his belly. "What do you mean?"

"Do you..." the man swallowed, started again. "What do you know?"

"Are you kidding me?" Webb said. "Who are you?"

The man swallowed. "Get security," he said to the woman who scurried from the room.

"Security?" Webb blinked as the medic backed off. Pulling out his IV, he threw the covers back and tried to stand. He stumbled against the wall, legs like jelly. "What's security for?" he growled. "*Where am I?*"

"Please... you must be still," the medic dashed around the other side of the bed and started rooting in a cupboard.

"You better start talking," Webb said, going for threatening even though he was having to prop himself against the wall. He made it to the door and locked it just as he heard raised voices approaching. "Tell me what the fuck's going on. Who are you people?"

The medic was too busy filling a syringe from a vial with shaking hands to answer. The door handle started to rattle, and then there were shouts from outside. Webb pushed himself up from the wall, staggered a couple of steps and grabbed the medic by the coat. The man squeaked, terrified, and Webb used his greater weight to pin him against the wall. He clutched at the man's wrist until he yelped and dropped the syringe.

"*Help*," the medic yelled, just as a banging began on the door.

Webb looked around. There was no other way out. He let the medic crumple into a heap by the bed and moved to the window. He was only one storey up and the window wasn't locked. He frowned, then turned back to the medic just as he started to crawl towards the door. He grabbed him by the collar, strength returning, and hauled him back away from the door.

"Pants," Webb hissed. "*Now.*"

The door handle rattled again and someone on the other side called for keys. Webb scowled down at the medic and the man started unbuckling his trousers. Webb shed the white medical-issue bottoms and pulled on the medic's trousers, too short and too big around the waist. "Coat too," he snapped and the man shook himself out of it. Webb went back to the window as he pulled it on. With one look back at the room and the medic, who was sat in the floor, eyes wide and mouth open, Webb leapt.

It wasn't a good landing. There was a car below the window and he dented the roof then rolled down the bonnet onto the ground. He lay there with the world spinning for a moment then got to his feet and ran, gravel digging into his bare feet. He threw one glance over his shoulder but it was a nondescript brick building with nothing to say what or where it was. The air was chilly and damp and the sky was grey. He took all this in in a flash then ran to the perimeter fence. There were no guard booths, no one on patrol, no alarm trips, just the wire fence and a couple of cameras. He hauled himself up and over, took one glance at the camera, and then was in the forest on the other side.

He ran. Every breath burned, but his legs seemed to remember what they were doing and he sped away between the trees, feet not making a sound in the soft fall of pine needles. He had to stop well before he knew he should and lean against a tree and cough. Everything was trembling. *What the hell is wrong with me?*

When he felt he was no longer going to retch he lifted his head and listened. There was nothing but silence. Utter silence. No whining of flyers, no roar of wheels on any nearby roads, no shouts or shots. He shook his head and pushed himself back to his feet and stumbled on.

A thirst unlike anything he had ever known threaded itself through his body. Once he had started to become dizzy, he heard the trickle of a stream somewhere near. He stood still, trying to pin point its direction but the sound was being bounced about among the trees. Just as he was about to give up and lie down in the pine needles, his feet splashed into a little creek. He dropped to his knees and started scooping up handfuls. It was the best thing he ever remembered tasting.

Once his thirst was dealt with, the knot of hunger that was his belly forced itself to the forefront of his attention. He shook water from the ends of his hair and cast about. Everything was silent as before with just a few birds calling their evening song somewhere high above his head. Night was starting to gather between the trees. He thought he could make out a darker patch of something further downstream and, not having anything else to guide him, made his way down toward it.

It turned out to be a large patch of brambles with mean thorns that clawed at his coat. There were black, knobbly fruits amongst the sandpaper leaves. He recognised them but for the life of him couldn't remember what they were, or if they were good to eat. His stomach clenched inside him. He cast about and saw that the bird droppings nearby were stained purple.

Well, if they hadn't killed the birds, maybe they wouldn't kill him. He put one in his mouth. It was sweet but with a bite and he swallowed and grabbed another. His mouth watered and he ate more and more. It was unlike anything he remembered tasting before, so wild and so real. He forced himself to slow down when his stomach cramped in protest and started gathering what remained into his t-shirt.

The shadows between the trees darkened further as he gathered the rest of the berries, then there was a great clattering noise as rain started pouring down. He was soaked in an instant. He got to his feet and peered around. It was only then the white light of flyer floodlights swept through the forest nearby. The engines hummed over the noise of the rain.

He cursed, praying the rain would dampen any heat sensors they might have and scrambled further down the slope until his feet connected with rock. The stream flowed over a tumble of stone then crashed down into a little pool before carrying on down the incline. He wiped water out of his eyes and climbed down to where there was a recess in the rock behind the little waterfall. He squeezed himself into the shelter and watched the lights sweep by and pass away. Then there was just the sound of the rain.

He sat and ate the fruit and watched the rain. Through the fog of fatigue he couldn't help but feel amazement creep through him. Everything was so *alive*. He watched the rain pitting the surface of the pool and reached out to let the water flow between his fingers.

Ø

If he thought he had been stiff when he woke the day before, it was nothing compared to how he felt after waking up from a night sleeping outside, on rock, in wet clothes. He managed to sit up before the trembling started. His teeth chattered and every muscle protested as he wrapped his arms round his knees and rocked back and forth, trying to warm up. He peered out into the grey dawn, fog wreathed amongst the trees like ghosts and he wondered if perhaps he should give it up and go back. Whatever the facility was, they had wanted him alive. There would be food and dry clothes. Maybe he had overreacted...

But he shook his head. Something wasn't right there. If he hadn't been a prisoner he had been about to become one and he didn't like the memory of the medic's needle, not one bit.

He had to get back to the *Zero*. He could figure everything else out from there. If he'd just busted himself out of a specialist medical facility,

242 Ø Chapter 15

well, he could apologise later.

He tottered out into the morning, still shivering though not so violently and, for lack of anything better to do, began to follow the stream downhill. As the sun strengthened he warmed and began to move a little easier though his hunger and thirst were both back with a vengeance. He drank from the stream and came across another crop of brambles but the aching from his insides demanded more.

He kept moving. He had to pause for rests and stopped himself several times from going to check his wrist panel. His feet padded over the pine needles and he wove between the trees like a zombie, letting the incline take him downhill.

Light that ebbed and sparkled up ahead brought him out of his dazed wandering some hours later. Stumbling forward, he finally came to the edge of the trees. He stood blinking and steadying himself against a trunk. A stony shore, narrow and steep, rolled down to a lake with a surface still as a mirror, dark water reflecting the blue sky and scudding clouds. A series of jagged hills rolled up on the far side, all grey grass and black stone. The huge metal blades of wind turbines spun soundlessly on the far side of the hill. It was wild and silent and amazing.

He stared until another cramp from his stomach brought him back to himself. He glanced up at the sun and tried to figure out whereabouts on Earth he might be but without being sure of the season he was struggling. He'd have to wait for the stars.

He glanced up the shore and tried to judge the distance around the lake to the turbines, feeling his heart sink. But as he looked further up the shore he made out a squat hut perched at the tree line, built from stone which was the same colour as the shore. There was an aerial and a rusted dish on the roof but no flyer, no car... just a wooden dinghy bobbing at a crumbling jetty. There was smoke rising from the chimney.

He approached it from within the trees, smelling the wood smoke as he got closer. When he drew level he tried to peer in the windows but ducked behind a tree as the door opened and a man stepped out. He was old, tall but thick-set with age, face obscured by a white beard and a faded cap. He closed the door and crunched off down the shore, disappearing around a bend in the tree line. Webb hung in the shadows a moment longer to make certain he had gone and then made his way down over the stones towards the hut.

The door wasn't locked. It opened onto a large room, deliciously warm from a low fire in a stone grate, with one door leading to a room in the back and a ladder up to a mezzanine under the rafters. There was a battered sofa and mismatched armchair, something he guessed was a stove, though he hadn't seen anything of the like except in pictures, and shelves full of clutter: plates, shells, bundles of net and piles and strings of mysterious objects he assumed were fishing gear. There was net hung on the walls and paintings of the lake and boats. There was no wall display or workstation.

He began pulling open cupboards. All the food was in tins, dry or uncooked. He felt frustration building until he happened upon a bowl of fruit. He grabbed an apple and started biting into it just as he heard the sound of boots on stone.

He swallowed, choking as quietly as he could and cast about. He tried the inner door but it was locked. With nothing else for it he scrambled up the ladder onto the mezzanine and sat in the shadows at the end of a large bed, as far back from the edge as he could. He heard the door open and shut. His heart pounded. He glanced about. There was a skylight over the bed. Clutching the apple in his teeth he started to crawl towards it.

"You know, son, if you needed help you only had to ask."

Webb froze.

"Come out now, lad. I'm not gonna hurt you."

Webb hesitated then, knowing his only other option was scrambling out the skylight and back into the forest, stood and came back to the top of the ladder. The old man had taken his cap off and was stood there with his fists on his hips. He wasn't as old as he had thought, he just had the skin of someone who had spent years in real weather. When Webb came into sight his tanned face flattened under it's beard and he openly stared. Then he gathered himself and beckoned him down. "Come down lad. You look like you need more than an apple." Webb climbed back down the ladder, munching, but hung back. The old man cast him a glance as he started opening cupboards. "What's the matter, lad? I don't bite."

"Who are you?"

"To you?" he said, looking him up and down with a lopsided grin. "Saviour, I'd say." Webb took another bite of the apple. "You can call me Mac. You from the Medic Centre?"

"Medic Centre?"

Mac looked up from an ancient refrigeration unit with a narrow glance. "Aye. Over the hill? You're wearing one of their coats."

"I guess..." Webb said carefully as Mac started chopping what Webb realised was real meat.

"What happened? Deserter?" Webb shifted, scouring his brain for a credible lie then Mac glanced at him and smiled. "Don't worry, lad. Just being nosy." His gaze raked over his dirty clothes and bare feet. "To tell the truth, I'm mostly wondering what kind of life you've come from that made you feel you had to steal food rather than ask for it."

Something shifted inside Webb and a rush of cold ran through him. Mac didn't press him.

"Come on, you look bloody pathetic just standing there like that. If you're not gonna help, get yourself up the ladder and have a look in the chest at the end of the bed. Some of my old clothes in there. They'll be too big for you," he said with another glance at him. "But they're dry at least."

Webb took another step towards the ladder and paused. "Why are you helping me?"

Mac's chopping never paused. "Not used to getting help, huh?"

"Not from people that don't owe me."

The old man looked up. His eyes were ice blue and seemed to look right into his head. "Well, you don't have to trust me. But make your mind up before I cook too much."

Webb examined him as he went back to chopping. He had started heating a pan on the weird stove and the smell of cooking meat filled the cabin. Webb climbed back up the ladder, stomach like a stone weighting his insides. By the time he had pulled out a pair of trousers (too big but with the medic's belt on the tightest hole they just about stayed up) and a threadbare jumper, he was feeling light headed again. It was only as he was pulling the jumper over his head he went to clutch for his crucifix to discover it, like everything else, was gone. He paused in the shadows with his hand at his throat feeling more lost than ever but shook it away. It took him a while to get back down the ladder where Mac gestured to the sofa then handed him a steaming bowl and a spoon.

It burnt his mouth but he didn't care.

"Slow down lad or you'll just throw it all back up again."

Mac sat in the armchair eating his own dinner and openly watching. Webb was too hungry to care and didn't look up until the bowl was scraped clean.

"Better?"

Webb nodded, wiping his mouth. "Fuck, that's good. Real meat?"

Mac smiled. "I hunt my own."

"You live out here all alone?"

"Just me and the fish and the deer," Mac said, finishing off his last mouthful. "Apart from the occasional student wandering in the woods for samples."

"Students?"

Mac stared at him. "Aye. From the Medic Centre. Didn't you come from there?"

Webb went still. He knew where he was. "The *Service* Medic Training Centre? In the Highlands?"

"That's right. You could spit on the Academy from the top of Bidean nam Bian." He nodded out the window towards the lonely, grey mountain on the other side of the lake then put his bowl aside, frown even heavier. "What exactly happened to you, lad? Don't you know where you are?"

Webb shook his head and rubbed his temples. "This doesn't make any sense..."

"You're telling me."

Webb rubbed his head, trying to force his thoughts to line themselves up but then noticed Mac was staring out over his shoulder.

"Speak of the devil."

Webb glanced out the kitchen window, saw Service uniforms, cursed and flung himself on the floor.

"Not company you're wanting, then?"

"I can't explain," he muttered, crawling to the lake-view window. "I have no idea what's going on... I just know I can't let them find me."

Mac looked to the door as someone knocked. Webb swore again and fiddled with the catch on the window.

"Relax," Mac said, putting a hand on his shoulder. "Here." He stepped to the door in the wall, took a key from a hook and unlocked it. The knocking came again as he pulled it open. "Get in."

Webb stared hard at him. But the knocking came again and he rushed in. Mac closed and locked the door behind him. Webb stood in the dark, breathing in the taste of dust. He put his eye to a crack in the wood just as Mac opened the front door.

"Good morning, sir," one of the Servicemen said. "We're sorry to disturb you."

"What do you want?"

"We're looking for an escaped prisoner," the same man replied. "Ran away yesterday."

"Prisoner?"

"He's a patient. Quite unwell. Mentally unstable. Could be dangerous."

"And you let him escape?"

There was an embarrassed pause. "Have you seen anything, sir?"

"Can't help you. Get it sorted. I don't want to be wandering around the forest with an escaped lunatic."

"No one's taken any of your vehicles?"

Mac shook his head. "Just come back from my garage. Nothing amiss."

There was a pause. Webb tried to see past Mac but he couldn't make out the Servicemen's expressions.

"You have the Centre's comm number if you see anyone or hear anything?"

"I do," Mac said. "Anything else?"

"Thank you for your time."

Webb stepped back, blinking as Mac unlocked the door again. "I'm not even going to ask," he said, shaking his head. "Just promise me you're not going to slit my throat in my sleep, huh?"

Webb came out, rubbing his forehead. "You know as much as me," he muttered. "Though, no, whatever sort of patient I was, I wasn't that sort. At least, I don't think so..."

Mac peered at him again and Webb felt a watery grin spread over his face.

Mac shook his head. "I know enough to know when I don't want to know the answers. You're welcome to stay as long as you need and I won't ask questions. Just don't do anything stupid like get me involved, okay?"

Webb frowned again as Mac cleared the bowls into a sink. "Why are you doing this?"

"Haven't we covered this already?" Webb searched the older man's face and then his own gut but found nothing unnerving in either. "Besides," Mac continued. "It's not as if you have much of a choice, is it?"

"I guess not."

"You got a name?"

"Webb," he said.

"A colony orphan, huh? Figures," Mac said, nodding. "Now come on. Since you're here, help me draw some water. You look like you spent the night in a cave."

Webb answered Mac's grin with his own and followed him outside.

"Wow," Webb said, leaning over the water pump.

"What?"

"Nothing," Webb said, jiggling the handle. "Just didn't think anyone lived like this any more."

"The Service keeps it remote around here."

"And they let you live here? Right between the Academy and the Medic Centre?"

Mac slung a bucket under the pump. "Something like that. Get on it then, lad."

Webb worked the pump handle. "Listen, Mac," he said as the bucket filled. "You got a panel or a workstation? Anything linked to the solar-net?"

"There's a unit in the back," he said. "Whether it'll still connect is another matter."

"Can I try?"

Mac gave him a look then nodded back towards the hut. "That keen to get back to reality, huh?" he said as they stepped back into the warmth.

"Huh?"

"Never mind," Mac said, taking the bucket from him and putting it on the stove. "Help yourself."

Webb watched him a moment longer but he didn't look up. Retrieving the key from its hook, he unlocked the back room and scrabbled around for a light. There was a switch on the wall that startled a bulb to life. The room was narrow, just filling the space under the mezzanine. And it was dusty, with no windows. There were lockers all shut up and odd shapes covered in blankets.

"Far corner," Mac called from the other room.

Webb moved through to a bundle in the furthest corner and pulled a sheet off a truly ancient workstation. He coughed and waved away the clouds of dust. After a couple of prods and a kick it hummed and booted up. He prayed under his breath and what seemed like an eternity later it engaged and he could see it was indeed still connected, though the link was so old it wouldn't be anywhere near secure enough to try and send a message.

He sighed and went about booting up a data search when he glanced at the corner of the screen and froze.

"Mac?"

"What?" Mac appeared in the doorway.

"Is this right?"

"Is what right?" Mac asked, coming and bending over his shoulder.

"The date?"

Mac peered where he was pointing and nodded. "Aye, looks about right. Why?"

Webb stared at the numbers, confusion chasing panic around his head.

"What's wrong?" Mac had to repeat.

"A year...?"

"What?"

Webb shook his head. "It's been over a year." He rubbed his eyes and looked again but the numbers still made no sense. "What... how...?"

"What's going on, lad?"

"It's not possible," he muttered, booting up a search and randomly scrawling the first new site that came up. "It can't be possible."

"Kid, you're not making sense."

"I don't know," Webb growled. "I don't know... I... Christ Almighty..." He covered his face, took a deep breath, willed himself to calm. "I got shot," he said into his hands. "I got shot and blacked out. Next thing I know I'm waking up up there..." he gestured at the wall in the vague direction of the medical centre. "And somehow... fuck. I've lost an entire year." Mac was silent. Webb blinked up at him. He was staring at the wall, jaw working. "I need to find my ship," Webb muttered, starting in again on the search. The connection was so slow and jittery that he couldn't skip between searches and he cursed, smacking the monitor.

"Calm down, kid."

"Calm down? *Calm down?*"

"You heard me." Mac's tone took on a dangerous edge. Webb took control of himself with an effort. "Look, obviously something's wrong here..."

"You fucking think?"

Mac's face hardened. "You're gonna buy yourself a whole new load of trouble if you go off half-cocked."

"What?"

"I'm saying, if you've been gone a year, lad, a little while longer's not going to make any difference. Offline and leave it. Get washed up and get some rest."

Webb shook his head. "Are you kidding me? I've got to find out what's going on."

"I think you'll agree that I saved your arse today?"

Webb blinked up at him again. "Yeah...?"

"Well then, in your terms, you owe me, right?"

Webb frowned. "I guess so."

"So here's how you repay me. Do as I say. Offline that machine and spend a night away from whatever fucked up reality you're from. Just one night. If you feel the same way in the morning I'll drive you to the spaceport myself."

Mac turned his back and left the room as Webb sat staring after him. He looked back at the workstation which had finally loaded some of his search criteria. His fingers itched. The *Zero* was out there somewhere. Maybe Hugo knew what was going on. Maybe he didn't. Maybe they all thought he was dead...

His hands hovered over the keyboard then he growled and got up and went back through to the main room. "What's this to you? Why do you care? And don't say we've covered it already."

Mac was stood at the stove with his back to him. "The water's ready."

Mac turned the stove off, nodded towards a tin basin on the counter then left the cabin, giving him one long look as he did. Webb's fingers clutched at the door jamb. He glanced over his shoulder at the workstation, heart thumping, then went back to it and turned it off, muttering curses as he did so.

Despite the mire of panic swirling just under his skin, the hot water still felt amazing. He washed his face and pressed a soaked cloth to his neck and shoulders. It eased the chords knotted from the night before. But when he looked down, the sight of his unmarked skin made him shiver.

Spend a night away from whatever fucked up reality you're from.

He drifted to the window that looked out over the lake. Loch, he corrected himself, and felt something catch in his throat. He reached to open the window, needing the smell of the natural air. But then the clouds shifted and the sun glanced off the turbines. His hand dropped. The Service Academy was just beyond that mountain. That made him think of Hugo, which made him think of the *Zero*, out there somewhere, running the missions the Service couldn't put its name to.

Without letting himself think why, he went to the door and stepped outside. The stones were cool under his feet. He padded around to the front of the cabin and sat on a bench propped against the stonework. The mountain blocked the turbines from sight. The breeze brought the smells of soil and pine. He sat and watched the water birds at the shore line and wondered at the numbness rising in his chest.

Ø

"Hey, kid. Wake up."

Webb gasped, sat up then swore.

"You okay?"

Webb bent over, rubbing at his neck. "Need to stop falling asleep outside."

Mac's beard shifted as he smiled. He had something slung over his shoulder. "Been to the smokehouse. You hungry again yet?" Webb's belly answered for him and Mac's grin widened. "Come on then."

Evening had drawn in whilst he'd been sleeping. The chorus of the birds clamoured in the air. Bidean nam Bian was a black cut-out against the pale sky and stars were starting to peak out over the trees.

The warmth of the cabin wrapped itself around him. Mac rattled around in cupboards for plates. The string of paddle-shaped pieces of fish that had been over his shoulder was laid on the side.

"Ever had smoked salmon?"

Webb shook his head.

"I'd never had it before coming here," Mac said, laying the pieces out on the plates. "Not the real stuff, anyway. You can get it synthesised on some of the Sunside colonies but it's nothing like the real thing."

"You're not from here, then?"

Mac clipped at some leafy plants on the windowsill, putting the leaves on the plates alongside the salmon. "Depends what you mean by 'from'. I wasn't born here. But this is my home now."

They sat and ate in silence. Webb loved the sharp flavour of the smoked fish. It tasted of woods and loch and sky. He had three pieces. "Jesus," he mumbled around a mouthful of salad. "I can see why you stay here."

"Can you?" Mac was looked at him keenly.

"What is it?" Webb said, narrowing his eyes at him.

"I'm getting on, you know. Could use a young back. Could show you how to fish. And hunt. And the Service folks don't come by often enough to be a problem."

Webb chewed, staring at him. "You're asking me to stay? You don't even know me."

"No," Mac said. "But I recognise you."

Webb almost choked on his fish.

"Not in that way, you idiot," Mac said, getting up and getting glasses from a cupboard. "Don't panic. It's just... you've got the look. The haunted look. Like you've seen too much. Done too much." He picked up a decanter from the sideboard and poured two glasses of amber liquid. "You've been given a chance, Webb. The same chance I got. You've been gone a year already...nothing to stop you staying disappeared." He added a drop of water to the drinks and held out a glass. "You could start again." Webb took the glass and stared into it rather than look at Mac. "Think about it," the older man said and drank.

Webb took a mouthful of his own. It made him cough but it was warm all the way down and tasted like earth and wind. "Real whisky?" He asked, swirling it around his glass.

Mac nodded. "None of the black whisky shit around here."

Webb grinned. "I know someone that swears by blask."

"Service, by any chance?"

"Something like that."

Ø

Despite his nap on the bench, when Mac turned out the lights and clambered up the ladder to his bed, Webb was feeling waves of exhaustion rolling through him again. The sofa was soft and the air was warm. But despite the weariness weighing him down like over-tuned gravity, he couldn't drop off.

He stared at the backs of his un-scarred hands in the light of the dying fire. He'd promised Mac one night. One night, just living and not thinking about the life that he'd left behind. The life that had left him behind.

But still he couldn't sleep.

Ø

"A promise is a promise," Mac said, though he didn't look at him as he closed the door behind them.

Their steps crunched as they paced down the shore. The early morning smelt like moss and dew.

"It's too late for me," Webb mumbled into the breeze as he trudged along behind Mac.

Mac didn't answer but just continued to lead the way down the shore then up a slope to a wooden building that held an ancient four-by-four. Mac drove in silence and Webb didn't break it. He watched the loch disappear in the folds of hills behind him, growing cold as he did so. They drove for well over an hour before the road broadened out and buildings rose around them.

"This is as close as I can get, kid," Mac said, pulling up at a junction where the towers of shuttle launchers looming up over the buildings.

"You're not allowed at the spaceport?"

"Remember the thing about questions, kid? Goes both ways." Mac smiled slightly at last.

"Seems you've figured me out without asking any questions."

Mac shrugged.

"Thanks," Webb said. "I mean it."

"I know you do. Watch your back, kid. You know where to find me if you change your mind."

Webb swallowed and nodded then climbed out of the car. He paused once to look back but Mac was gone.

XVI

"I can't go any lower, Hugo," the fence muttered as he leaned over the table. "My dealer is likely to lynch me as it is."

"This is shit," Hugo muttered, chucking the sample of metal back on the table. "I bet your dealer would sell it to me direct at half."

The fence glowered. "Too bad. He doesn't deal direct."

"Maybe I'll ask him anyway."

"He isn't here."

"Isn't he?" Hugo looked around the bar, letting his eyes linger on the more shadowy booths. The man glowered harder but Hugo hadn't missed the slight paling of his face as Hugo had looked toward the corner. "Ah," Hugo said, got up with his beer and turned towards the corner table but the fence put his hand out.

"Wait," he hissed.

Hugo paused then sat back down.

"Fine, fuck it, fine. A third the street market value. Final offer. And I'm warning you, you try to get it for any less from Lucwitz I'll have your name blackened from here to Sunside."

"A fifth," Hugo said, lowering his head to look right into the man's eyes.

The fence ground his teeth, glanced over to the booth in the corner then growled and drained his beer. "Fine. A fifth. If you transfer the credit now."

Hugo nodded, took the panel the greasy man pulled out of his coat, keyed in the dummy account codes and handed it back. The man glanced over it and threw him a keycard. "Locker 647. But listen here Hugo: if you ever want to do business in Pole-Aitkin again, you better not come to me."

"Did you get that name, Rami?" Hugo mumbled into his wrist panel after the fence had stalked away.

"Aye, Captain," she said in his earpiece. "Lucwitz. Noted."

"He's in the corner booth. Can you get a visual?"

"The cameras aren't great, sir."

"Just get a screenshot of his face. The Analysts will have to make do."

"Sir...?"

Hugo frowned. Her voice had changed. "What?"

"Someone's tripped the *Zero*'s access alarm."

"What?"

"I've got a reading on my panel."

"Could it be the crewmen?"

"Unlikely, sir. They only left for the trading district twenty minutes ago."

"How close are you to the dock?"

"Ten minutes, sir."

"Get there. Now. Take a weapon. I'll be there in twenty."

Ø

The lights were all on in the *Zero*'s corridor. Hugo took a step further in and heard movement from the galley. He pulled out his gun, not letting his boots rattle the grill flooring as he approached. Flattening himself by the galley door, he strained his ears but all he could make out was someone mumbling and shifting about. He stepped around into the galley, gun ready, to see Rami sprawled on the floor with a tall figure bent over her.

"Hugo," the man said. "Thank Christ. Quick, help me. She stumbled...I think she hit her head."

It felt like someone had dumped first scalding then icy water over his head. He pulled in a ragged breath then levelled his gun. "Who are you?"

"What?" The figure frowned. "Hugo, what are you playing at?" It was his voice. His accent.

Hugo took a step closer, gripping his gun in both hands to try and stop it trembling. "What is this?"

"What the hell? Hugo, it's me. Put the gun down."

"What the hell is this?"

The man stumbled back but Hugo stepped forward until he had him backed against the wall.

"Hugo, what the fuck?" His face was dirty and he was a touch too thin. His hair was only just long enough to fall in his eyes and there was something different about his face too, something that made him look younger. But the expression was his. The person looking out of his eyes was him. "What the fuck is with everyone?"

Red engulfed Hugo's vision. When he could see again, the man was on the floor and Hugo was on top of him, arm raised and knuckles stinging around his grip on the gun. The man was spluttering blood and cursing, arms up to ward off another blow. Hugo grabbed a handful of his hair and pressed the muzzle of the gun hard enough against his temple to bruise. Every instinct in him was screaming at him to fire. This was not who he thought it was. It couldn't be. He must be an enemy.

But his hand trembled. The face of a man who had once been a friend looked up at him through the dirt and the blood and all Hugo could do was curse everything he could think of as memories of all that had happened to him since he first stepped aboard this ship rose up in a hot wave of fury.

"*What the fuck is this?*"

There was a confused clamour of voices and then hands were pulling at him. Bolt hauled him off the man and Sub pulled him out of his reach. Rami murmured and sat up and then a silence like a vacuum filled the room whilst everyone stared.

"Put him in the brig," Hugo snapped, holstering his gun. "And get everyone back. We're launching."

"Sir -"

"*Now.*"

Ø

Once they had got far enough away from Pole-Aitkin for the harbour control's angry comm call to be cut off, Hugo had More cue up the video feed from the brig on the bridge viewscreen. The stranger was pacing back and forth, shaking his head and muttering.

"Fuck, you weren't kidding," Sub muttered. Rami tensed. The man that looked like Webb looked up at the camera then and tapped his ear, mouth moving.

More looked to Hugo.

Hugo clenched his fists. "Cue sound."

More typed in a command.

"-thanks for the pistol-whip, Hugo. Fucking nice welcome back that was."

"Who are you?" Hugo grated.

The man on the display raised his eyebrows. "You're kidding me, right?"

"I'm not going to ask again."

The man ran his hands through his hair and made an impatient noise. The familiarity of the gesture made a chill wash through Hugo.

"You've gone space-crazy. Let me out."

Hugo glared at the screen but didn't speak.

The man scowled up at the camera. "You might as well, you idiots. I programmed the codes for the door."

"You will sit down and you will stay fucking put."

"Or what, Hugo? You'll ventilate me? And the hull at the same time?"

"Sit down and shut up. Cut off sound. Rami, reset the brig codes."

"It's not possible," Rami mumbled as she typed. "I...I don't understand..."

"We're the only ones that know Webb's dead," More said. "Maybe he was sent to infiltrate us?"

"Not even the best re-constructive surgeon could produce a likeness like that," Rami said, gesturing to the feed that showed the man sprawled on the bench, scowling at the floor. "And even if they could, if you had gone to all that effort and expense, don't you think you'd match up his scars?"

"His tattoos are missing too," Kinjo said. She was stood in the corner furthest away from the screen. Her body was strung like a bow and her face was blank.

"Who the fuck is he, then?" Hugo growled.

"He seems to think he's Zeek," Rami murmured.

"Bullshit," Hugo said. "It's an act." But even as he said it, he watched the way the man gingerly touched his split lip, frowned at the blood and muttered and felt another shudder run over his skin. He gathered himself with an effort. "Could he have had a twin?"

"It's possible," More murmured. "Though Rami's point still stands. He looks like him alright, but not enough to convince anyone that knows him."

"Ask him." Bolt said. "Ask him what he remembers. Ask him where he thinks he's been."

Hugo stood grinding his teeth a moment as everyone looked at him. He cued the mic again. "Where have you been?" he asked, managing not to make his voice catch.

The fake Webb looked up. "What?"

"It's been over a year. Where have you been?"

"Uh... honestly? Not a clue."

"What?"

"I know it sounds weird, guys," he said, rubbing his eyes. "And I know I look weird too. I can't explain it. The last thing I remember is X6-119," Kinjo stiffened. "Next thing I know I'm waking up at the Service's Medic Training Centre, medics are freaking out around me and I'm panicking and jumping the fence. Then I find out it's a year later and there's nothing anywhere to tell me what's happened."

"That's all you remember?"

"Yes," the man shrugged. "Look," he said, getting up and wandering up to the camera. "I don't know what's got you all so freaked out... I'm a little freaked out myself... but you have to believe me. It's me."

"Cut it, More." Webb's face vanished from the screen, though his voice still echoed in Hugo's ears. Kinjo had gone very white. Rami was staring at the floor.

"I don't think it's an act," More muttered.

"It has to be," Hugo said.

"Spinn?" Rami said and the doctor looked up. He had been sat in the corner this whole time. His eyes were glassy and skin clammy. "Didn't you work in the bio research division on the *Endeavour*?"

"Yes."

"Could he be...?"

Hugo looked between the two researchers. Spinn swallowed heavily.

"They did take his hair..." Rami went on.

"For proof," Bolt said. "Whoever set us up wanted proof the job was done."

"Maybe not," Rami said. "I never did track down the details of the contract on him."

"So what then?" Hugo barked.

Rami's gaze was steady though her eyes were weighted. "Maybe they wanted his DNA."

"What exactly are you suggesting?"

"Spinn?" Rami prompted.

"Duplicating has been around for over a hundred years, Captain," he said. "In theory, at least. Though the technology and costs for cloning a human were always too extreme for the Service to consider funding proper experimentation."

There was silence for a moment. Hugo felt his fingers digging into the palms of his hands.

"Why would anyone want a clone of Webb?" More said, dark brows in a heavy frown. "He's a nobody."

"Is he?" Hugo said.

More shrugged. "We're all nobodies, Captain. That's the point. I can't see how his DNA is worth anything to anyone."

"Do we know who his parents were?"

"He didn't have any, Captain," Rami said. "His earliest memories are the streets and maintenance ways on Lunar 1."

"*Someone* produced him," Hugo said. "Has he never tried to find out?"

"He never wanted to," Rami said.

"Run a DNA test," Hugo said. "First to see if he is a match to Webb and then to see if his parents are registered anywhere. If he is a clone, he's important to someone. And it's not for piloting or picking locks."

"I'll do the test, Captain," Spinn said, standing.

"This is too weird," Bolt said, running a hand over his head. "Permission to get back to the hold, Captain." The crewman looked stiff, face tight.

Hugo nodded. "Kinjo?" She jerked her head up. Her eyes were dry but wide and he could see her knuckles were white where her fingers were digging into her arms. "You go with Sub and Bolt. Keep it together."

She gave a stiff nod and filed out with the crewmen.

"Rami, if this turns out to be true..." Hugo took a deep breath. It shuddered in and out. "If he is... has been... cloned... that explains the way he looks and moves and thinks, but how does he seem to know everything? The codes, our last mission?"

"Someone could have researched it," Rami said, gazing off in the direction of the corridor that lead to the brig. "Though how anyone knew what happened on the satellite is beyond me."

"So?"

Rami shrugged. "If Spinn is right and cloning a human has never been attempted before, Captain, it's possible no one predicted he could just... wake up with his memories."

"You think that's what happened?"

Rami took a breath but still didn't look at him. "That certainly seems to be what he thinks has happened. My guess is whoever did this thought they'd just be getting a body. It would have his potential for skill and intelligence. Maybe thy hoped they could teach it like a child, but I don't know."

"What for?" More said.

"Fitzroy...?" Rami mumbled, eyes widening.

"What?"

"Sir," she started, paling. "Didn't you say that Governor Cho-Jin's aide had been trying to recruit Webb to the Lunar Independence League on the run up to that AI mission?"

Hugo swallowed. "That's what he told me."

"I wonder how badly they wanted him?"

"LIL had no reason to want him that badly," Hugo said. "You said so yourself."

"Something's been stirring in the Lunar Strip though, Captain," More said. "I don't think we really know how strong they are, or what they want."

"There were rumours in Pole-Aitkin..." Rami began.

"And Cho-Jin did another speech last week," More said, skimming through data on the screen display. "Bigging up this conference they're having in Tranquillity. He's falling over himself to declare his loyalty to the Service."

"He must suspect something's going on," Rami said.

Hugo shook his head. "This is too big. We can't go declaring the Lunar Governor is a rebel and insurgent, or even an accomplice to one. And even if it's true... to go to the effort and expense of killing our commander and then cloning him? Where's the reasoning?" More and Rami exchanged glances. "Besides," Hugo continued. "He said he woke up in the Medic Centre at the Academy..."

"Any number of institutions commission work from the Medic Centre, Captain," More said.

"And their data is some of the most secure in the entire Orbit," Rami said quietly.

"I don't like this," More murmured.

Hugo slumped into the command chair and rubbed at his face, feeling wetness on his eyelids. "This isn't fair," he said into his hands. "After everything... him coming back..."

Rami turned away towards her workstation then, shoulders tense. More looked on impassively though there was a hardness in his eyes. "So what do we do?"

"We run the test," Hugo said, straightening. "Then we'll go from there. But no one tell him. If this is true, he clearly doesn't know..."

They all looked at each other, faces drawn.

"Rami," Hugo said after the silence had deepened. "Get ready to get me a connection to the colonel."

Ø

"Are you sure about this, Hugo?"

"No, sir," Hugo said. "I'm not sure about anything. All I have is what he's told us and what the DNA test showed."

"Which has him a match?"

"An exact match, sir. He is genetically a copy of Ezekiel Webb. Though beyond that, we found nothing."

Luscombe's frown was heavy. "This doesn't make any sense. The Service Medic Training Centre, you said?"

Hugo nodded. "So he says. Sir, don't you think this is enough to justify looking again at what happened on that satellite?"

Luscombe looked at him for the longest time. Hugo felt the blood pulse through his head and a thread of panic wove it's way through him. He stared hard at the colonel and tried to figure out if he'd made a mistake.

"Do you have a picture of this man?"

"Yes sir," Hugo said. "We've got the camera in the brig monitoring him."

"Send me some footage so I can see for myself. Then I will have Hudson look into this."

"Sir -"

Luscombe held up a hand. "You leave this alone, Hugo. Send me everything you have and then continue as normal. No one is to know."

"And what about the clone, sir?" Hugo forced himself to ask.

"He really doesn't know?"

Hugo shook his head. "It doesn't appear so, sir."

"Well then, as you have been so fussy with filling the commander's position you can use him to get the *Zero* back to full capacity."

"Sir," Hugo said, once he'd found his voice again. "Sir, once he finds out what's happened I doubt very much if he will be willing to help us."

"Then don't tell him."

Hugo swallowed. "Sir... it would be very hard on my crew..."

The understanding that had been in Luscombe's face a moment ago evaporated. "He is a valuable commodity, Hugo. And we need to keep him secure until we know who made him and what to do with him. You either use him or I stick him in the Command Centre brig until we've figured this whole thing out."

Hugo was tempted. Sorely tempted. The thought of having to work beside the clone made cold wash through him. But then he thought of having to tell him the truth and swallowed. "We'll keep him on, sir," he said, voice tight.

Luscombe nodded. "Good. Keep him close and use him while you have him. I'm impressed with your work of late, Hugo, but Webb was one of a kind. Try and get as much information about his networks and contacts while you can."

Hugo stared at the screen for a long time after the colonel had signed off. He felt ill.

Ø

"No, Captain," Rami said, shaking her head. "Keep him on? Pretend nothing happened?"

"These are our orders, Lieutenant," Hugo said. Rami's lips flattened into a thin line. Kinjo had gone stiff in her seat and was glaring at the galley wall. Sub and Bolt shifted uneasily and Spinn and More just stared at him with unreadable expressions. "We need a commander," he continued.

"This isn't fair," Rami said.

"Has anyone considered what's fair to him?" More said.

"To who?"

"The duplicate," More said calmly. "How can we let him carry on, not knowing the truth?"

"You want to explain that to him, Thomas?" Bolt said.

More looked at the crewman, jaw working, but didn't answer.

"We have our orders," Hugo repeated. "This is not our case."

"Sir," Rami said, voice steady now. "With all due respect, if the Service are investigating this... we may never find out why this happened."

"We are following orders, Lieutenant," Hugo said crossing his arms. "I am not risking getting any more mixed up in whatever this is. Take five minutes back at your posts to get your heads round it because I'm letting him out of the brig in ten. Dismissed."

Everyone stood and filed out of the galley in silence. Hugo didn't look at them as they did, instead trying to sort his own muddled thoughts.

"Captain?" Hugo turned. Kinjo was at his elbow. Her face was pale but her hands were clenched at her sides and she wasn't blinking. "I'm resigning my commission."

"Kinjo?"

"I'm sorry sir," she said.

"Midshipman, no," Hugo tried. "I know this might be difficult -"

"With respect, you don't know, sir," she said, voice shaking.

"I think I do, Midshipman. He was my friend too."

"Captain," she began again, voice no longer shaking but forced and cold. "I was born on Haven. I worked in the bloodgrease refineries since I was four. I didn't even know what living was until Webb came and took me away. He gave me my life. He gave me everything. And now I wake up from nightmares and find myself at the sink, scrubbing his blood off my hands again and again. I cannot do this. "

"It wasn't your fault," Hugo tried.

"I cannot work on this ship with that thing," Kinjo continued. "I cannot. I resign, effective immediately. I will stay in my cabin until I can disembark."

Hugo wanted to argue further but, though her jaw was clamped shut, her eyes were screaming.

"You were going to make Sub-Lieutenant in a few months," he said, though he knew it was useless.

"There's a resource satellite on the heading More has us on, sir," she said. "Please drop me there."

Ø

"What do you want now? A stool sample? Or have you come to hit me again?"

Hugo made himself stand straight and look the man in the eye. "I'm sorry."

"Are you?"

"Yes."

The clone frowned. "So, what? You believe me now?"

"I do."

"And all I had to do was beg, cry and bleed, huh?"

"I'm sorry. You've been... gone a long time."

The double sat up straight, looking him right in the eye. "You guys thought I was dead, didn't you?"

Hugo stiffened but made his face stay blank.

The clone sighed and got up. "Well my jaw is sorry too. Maybe I should have got on the comm before letting myself into the ship."

"Why didn't you?" Hugo said, still concentrating on keeping his tone flat.

"Honestly?" The clone grinned. "I was hungry."

There was a sickening moment when seeing the grin spread across that face made the heat bubble up inside him again. He could feel rain on his skin and smell the fresh turned earth.

"Captain?"

Hugo shook his head and he was back in the present. He gestured out of the brig. The clone looked at him a moment longer then preceded him out the door.

"So what do we do now?"

"What do you mean?"

"I mean," the clone said. "Where do we begin figuring out what the hell's gone on here? You're the one that's been around the last year... what even happened after I blacked out anyway?"

"The satellite destabilised," Hugo said, hoping his clenched jaw wasn't noticeable. "We had to abort -"

"It's okay, Hugo," Webb said, a half-smile spreading on his face making Hugo's gut ice over. "I agree with the whole no-retrieval-of-the-dead thing. A shot to the back would have convinced me too. And I'm damned if I can guess what's happened, but I know it's not your fault. So where do we begin? AI?"

"We're to leave it alone. Luscombe's investigating."

"Luscombe?" the clone stopped. "Does he know what might be going on?"

"No."

"Are you sure?"

"Yes."

The clone scratched his head. "Hugo, are we sure that's the best way to actually get the truth? I did wake up in the *Service* Medic Training Centre."

"We can trust Luscombe."

"How can you know that?"

"Webb..." Hugo paused, swallowed. "*You* always trusted him before."

"That was before I came to in a Service-owned facility after having lost a year and no one wants to tell me what happened."

"Just leave it," Hugo said, turning toward the bridge. "Let Rami check you over then report to the bridge."

"Hold up. Hugo, *hold up.*"

Hugo stopped as the clone grabbed a hold of his elbow. He felt his pulse hammer and he turned and looked into that face again, feeling himself go pale. "What?" he managed to say in a steady voice.

"What the hell's going on that you're not telling me?"

"Nothing."

The clone frowned. "Something's not right. Since when are you happy handing everything over to Luscombe without even knowing what you're handing over?"

Hugo searched for words. Having the double close enough to be able to see the lines of his frown under the dirt on his face was unsettling. He clenched and unclenched his hands and the frown on the double's face grew deeper. Hugo pushed everything back and made himself think of him as Webb. He had to believe that, somehow, it had been undone. He had a second chance. He had come back.

If he thought of it that way, maybe he could get through this façade without hitting him or having a breakdown. He blinked until he could look at the man without double-vision overlaying his sight and pushed back the chill of guilt that ghosted around his insides. "Look, Webb," he said. "I tried to get Luscombe to investigate after everything on X6-119..."

"And?"

"He said there wasn't enough evidence. The circuit board we got from the quarry got broken in the fight... as for everything else, he just didn't believe me. Whatever's going on here, Luscombe's not involved."

"He didn't believe you?"

Hugo shook his head. "We investigated everything to do with those missions and that contract out in your name. Anything that we could use to make Luscombe feel justified to look closer to home. But we found nothing. Nothing solid led back to the Service."

"Someone had a way of knowing where we... I... was going to be."

"That's what I thought," Hugo said. "But how and who, it didn't look like we'd ever know."

"And now?"

Hugo looked at him, swallowed again. "It seems finally Luscombe has something to move on. But we're leaving it to him."

"So we're supposed to just soldier on and pretend nothing's happened?"

Hugo gave a shrug. "It's like you said. You get screwed, you take your pay and hope you're still useful in the morning."

A wry smile tugged at the clone... Webb... Webb's face. "Wow, Hugo. You've gone native."

Hugo didn't smile. "Get changed, wash up and report to Rami. Then I need you on the bridge, Commander."

Ø

"Hey there."

Rami didn't turn round. "Sit."

Webb watched her not looking at him for a moment then sat on the medbay bunk.

"How do you feel?" Rami said, finally turning to him and examining his jaw.

"Feeling like I don't want to piss Hugo off again any time soon."

"Anything else?"

He blinked. "Fine, I guess. Tired. Hungry."

"There's some muscle wastage," Rami said, kneading at his shoulder. "How long were you in that bed for?"

"No idea. Long enough for them to do some weird overhaul. All my old aches are gone, Anita. They even gave me some real teeth, see?"

She glanced in his mouth then away again. "Have you been dizzy?"

"I was when I first woke up...but not now. Anita..." Her fingers froze as they felt their way down the muscles in his arm. "I'm sorry."

"What for?" she said. Her voice was quiet.

"For whatever's happened," he managed, feeling his throat go tight. Something went out of her and her face was washed with despair. He felt his chest tighten. He opened his mouth to try and say something, but she crumbled and flung herself into his arms. He held her tight and felt her cling on to him desperately, trembling.

He felt uncertainty fluttering under his belly again. Rami didn't do desperate.

"I'm back now," he said into her hair. She didn't pull away for a long time and he let her hold him, breathing in her smell and wishing he could ignore the claw of doubt that was digging into the pit of his stomach.

Ø

He felt a little better after a couple of protein drinks, a shower and a change of clothes. More's stuff was a better fit than Mac's at any rate, though he had to put a belt on its tightest hole again to convince the cargo pants to stay up. It was odd walking around the *Zero* seeing new posters and cargo moved or changed. The air tasted different. Hugo must have had the generator upgraded at last.

"Hey Sub," he said as he caught up with the large crewman in the corridor. "Are you picking up supplies? Think you could get me some shoes and pants that might fit?"

"I reckon so, Commander," Sub said, without looking up from his panel.

Webb watched him walk away, trying to pick apart the exchange for anything wrong. He shook his head and padded up to the bridge. Hugo was in his command chair, which had been scuffed enough in the last year to match the rest of the bridge and More was at the controls. The familiar bleep and whirr of the ship in flight made his spirit lift back up a rung.

"Where we heading?" Webb asked, sitting in his chair.

"Resource Satellite X10-899," More said.

"We should pick up some ore whilst we're there," Webb said. "We could name our price on Lunar 4... hey... what the hell?" He wiggled around in the pilot's chair. "Who the hell has been sitting here?"

"Sub," More said.

"Jesus, no wonder my ass-groove is all out of shape. And what's this?" He bent over the control panel, started keying in commands. "Who's re-calibrated the drive feeds?"

"Is there a problem, Commander?"

Webb scowled over his shoulder. "What the hell have you done to my ship?"

Something flickered in Hugo's face but then it flattened out again. "It's standard Service protocol, Commander. It allows for a smoother response."

"Screw smooth response," Webb muttered, starting to reprogramme the panel. "I want to feel my ship." He didn't get the argument he was expecting which made him uneasy but a glance in More's direction showed he had the slight tightening of his cheeks which was the closest he ever got to showing amusement. "See?" Webb said, still re-routing command signals. "Thomas knows what I mean. I can't believe you let him do this to the *Zero*, More."

"Sorry, Commander," More said. "We're coming into the satellite's space now, Captain."

"Hail and get us a dock, Sub-Lieutenant."

As More was getting the satellite's control on the comm, Webb went further into the command controls. It was like coming home. In terms of time he was aware of, he'd only been separated from the *Zero* for a few days. But it felt like his fingers were rediscovering everything, like they knew he had been away for months and months. It soothed him and he immersed himself in it, not even realising when More had handed control entirely to him. He guided them into dock, feeling every inch of the ship respond.

There was a clunk and a shudder as the ship berthed. Webb took a moment longer with his hands on the controls just enjoying the feel of it and refusing to think about anything else.

"Hey," he blinked out the viewscreen as the midshipman came into sight, crossed the dock towards the exit with a heavy pack. "Where's Kinjo going?"

"Leave her."

Webb frowned at Hugo. He wasn't looking at him. "What's going on, Hugo?"

"I said leave her, Commander. That's an order."

Webb ignored Hugo's barked protest and ran from the bridge and scrambled down the ladder into the hold. "Kinjo," he called as he ran down the ramp and into the dock. "Wait up!" She increased her pace but so did he and caught her by the elbow before she went through the exit. "Kinjo, what's the deal?"

"Let me go," she said, not looking at him. Her eyes were hard as she stared at the door.

"You're leaving?" he panted. "Why?"

"I..." She stopped, hoisted her pack higher on her shoulder and tried again. "I can't stay."

"Why?"

She looked at him then. He flinched at the hardness in her eyes. "Let me go."

"Not until you explain what the hell you're doing."

"You don't understand."

"You're telling me."

"You promised me," she cried out after a long pause. "You *promised*..."

"Iena..."

"Don't." She breathed in and out and he let go of her elbow. She stared at a spot over his shoulder. "Webb...*you* promised me I would never be scared and alone again... you promised me that. And then you were... you were gone."

Webb felt his throat tighten. "I'm sorry," he managed. "I didn't mean for that to happen."

"Of course you didn't," she spat. Her eyes burned. "You never think... never think what it would be like for those you leave behind."

Webb felt like he'd been kicked in the stomach. He looked at the anger flaring in her eyes and felt it singe his skin. "But it's okay, Iena. I'm back now. I can protect you again."

She shook her head. "You can't. Not now."

She swept through the hatch into the corridor beyond. The door hissed shut behind her and he stood there feeling boneless.

"She took it hard..." Webb blinked at a burning around his eyes and looked back at Rami stood behind him. "We all did." He stared at the lieutenant, trying to untangle the emotions warring in her eyes. But his chest was aching and his head was spinning. "Come on," she said. She hesitated the barest second then held her hand out. He looked at it for a moment then took it and allowed her to lead him back aboard.

Ø

Most of their dealings on X10-899 passed Hugo in a daze. Some part of him marvelled that he was able to negotiate trade without having to concentrate. He tried to sink himself in overseeing the exchanges and some much-needed maintenance on the *Zero*'s engines to distract himself from the cloud of uncertainty that hung around him.

Webb went quiet for a time after Kinjo left and this had Hugo on a knife edge, concentrating on trying to act normal but watching the clone for any sign he was suspecting something was wrong. But when the clone eventually eased and became more himself again, this only muddled Hugo's emotions further. It was like he'd learned to live without a limb, only to have it grow back overnight. It was getting under Hugo's skin. He was glad when they were back in drift and he had a mission to anchor him.

"There are plenty of traders along the Earth-side rim that would give us a good price," More was saying as he adjusted their course towards Lunar 4.

"Get us a dock on one of the spokes," Hugo said. "We need to check in on Calle and Javi whilst we're here."

"Do you think they'll have anything for us yet?"

"They'd better," Hugo muttered.

"Jesus, Hugo," Webb said. "When did you get so good at this?"

"Whilst you were off doing your sleeping beauty act," Hugo said. "Adjust course and get ready on the comm." Webb chuckled and Hugo felt a small smile of his own creep over his face.

Ø

"Are you sure about taking him onto the colony, Captain?" More said as he shouldered his pack and glanced across the hold to where Webb was examining one of the new motorbikes.

"Whoever made him will want him back," Hugo replied. "We need to draw them out."

"Very well, Captain."

"What is it?"

More shook his head. "Nothing, Captain."

"I know when you're thinking something you won't say, More."

More sighed. "It's him, Captain," he said with a shrug. "I know it's *not*. But it *is*. It feels like we're lying to *him*."

"I know," Hugo said. "But we have our orders. And if we ever want to track down the sons of bitches that killed him, we'll have to deal with it."

"Yes, sir."

"Glad to see you've not let *everything* go to shit, Hugo," Webb called as he re-attached the cover over another bike. "Though I think we need to have words about your stock in the galley."

"Fruit packs are healthy, Commander," Hugo growled, weaving his way towards the Jeep and climbing into the driver's seat.

"Healthy's for the dying," Webb said, getting into the passenger seat. "We're picking up turkey jerky while we're here."

"That was something I didn't miss," Sub grumbled as he climbed in the back.

"Aw, Sub," Webb said, twisting in his seat. "Does that mean you missed the rest of me?"

Sub grumbled and Webb laughed. Hugo felt something ease in him. He knew it wasn't real. He knew it wouldn't end well. But right now, it was like his crew was whole again.

Just so long as he didn't think of Kinjo... Kinjo covered in Webb's blood.

Hugo shook his head and started the engine. "More?" he called out the window. "Are you joining us?"

"Yes, sir," More said, pocketing his panel and clambering up into the back of the Jeep with Sub.

Lunar 4 customs took a thorough scan of the Jeep and a download of the inventory. The officers were efficient but surly, frowning over their fake gun licenses, and Hugo was shifting in his seat and growling by the time they had got through onto a groundway that lead to the colony intersections.

"I love Lunar 4," Webb said, smiling as they came out into the dull light of the start of the day cycle. "Everyone talks funny like More."

"This from the colony-born Yank," More muttered.

Webb laughed. "Hey, who are Calle and Javi anyway?"

"Just some fences," Hugo said. "We're coming up towards the industrial intersection now. You and Sub go with the ore. Remember we need lifter giros. Stay on the comm."

"Trade?" Webb whined. "Come on, that's boring. Let me come deal with the fences."

"Negative, Commander. They don't know you."

"I'm a likeable guy. Come on, Hugo. I wanna see what kind of points you've picked up on your own."

"Go with the crewman, Webb," Hugo growled. "That's an order."

"I see you haven't had the rod removed."

"And I see your near-death experience has not improved your attitude any. Let Sub broker the deals and sit in the background and be quiet. You have been out of the game too long. Listen and learn."

"Listen and learn," Webb snorted. "Not like I was in the game for fifteen years before that or anything..."

Hugo pulled the Jeep over and glared at Webb until he climbed out, grinning. "Come on then, Sub. Let's go have some fun."

Hugo pulled the Jeep back into the thin traffic of the mid-level groundway. He saw More watch out the back until Webb and Sub were out of sight. "Do we have anything to barter with, Captain?"

"They were looking for baranium traders last time we were here."

"Lucwitz won't be in business for much longer."

"Calle and Javi don't know that."

More nodded and lapsed into silence.

The Jeep drove into the shadow of Carlisle Block and pulled up outside *Su Casa*. The boarding house sign had been repainted in the last four months but otherwise the only difference was that another of the windows on the lower level had been boarded over. Calle himself was behind the counter in the gloomy reception, feet propped up on a broken air conditioner, watching zero-g handball on a display too large for the reception booth.

"*Hola.* Twin or double?" He looked up with a grin, took in More and Hugo and his face shifted. "Well, well. Back again? Business or pleasure?"

"Javi here?"

Calle's eyes narrowed. "Business, then?

Hugo stood with his arms folded.

Calle sighed. "Allana," he called over his shoulder. "Cover the front. Come on then, Captain."

Hugo glanced around then followed Calle through a door behind the counter. They went through the darkened kitchen then through another door into a room far more lavishly furnished than the rest of the building. Calle's twin was there, talking in Spanish to a video display in the wall. He looked over his shoulder as they came in, paused, muttered a few more words to a rather startled looking person on the other end then cut the feed.

"Kaleb? And Thomas too?" Javi said, smiling to show perfect white teeth. "I didn't expect you back this soon."

"Do you have anything?"

Javi came forward with an exaggerated shrug. "Come now, Captain. The sort of information you want takes time. Fences don't give their contacts up just like that, you know."

"I thought you said you could talk your way round anyone?"

Javi clasped his hands together, smiling yet more broadly. "Of course I can. And your collateral is worth it, I know. Patience, *amigo.* You will get your names."

Hugo glanced at More who was stood silently behind him with hands clasped behind his back. He wasn't sure what he was expecting to get from his sub-lieutenant, but whatever it was, he didn't get it and had to bolster his courage on his own. "I have something else to add to my collateral. If you can give me something now as a show of good faith."

The brothers took on the same carefully guarded expression.

"Good faith, you say?" Javi said. "But where are my manners? You think living on Lunar 4 with the colony Anglos for this long would have improved them. Calle? Wine?"

"No, thank you," Hugo said as Calle moved to a handsome cabinet in the corner.

"Are you sure? We have the real deal, you know."

"I don't doubt it. But we're in a hurry."

"You always seem to be in a hurry, Hugo," Calle said, pouring red wine from a decanter. "You should learn to slow down occasionally. Live a little."

Hugo ground his teeth, but breathed through his immediate reaction seeing Javi watching him.

"Go on then, Kaleb," Javi purred. "What have you got to tempt us with?"

"The name of a baranium dealer."

Javi and Calle were quiet for a moment whilst Calle handed a glass to his brother. "Just a name?"

"And a location," More said.

Javi sipped, dark eyes boring into Hugo. "Can this name be linked back to you?"

"Does that matter to you?"

"Why, Kaleb," Javi said, swilling his wine. "I'm hurt. Your welfare is very dear to me."

"Do you want the name or not?"

"Well," Calle said, perching on one of the deep couches. "That all depends. What is this show of good faith you expect us to extend?"

Hugo swallowed. "Just a name. Let me know if you've heard it recently."

"A name for a name?" Javi said and looked at his brother. "Seems fair."

"Go on then, Hugo," Calle said. "What name are you hoping we haven't heard?"

Hugo hesitated long enough to look at More. His face was still impassive, though he did meet and hold Hugo's gaze.

"Come, come, gentlemen," Javi urged, perching next to his brother. "No division in the ranks I hope?"

"No," Hugo said. "It's just a delicate matter."

"They are our speciality."

Hugo took a breath. "Ezekiel Webb." The twins took a mouthful of their wine. Javi looked at Hugo. Calle looked at the wall. The seconds ticked by and Hugo felt his heart beat rise. "Well?"

"He was your commander, wasn't he?" Javi said. "The one with a contract out on him about a year ago. Disappeared, didn't he?"

"Yes."

Javi and Calle looked at each other then. Hugo held his hands at his sides with an effort.

"Calm down, Kaleb," Javi said, looking at his expression. "You'll give yourself an aneurysm. In what context might we have heard his name, do you think?"

"Just tell me, yes or no," Hugo said.

Javi sighed and sat forward on the couch, elbows on knees and looking up at Hugo through his fringe. "This is a big show of faith, Hugo, I hope you realise this?" Hugo kept quiet and just swallowed against his dry throat. Javi looked back at his brother. Calle took another sip of wine then gave an infinitesimal nod. Javi sighed. "Yes, Hugo. We've heard the name. There's another contract out on him. Different terms this time."

"What terms?"

"Live capture only," Javi said.

"Whereas before?"

"If you want details of the first contract, Hugo, you're going to need more to trade with."

Hugo clenched and unclenched his fists. "Who?"

Calle sighed. "That's as much as we know, Hugo, and I'll tell you this for free, in good faith, as you say: we didn't know who put the contract out first time, either. Just the terms."

"Granted we didn't try too hard to find out," Javi said, getting to his feet and moving back to the wine cabinet. "But no one asked us to. If only you'd run into us a few months sooner, eh, Hugo?"

"That's all you have?"

"That, and this," Javi said. "You might want to find him before anyone else does. The return is worth anyone's while. You're lucky we like you or we might have put feelers out of our own." Javi smiled again, though there was an edge there this time.

"Now, Captain Hugo," Calle said. "This dealer?"

"Lucwitz," Hugo said. "Pole-Aitken, Southern Quarter. Ask at the Crescent Inn."

Calle drained his glass whilst Javi nodded. "Thank you, Kaleb," he said with another smile. "Pleasure doing business. Now, you'll both stay for dinner, yes?"

"Thanks, no," Hugo said, already heading towards the door.

"Come again soon," Javi said as the door closed.

"Captain, I think we need to get the clone back out of sight," More muttered as they hurried down the pitted walkway. "If the contract is as lucrative as they're saying, we'll have a hard time keeping him safe."

Hugo was already tapping a command into the comm on his wrist panel. "Commander? Webb, do you read?"

No reply. More tried too and still no response.

"Sub? Crewman Subune, do you copy?"

"Captain?"

"Webb? Why are you whispering?"

"Ran into a bit of trouble, Captain," came Webb's mumbled reply.

"We're hidden... oh shit." There was a muffled shout and the sound of Sub cursing and a crash and the link went dead. Hugo tried to reconnect with no luck.

"Come on," Hugo called over his shoulder, running down the walkway and splashing through puddles of grey water before scrambling back into the driver's seat of the Jeep. "Can you get a trace on their wrist panels?"

More was tapping at his panel. "It's always been difficult on a colony. The metal interferes with the signal... wait... got him. Head rimwards, captain. They're still in the industrial markets."

The groundways were getting busier with the rising day-cycle. The sky-ways hummed above them and the intersections in the trading areas were already rammed. Hugo cursed and swung them onto emptier side streets, More shouting directions and attempting to raise the others on the comm.

They rounded a corner and came up against a solid fence surrounding an industrial lot, the stalls still shut up. There was an alarm blaring some-where in the distance.

"They're in there somewhere, Captain," More said, checking the read-ings on his panel.

Hugo growled, climbing out and drawing his gun. More followed, clambering over the wire fence at Hugo's side and hauling himself over the top. Hugo dropped to the ground a second after him and let him take the lead. They raced across the tarmac, weaving between the stalls. A sleepy stall owner opened a window to peer out as they ran by, but pulled back with a squawk as gunfire rang out somewhere up ahead.

As they continued to weave amongst the maze of stalls Hugo began to think they would never find their way out again when there was a familiar voice shouting and Webb and Sub came stumbling round a corner. Hugo and More skidded to a halt and they ran up, panting.

"What happened?" Hugo said but they didn't have time to answer when a yell and the sound of an engine revving came from around the next stall. "Split up," Hugo barked. "More, you and Sub head that way, we'll go this. Whoever gets to the Jeep first get it the hell away from here and wait for the others to come in on the comm. *Move.*"

Hugo didn't wait but squeezed down the space between two closed up stalls and was then pelting across another storage lot, piled high with sealed cargo crates, with Webb at his heels. The sounds of whining mo-peds faded as they put more metal in between them and the main section of stalls but it didn't disappear and was soon joined by another.

"They're fanning out," Webb said between breaths as they vaulted a wall. They dodged a flyer, the pilot sounding his horn and swerving, then ran down another alley.

"What the hell is going on?" Hugo panted as they pounded down the alley.

"I was just getting us the best price," Webb said as he skidded around a corner and paused to catch his breath.

"Explain," Hugo growled.

"There's a couple of dealers I knew from from way back, always after good ore."

"You went to people that know you?"

"Yeah," Webb said, frowning. "What's the problem?

Hugo shook his head. "Never mind. This way," he said, with a quick glance at the wrist panel. The sound of traffic faded and they came out onto a trading walk. A few of the warehouse doors were open with lifters and mopeds coming and going and Hugo wove between them, Webb following close behind and glancing around.

"So you went to see these points?"

"Yeah," Webb said. "All was hunky-dory until they call in this new guy. He takes one look at me and draws his gun and starts shouting for binders. Whoever I've escaped from must have put word out. I'd be flattered if I weren't pretty sure it can't be for anything good."

Hugo didn't look at his commander but kept moving up the trading walk, glancing at his display for bearings. He was just about to put a call in to More to come and get them when there was a whirr and whine of moped engines and shouts from behind them.

Both men swore and broke into a run. Traders scattered out of the way and Hugo ducked down the first gap between the warehouses that was too narrow for the mopeds.

"Fuck," he swore as they skidded to a halt at the bottom of a ten-foot concrete wall.

"Give me a leg up, Hugo," Webb said and Hugo knelt and boosted the commander up. Webb hoisted himself up to straddle the wall then reached down for Hugo. Hugo took a hold of his arm and scrambled up. Webb managed to haul him up and they both tumbled off the wall onto a flat roof.

He took the barest second to glance around the scrap yard they were in then jumped off the outbuilding. Webb was panting behind him. They ran towards the gate then heard moped engines from the other side and skidded to a halt, glancing round.

"There," Webb snapped, pointing, then scrambled up a pile of scrap. Hugo muttered and followed over the top and dropped himself into the narrow space between the scrap pile and the wall.

"Webb?" he hissed. "Where are you?"

"Here," came Webb's whisper and Hugo bent and saw that the commander had managed to crawl under a gap made by some angled girders. Hugo shimmied underneath, not liking the sound of the metal groaning around him, and squeezed through into a space just big enough for them both to crouch in. Their panting breaths sounded intolerably loud in the small space and beyond that he could hear voices on the other side of the wall.

"They went in here," someone barked.

Hugo willed his breathing to calm and saw Webb close his eyes to do the same. There were more muffled sounds as men paced around the walls or rattled at the gate.

"Hugo," Webb breathed. "Can I ask you something?"

"What?" Hugo hissed, straining his ears.

"Is there something going on with the crew?"

"What?" Hugo snapped again as someone swore and banged on the gate.

"I don't know. More seems okay... but everyone else... Rami," Webb shook his head. "I've never seen Rami cry before, Hugo. And now she looks like she wants to cry every time she looks at me."

"Do you really want to get into this now?"

"I just want the truth," Webb said barely above a whisper. He looked at Hugo in the gloom. His face was still, his eyes were steady but there was desperation in them.

"The truth?" Hugo said. Webb nodded. More rattling from the gate and sounds of scrabbling as someone was boosted up onto the wall.

"Please, Hugo," Webb said. "Am I not owed that much?"

Hugo felt his throat tighten and was grateful for the semi-darkness. He pretended to be listening for a second. "The truth, Commander," he said, slowly, "is that everything on X6-119..." he paused, gathered himself. There was the sound of someone wrenching open the door of the outbuilding and a curse as they slammed it shut again. Webb watched him. "Let's just say I did not handle what happened well. The crew had to hold the *Zero* together. They had to hold me together." Hugo paused again as footsteps came closer to their scrap pile then faded away again. "After all that," he went on in an even lower whisper. Webb was still looking at him expectantly. "After fighting that hard to find a way to live with what we thought had happened... I suppose it's just difficult for them to believe..."

"Believe what?"

"To believe that you're back."

Webb looked away then. The men were shouting to each other and the increasing level of noise started to bleed through from the trade walk and nearby groundways. "And what about you?"

"What about me?"

"So the guys are having some trouble getting their heads round it all. They think I've been dead for a year. I can give them some time to come round. I owe them that. But I need *someone* to believe me. To believe *in* me. I need... you... to believe in me." Webb looked back at him. "Do you?"

Hugo breathed in and out, tasting iron, rust and dust. He felt his eyes burn and his spine crawl. It was Webb staring out of those eyes, but Webb as he'd never seen him before. He looked... vulnerable. It made him angry.

He was stood in the mud at the graveside again. He could taste the pine and the rain. His commander and friend was buried in a forgotten stretch of lake shore at his feet and no one knew. No one cared. And yet here he was, cheated even of a peaceful end and desperate to be lied to without realising it.

Hugo opened his mouth, then closed it. Webb blinked, face falling. "Yes. I believe in you." Hugo managed.

The clone closed his eyes and let out a breath, nodding. He surprised Hugo by grabbing him by the back of the neck, pulling him close and pressing their foreheads together. Hugo felt the hand on his neck trembling. Then he broke away and Hugo was left with guilt swilling around his belly like ice water.

They both froze as a shuffling clank sounded above them, then a muttered curse and a pair of boots appeared in the gap they had crawled through.

"Fuck this," someone growled. "They're not here. Get back to the market. Track down that fucking ship."

There was a shuffling and boots stomping and the metal around them shifted and groaned as the man clambered back over their heads. Presently there was the sound of them climbing back over the wall and the whine of moped motors starting up and fading away.

Hugo moved to crawl back out the gap when Webb stopped him with a hand on his elbow. Hugo looked back, keeping his face as blank as possible.

"You're a good captain, Hugo. And they're a good crew. I'm glad they came through for you when you needed them."

Hugo nodded, trying to ignore the ache in his throat. "We've got to get moving."

Webb nodded and they clambered out, jogged back to the outbuilding and hoisted themselves onto the roof and over the wall. Hugo hailed More on his wrist panel.

"We're not far from you, Captain," More answered. "Bear towards the rim and we'll pick you up."

Ø

More accelerated the Jeep away even before Webb and Hugo had closed the doors behind them. The groundways were busy but More got them back to the harbour in record time. Hugo struggled to stop himself fidgeting as customs once again inspected their vehicle. The officer gave Webb and Hugo, sweaty and scuffed with rust and dirt, a prolonged look before nodding them through.

Bolt stared at them as they all exited the Jeep back into the hold.

"Close the hatch," Hugo snapped. "We're launching."

"Sir, she's got to refuel," Bolt protested.

"Just do it," Hugo barked and climbed up the ladder behind Webb. "Get her in drift, now."

More nodded and jogged up the stairway to the bridge. Hugo hurried to the medbay. "Rami?" The lieutenant span round, startled. Spinn blinked in the corner. "Get me a secure connection to Luscombe. And do it fast."

"Yes, sir."

"And strap in. We're launching," he called over his shoulder as he hurried to the bridge.

"Just once I'd like to leave a colony without someone trying to kill me," Webb muttered at the controls as he input start-up checks. More got harbour control on the comm. Hugo itched as he had to talk them round their unscheduled departure.

"You'll have to file a cancellation proformer, *Zero*," the dreary voice sighed. "And submit your manifest again."

"Just do it, More. Quick."

More and Webb bent over the command panel, hands flying. Control finally relented and opened the dock doors. Hugo watched the commander closely, but he went through all the launch sequences with the same practiced ease Hugo remembered. He cracked jokes with More and grinned at Hugo over his shoulder as he did so, seeming generally more himself than ever. Hugo felt guilt wash up against his insides again and looked out the viewscreen, issuing launch orders he didn't need to issue, just so he had something to say. The *Zero* dipped and lurched as the thrusters pulled them from the gravity field and then they were easing forward into space.

"Heading, Captain?" More said.

"How much fuel do we have?"

"Not enough to get out of the Lunar Strip."

Hugo chewed his lip for a moment but then the comm on his command chair bleeped.

"Captain?"

"Lieutenant?" Hugo responded.

"The Colonel's not at Command, sir. He's already left for the Tranquillity conference."

"Have you tried his personal comm?"

"Yes, sir, but he's not responding."

"Keep trying," Hugo said and shut the comm off.

"Heading, sir?" More asked again.

"Just get us to the nearest colony. Webb, you will stay on the ship."

"For once I ain't gonna argue," Webb said and set about keying in course commands.

"Heading to Lunar 3, Captain," More said. "Approximate arrival in two hours."

Hugo nodded then watched long enough to see the men finish programming the course then shut himself away in his cabin.

The low fuel protocol kicked in and the overhead lights dimmed as he sat down at the table. He glared at the stubbornly blank wall display and spent the time servicing his guns and running through the ships systems and inventory. He was just stopping himself from pacing the cabin when his display began bleeping.

"On screen."

"Hugo." Luscombe's face was heavier than usual. He was bent close to the screen and his voice was low. "I'm in flight. Make it quick."

"Sir," Hugo said. "There's another contract out on him."

"On who?"

"Webb."

"You mean the clone?"

Hugo nodded.

Luscombe glanced around, leaned in closer. "Hugo, this clone theory is a giant tangle of dead-ends. There is no record of any such experimentation at the Medic Centre, either Service or civilian commissioned, let alone anything to do with Ezekiel Webb. Are you sure of what's going on here? Are you sure he's not some sort of agent?"

"The tests, sir," Hugo said with an effort to stay calm.

Luscombe shook his head. "Yes, yes, I know. Look I can't talk about this now. Come to Tranquillity. Someone wants him back bad enough to put a contract out, there must be a neck-level shit-storm brewing. Maybe it's best I take him into custody until we know more."

"Is that fair on him?"

Luscombe frowned. "Hugo, if your theory is right then that man is nothing more than the result of a potentially dangerous medical experiment. Keep him under control until Tranquillity then we'll find a way to secure him."

"Sir, you can't..." Hugo gripped the table, feeling his knuckles ache.

Luscombe's frown got heavier. "Someone like Webb turns up and you go right back to arguing with your orders, Hugo. The sooner we get him off the *Zero* the better. Dock at Southside Harbour and await my orders."

Hugo stared at the blank display after the colonel had signed off, breathing through his teeth until he felt the heat ebb from his face. "Hugo to bridge."

More's face appeared. "Yes, Captain?"

Hugo paused long enough to make More frown. "We have a new heading." he said. "Get us to Tranquillity."

More's eyes flickered. "We'll have to downgrade to sub-economy mode, sir."

"Do it. Where's Webb?"

"In the crew cabin I think, sir."

Hugo paused and looked away for a second, jaw working. Then he nodded. "Get us to the moon and get us docked."

"Yes, sir," More said and signed off. The lights dimmed still further and the air stilled as the cabin's air conditioner shut down. His breathing sounded loud in the ensuing silence as did the sound of his own voice arguing with him in his head.

Ø

"Descending now, sir," More said as the ship shuddered through the gravity field.

"Do you need a hand?" Hugo asked, seeing that Webb had not come back to reclaim his pilot seat.

"I should be fine, sir. Nearly there."

The orange-black sky of Tranquillity filled the viewscreen, criss-crossed with the glowing bands of skyways. The spacescrapers towered up against the dull backdrop. Southside Harbour was wide and orderly with hangers and a control centre as almost as big as a spacescraper towering over the berthed ships. He tried to decide if it was a relief not to be returning to the Northside Harbour and all the memories it might stir.

"Docked, sir," More said after the landing gear had clunked into the berth. "Running shut down -" More broke off, frowning as a light started flashing on his control panel.

"What's that?"

"The starboard hatch, sir. Someone's left the ship."

Hugo frowned. "Already?"

More nodded.

"Hugo to hold."

"Sir?" Sub's voice filled the bridge.

"Has Bolt gone to organise fuel already?"

"No sir," Sub said after a moment. "He's here with me."

More met his puzzled gaze with one of his own.

"Hugo to Webb."

More's face flattened when no one replied.

"Repeat," Hugo said. "Bridge to Commander Webb."

Hugo listened to the silence again and then went through to the crew cabin but it was empty. "Hugo to Rami," Hugo snapped into his wrist-panel as he jogged back past the cabins.

"Sir?"

"Is Webb with you?"

"No, sir."

Hugo cursed again as he ran back across the bridge then jumped down the stairway two at a time. The galley was empty and the medbay only contained a startled looking Spinn and a tense Rami. He ran to the hatch but it wouldn't open. He cursed, keyed in the code again. *Incorrect lock code* flashed on the controls. He kicked it and stormed back through to the medbay. "Rami, he's locked us in."

"Who has?"

"Webb. Scan the systems, find out what he's done and override his lock commands. Now."

Rami's jaw tightened and she sat herself at a workstation and began entering commands. Spinn blinked in a corner, clutching a panel to his chest. "Doctor?" Hugo snapped. "Do you want to help her?"

Spinn swallowed and started typing into the panel, forehead starting to gleam with sweat.

"Bolt to Captain Hugo."

"I'm here, Crewman," Hugo said and the wall display next to Rami's workstation flashed on to show Bolt looking stormy. "Sir, we can't open the hold doors."

"We're working on it."

Bolt took one look at his face and then shut off the connection. "Anything?"

Rami shook her head. "I can get around his locks, sir. It's just…"

"What?" Hugo said, roping together his patience.

"The history system's a mess. It looks like someone's been digging through everything."

Hugo went cold. "What specifically?"

"Well, our data banks and camera feed history look to have been rifled through. And it looks like someone monitored your last conversation with Luscombe."

Hugo felt himself pale. "Can you tell who it was?"

"No sir," Rami said. "But it was someone on the ship."

"Get those doors open. *Now.*"

Hugo stood and glared at the hatch, stopping himself from kicking it with an effort, replaying the conversation with Luscombe over in his head and trying to convince himself he was wrong about where he suspected Webb had gone. The red light still blinked on the controls and More stood with a panel, monitoring Rami's progress. After what seemed like an eternity the light changed to green and with a hiss the hatch slid open.

"I'm going after him," Hugo said. "You stay here."

"Sir," More began. "Shouldn't you take some transport?"

"We can't wait until Rami's unlocked the hold. Get her digging through any moonframe security systems she can get into. Try and find out where he went."

"Sir… if he doesn't want to be followed we won't find him."

"Do it anyway."

The customs agents at Harbour Control had no record of Webb. Rami confirmed there was no footage of him on any of the Control Centre's cameras. Hugo got through after an eternity of checks that made him want to kick things even more and then ran out onto a walkway, looking this way and that feeling utterly lost. He took a breath and closed his eyes and forced his brain to work. Then he turned left and struck out for the nearest shuttle port with a line heading Northside.

Ø

"Captain Hugo," Jaeger said, looking up from his bar display. "Long time no see."

"Have you seen Webb?"

"Who?" Jaeger said, just a little too casually.

"You know damn well who," Hugo growled.

Jaeger shook his head. "Look, Hugo, don't go getting me involved in whatever this is."

"He's been here?"

Jaeger shrugged.

Hugo leaned over the bar so that his face was right in the barman's. "Listen to me," Hugo tried to keep his voice level. "He's about to do something very stupid. You better tell me what you know."

"Had I?" Jaeger said.

Hugo ran both his hands through his hair. "Look..." he took a breath, steadied his voice and looked up. "Look," he said in a calmer voice. "Please. I just want to stop him getting executed for mutiny. What did he want?"

Jaeger regarded him a moment, jaw working then he leant on the bar. "I don't ask questions of my guests, Hugo. I listen to what they tell me, I serve them what they ask for. But I never ask questions."

"He asked for something?"

"I set him up with a point. That's all I'm saying."

"A weapons dealer?" Hugo felt the blood drain from his face when Jaeger nodded. Hugo pelted from *Sturm Hafen* with the drinkers staring after him.

Ø

He cursed himself for the thousandth time for not bringing a motorbike. He clambered off the First Class shuttle at Tranquillity Hall, earning disgusted looks from the finely-dressed guests disembarking at the same stop. The groundway was packed with classy low-flyers, hover craft and even a couple of vintage wheeled vehicles. The steps up to the entrance were teeming with more people dressed in expensive gowns and suits, all velvet and silk and glints from polished shoes, diamonds and medals. He searched for Luscombe without success.

Hugo took a step back and surveyed the tall moon-stone building. It glowed like a star in the white up-lighters. Projectors were beaming swirling starscapes on the sides of the building along with the words *Lunar Conference Welcome Ball. Building a Brighter Future.*

Uniformed sentries were checking invitations at the main entrance and all the other doors were guarded. He wove between the many guests and Tranquillity residents who had paused to gape at the spectacle, then dashed across the groundway and dodged between the surrounding buildings to approach the hall from behind.

There were no up-lighters here. No projections or limos. Servicemen there were, however. They patrolled the walkways around the hall with rifles on show. Hugo scanned it all, heart pounding. Part of him was nagging to just go on up to one of the guards and tell them what was going to happen. A year ago he would have done so without blinking. But the idea evaporated before it had even properly formed and he slunk through the shadows towards some trash skips that were tucked tastefully away in the shadows. He clambered up onto the them and pulled out his multitool. Keeping a careful watch on the nearest Service guard, he began unscrewing a rubbish chute hatch in the wall.

The security was good but Hugo wove through the blind spots without having to think. He checked the anterooms at the entrance, the cloak-rooms and all the alcoves in the entry hall, only feet from the arriving guests, but there was no sign of Webb anywhere. Hope that he had made a mistake tried to creep up on him again but he pushed it away. It was just that Webb... in whatever incarnation... was better at this than he was. Way better.

He slipped around a corner heading towards the ballroom, squeezed through a narrow gap meant for ventilation and found himself behind a heavy curtain. Beyond it was the clamour of voices, laughter, the clinking of glasses and swaying music. He edged along until he came to a sliver of light where the curtain ended and peered out. Arriving guests were be-ing plied with wine as they entered. They mingled on the wide, under-lit dance floor, expensive shoes clicking across the plexi-glass. Hugo could smell the wine and the food and the expensive perfumes. But he could also see the swathes of white velvet draped around the walls, creating a hundred shadowy hiding places.

He peered around, trying to detect any ruffle of movement out of place. His heart hammered in his chest as he spotted Luscombe at the edge of the dance floor, a handsome woman on his arm, talking and smiling with Governor Cho-Jin.

He tried to judge every angle in the room that had Luscombe on a direct line and noticed the first floor balcony that overlooked the dance floor, swathed in shadow from the curtains.

Hugo sank back out of sight and moved as fast as he could back toward the corridor without ruffling the velvet. He increased his pace and had to skid back out of sight just in time as a Serviceman rounded the corner. He waited out of sight, breathing and willing himself to be calm, before pushing on and casting about for a staircase.

The double doors onto the balcony were locked. He tapped away at the keypad, remembering the elementary hack combinations Rami had taught him and was satisfied when there was a click and the door popped open. He crept onto the darkened balcony, the noises from the ballroom echoing oddly in the curtained corner. He scanned the dimness, praying that even now he was wrong.

Then he saw him.

He had his back to the door and was knelt in the deepest shadows, Haven-made rifle poised on the rail. He was so still Hugo couldn't even see him breathing. There was a black cap pulled low on his face, the sight of which made something jolt inside Hugo.

"Put it down, Webb."

"That's not my name."

Hugo swallowed, took a step closer. The man didn't move. "Put down the gun."

He still didn't move. The people below were drifting into couples and starting to glide around the dance floor. Luscombe came into sight again, leading his partner amongst the dancers. Webb stiffened.

"You left a system trail," Hugo said. "You wanted me to stop you. I could have raised the alarm but I didn't. You don't want to do this. Do as I say and put the gun down."

"You're not my captain," the man's voice was heavy and it shook. He put his eye to the rifle scope.

Hugo dove. The shot went wide. A scream rang out below and the music stopped to be replaced by a slowly mounting hum of confusion and panic. Hugo was barely aware as he tried to wrestle the rifle from the clone. Hugo flipped himself over, using his weight to pin the slighter man to the floor. The face was no longer one he recognised, the rage in it was so fierce it twisted it into an inhuman mask.

The rifle went off again. More shouts came from amongst the scattering guests below. Hugo's ears were ringing from the shots. The clone managed to jab a knee into Hugo's gut and he rolled off, winded. The younger man scrambled away and stood breathing over Hugo.

"You fucking asshole," he ground out. "All the self-righteousness, all that honour. And what are you? A liar and a coward."

There was shouting somewhere nearby and someone was battling with the door.

Webb dropped to his knees, grabbed a handful of Hugo's hair then hissed into his ear, "This isn't over."

Hugo tried to scramble to his feet after Webb but he couldn't get enough breath into his lungs. The next thing he knew people were clamouring around him and he was being hauled to his feet, the rifle was wrenched from his hands and he was bundled back out into the light.

XVII

"You let him get away?" Luscombe thundered. "First you let him find everything out, then you let him loose in Tranquillity with murder in mind, and then you let him escape...*again*."

"He overpowered me, sir."

"Bullshit," Luscombe scowled. "You let him go."

Hugo stood holding Luscombe's gaze but not speaking.

"Find him. Now. Before someone cashes in his contract or he tries anything else."

Hugo swallowed, heat warring with ice in his gut.

"Captain?" Luscombe hissed. "Acknowledge."

"Yes, sir."

Ø

"Anything?"

"No, sir," Rami said, fingers flying over keys.

More stood at her shoulder but he was watching Hugo and not Rami. "He won't stay on the moon."

"He has to get off this rock somehow. Keep checking the launches."

"Sir," Rami said. "We have a problem."

"Another one?" Hugo said, kneading his temples.

"The Service have issued an official arrest warrant for him."

"What?" Hugo snapped and bent over her shoulder to blink at the warrant on the screen. "Luscombe... that bastard."

"Every Service member in the Lunar Strip will be looking for him," Rami mumbled.

"He did try and assassinate a Service Colonel," More pointed out. "I don't think even Luscombe could have talked the Analysts out of issuing a warrant."

"Sir," Rami said. "At least on the *Zero* we could keep moving and keep him hidden. But if the Service get to him first, whoever's got the link inside will find him for sure."

"Keep looking, Rami. He's... close to unhinged. He might make a mistake. More, come with me."

"Where to, sir?"

"To see Dolgorukov."

Ø

The Jeep ride to the scrapyard was silent. More called Dolgorukov on his personal comm once they pulled up under the floodlights at the gate. The small man was there to meet them when they drove through.

"Webb's not with you, then?" he said, peering in the windows of the Jeep.

"What have you heard?" Hugo said, climbing out.

"What haven't I heard," Dolgorukov said, eyes wide. "Hugo, it's all over the newsfeeds: a failed assassination at the conference welcome ball. The Service is up in arms and Cho-Jin is spitting blood."

"Has Webb been named?"

Dolgorukov nodded. "They've issued an old picture, but it's definitely him. There's a contract for his detention, an *official* one. I couldn't believe it. He's been missing for over a year and now this? What in the name of holy fuck has happened?"

"More than we can afford to tell you, Anton," More said. "We just have to find Webb before the Service do. Have you seen him?"

Dolgorukov shook his head. "Sorry, folks. I want to help, I do. But he's not been here."

"Are you sure?" Hugo said, staring at the point but his eyes were clear and the only thing showing on his face was confusion tinged with fear.

"Positive. I'd be worried if I had, the kind of trail he'll have on him now. I don't understand," he said, shaking his head. "This could have sparked another war. Why did he do it?"

Hugo glanced at More but the sub-lieutenant just looked straight ahead. "Will you let us know if you see him, Anton? Trust me, it's in his best interests that we find him before anyone else does."

Dolgorukov bit his lip, considering it then nodding. "Okay, folks. Only because I remember him being a good kid and that this can't be the real him."

"Thank you, Dolgorukov," Hugo managed. "We owe you."

"No you don't," Dolgorukov said, waving his hands. "Not for this one. I'd rather associates of the suspect weren't seen to be owing me favours. Nothing personal."

"We understand. We'll steer clear. Please just get the *Zero* on the comm if you hear or see anything."

Dolgorukov nodded, still looking pale. He looked from More to Hugo then looked over his shoulder but all the yard workers were out of earshot. "Listen, Hugo... I heard something else, not so far back... something it might be worth your while to know..."

Ø

The rage burned so strong and hot that it was like his being was carved from it. He could measure himself from his ankles to the tips of his fingers with the breadth of the heat. It swirled red-hot in his brain and he couldn't see straight.

Part of him was aware he was staggering blindly around Tranquillity and kept him to back streets and alleys out of instinct. There were shuttle rides and perhaps even ship flights too but he never pulled himself together long enough to figure out where he was going or what he was doing.

He ached to scream and yell and cry and kick and bleed. He came to himself long enough at one point to register he was standing in front of a mirror. There was graffiti on the walls and piss on the floor. There was a knife in his hand. He was staring at himself in the glass, breathing like he'd run the length of a flagship, and his eyes were red and his skin was clammy. There was a foul taste in his mouth.

The face in the mirror. The one staring back at him impassively. It was someone else's face.

He watched himself grab handfuls of his hair and slice it off at the roots. Seeing it fall in dark clumps into the metal sink hurled him back to the moment when they had sliced off his hair before the shot.

He snarled and covered his face with his hands, the metal handle of the knife pressing into his forehead. That wasn't his memory. But it was there, it was burning. He saw it, felt it. He knew the smell of the rock and iron and the feel of the gravel digging into his knees and the heels of his hands and the burning blankness as the bullet went through him. He knew it all, felt it all, carried it all...everything that made up someone else and it screamed and clawed at the inside of his head.

He blinked, breathing hard and noticing pain swelling in his hand. Shards of glass lay in the sink with tufts of black hair like debris strewn across space. He kept cutting away at what was left, desperate to make himself look less like the man he wasn't, feeling blood trickle into his collar from the cuts made by his shaking hand.

After that brief snap of clarity, reality became throbs of cogitation between pulses of confusion. At one point he was crouched between crates with the sounds of a ship in drift thrumming around him. Then he was stumbling through streets again. The taste of the air was trying to bring him back but he shied away, resisting the pull of memories that weren't his. But it got into his lungs and in his blood and he blinked to find he was staring at a door he recognised.

Doll opened the door. Her face went white. For a minute he thought she might faint. She stared at him and all he could do was stare back. And then it all went black.

Ø

"Look what they've done to me, Doll," he said in a cracked voice he didn't recognise. He couldn't tell how long it had taken to come back to himself but he was still shaking. "Look what they've done..." He sat at her table with his forehead pressed against the metal, head covered with his arms. He sat there, breathing into her silence for several moments. "I've shit you up, huh?"

"I don't know how to talk to you."

He raised his head and tried to smile, but from the look on her face he guessed it came out even more ghastly than it felt. "I know everything he knew. Remember everything he's seen. I *feel* it all. And none of it is mine. It's not real." She stared, face grey. Guilt surged through him to swirl and mingle with the mess that was everything else. "I'm dead, aren't I? I mean, the real me. *He's*...dead?" She managed a stiff nod, lips pressing together. He lowered his head back down onto his arms. "They didn't even let me die. After everything... after *everything*... they couldn't even let me just die."

"What... what are you?"

Webb stared laughing, shoulders shaking. "A clone. An experiment. A nothing."

There was silence then. He blinked his sticky eyes in the darkness of his arms, feeling himself slide towards oblivion.

The sound of her chair scraping made him jump. He sat up and saw she'd left the room and everything ached, right to the core. He stared around, knowing exactly where to look to see the deck of cards that Hugo had played Dead Man's Candle with, knowing in which book Doll kept a hard-copy wedding photo of her and Duran McCullough and knowing that the workstation in the corner sometimes needed to be re-routed through a back-up connection to access the solarnet. He felt sick knowing he'd never actually been in this room before.

The click of a gun-hammer behind him made him turn. Doll stood at the door, hands steady around the gun but face tortured. There was wetness on her cheeks.

"I won't let them use him... I can't let them... have you," her voice shook. "I'm sorry."

An odd calmness settled in him as he looked at the gun. "It's okay, Doll," he said, feeling a more genuine smile spread across his face. "It's okay..." She stood there and kept the gun level with his face and he kept on smiling. "Do you..." his voice caught. He swallowed and tried again. "Do you want to do it outside? To avoid the mess?"

Her eyes widened then her face scrunched up and she dropped the gun then slumped against the wall, covering her face with her hands. Great sobs racked her. He wanted to go to her, to put his arms round her, to bury his head in her shoulder and sob with her. The urge was so strong he almost choked on it. But it wasn't his urge.

He got to his feet and staggered back outside, across the alley, through into the abandoned lot. The maintenance hatch in the corner was almost too heavy for him after so long with no food or sleep, but he got it open and dropped down into the dim passage. He drifted along, head spinning, eyes blurry. He knew where he was but that just made him hold his aching head in his hands and want to scream.

He stumbled round a corner and came up against a railing. The air was filled with humming and clanking and the smell of exhaust. He blinked until the pit below him came into focus. It was filled with whirring and spinning machinery: the rusted heart that pumped the sickened blood of Lunar 1.

He stared into the maw and leaned over and further over and still further. He leaned so far that his feet left the floor.

Just let go... let go and it will all be over.

He hung there with the taste of Lunar 1 in his throat and its dust in his eyes and its wheels and giros and pumps throbbing and whirling and grinding below him for what could have been seconds or hours. Then he staggered back and collapsed against the wall. He stared at the oil-streaked metal surrounding him and breathed through the bile rising in his throat.

The grey wash of despair was being swamped by a returning tide of anger. He kicked at the wall, swearing. They'd screwed him over, then they'd killed him then they'd brought him back just to screw him all over again. Well he wasn't giving them the satisfaction of driving him over the edge. They hadn't before and they wouldn't now.

Shakily, he got to his feet and closed his eyes. He tried to pretend the gusting air was actually the breeze off the loch. His brain did somersaults when he tried to decide whether it was a second or a first chance he had been offered, but either way it was a chance. He thought of the little hut by the water and the boat and the taste of real fish.

"Hey," a shout cut through the hum and clank of machinery and Webb started and blinked round. A man was coming towards him, face grimed with oil, waving a spanner. "Who are you? You shouldn't be here... hey!"

He ignored the shouts fading to nothingness behind him and wove this way and that amongst the maintenance tunnels, staggering occasionally until he found somewhere dark he could curl up in. Now he had made up his mind the pain and the anger and the confusion ebbed to a dullness in the back of his awareness, to be replaced by everything else: gnawing hunger, sore limbs and stinging from the cuts and bruises where he'd staggered into things and cut his hair and a thirst so strong it felt like he was being turned inside out.

But he could deal with all that when he had the strength to move. Right now it was enough just to be still, inside and out. He breathed more steadily and let everything go black.

Ø

Another mouthful of the oily coffee helped Webb bring the screen into focus. The fact that the display was warped was doing nothing to help his headache. But he roped in his concentration, determined he could pull together enough fake credit to get him started without Rami recognising the pattern.

He pushed away any further thoughts of Rami and bent to his task. He could feel the café owner's eyes boring into his the back of his head and kept his movements as smooth as possible. He blinked a few more times to be sure he had done it then got up from the workstation with what he hoped wasn't too obvious a stagger and turned his grin on the owner.

"Thanks, buddy," he said, keying the account codes into the panel he handed him. "Don't suppose I could use your bathroom?"

The owner jerked his head at a door in the corner and Webb moved through, the coffee roiling in his stomach but providing some welcome heat and substance.

He looked in the mirror and flinched. The owner probably thought he was drug-addled at the very least. He washed his face, cupping hand-fuls over his shorn hair to rinse away the dirt and dried blood as best he could. When he looked back he looked slightly less grungy though the last few... whatever it had been... days?... had left dark circles under his eyes and his cheeks were sunken and pale. He almost didn't recognise himself. Almost.

He shook his head, then moved back out through the coffee bar, snagging a pastry off the counter whilst the owner was distracted. The day cycle was already halfway through. He looked back and forth down the street to get his bearings, forcing himself to eat the pastry slowly.

Now he just had to find a ship running to Earth and barter a place without leaving a trail. It would have been a piece of cake for Webb, but with the fatigue that gnawed him right to the soul and lack of food and sleep, it was taking a great effort of will just to make sure he avoided the parts of the sector where he was likely to be recognised.

He steered away from the trading streets and headed towards Aurora, the nearest megablock and one he hadn't been to in years... the former him anyway.

The express lift ascended on the outside of the structure and the whole of the sector was laid out in front of him. He swallowed when he saw Houston Block against the backdrop of the steely colony horizon. He told himself not to react... those memories weren't his.

Webb wandered around Aurora's spacer level, swallowing some noodles from a vendor on the food court, trying to figure out which crews would be dishonest enough to smuggle him to Earth but not dishonest enough to want to cash in on one of his, probably by now, numerous contracts.

As he finished the noodles and downed a third cup of water from a fountain he began to feel more in control. It was all still there, seething just below his belly like a pit of snakes, but he controlled it, picking carefully through his brain for just what he needed and refusing to look any deeper.

After asking a few guarded questions of a few even more guarded company frontmen in the Earth-runner quarter, he heard of a new company that did runs to Old Europe. A little more digging turned up that they hadn't been around long enough to want to try anything too daring that might cut into more established runners' turf, but stretched to skimming through an occasional illegal immigrant to make ends meet.

He got to the right level and wove through the corridors until he found the booth. It was small, nestled between a bar and... another bar... across from a few booths' worth of boarding pods. All the letters were lit up in the sign and a glimpse into the dark interior revealed a plain servicing desk with displays on the walls reeling prices, routes, ship capacities and timetables. It was empty.

He wandered in, allowing his instincts to rise to the surface just enough to judge how closely he was being watched, but the only camera he could see looked old and broken.

He stepped up to the counter just as the door behind it swung open and Kinjo stepped out. The smile fled from her face like it had been tugged off with wire. She stood and stared and he tried to untangle his tongue or find the strength to turn and leave but managed neither.

"You..." she said.

"Sort of," he said before he could stop himself. She stiffened. "Sorry," he said with a weak laugh. "I'm sorry. I'll go."

"No," she said, looking up from the floor. She looked him up and down then right in the eyes. She paused a moment longer then said again, "No. Don't go."

They stared at each other for longer than was comfortable. "I'm sorry, Iena," he said eventually, from a different place inside him. "This is all a bit fucked up, huh?"

"So you know?"

He nodded, running a hand over his untidy mess of cropped hair. "Yeah. Yeah I know."

"What happened to you?"

He shook his head. "Oh, went to hell and back."

"Do you have to talk like him?" she snapped. Her eyes widened. "Sorry," she said, putting a hand to her forehead. "I'm sorry. That wasn't fair. I'm not angry with you."

"I just happen to be the closest approximation to who you are angry with," he said again, trying another grin.

This time she smiled a thin smile. "Something like that. So you ditched the *Zero*, then?"

Webb attempted to ignore the flare of pain this sparked in his chest. "I guess so. Though does it count as ditching if you never really belonged there?"

She shrugged. "Maybe not."

"So this is where you ended up, huh?" Webb said, glancing around the booth. "Not bad for Lunar 1, I guess."

"Better than Haven," she said.

"Aye," Webb muttered. "Look, Kinjo. I want to get to Earth. I'm going to disappear. It's best for everyone."

"Whereabouts?"

"Old Europe," Webb hedged, watching her closely.

She started tapping some things into a panel in the counter. "Well, you're in luck. We've got a run scheduled..." She paused, glaring at the panel, her hand over it, frozen. "I... I think I owe you an apology."

He came forward and, ignoring the part of him that told him it was a bad idea, took her hand in his. She stared at it. "We're both sorry. But I think I'm more sorry. I'll find another runner -"

"No," she raised her head and looked at him with steady eyes. "No... look... it's just. Damn it this is just too... I don't know."

"Don't beat yourself up. I don't think there is any established etiquette for how to converse with a clone of your dead crewmate."

She looked so pained for a moment that the regret swamped him. "I guess not."

"I'll go," he said.

"No, wait..." she floundered. "How about a drink?"

He blinked at her. "A drink?"

"Yes, you know," she said. "Liquid, preferably with alcohol, that you put in your mouth and swallow?"

He smiled. "Yes, yes, Kinjo. It's just... is that a good idea?"

She let the corner of her mouth twitch. "I think I can handle it. If you can?"

"Okay. Sure. I'd like that."

Kinjo nodded. "I'll meet you in *Armstrong's* next door. Just give me a minute to close up."

When he was sat sipping at a bottled beer, glancing around the grimy hole that was *Armstrong's*, he wondered whether he'd made a massive mistake. But the place was next to empty and was so dimly lit that even if someone else came in he doubted they'd be able to recognise him. Kinjo came in and tapped her order into the bar without speaking. A panel slid aside and she grabbed her beer but then just sat on her stool, pulling at the label.

"I don't want to say I told you so..." Webb said when she still hadn't said anything.

"I felt like we should talk," she murmured, still staring at her drink.

"I don't know if I'm going to be able to tell you anything that will make you feel any better."

She closed her eyes a moment but then opened them and looked at him.

"Except," he continued after pushing down memories of Kinjo as a little girl, bruised and terrified, clinging to his leg and begging him to take her with him. "I can tell you that he loved you. He cared for you. If he knew he'd hurt you-"

"I know," she cut him off, swallowing a mouthful of beer. "I already know all that, I think. But you're right. It doesn't make it any better."

"Do you think..." he began, looking at his bottle and not at her. "Do you think we might just possibly be the two most shat-upon fuckers in this whole fucked-up Orbit?"

She gave another weak smile. "I think we're close contenders, at least."

He nodded, drank again. "Iena -"

"Don't," she said, a little firmer, looking over her shoulder. "Don't say any more. I wanted to come here to get a chance to say I'm sorry. Properly."

"You don't need to be sorry."

"Yes I do."

He frowned. She was glaring at him, knuckles white around the drink, eyes shining and lips thin.

"What's going on??"

"You aren't Webb. You can't carry on pretending you are."

"I'm not... I'm not pretending," he said. "I'm trying, Christ, I'm trying, to untangle myself from him... but everything I know and think and remember is-"

"Stolen."

He blinked at her, feeling coldness wash up under his stomach. She stood, leaving her beer on the bar. Webb looked over her shoulder to see two large men in suits stood in the door. They scanned the empty bar then walked over. Kinjo backed away, not looking at him.

"Has the credit been transferred?" she said as they took up position between him and the door.

"Is this definitely it?" one of the men said, eyeing Webb suspiciously.

"It is."

The first man nodded to the second and he pulled a panel from his pocket and tapped a few keys. "Then it's done."

Kinjo nodded, threw him one glance that struck him like a blow and left. The bigger of the two men pulled out a gun and let it dangle at his side. "Now. We can do this the easy way or the even easier way."

Ø

"Are you sure that's him? I never saw the Ezekiel I remember in such a state."

"You never saw him brought back from the dead just to be fucked over."

Evangeline came forward with a wrinkled nose. "Well it certainly sounds like him."

"The girl said it was," one of the men said, shoving him further into the room.

"And she would know," said Evangeline in a soft voice. "My dear, what on earth have you done to yourself?"

Webb glowered at her.

"It is all a great shame, really," she continued with a sigh. "I was rather fond of him, you know."

"So you know everything?"

"Oh yes, darling, I know. One of the few who do, I suspect. Most people he knew haven't a clue he's even gone. Tragic, really, when you think about it. How did it happen?"

Webb ground his teeth, heat pulsing behind his eyes. He tested the binders again but they didn't budge.

Evangeline shook her head and turned to a black marble bar in the corner of her office. "But yes for the record I do think this is a miserable business. But one can't be too choosy. A girl's got to eat, you know. And after that little snafu with your crew... sorry," she smiled. "*Webb's* crew and the Splinters' warehouse... well, darling, that left me in a bit of a spot. Have to make amends somehow."

"It's the same people who recruited the Splinters that are looking for me?"

Evangeline arched an eyebrow, dropping a slice of lemon into her clear drink. "Come, come, my love. I thought you were clever."

"Who?"

A slow smile spread across her mouth. She stirred her drink with a black cocktail stick and paced forward, pale eyes measuring him. "You really do remember everything he does, then? How curious. I'm almost sorry I've got to give you up. It's all rather fascinating, don't you think?"

Webb spat on the floor at her feet. The men grabbed him and slammed him against the wall. Evangeline took a sip of her drink then shook her head.

"Dear, dear. And you used to have such charm. Still, I can't say I wouldn't be upset too. I've seen all I need to. Lock him in the small conference room and let our contact know they can pick him up at their earliest convenience. And whilst you're at it," she called as the men started to hustle him towards the door. "Remind them that this is us square. I do not take kindly to the way they have handled this matter."

She turned her back and he was manhandled out of the room and down the corridor. They went through a door and another and then he was bundled into a room so bright it made his head ache. There was a table and chairs, a wall display and a camera. They locked the door behind him.

Dizziness overtook him and he sat down heavily on the floor. He sat with his forehead pressed to his knees, not even able to summon the will to have a look at the door lock. There was the sound of someone coming in and something being put on the table but he didn't raise his head until they'd gone.

He made himself get up. There was a tumbler of water, a hard biscuit and a couple of ration bars on the table. He made himself eat slowly, fumbling a little because of his bound hands and sipped the water. He felt his head clear and his insides stop aching. He stole glances at the camera as he ate and his fingers itched for a multi-tool.

Swallowing the last mouthful he wandered to the wall and turned away from the camera, pretending to examine a digiprint of a starscape. He took a deep breath then folded his thumb in until it strained against its joint and pulled, taking care to try and not let the exertion show across his back. The tendons in his wrist and hand screamed and the skin split but the blood helped slick his wrist. He twisted it a little, biting down on the inside of his cheek and with a jerk he nearly didn't manage to disguise, his right hand slipped free. After taking a second to breathe through the pain of his thumb slipping back into place, he wandered to the corner furthest away from the camera and slumped to the floor with his hands in his lap and his forehead on his knees. He kept still enough to look like he'd fallen asleep but sat and listened, his breathing shallow.

He needn't have strained his hearing. The heavy boots of the approaching spacers could be heard well before they opened the door.

"That's it?" someone grunted. "Jesus what a pathetic sack of shit. They've got their work cut out for them, that's for sure."

"Alright you," a woman's voice commanded, and then he felt the muzzle of a gun poking him in the shoulder. "Up you get."

Webb leapt to his feet and wrenched the gun from the woman before she even had time to swear, then kicked her feet from under her and fired at the second mercenary. But his aim was sloppy and the man ducked out the way. Webb ran for the door. One of Evangeline's hulking bodyguards was in the room beyond but Webb managed to duck under his grasp and then was pelting down the corridor.

Shouts and swearing clamoured after him. He wove down the corridors, finding a metal stairway down to the lounge of the Seven Sisters. He burst out a door behind the bar, someone nearby shattering a glass as he vaulted over it and made for the exit.

He was so focused on the open doors that he didn't see the second of Evangeline's guards stood in the shadows until it was too late. He tried to skitter to the side but tripped and the man brought him down and pinned him to the floor. The wind was knocked right out of him and spots danced before his eyes. More hands grabbed at him and he kicked and punched and scratched, blind and furious, but there were too many and he was too dizzy and someone landed a blow on his temple that sent him reeling.

When he came to, head pounding, he was being shoved into the back of a large flyer with the mercenaries, each with a gun ready.

"Don't even fucking think it," the man hissed, seeing him coming back to himself. This time his hands were bound behind him and it was all he could do just to stay upright.

When his vision had stopped swimming he tried to get a closer look at his captors, but nothing about their clothes, faces or flyer gave him any sort of clue of who they might be. He peered out the window but his head hurt too much to make sense of their direction..

He must have passed out again because the next thing he was aware of was the clunk of the flyer engine shutting down and being manhandled out the door. He blinked up and around the huge hold he was in, packed with flyers, fighters and cargo. Crewmen and technicians watched them as they passed and their heavy gazes sent a finger of fear crawling up his spine.

He was forced out of the hold and down a corridor, though his escort had to support him as he struggled to get his feet under him, cursing and shaking him as they did.

"You do that all you want," he mumbled at their feet. "But I'm telling you now, when I hurl it's going on your shoes."

"This is really him?" the man on his right mumbled when he'd finished swearing but the woman shushed him.

More glances from the crew lingered on him as they passed. About the third time Webb saw a crescent-moon pin on their jumpsuits, the creeping realisation gathered strength. When he saw ship's name, *Tide*, flashing on the screen of a workstation he felt his stomach tie itself in a knot.

The floor shook and the humming of the ship took on a higher note. They passed a viewscreen just in time for him to see Lunar 1 fall away into the inky blackness like a pebble dropped into a pit. A dizzying series of passages later and they took him through a door guarded by a man with a large gun who only nodded them through once his escort had turned up their lapels to show two more crescent-moon pins.

"You're fucking LIL, aren't you?" he growled and earned another shake.

"Wait, wait," someone called behind them.

"Oh hell," the man muttered.

"Be careful!" The shrillness of the voice struck a chord of memory and Webb craned his neck. He recognised the flushed face and small stature of the man from the Medic Centre he had stolen clothes from.

"Look, doc, you can look at him once he's secure."

"What have you done to him?" the small man cried as he ran up to them.

"Open number three," the woman called and one of the doors slid open. The cell contained nothing except a hard bench and a camera.

Webb was shoved in.

"*Careful*," the medic hissed again. "Look at the state of him." He tutted as he pulled Webb round to look at him.

"What the hell is going on?" Webb snapped.

The medic tutted and took a hold of his chin, turned his face this way and that, looking in his eyes and muttering over the healing cuts on his head and bruising on his face. "This is not good enough. Look at this, and this!"

"Look, doc," the woman growled from the door. "The little shit was already in a state when we got him."

"And he fights like a rat," the man added rubbing at scratches on his neck. "You're lucky it's not worse."

"Sit," the medic said, indicating the bench. Webb just glared at him. The little medic looked confused, chewing on his lip. "Sit, please."

Webb glanced from the twitchy medic to the two mercenaries scowling in the door and slumped down on the bench. The medic proceeded to poke and prod at him, mumbling to himself in Japanese and entering notes into a pocket-panel. He shook his head sadly. "And he was next to perfect."

"Well, doc, maybe you shouldn't have let him escape."

"I did no such thing," the medic grumbled. "This had never been done before. There was no way to predict -"

"No security, you said," the woman growled. "He'll wake up like a newborn, you said."

The medic span. "I had twenty years of research behind my decision. I also know that when security is involved, this is what happens," he said gesturing at Webb's face.

"Hey," Webb snapped. "I'm a clone, not a moron." The medic blinked at him and the two LIL mercenaries glowered at him. "Do I even get the courtesy of being told what this is all about?"

"You know, Ezekiel... I've suffered a lot of disappointment in my life but I think you were the worst."

"Fitzroy?" Webb stammered as the short man stepped into his cell. The medic ceased poking at him and backed into a corner, turning his panel over in his fingers.

The bald man folded his arms and shook his head, a vaguely disgusted look on his face. "You were a pain in the ass then and an even bigger one now."

"*What is going on?*"

"I gave you, well, *him*, a chance, Webb. A real chance. He could have been Governor. He could have led the colonies to independence. But no. And now look at you. Even when created from scratch you're still a gutter-shit."

"Governor? You were going to make Webb Lunar Governor? That was your plan?" Webb laughed. "Herman, when was the last time you had a psych evaluation?"

"You know, I really thought you knew. I thought that was why you wouldn't listen or return my comm calls. I figured you knew and were running from it. But you really haven't a clue, have you?"

Webb frowned, trying to read the piercing eyes whilst a chill continued to spread through his insides.

"So, Doctor Yoshida," Fitzroy continued, shifting his focus to the medic. "What do you think? Can he be salvaged?"

The medic muttered, scanning his notes then blinked over the top of the panel. "There appears to be no permanent damage. I will need to perform a further examination and do a brain scan -"

"Answers, Yoshida. Can you reset him?"

"*Reset* me? What?"

The medic blinked at him a moment then nodded. "I believe it can be done."

"Good," Fitzroy said, pale eyes taking on a dangerous gleam. "You deliver on this promptly, Yoshida, and our positive opinion of your services may be restored."

The two guards at the door grinned and Yoshida paled.

"Fitzroy," Webb growled.

"Relax, Webb," Fitzroy purred. "Soon you won't remember any of this."

Webb blinked, opened his mouth then there was a bleep. Fitzroy frowned at his wrist panel and then his face flattened. He pushed a button. "Yes, Admiral? Yes, we have him. He appears... very well, Ma'am. Yes, Ma'am. Cell 3."

Fitzroy mumbled some orders to the two at the door who nodded and left, shutting it behind them. Fitzroy moved over to Yoshida and bent to talk in his ear. Webb just gazed at the wall. The room had started to spin again.

When the door slid open and Admiral Pharos walked in, standing tall and with a grim expression on her face, all Webb could do was sit there and stare.

She eyed him critically. "So? This is it, is it?"

"Yes, Ma'am," Fitzroy said, falling in next to her.

"What the hell happened to him?"

"He appears to have gotten himself into some scrapes since escaping from the Medic Centre, Ma'am."

"We will have to get the worst of it healed before we can initiate this part of the plan. Doctor, you're lucky I don't drift you."

Yoshida bobbed his head, mumbling over his panel. "I can restore him, Admiral. He will be good as new."

"We've waited a year already," she said, voice dangerously low. "AI have only just managed to scrape through this latest investigation into their production of phozone for your projects, Doctor, as well as the over-production of the equipment they have supplied us with. They will not wait any longer for their return, and neither will I. Every day we delay is another day the Lunar Colonies spend in the Service's stranglehold. I want everything putting in motion *today*."

"Ma'am -" Fitzroy began.

"We use *him*-" Pharos indicated Webb with a wave of her hand "-the second he's fit to be seen. But my fleet and troops are on standby. We move today."

"Pharos?" Webb finally managed.

She glared at him. "And get his memory dealt with immediately. Ezekiel Webb has managed to put spanners in all our plans so far. The sooner every trace of his former self is eradicated the better."

"Yes, Ma'am," Fitzroy said. "Can I just suggest one thing?"

"What?"

"This clone somehow knows everything he knew. Everything. Points, contacts, deals with bent Service reps, not to mention things Kaleb Hugo might have told him. We may yet be able to turn this setback into an advantage."

"I have all the information we need about the Service," she replied.

"Yes, Ma'am," Fitzroy said. "But Webb knew everything you weren't to know. I'm prepared to bet he knows things, say, where top-ranking Colony Enforcers and Service informants are concerned that could prove useful, particularly to bring Lunar 1 to heel."

Pharos eyed him again. He tried to scream at her but the rage choked him. "He won't talk. I knew this man. Stubborn doesn't begin to cover it."

"Oh, there are ways though, Ma'am."

"No," cried Yoshida. "No interrogation. You'll ruin him. Admiral, please."

Pharos rubbed her chin, her iron-coloured eyes never leaving his. "Do you have a blade you can trust?"

Webb felt himself pale. Fitzroy smiled. "Ariel can be here from Haven within a few hours, Ma'am."

"No, please, Admiral." Yoshida came forward, clutching the panel and stammering. "You need him to stand tall and strong, he needs to look like a leader. We can't have him broken."

"But you can wipe his memory, yes?" the admiral asked coolly.

The medic swallowed. "I believe so."

"Then we break him and start again. So long as the blade is issued instructions to avoid permanent damage, it is worth the extra time to try and retrieve something from this disaster. Call in your blade, Fitzroy. But do it quick. Our timing is crucial."

"Why?" Webb managed, though it came out as more a strangled choke. "Why me? Why him?"

Fitzroy looked at the admiral. Her jaw had hardened. "You deluded fool. You who thought you were so clever, so canny. Didn't you ever wonder why the *Zero* was commissioned in the first place?"

"To do your dirty work."

The edge of something tugged at the corner of her month. "An added bonus, nothing more. The *Zero* was commissioned for Webb... to keep him under my eye but out of the eye of the Service. The only person more deluded than he was is that idiot Luscombe. Or perhaps that arrogant fool, Hugo, turning the *Zero* into his own private chance to prove himself. No, Webb. The *Zero* was to keep the original you both watched and hidden."

"Who was he?" His voice sounded cracked and far away in his own ears.

"Can't you guess?" Pharos growled. "Even now? Did we not train you better than this?"

Understanding slammed into his gut. He was left swaying and dizzy and bent over until his forehead touched his knees.

"He's got it," Fitzroy muttered..

"Good," Pharos said, glancing at her wrist panel. "Maybe there's hope for his capacity for intelligence after all. Now I have to get back to the *Resolution*. Get it done."

"Yes, Ma'am," Fitzroy said. "I won't let you down."

"You had better hope you don't."

"You know, Webb," Fitzroy said into the silence that followed Pharos's departure. "You'd save us all a lot of time and you a lot of unpleasantness if you just told me everything now. You don't really want to protect all those you know about, do you? Remember, you don't even know them. You've never even met them. And tomorrow you won't remember them."

"Go to hell," Webb croaked out.

Fitzroy sighed. "Very well. You always did choose the hard way."

"And to think you call other people deluded," Webb growled.

"I see things far clearer than you do, my friend."

"Revolution's your answer is it?" Webb spat, sitting up. "After it worked so well the last time?"

Fitzroy regarded him levelly. "Some things are bigger than the people involved. You should know that. The Orbit would be a very different place right now if Governor McCullough had succeeded."

"Yeah. There'd be more debris."

Fitzroy's cool expression didn't falter. "Do you want to know what deluded is, Webb? You've crawled through the sewers of this Strip and can't smell its shit."

"Well getting everyone in it killed is certainly one way to solve their problems."

"Nothing worth having comes without sacrifice," Fitzroy barked. "I am willing to sacrifice. The Lunar people are willing to sacrifice."

"Are they?"

"Yes. The Service is a cancer. It kills, slowly, from within, without you even seeing it. It strips you of your freedom and identity. It takes away who you are. You've been doing their work for the last fifteen years. You look me right in the eye now and tell me you don't agree."

Webb narrowed his eyes at him. "There's one thing you forgot to say about the Service, Fitzroy."

"What?

Webb felt a death's-head grin spread over his face. "It's big. Fucking big. With a lot of guns. And ships. And men."

"So are we."

"You're insane."

"I'm saner than most. Sane enough to see that the only thing worse than a colony in the stranglehold of the Service is one they've left behind to rot."

"And the good admiral believes all this too, does she?"

"Pharos believes in McCullough. In his vision, in the future he planned. The people believed in him too. As they will believe in you. Once we stand united, they won't take us down. Not again." Fitzroy lifted his hands, smiling. "We've already won. We've got power. We've got faith. And we've got you. The Lunar State will be a reality again. You should be proud."

Webb's anger blazed white hot and swamped anything more he could think of to say. Fitzroy's smile in his hairless face widened. "Now...there is one more thing you can do for us in your current incarnation..."

"Sir," Yoshida finally found his voice and unpeeled himself from his spot in the corner.

"No more protests, Doctor. I will allow you to be present to oversee the interrogation. But the information in that head is too valuable to wipe without looking at first."

Ø

One thing that was in Webb's head, apparently, was how to sink away from his physical awareness. Unfortunately, he also knew why he'd learnt this trick, but steered away from those memories and just concentrated on pulling in deep breaths and sinking himself into the feeling of the cold metal table under his bare back. The steel binders at his wrists and neck holding him down made him shiver but he wrapped himself in the chill, visualised it as an impenetrable blanket around him. Yoshida hovering in the corner, muttering to himself and the hiss of the door opening were only brushes at the edge of his awareness.

There was a figure moving around the room. He was talking. His voice was nasal. Whiny. There was a question but Webb just stared at the ceiling and breathed.

Somewhere, there was the prick of a needle and something crawled under his skin... like heat but sharper. It made his heart speed up and goosebumps rise on his skin but he just breathed and stared up, willing the white ceiling to blank out his mind.

A face came into view. A pale face. Thin lips, darting eyes. Short hair, neat and tidy and fair. So fair it didn't look real, especially set against what seemed like impossibly dark eyes.

The heat under his skin was strengthening and spreading, searing his body from the inside. It pulled him back from his protective place and made everything sharp and real. The very air felt heavy against him and the binders against his skin began to burn.

"There now, are you with me?"

Webb breathed in and out through his teeth, every inch of his body crawling and scalding and stinging.

"That's better," the pale man said. "Now. Some of my counterparts like to start with a relatively inconsequential issue and build their way up. There's some argument for the advantages of that process. But me, I like to start with something big and gauge the reaction. There are various schools of thought on the subject, you might be interested to know. But I've always had great success with this method. So..." he hesitated, a faint frown appearing between his white eyebrows. "What shall I call you?" He tapped his lips, staring unblinkingly down at him. "Let's just stick with Ezekiel for now, shall we? It's what you know, as I understand. It should keep you focused. And focus is a big part of this process. So, Ezekiel..." The man pressed his fingertips together, dark gaze boring into his eyes. "Special Commander Hugo. I believe you know... or your former incarnation knew... her son quite well. Let's see what you know that might be of interest. Any offers?"

"Go screw yourself," Webb hissed.

The man shook his head and tutted, pulling a scalpel from his breast pocket. "Very well." The first cut went down his ribs. Some part of him knew it was only shallow, but with his skin aflame from the inside, it felt like it was gouging right through to the bone. He clenched his teeth together and forced himself to keep from making any noise, shuddering with the effort. The slicing stopped but left a burning trail. The warm blood trickling down his rib cage felt like liquid fire, scalding and peeling away his skin.

"Shall we try again? Captain Hugo. Let's start with some details of your little jaunt on Lunar 1."

"Fuck you."

The man frowned again, looking hurt. "Dear, dear. You surely understand how misplaced your loyalty is? I was given to understand you were quite the independent individual. I assure you this is the worst time you could choose to grow a sense of fidelity. Now. Again. Lunar 1. Was Hugo in the team that destroyed the apartment block? Hmm?"

Webb blinked at the ceiling, wishing his blood would cool on his skin. The blade sighed and bent with the scalpel again.

"Ariel..." Yoshida had stepped up twisting his fingers together. "Please be careful."

"I'm a professional, Doctor," Ariel said as he sliced another blazing line down his ribs. Webb bit his tongue against the red waves of fire blazing through his chest but at no time did his awareness blur, no matter how much he willed it to. "There will be no permanent damage. Now, Ezekiel my friend. The good LIL Commanders may have given you to understand that they are on a deadline, but such things are of no matter to me. I have a reputation to consider, built on the quality of the information I obtain. Therefore it makes no difference at all to me if we're here ten minutes or ten days. So..." he bent close enough over Webb's face that he could feel his breath on his face. The scalpel hovered next to his eye. "Shall we try again?"

XVIII

"He's around here somewhere, sir," Rami mumbled as they kept their heads down and paced along the crew passage. "They disappeared from the camera feeds right around..."

Hugo had to back pedal to stop from slamming into Rami who had stopped still in the middle of the passage. Hugo followed her gaze through a window and felt his blood run cold.

"Quick," he hissed. "Lieutenant, pull yourself together."

Rami visibly gathered herself and Hugo moved past her and palmed the door control. There was a small man with a worried face in a lab coat in the corner. He looked their way almost hopefully as they came in. The very thin man in the gloves straightened from where he was bent over Webb's prone form, fair brows drawn together.

"Yes?"

"Sir, Mr. Fitzroy needs you right away," Hugo chanced.

"He does?" the thin man narrowed his eyes. "Can you not tell him I'm occupied?"

"He was rather insistent, sir," Hugo said, keeping his hands clenched together behind his back and his gaze lowered. The man's dark eyes stayed on him for a second longer, then he sighed and placed the scalpel delicately on a metal tray and removed his gloves. "Very well. It's his credit he's wasting more than my time."

He swept out and then only the little medic was left. Hugo was just considering pulling his gun when he trotted right up to Hugo, eyes round. "Listen, soldier," he muttered. "Could you get this man out of here?"

"Sir?"

The medic, twisting his fingers, glanced behind him at Webb. "Just... get him away from this room. Somewhere safe. I will smooth it over with command, I assure you. You won't incur any blame. If the interrogation continues I fear there will be damage that cannot be undone and then all is lost. I will find you when I can and take him back."

"Okay, sir," Hugo managed and the doctor let out a shuddering sigh and smiled weakly at them.

"Thank you," he said, then scuttled off.

Rami drifted over to the table looking dazed.

"We need to move quickly, Lieutenant," Hugo muttered. Rami nodded and started examining the table's binder controls whilst Hugo shed his coat. "Webb?" Hugo muttered. "Zeek, can you hear me?"

"Hugo?" Webb's voice was thick, his eyes didn't seem to want to focus.

"We're getting you out of here. Try and stay awake."

Rami got the binders open and Hugo laid a hand on the commander's shoulder to help him sit up but Webb twisted away, whimpering and mumbling.

"Bastards..." Rami hissed.

"What?"

Rami was staring at the vials on the tray next to the scalpel and a neat row of syringes. "They've given him a neuro-enhancer." She looked at the shallow cuts that ran down his ribs, over his chest and behind his ears and shook her head, going pale before turning back to the tray. "You'll have to wait, Captain."

"We need to move before the *Zero* shows up on their scans."

"We can't even touch him in this state," Rami replied, looking through the vials. "They should have a suppressant... if they were planning to keep him alive, that is."

Hugo glanced between Rami and Webb and the door, feeling seconds slip by. "Hurry, Lieutenant."

Rami found a vial and filled a syringe. She hesitated with a hand over Webb's arm.

"Do it," Hugo snapped.

Hugo saw her swallow, grab Webb's wrist to hold his arm down. He cried out and tried to pull away. Hugo helped her hold him down but every touch made the clone tremble and writhe. Rami went even paler but she managed to administer the injection and Webb gradually calmed.

"Zeek?" Hugo asked.

Webb blinked at the ceiling, looking a little more focused.

"Quick, Rami," Hugo said and Rami helped him sit him up. He whimpered but Hugo managed to get the coat on him and cover most of the blood. "Webb, try and stand."

"That's not my name," he mumbled, staring at his knees.

"It is for now," Hugo growled, pulling the slighter man's arm over his shoulders, ignoring the responding shudders. "Rami, your hat."

Rami pulled her cap off and placed it low on Webb's shorn head to hide his face. He gazed blearily at her. "Anita?"

Rami swallowed, jaw tight.

"Lieutenant," Hugo snapped. Rami shook herself, taking Webb's other arm and helping him to his feet. They shambled to the door. "You go first."

Rami looked up and down the corridor then waved them out.

They made their way back through the corridors of the *Tide*, Rami guiding the way. They managed to shuffle out of sight around corners whenever someone came their way and Webb managed to take more of his weight as they got down to the level of the docking holds. These corridors were busier and they drew a few looks as they shuffled along, hands out to stop Webb stumbling.

"We need to hurry," Hugo said. "It won't be long before someone reports this."

"The dock is just around this corner, sir," Rami said, checking her wrist panel. They came around a corner onto a more familiar hallway and ducked through an entryway into the wide, bright dock, busy with berthed fighters and flyers and a bustling tech crew.

"Oh no," Rami muttered, drawing up short. Hugo looked up and saw some of the engineers stood around *Son*, frowning at the reg code and at a computer panel.

"They'll be checking the docking schedule," Hugo muttered.

"I got *Son* on it, sir," Rami whispered, shifting a step forward to hide Webb from view. "But who knows how they work from day-to-day on here."

"Webb," Hugo said. His head was hanging and Hugo was afraid for a minute he'd passed out. "Webb, you need to try and walk."

The clone lifted his head. His eyes looked far away. "What's the point?" he mumbled.

"What?"

"There's nowhere to run."

"What are you talking about?"

"Sir," Rami said, pointing. The dock workers were shrugging and moving on to the skiff berthed next to *Son*.

"Webb, you have to try and stand."

Webb shook his head but pulled some of his weight off Hugo. He swayed but Rami steadied him and he nodded. Hugo took a breath then stepped out onto the dock area and started walking over towards *Son*. He fell back to walk beside Webb, ready to grab him if he fell, and Rami paced just behind. One of the tech crew at the skiff paused to watch them approach. He consulted his panel again, frown deepening.

"Quick," Rami hissed, keying the cockpit control.

"Hey," the tech called.

Rami scrambled up the fighter then reached down. "Zeek, quick," she said, reaching for him. For one horrible moment Webb just stood and stared at her. Then he reached up grabbed her hand and allowed her to help him up into the squat space behind the pilot seat. There was another shout from the tech but Hugo was up and in the seat before he reached them. He fired the engine and the man fell back, staggering with the force of the thrusters. *Son* lifted from the floor then blasted out the drift shield into open space. A light on the control panel started blinking as the *Tide* tried to hail them.

"More," Hugo said, pushing the comm button. "Bring the *Zero* round and open the hold."

"Yes sir. What's your status?"

Hugo glanced over his shoulder. Webb was curled up against Rami, head on her shoulder with his eyes closed. She was holding him but her eyes were dry and angry.

"We've got him," Hugo said.

"Sir, the *Tide* is moving to engage you."

"I see it," Hugo said, scowling at his instruments. "Just get to the rendezvous."

The *Tide*'s cannon fire seared past his wing but *Son* was far more manoeuvrable. He increased their speed and the bigger ship fell away behind. Fighters started to deploy but the *Zero* pulled into their path and Hugo manoeuvred them into the hold. "More, full thrusters, *now*."

They felt the *Zero*'s engines scream and they thundered away from the oncoming LIL fighters.

"Webb, wake up," Rami said as the hold pressurised around them and *Son*'s cockpit opened. "Sir, can you help?"

Hugo swallowed and reached around the pilot's chair to try and help manoeuvre Webb out of the squat space. Bolt and Sub came running up to the side of the fighter and helped hand him down.

"Take him to the medbay," Hugo said and they nodded and headed towards the ladder. "More," Hugo said into his wrist panel as he followed. "Are we away?"

"Out of the *Tide*'s range now sir. Any heading?"

"Anywhere away from here. And fast."

"No," Webb croaked, pulling himself from Sub's grip and trying to turn and face him. "Hugo, no, we need to get out of Service space."

"What?"

"Just -" Webb swayed and clutched his head.

"Get him to medbay."

"Kaleb, get out of Service-controlled space. Trust me."

Hugo stood frowning at him for a second, but through the bleariness and the pain he saw certainty haunting his eyes. "More," Hugo said again.

"Sir?"

"Take us out into neutral drift."

A pause. "Sir?"

"Just do it."

"Yes, sir."

Sub and Bolt managed to help Webb up the ladder then Rami was ushering him through to medbay.

"It was LIL all along," Hugo said as Webb was perched on the medbay bunk and Rami peeled off his jacket and cap.

"How did you find out?" he murmured.

"You were right to stay in Anton's good graces. He was the first one Evangeline tried to make a deal with when LIL issued the contract for your recapture. He knew about them using the *Tide* as their flagship, too."

Webb just nodded in response, staring at the floor.

"Why did they interrogate you?"

"Sir, he needs to rest," Rami said.

"Leave us for a minute, Lieutenant."

"Sir -"

"It's okay, Anita," Webb managed a weak smile. "Go help More. He's going to need a co-pilot once we hit the Belt." She hesitated a moment longer, looking angry and confused, then put down her medkit and left. "Fitzroy ordered it," Webb continued, reaching for some sterilising wipes and wincing as he cleaned some of the blood off his ribs. "He wanted information to use against the Service before they wiped it all out of my head."

"Wiped it?"

Webb nodded, throwing a bloody wipe on the floor and taking another. "They never wanted another Webb. Not after he so obviously wouldn't play their game. They just wanted something that looked like him that would pass a DNA test."

"A DNA test?" Hugo frowned.

Webb looked up at him. "Webb... the original Webb," the clone managed a half-grin. "Governor McCullough's son." Hugo stared at him. The clone's weak smile widened into something that looked like a leer. "Didn't see that one coming, huh? Though, to be fair, neither did Webb."

Hugo stared at the face. His blood ran cold. This broken, bloody and defeated Webb - not in a hundred years would he have associated him with the Governor McCullough from all the history reels. But the old Webb... his commander...? He thought of the determination, the fire, the energy.

He sat down heavily at the workstation. "This is not possible."

Webb shrugged. "Apparently it is."

"Doll?"

Webb shook his head, not looking at Hugo. "Doll's sterile. It was probably the result of some roll in the hay with some poor, bedazzled low-life on Lunar 1. Kind of explains why Doll did all she did for him," he shook his head, looking pained. "He was her husband's son..."

"She knew?"

"Judging from the way she reacted when I turned up on her doorstep..." His eyes went far away again. "Yeah, I'd say she knew."

"But we ran a DNA test," Hugo said. "Spinn ran one and didn't..." Realisation slammed into him. He snarled and turned to the medbay workstation. "Spinn," he barked into the comm whilst rooting through the medbay data.

"Captain?" Spinn's reply sounded nervous.

"Medbay. Now," then Hugo cut off the connection. He turned back to the figure on the bunk who was staring at the bulkhead again. "LIL are planning an uprising?"

Webb nodded. "Using Duran McCollough Junior as a figurehead. Fitzroy thinks it will unite the Lunar Strip and make them willing to throw themselves on Service swords. But Hugo...there's more."

Hugo felt his skin go cold. "To do with why we had get out of Service space?"

Webb turned his gaze on him, glassy and tired. "Admiral Pharos is LIL."

Hugo took a second to find his voice. "What?"

"This whole thing... it was her. Her and Fitzroy."

Hugo stared at him. "No."

"Saw her with my own eyes, Hugo," Webb said, cleaning more cuts and flinching. "She was all for having my memory wiped and using me as a puppet this evening."

"But... she... she gave us our missions..."

"They came from Luscombe," Webb countered.

"Under her supervision."

Webb shrugged. "I'm willing to bet she didn't know about the Splinter operation. Hence her jumping on your case when it was over. And as for AI... well... didn't you get the feeling we weren't supposed to come back from that?"

Spinn came in then and stood against the bulkhead, glancing between Hugo and Webb. It was a long time before Hugo could trust his voice to be steady. "Spinn," he grated.

"Captain?"

"You knew?"

"Sir?"

Hugo sprung to his feet. "You knew who Webb really was?"

Spinn looked between them again, eyes widening. He swallowed. "I'm sorry, sir."

"You knew all along?"

Spinn took a step back, though Hugo hadn't moved. "Sir, Pharos commissioned me to track him down when he was still a child. I was the one charged with... with..."

"With keeping him watched?" Webb's didn't look at the doctor.

Spinn swallowed again. "I was keeping him safe."

"Safe?" Webb laughed then. It was a horrible sound.

"Why didn't you say anything?" Hugo growled, taking a step closer to the researcher. "From the minute we heard LIL were trying to recruit him, you must have known why."

"I -"

"We could have saved him, Spinn," Hugo closed the distance between them and shouted in his face. "He'd still be alive, if we'd known. You bastard. You spineless, treacherous bastard."

Spinn's jaw worked and his body stiffened. "Fifteen years I've lived with this, Captain. Fifteen years I watched More, Rami, and others, poor nobodies, bleed and die for this blasted ship - for the Service - when the whole time I knew they were just using us. Using every one of us to keep him hidden but alive, while they bided their time until he became a political advantage, or a loose end to scrub out. Fifteen years I had to watch and say nothing." His face took on an imploring expression as he looked over Hugo's shoulder to Webb. "The minute I said anything that would be it. His ignorance - all of your ignorance - was the only thing that kept him alive as long as he was."

"I want you off my ship," Hugo growled.

"Hugo," Webb said.

"The next colony, satellite, fuck it, you can get off at Haven for all I care. You're done. I never want to see your face again."

Spinn's gaze didn't waver. "If those are your orders, Captain, I will follow them. Though Admiral Pharos was the one who commissioned me.

The *Zero* will be finished if she finds out you've relieved me."

Hugo ground his teeth. "Admiral Pharos has joined LIL."

Spinn's brow clouded.

"It's true, Spinn," Webb said, throwing another sterilising wipe into the disposal. "This clone thing was all her idea."

"No," Spinn shook his head. "No. The Admiral charged me with watching over Webb. To keep him safe... exactly so he couldn't be used in this way by the enemy. She would never -"

Webb sighed. "She's dicked you, my friend. Dicked us all. She put out the contracts. She recruited the Splinters."

"That was her too?" Hugo said, heat washing through him.

Webb nodded. "Through untraceable back channels we gave her, most probably."

"Why?"

"Lunar 1 would never fight for anyone, LIL or Service. She knew she'd have to take it by force if she wanted a united Lunar Strip and there was no way she'd get enough Servicemen aboard to do the job without drawing attention."

"This isn't true," Spinn said, shaking his head. "X6-119 was the source of the Splinters' credit. She ordered it destroyed -"

"To cover her tracks," Webb said, staring at the bulkhead. "Under a rather convincing cover of an official mission, of which there will be a record, somewhere. I bet she knew we'd exceed the orders and send crew aboard too, Hugo. And that I'd be with them."

Hugo went cold. "That's why it was so heavily armed. And why every knew who we were. And... and why they..."

Webb nodded.

"No," Spinn was still shaking his head. "She admired Duran Mc-Cullough. I know that's true. That's why she wanted his son kept safe. But she's a loyal Service Officer. She would never side with rebels. She fought against the Lunar rebellion..."

"Did she?" Webb stared at his hands.

Spinn just stood there blinking.

"She was a captain then," Hugo mumbled. "Captain of a relief team that was charged with clean-up work on the moon and colonies. Her unit never fought in the battles."

Spinn was staring into space, looking dazed.

"Spinn," Hugo said, quietly. He pulled his gaze round, wide and distant. "My orders still stand. Lock yourself away in the brig. If you're lucky we'll wait until we can get back to the Orbit before we throw you out."

Spinn blinked at him a few times. For a moment he thought he might say something more but he just turned and left the medbay, moving like someone in a waking nightmare.

"Hugo. They may have lost their toy dictator, but they're not going to stop now. Pharos issued the assault order whilst I was there."

"We have to warn someone."

"Who?"'

Hugo balled his fists and uttered a wordless exclamation. "We can't just let them declare war without warning anyone."

"Luscombe..." Webb mumbled.

"How do we know he's not in on it all?"

"The good admiral mentioned him whilst I was there. It doesn't look like she thought highly enough of him to include him in her schemes."

"Luscombe then," Hugo muttered, sitting himself back at the workstation.

"Then what?"

"We'll see what his orders are."

"No," Webb said. "Then what with me? Is what the Service has in mind any better than what LIL were planning? Because if not, I'd just as soon take my chances in the Haven shipyards too."

Hugo turned in his seat. His throat felt tight. "I would have come for you anyway," he said, quietly. "Whether Luscombe ordered it or not."

"Would you?"

Hugo nodded. "I don't care whose son you are. You've spent your life as a soldier of the Service. And you are my crew."

Webb was shaking his head. "The man you're thinking of is dead, Hugo. It's not me."

"I lost him and then I used and lied to you and almost lost you too. I've made a lot of mistakes, Webb. But I'm going to try and make them right."

"Just as soon as you've saved the world?"

"Not that I'm sure the world deserves it," Hugo muttered.

Webb stared at a point just over his head for a minute. "I'm sorry, Hugo."

"What for?"

Webb looked at him then. "I told you in Tranquillity Hall that it wasn't over. But it is now. All of it. I shouldn't have said those things."

Hugo swallowed. "I think I deserved some of them," he said quietly.

A half-smile played about the clone's mouth. "How did you know what I'd do?" he said, barely above a mumble. "In Tranquillity, I mean?"

Hugo swallowed and looked away. "Because it's what I would have done."

"He believed in you, you know," Webb said after a heavy silence. "Webb, I mean. The real Webb. He thought you were a good captain." Hugo tightened the grip he had on the back of the chair, blinking through the heat behind his eyes. "A stubborn asshole," Webb added, another ghost of a smile lingering about his mouth. "But a great captain."

Hugo felt a corner of his own mouth turn up but then he stared hard again at the clone. "Why didn't you talk?"

"What?"

"When we found you," Hugo mumbled, keeping his voice steady with an effort. "The blade was still working. You hadn't talked. Why?"

Webb's smile widened. "Because I'm an even more stubborn asshole than you?"

Hugo out-and-out grinned before he could stop himself then shook himself and stood. "Lie down before you keel over. I'll send Rami down to fix you up. I want you fit to accompany me when we get to Command."

"Service Command?"

"Yes," Hugo said. "You know, I'm beginning to suspect Luscombe's the only one in this whole damn Orbit on our side."

"I guess we better hope so."

He ordered Rami down to medbay from the bridge and took over at the controls. "How are we doing?"

"Okay, Captain," More said, eyes locked out the viewscreen. They were just skirting the edge of the asteroid belt and More was steering them between the scattered rock. Hugo glanced at the course overview on the display and helped compensate the port. "Though you ought to know that we're entering Haven space. There's a mining team rigging a satellite about fifty clicks to starboard. We'll be showing up on their scanners soon."

"Head towards them."

"Sir?"

"We're dumping Spinn."

More threw him a confused glance. "Sir?"

Hugo ground his teeth. "The man's a traitor. He knew all along who Webb was and why he was targeted."

More blinked again. "Who was he?"

Hugo swallowed. "He's... was... McCollough's son. LIL wanted him as a figurehead for a new revolution."

More stared at him a moment, his normally stoic face open with shock. He shook his head and pulled his attention back to the controls just in time to avoid a collision. "And Spinn knew?"

"He was Pharos's man...charged with tracking Webb down and keeping him watched."

"*The admiral* knew?"

Hugo nodded. "Knew. Knows. Is planning a revolution with the knowledge."

More shook his head again, staring out the screen and looking pale.

"I take it you didn't? Know, I mean."

More threw him a baleful glance.

"Thank God. That's at least one person in my crew who hasn't been lying to me."

"What are we going to do?"

"We're getting the mutinous scum off this ship," Hugo grated. "Then we're getting back to Command to warn them. What's that look for?"

"Nothing, sir."

"Thomas," Hugo growled.

More was silent for a second, not looking at him. "Permission to speak freely, sir."

"Just spit it out."

"Spinn was following orders, sir."

Hugo felt heat flare. "He betrayed us. It's mutiny."

"If you say so, sir."

"More, I don't understand you. Webb is dead because of this. None of this would have happened if he'd spoken out as soon as LIL reared their head. It's wilful treachery, mission or not. You do not treat your crew this way."

"Not even if you were ordered to?" More gave him a glance that Hugo couldn't read.

"I'm not letting this go," Hugo said after a difficult pause. "I can't believe you even want me to."

"I don't sir," More said mildly. "I'm just thinking dropping Spinn with a Haven mining crew might not be the best course."

"What would you do then?"

"Take him back to Command. We're going to need some evidence on our side if we're going to report on Pharos."

Hugo chewed his lip. The anger was still burning hot. He could see the flashes and dust in the distance that indicated the presence of the mining crew on one of the asteroids. A hail started bleeping on the control panel.

More glanced at it then at Hugo.

"You're not just wanting me to spare him because you like him?"

"I've known him a long time," More hedged. "And thought him a good man. But either way... I think my point still stands."

Hugo glared at the blinking hail light. "Turn her round," he said. "Plot a course that will get us to Command. But avoid the Lunar Strip, for fuck's sake."

"Yes, sir. I can do that. Just one thing, though..."

"Another?" Hugo said, kneading his temples to try and ease the pounding there.

"The minute Luscombe knows we're coming with the clone they'll have us surrounded and a boarding party dispatched. I don't know if we'll get word through in time if we're boarded."

"We'll have to get docked without him knowing."

"So we're not turning the clone in?"

"No."

More nodded, seeming slightly easier than before. "Quinn in supplies can get us in, I'm sure."

They increased their thrusters to full capacity as soon as they were clear of the Belt, but cast their sensors wide to manoeuvre around any approaching ships and the Lunar Strip sensor nets. Hugo had to stop himself from pacing as they skirted around the edge of the Strip.

It seemed an intolerably long journey back to Command. He double and triple-checked their engine capacity to see if any more power could be re-routed from anywhere but More had seemingly already thought to that. He itched to try and hail Luscombe but knew More was right. The minute he knew they were on the approach he would want the clone secured and ready to face trial before he would listen to anything else.

Slowly, however, Earth gained size and definition. Hugo filled the hours trying to find anything in the newsfeeds or Lunar status reports to suggest Pharos was making her move but all seemed normal. Painfully normal. It made him feel cold inside when he visualised the *Resolution* in orbit around the colonies.

"In hailing distance now, sir," More said.

Hugo almost jumped to the comm and started keying in the commands to get a connection.

"I don't know, Hugo," Quinn sounded distracted over the comm. "I don't like how many people seem to know the name *Zero* all of a sudden."

"Look, Quinn," Hugo kept his voice as neutral as he could. "Just get us your usual clearance through the patrols. Please."

"After all that happened at Tranquillity Hall? I'll get discharged."

Hugo ground his teeth. "Quinn, you have to trust me. We have information. Important information. Something big is coming."

"Is *he* with you?" she said after a pause.

"Who?"

"You know bloody well who. That maniac commander of yours that tried to ventilate the colonel."

"Yes, he's with us."

"Then forget it, Hugo. There's a contracted warrant out on his head. No way can I let you sneak him aboard."

"Quinn, I can't explain right now but you have to believe me that Webb's little stunt is the very least of our worries. I have a contact on Command who needs this information we have."

"So get *them* to give you clearance."

"We're approaching the edges of Command's sensor net now, sir," More said.

"Quinn, you do this and I won't forget it. Believe me, you'll regret it far more if you don't."

There was a pause and then a noisy sigh. "I don't know why I listen to you, Kaleb Hugo. My mother warned me against types like you. She always said sincerity is the worst deception of all."

"I swear, Quinn, on my life, that our contact is going to need and be grateful for what we have."

"Fine, fine. Transmitting clearance code now. But I don't want to see or hear from you ever, ever again, understand?"

"Thank you," Hugo unclenched his hands and started feeding the clearance code into their ID transmitters. "Berth U-276, More."

"Yes, sir."

"Sir?"

Hugo turned in his chair. Rami was stood at the entryway.

"How is he?"

Rami nodded. "He's doing better, sir. They were all superficial wounds. The neuro-enhancer was the cruel part and it's out of his system now. But, sir...?"

"Yes, Lieutenant?"

"Are we turning him in?" She was gazing out the viewscreen to Service Command looming against the star-specked back drop.

"No, we're not," Hugo said, standing. "The Service has no more right to him the LIL do. We are keeping him safe until all this is over. What he does then is up to him."

"Very well, sir," Rami said, dropping her gaze to the floor.

"We can't make him stay, Lieutenant," Hugo said in a low voice as he came closer to her. "And we can't use him to ease our own -"

"I know, sir," she said, quickly. "I know that."

Hugo nodded. "Good. Now help More ward off any invasive scans you can, and keep an eye on our clearances and docking registration. Webb and I are going in."

Ø

Webb was in the crew quarters, pulling on a t-shirt, cap and his old cargo jacket. "I can't believe you kept this," he was saying. It hung a little loose on him now.

"More wouldn't let it go."

Webb smiled, but then his hand went to his throat and his face fell. "I don't suppose...?"

Hugo shook his head. "The pendant went with him. Sorry."

Webb nodded, tugging on the brim of his cap in a gesture so familiar it stirred up the pain all over again. "Are we ready?"

"As we'll ever be. We'll have to move quick. It's only a matter of time before one or both of us gets recognised."

"I don't think Luscombe will exactly be pleased to see me, you know."

"You need to tell him everything you heard and saw. LIL could declare revolution any hour now."

Webb was staring at his boots.

"Webb..." Hugo said then paused, swallowing through a tight throat. "Zeek... you do this and I'll make sure the Service doesn't get you. LIL either. I'll make sure you get to go your own way."

"That all rather depends on us surviving."

Ø

Hugo kept his head down as he paced through Command's corridors. They were already drawing looks though he couldn't determine whether it was people that recognised them or if they were just confused by their lack of uniform or their fevered pace.

"Do you even know where he is?" Webb said, jogging to keep up.

"I've got a good idea."

Hugo took them to a bank of express lifts and got them to the conference level. The armed guards gave him confused glances as he keyed in the codes for the doors without hesitation, recognition mixed with uncertainty in their faces, but Hugo kept them moving quickly enough so that none of them had time to make up their minds. Finally, they were moving down a corridor of black metal, display screens reeling status reports and statistical data. He turned a corner and passed a startled Commander Hudson who stood from her desk and scrambled after them, protesting as Hugo walked right up to some double doors and started keying in codes.

The doors hissed open and Hugo stepped in, Webb at his shoulder. A dozen people in grey uniforms and a myriad of pips, insignia and medals between them looked up and fell silent when they burst in. Every face froze.

"Hugo?" Luscombe stood from the head of the conference table, face pale with anger. His eyes slid from him to Webb and his cheeks flushed red. "What the hell?"

"Colonel, we have to talk to you."

"Luscombe," one of the other officers frowned heavily. "What's going on here? Is that Kaleb Hugo?"

"Hugo, get out of here. Now."

"Colonel, you have to listen. LIL -"

"Hudson!" Luscombe shouted. The other officers were exchanging confused or dangerous glances.

The commander appeared at their side. "Sir?"

"Get security immediately."

"Got some unexplained troop movements there, by any chance, Colonel?" Webb stood with his arms folded, nodding towards the Orbit maps on the wall displays.

"Colonel Luscombe," the man who had already spoken stood. "What is going on here? I've had troops out with the contact to arrest one of these men for your attempted murder."

"It's under control, General," Luscombe growled.

"Colonel," Hugo said. "Please listen. The Lunar Strip is going to declare another Lunar State. "

"What's he talking about?" another officer demanded.

"Hugo, you can go with Hudson to the brig quietly or you can be dragged out of here by security. It makes no difference to me but you may want to think hard -"

"Christ Almighty, Marcus," Webb snapped. "You wanna live out the week? Pull your head out of your ass for five fucking seconds, will you?"

"Zeek," Hugo growled as eyes widened and jaws set around the room. "Colonel, he's been aboard the *Tide*..." Hugo started, but then tailed off and stared at the wall displays which had begun to flicker. The Orbit maps and stats vanished and were replaced by an oriental man's face. He looked down from every screen, expression grave.

"What's going on?" someone muttered.

"It's Cho-Jin. What the hell...?"

"Quiet," Luscombe held a hand up as the governor started talking.

"The time has come to embark on a new future. Too long have Lunar Colonists lived under tyranny and military control. The Lunar Strip will no longer bow to the Service yoke." The image cut to scenes of smoke and fires, buildings under siege, people running and taking shelter, skies and colony backdrops a blaze of laser and gunfire. Someone in the room muttered an oath.

"What you're seeing is a fight for freedom. We are declaring an independent Lunar State. We are purging the poison from our colonies. The Service have 12 hours to surrender and abandon all outposts in the Lunar Strip before we declare full war."

The screens went black. There was a moment of strained silence then every officer around the table stood and started barking orders into wrist panels and comm units. Commander Hudson stood at Hugo's side staring at the black screens, mouth open. Luscombe's face had gone very still.

"Get the Sunside flotilla mobilised immediately," someone was muttering. "And someone get Pharos on the comm."

"They knew," the officer that had recognised them pointed. "These men knew, Colonel. Get them into custody immediately."

"Wait, Colonel, there's more," Hugo started but then he was grabbed from behind by armed guards. "Colonel, you must listen. Admiral Pharos -" he tried to protest desperately, but then a stunner was pressed to his neck and everything went black.

Ø

"Well. That went well."

Hugo sat up, groaning, glaring at Webb who was staring at the ceiling of their small cell. "Did you manage to tell him?"

"Tell him what? That their precious flotillas are not only going to meet an entire Service fleet at the Lunar Strip but the *Resolution* as well?"

"Well?"

"No, Hugo. They didn't give me much of a chance to discuss it in between getting arrested and getting stunned."

"Shit," Hugo spat, standing and kicking the wall. "They'll be massacred."

Webb kept a stony silence, glaring at the opposite wall. "You think LIL threatened or paid Cho-Jin?"

"He's always been weak. I'm betting that's why the Service had him elected."

"Well, that came back to bite them on the ass."

"Oh no..."

"What?"

Hugo stood on tip toe to try and get a better view into the brig corridor through the narrow window in the door. "Sub and Bolt... and Rami... Spinn too."

"They're here?"

Hugo nodded. "In binders, getting locked up further down."

"So much for being valued members of the Service." Webb put his hands behind his head and stretched his legs out in front of him.

"We have to try and make them understand..."

"Haven't you got it yet, Hugo? We're nothing. Scum. They don't want our help."

"So that's it, is it? You're giving in?"

Webb blinked at him, slowly. "It's not like they've inspired much faith in me of late."

Hugo felt his face flush. "And what about me? What about my faith?"

"Huh?"

"I told you I believed in you."

"You were lying. We've been through this, Hugo. I'm not Webb."

"I know that, you idiot," Hugo paced over and stood over him. "Don't you think I know that? I *buried* him. You may have lived it but I had to watch and lie and scream in silence because I thought it was the right thing to do. I was wrong, but I stopped you from killing Luscombe and signing your death-warrant. I busted you out of the *Tide*..."

Webb's face was very still. "To stop the war."

"No."

"No?"

"No. Not to stop the war."

"Then why?"

"Because I *do* believe in you. I believe in the person you were made from and can be."

Webb swallowed. "Jeez, Kaleb. If I knew you were gonna get all mushy on me -"

"He was a good man. And you've got that in you too. You won't let thousands of people die because of a personal grudge."

Webb held his gaze for a moment. "You don't know me as well as you think you do."

Hugo opened his mouth again but the cell door hissed open and Luscombe came in. He crossed his arms and glowered. "Well, thanks for the heads up, Captain. A whole three minutes warning you managed to give us there."

"Sir," Hugo said. "My crew?"

"You left me no choice, Hugo. Sneaking in through the clearance checks, barging right in on a private conference with a wanted man in tow. I have to keep up appearances. For now anyway. But you and I know we have bigger things to worry about. You're now going to convince me that you didn't deliberately leave it almost too late to allow Cho-Jin to get the jump on us."

"Sir, we only knew their plans when we managed to get Webb back."

"Back from where?"

"The *Tide*," Hugo said. "It's under LIL control."

"LIL engineered the clone?"

"Certainly did," Webb said, picking his fingernails.

"What the hell for?"

"Why don't you ask the boss?" Webb said.

Luscombe's jaw was working. "Explain."

A corner of Webb's mouth raised. "You've been fucked, my friend."

"It would seem, sir," Hugo added quickly. "That Webb saw Admiral Pharos aboard the *Tide*. It would appear... it seems that..."

"She's shafted you, Marcus," Webb said, standing and grinning. "Royally."

"You have proof?" Luscombe said after a moment of stony silence.

"You believe us?" Hugo asked.

"There have been... indications. Not enough for me to really understand what I was seeing. That's what that conference was for. I was trying, until you came barging in, to make all the other commanders see there was something going on. So, any proof?"

"What, other than hearing her say that should couldn't wait to have her little war?"

"Webb, clone, whoever you are..."

"Ezekiel will do for now, Marcus," Webb grinned.

"Christ," Luscombe growled. "You're as infuriating as ever. Yes, more proof than hearsay."

"I say if you want proof," Webb said. "Just keep your ships heading towards their rendezvous with her fleet. The *Resolution* will make you feel very welcome."

Luscombe looked fractionally paler but his steely gaze never shifted from Webb's face. "And where did you fit into this shit-storm?"

Webb's face took on a frozen look.

"Webb was the late Governor McCullough's son, Colonel," Hugo said.

It took a moment for Luscombe to stop blinking. "I beg your pardon?"

"It's true. And Pharos knew. She had the whole *Zero* project commissioned to keep him contained. Ostensibly to keep him safe but now it seems just to keep him hidden away until they could use him."

"But they killed him..." Luscombe said, glancing at Webb who was standing very still.

"He didn't want to join. When it came to it... he didn't want any part of another war," Webb said.

Luscombe grimaced. "So they killed him?"

"And cloned him," Hugo said. "Hoping they could get an empty-brained double that would look like McCullough and pass DNA tests. A figurehead for another revolution. Only this time with a Service Space Corps fleet on their side."

"Pharos," Luscombe said, clutching at his forehead. "Fuck."

"That about covers it," Webb said, smile bitter and arms folded. "If it's any consolation none of us had a fucking clue either."

Luscombe glared. "Stop joking. This is serious. Her fleet would sail into the maw of a black hole if she ordered them to. We won't get any quarter from them. And it's already started. Communication channels are going down all over the Lunar Strip. This is going to get a whole lot worse before, and if, it gets any better."

"Don't we fucking know it."

"As for you," Luscombe said, glowering at Webb. "Don't think this makes everything alright."

"Yeah, sorry about the whole trying-to-kill-you thing," Webb's tone was mocking but his face was still and dangerous. "I lost it a little there, I admit."

Hugo wanted to intervene but couldn't think of anything to say. The two men glared at each other for a moment longer.

"We don't have time for this," Luscombe barked. "Everything's out in the open now. I want all the data from the *Zero*. All of it. The contracts you investigated, then and now, any readings you got from the *Tide*, data from the AI missions, everything. We need to rally the entire corps and I can't afford to waste time convincing everyone I'm not space-crazy."

"Sir, Dr Spinn knows more than the rest of us put together. He was Pharos's man from the start."

Luscombe's face flattened. "He knew this whole time?"

"He didn't know what she'd do," Webb put in, sending a narrow glance at Hugo who was grinding his teeth. "Only what she told him."

"Very well," Luscombe snapped, rubbing his forehead. "That's still more than we've got now."

"Sir," Hugo said. "This will mean -"

"I know," Luscombe said, looking at Hugo. "There's no helping it now. The *Zero* game is up. You're working with me now. Both of you."

"Hang on just one -"

"Stow it, Webb," Luscombe snapped. "I haven't got time to make you understand the depth of crud you are in. But do your bit and we'll see what can be done about the whole attempted murder, life-sentence, death-warrant thing."

Webb glared a second longer but didn't say anything.

Luscombe gave Hugo a heavy look. "Captain. Your job is to convince Special Commander Hugo that one of her admirals is a turncoat... and that you shouldn't be shot for mutiny."

XIX

Despite the knowledge of what was going on in the Lunar Strip being an almost physical weight at the back of Hugo's mind, the feeling of his heart in his throat was the sensation that over-rode everything else as he paced behind Luscombe through Command's corridors. People were rushing about as orders were being shouted across halls and were booming through overhead speakers. Out of every viewscreen he could see white streaks of ships and fighters at full thrust heading out towards the Lunar Strip. But it all seemed to be happening on the other side of a misty film of plexi-glass.

Webb kept pace beside him. His face was set but Hugo didn't have the focus to try and work out what he might be thinking. They turned a final corner and Hudson was waiting to usher them into a chamber with workstations around the walls manned by Service troops, muttering into comm units and keying commands into the control panels. Data scrolled on a myriad of wall displays in between the workstations and a giant screen on one wall was showing footage of the fighting still being screened from the Lunar colonies.

His mother was bent over a display in the wide central workstation, flicking through data feeds and mumbling to an admiral and a general on either side of her. She straightened as they came in, lips pressing together and eyes hardening. There was a lull amongst the hubbub as people craned their necks to look from the Special Commander to Luscombe and Hugo before commanding officers barked at them to get back to work.

"Colonel Luscombe, Ma'am," Hudson announced.

"Yes, Colonel?" she said, eyes never leaving Hugo. "What is the meaning of this?"

"Special Commander," Luscombe said with a slight bow. "Captain Hugo and his commander have some urgent news to report."

There were more surreptitious glances, apart from the two commanding officers either side of his mother who openly stared.

"Colonel, I have an Orbit-wide crisis on my hands. This is no time to be peddling information from pirates."

"Ma'am...they're not pirates," Colonel Luscombe said, managing to keep his face neutral and ushering them forward. "They work for me."

Her ice-pale eyes slid from Hugo to the colonel. "Explain."

"Red-level special ops, Ma'am. The *Zero* is an undercover vessel."

Both the men on either side of his mother looked from Luscombe back to her expectantly but she didn't speak.

"Ma'am," Hugo started, but his voice cracked. He coughed, took a breath, straightened his back, met her eye and started again. "Ma'am, we have vital intel. Our ships will meet more resistance than they are prepared for."

There was a dangerous pause when she weighed him up. "What sort of resistance?"

"The *Resolution* and Admiral Pharos's fleet, Ma'am..."

"What about them?"

Hugo tried to make the words come out but his mother's stare froze him over.

"Last reports showed Pharos in position to move in with the *Sincerity* as soon as our inbound craft arrive at the rendezvous, Ma'am," the general said.

"Ma'am, she is not there to move against the rebels. She is going to turn on your ships."

The special commander's eyes narrowed slightly whilst the general and other admiral started protesting loudly.

"The boy's space-crazy," the general muttered.

"Kaleb." His mother didn't say it loudly but both the men clammed up. "Explain how you know this."

Hugo took a step forward. "Ma'am...my commander has been at the centre of a conspiracy which Pharos has engineered in order to declare an independent Lunar State. There is not enough time to go into the details-"

"I will provide a full report in as soon as there's time, Ma'am," Luscombe put in.

"-but for now, your outbound fleet depends on you believing us."

"And what does *he* say?"

Hugo looked over his shoulder at Webb who was still hanging back with Hudson, shoulders hunched and arms folded and staring at the floor. "Zeek?"

For one sickening moment Hugo thought he wasn't going to say anything. The commanding officers glowered and his mother's brow clouded.

"It's true, Special Commander," Webb eventually said, though he didn't look up. "I heard her outline her plans myself."

"Ma'am," one of the duty officers called from the workstations.

"Yes?"

"We've lost communication with one of our scouting parties."

She hesitated and glanced back at Hugo. "What was their last location?"

"They were just entering Lunar 1 scanning range, Ma'am. But there is no enemy activity reported that far out from the Strip."

"It's Pharos," Hugo said.

"This is preposterous, Ma'am," the admiral muttered. "Mutiny, even."

Hugo kept himself still, holding his mother's calculating gaze.

"Admiral Wilson," she said, breaking eye contact. "Call back your fleet."

"Ma'am -"

"That's my order. Call back your fleet, unless you want them massacred. Issue evacuation orders to all Service outposts in the Lunar Strip. General Ling?"

"Yes, Ma'am?"

"I want every space-worthy ship you have on Earth in drift in the next four hours. They are to provide cover for the evacuation whilst we reform what fleets we have left."

"Ma'am, some of those units are engaged -"

"Earth will have to look after itself for the time being. And someone get the Analysts on the comm. Colonel Luscombe?"

"Yes, Ma'am?"

"Get the Command Staff to issue a recruiting call. We're going to need all the help we can get."

"Ma'am," Luscombe said and left, Hudson close on his heels.

"Ma'am," Admiral Wilson ventured, visibly steeling himself. "I don't want to suggest that your personal involvement with this man may be clouding your judgement -"

"I should hope you aren't, Admiral," she said, levelling her gaze at the man. "Not as someone who values their position, their command and a future not spent in the brig."

A few glances were exchanged then a renewed flurry of activity broke out. The jabbering of officers into comms and the tapping of workstation keys increased and General Ling and Admiral Wilson began shouting orders at aides who scrambled to obey.

Amongst all this, Erica Hugo came forward to Hugo and Webb. She stood eyeing them up for a moment. "This whole time? Special Ops?"

"Yes, Ma'am," Hugo managed.

"Best captain *Zero*'s had, Ma'am," Webb mumbled. "You should be proud."

Hugo flushed, opened his mouth but his mother silenced him with a look. He swallowed but then a ghost of a smile went across her lips.

"I am," she said. Then she pulled a computer panel off the nearest aide and started typing in commands. "Here. This is an official pardon for you and your crew."

"Ma'am?"

She handed over the panel with a narrow glance at Webb. "The recent unpleasantness on Tranquillity can't be overlooked..." Webb folded his arms but said nothing as he was weighed up. "And I will need to get more details from Luscombe to correct your Service records when all this is over. But this will be enough to get your crew out of the brig. Kaleb, report to the assembly deck. You and any of your crew who are willing to engage will be assigned a role. This is not an order. This is a... request."

Hugo nodded. "Yes, Ma'am."

His mother glanced at Webb. "Commander?"

Webb's eyes flashed and for a second Hugo thought he was going to scowl. But he smoothed his expression back out so quickly it was a little unnerving. "Will this help my chances with the whole Tranquillity thing?"

"It certainly can't hurt them."

Webb carried on holding the special commander's hard gaze a moment longer then nodded. "Of course, Ma'am. Anything for the Service."

Hugo frowned, searching Webb's face but he kept it blank.

"Good," his mother said, looking back to him. "Report to the assembly deck. You will be re-joining Gamma Company."

Ø

"So that was Mom, huh?"

Hugo threw a sideways glance at Webb. "Yes. And?"

Webb shrugged but he was grinning. "Nothing."

"I can tell you want to say something."

"Not at all," Webb grinned wider. "Just..."

"Yes?"

Webb chuckled. "Well, I now know where the rod came from."

"Can you focus, please?"

Webb laughed. "Come on. Sub and Bolt won't like being locked up."

Hugo trotted to keep up with Webb's increased pace. His commander was smiling easier, looking almost smug. He made mock salutes to the armed guards at the entranceway to the brig as they inspected the pardon.

"You're enjoying this too much," Hugo muttered.

"Hey, whichever way you look at it, I've been a wanted man my whole life. This absolved-thing feels alright. Let me enjoy it while it lasts."

"While it lasts?" Hugo frowned, pacing up the corridor of cells.

Webb just shrugged and carried on. Hugo felt something unclench inside him as they arrived at their crewmates' cells. Hugo glanced at the Pardon Notice and keyed in the release codes. The door slid open and Rami and More looked up. They looked grimy, bent and tired against the white polyfibre of the cell.

"Captain?" Rami frowned. "What's going on?"

"Fall in," Hugo said. "We've got work to do."

Webb took the pardon down to the next cell to release Sub and Bolt.

"Leave Spinn where he is," Hugo growled.

Webb hesitated with his hand on the keypad of Spinn's cell then let it drop without looking in the window.

"Let's go," Hugo said as the rest of the crew gathered in the corridor. "I will explain on the way."

Ø

By the time they were back out in the public corridors of Command, Hugo had become used to the glances they were drawing. He recognised more than a few faces and saw them recognise him in return. He carried the pardon on him but no one came up to them.

It was only as they neared the express lifts that he noticed some of the wall displays were scrolling details about the *Zero* and their pardon. Their faces went by on a loop, lingering on Webb's and Hugo's with concise details listed alongside them. He felt himself flush and moved on swiftly.

"Gamma Company are a good unit," Hugo said as they approached the assembly deck. "Fighter unit. *Father*, *Son* and *Ghost* will be a worthwhile addition. Sub and More, you pilot the *Zero* -"

"Sir..."

Hugo paused, realising More had stopped. The foot traffic flowed around them. "Yes, Sub-Lieutenant?"

More swallowed. "Sir, I will do this. I will fight. For you. You are my captain and I will follow your orders. But only if you look me in the eye and tell me we're fighting on the right side."

Hugo glanced around his crew. Rami was watching him, dark eyes steady. Sub and Bolt were watching him too, though they glanced at Webb as well. Webb stood a little to the side, arms folded and jaw set. His gaze was the most intense of all.

Hugo took a breath and looked back to More. "LIL started this. The Service is the only thing that can end it. We don't need any more killing.

The Orbit needs peace. Balance."

"More than freedom?" Webb asked.

Hugo glared at him. "What's the use of freedom if you're dead?"

"You're asking the wrong guy," Webb said, smile unpleasant. He strode away through the doors to the assembly deck before Hugo could think of a response. Rami, Sub and Bolt followed him with glances back at Hugo. Hugo watched them go, uncertainty niggling at his resolve. When he turned back, More was still looking at him.

"We've said before how there really are no sides," More said. "Just who you trust. If you trust the Service to do the best thing for the Orbit... I will fight at your side, Captain."

Hugo nodded. "Thank you, More."

More ducked his head then gestured for Hugo to lead on.

Hugo strode out onto the assembly deck trying to ignore the roiling in his belly. His crew were stood together, blinking about, looking awed. Even Webb was staring with his mouth open. The deck was wide and open with scores of uniformed officers and soldiers rushing back and forth, gathering into units, exchanging orders, consulting panels and the dozens of workstations that were wired in around the edge of the huge hall. The lights were on full so the metal walls were an almost blinding silver and the display that dominated a raised platform along one wall was streaming manoeuvres and Analyst data. The dozens of other screens around the room reeled individual unit commands, yet more Analyst data, more footage from the newsreels and he noticed one was looping the report about the *Zero*.

Arching over all this was a vast plexi-glass ceiling that looked out onto the infinite roll of stars and space. It was criss-crossed with thruster tracks as Service fighters and ships assembled or manoeuvred to units or were dispatched elsewhere. The two remaining flagships, the *Assertion* and the *Sincerity* loomed, cut about with light and shadow, directly in line with the assembly deck, their squadrons and units gathering around them in a flashing cloud of thrusters and reflected starlight.

It brought back a feeling Hugo had forgotten: the feeling of being small, being a grain of sand amongst the tumbling dunes of consequence. He had taken comfort in that feeling once, of being part of a whole far greater than himself. Now it made everything that ebbed and flowed inside him even more difficult to pin down.

He shook his head and scanned the throng for Gamma Company, just as a figure disengaged himself from the melee and trotted over.

"Commander Hugo," he called when he came up, eyes bright. "I mean,

Captain? I mean..."

"Fraser," Hugo said, unable to stop a smile. "Hugo is fine for now, Commander. Where's the rest of the unit?"

"Over there, sir," Fraser said, indicating a formation of soldiers, most of whom he recognised, forming into lines near the platform. "It's an honour to have you back, sir. I mean, when we got the news... well... I had always said it was a mistake for them to let you go."

"They didn't."

"Yes sir," Fraser ducked his head. "We know that now. The whole company got the message about twenty minutes ago. I'm sorry..."

"There's nothing to apologise for, Commander."

Fraser ducked his head again then glanced over Hugo's shoulder. "Is this your crew, sir?"

"Yes," Hugo said. Fraser looked doubtful. "They are Service-trained, remember, Commander. And more besides. You couldn't hope for better pilots or gunmen."

Fraser brightened. "Yes, sir."

"And less of the 'sir'. This is your unit."

"That's what I came to talk to you about, sir," Fraser said. "I... well... we..."

"Yes?" Hugo prodded, aware all the rest of the companies were almost assembled. The lights were dimming and Admiral Wilson was moving up onto the platform.

"It just feels wrong, sir," Fraser said, "you being back and not commanding the unit."

"Commander..."

Fraser raised a hand. "We need you to command, Hugo. This..." he gestured toward the giant display which was mapping out predicted positions of Admiral Pharos's fleet. "It's big. We need you."

Hugo glanced behind him. Sub and Bolt and Rami were talking together, pointing out information from screens and More was gazing at the main display. Webb was watching him. "Very well, Commander. Lead the way and make sure everyone's present."

"Sir, yes sir," Fraser said with a smart salute and disappeared back into the crowds towards Gamma Company.

The unit was lined up with backs straight and eyes on the platform, but he felt eyes slide his way as he got closer. He got nods and even a few handshakes and some low words. Webb and the others got uncertain looks. Hugo drifted to the front and took the Commander's spot next to Fraser, reaching inside himself for some certainty.

"All units, to attention," Admiral Wilson's artificially amplified voice rang out through the assembly deck. The room fell quiet. All eyes were focused on the platform as the silent ballet of ships went on above them. "By now you should have all have assimilated the situation. At this present moment the Second Fleet is on its way back to Command and will arrive in approximately two hours. All units are to attend to their flagship." The Lunar Strip appeared on the main display, divided up with a 3-dimensional grid. The same image from a different angle overlaid the plexi-glass above them, real space providing the backdrop for the approach vector lines and formation simulations.

"With the *Resolution* and her fleet on the opposing side," Wilson continued, "we will be adopting class 2 assault tactics. We shall approach with a pincer movement..."

Hugo felt Webb shifting next to him. He glanced at his commander in the gloom, the light from the screens paling his face. He was staring at the image of the Lunar Strip under attack with fire in his eyes. Hugo glanced around at all the still and stalwart faces focused on the admiral, and elbowed Webb in the ribs.

"What?"

"Are you sure you want to do this?"

Webb just nodded.

Hugo opened his mouth to say something else but then Wilson was dismissing them and the lights went back up. Hugo shook himself, looked away from Webb's unnerving blank stare and turned to his company.

"Form up and proceed to the fighter bay."

Gamma Company moved on their heels as one and marched across the assembly deck to line up with the other companies leaving the hall. The *Zero* crew followed at a jog, only Rami glancing back over her shoulder to see if Hugo followed. Hugo waited a couple of heartbeats to see if he could figure out if he should be worried about Webb, then shook himself and followed. He felt his gait fall back into the regimental step of the marching company and kept at the rear, barking orders from instinct as they wove amongst the wide corridors towards the fighter bays.

Fraser dropped back to march beside him. "We're in Bay 4, Commander," he said, consulting his panel.

"Good. Make sure everyone is fuelled, loaded and charged to full. We don't join the *Assertion* until everyone's fighter is ready and fully compliant."

Fraser glanced at him then looked away. "Yes, sir."

"I don't care about immediacy. My company aren't going into battle unless every fighter is fully energised and armed."

"Very well, Hugo," Fraser said. "I agree, it's just -"

"I'll take the rap. I'm used to that by now."

That managed to draw a smile from Fraser and he skipped ahead to start relaying orders to the marching company. They were approaching the fighter bays and Hugo called away the *Zero*'s crew as they came towards a turn off towards the supply levels.

"Get back to the *Zero* and our fighters. We need their speed and fire power. But I want you to hang together and at the edges of the engagement. Don't get in the middle."

"Captain," Rami said, drawing herself up. "We are perfectly capable -"

"I know you are, Lieutenant," Hugo said. "Probably more capable than most of the company. But these officers have drilled and trained together under Service regulations. They don't do -"

"Creative thinking?" Webb put in.

Hugo shrugged. "They would struggle accounting for an unorthodox ship with unorthodox methods in their formation. It will do more harm than good if you try to fall in alongside."

"Very well, Captain," Rami said, a little less stiffly.

"Good. Now. Be prepared. Pharos will throw everything she has to stop anyone from getting anywhere near the strip whilst they're taking it under control."

"She'll prioritise defending Tranquillity," More put in. "That's where Cho-Jin is. That's where Fitzroy is."

"It's also where the central servers for the moonframe are," Rami added. "The newscasts, info sites and communication grids are controlled from Tranquillity. She won't want it taken or damaged."

Hugo nodded. "See, you're used to reasoning. Use it. But don't get caught up in the inter-unit fire. Hang back and to the side and engage renegades and assist evac. Keep eyes and ears open and stay on the comm. Webb?"

"Captain?"

"I'll leave the *Zero* company in your command." Hugo watched him for any sort of reaction but Webb's face stayed blank.

"Yes, sir."

The formality made Hugo go cold, but he couldn't think what else to do. He looked between the faces of his crew. He tried to speak, swallowed then tried again. "Come back from this," he said. "All of you. I think it's time you got some recognition for everything you've done."

The responses on the faces were mixed. Sub and Bolt looked uncertain,

More looked doubtful. Rami's face was still and calm and Webb's face held a twist of anger before he smoothed it out again.

"Go," Hugo said, gesturing down the corridor. "Report to me and only me. Rendezvous at the *Assertion*."

"Yes sir," everyone muttered then jogged away. Hugo watched them go, suddenly feeling very alone in the thronging hallways.

He was just turning towards the doors to the fighter bay when Quinn came trotting up the supply corridor, heading right for him and calling his name. "Hugo, you bastard," she said as she drew up and jabbed him in the chest. Her face was flushed and she glanced at everyone that passed by. "You were Service all along? When I've been sneaking you through patrols this last year?"

"We couldn't tell you, Quinn. We couldn't tell anyone."

"So you've been reporting on me?" she hissed.

"No," Hugo shook his head. "You don't understand."

"I helped you screw procedure..." Her mouth was tight with actual fear. "And all along -"

"Quinn, quiet," Hugo snapped seeing people start to look at them. "I'm not going to report you. My remit... well... we were closer to the other side than this, if you see what I mean."

"Huh?"

"It was the trouble outside the Service they were interested in. Not problems at home."

She pressed her lips together and stared hard at him. Then she nodded. "Okay. Well. Thanks, I guess. But I would take it kindly, now that you're commander of Gamma Company again, if you forget that we ever met. Deal?"

"You can trust me, Quinn."

"Well, I bloody well hope so."

"You can," he insisted.

She sighed and he thought he saw relief slump her shoulders. "Good." Then she looked around at the chaos around her as if just noticing it. "I guess, considering, it would have been better if they had," she mused "kept a closer watch at home, I mean. Not better for me, mind, but for the poor bastards in the Lunar Colonies."

"There's still time to fix it."

She made a noise, gazing at the wall display behind him. Then she looked back. "Good luck, Hugo," she held out her hand. He shook it then she turned and disappeared into the crowd. He watched her go with something shifting inside him, trying not to think about how many more people might look at him that way before all this was over.

He found Gamma Company in the bay, swarming around a unit of pristine fighters. The other units were already launching, but he was pleased to see Fraser was making sure his orders were being followed and that every fighter was having a full series of checks. Technicians were running amongst them all with fuelling lines, panels, tools and charge readers, obeying the many and impatient commands of the pilots.

"How are we doing?" Hugo asked Fraser as he came trotting up with his panel full of reports, accompanied by a harried tech with arms full of vacuum suits.

"Nearly, there Commander," he said, though he was eyeing the other fighter units dwindling as more and more ships launched. "All fighters are almost compliant and we have 84% pilot capacity."

Hugo frowned as he took a suit from the tech and started climbing into it. "Where's everyone else?"

"Part of the company was dispatched to Earth last week to increase manpower around the North America border disputes."

"Have they been recalled?"

"Yes, sir. But they won't be here for hours yet. Civilians are answering the recruiting call, though," he said, managing to sound disproving. "We've managed to fill four more fighters."

"And I'll take one more."

"Commander?"

"I'm not going to sit staring at Analyst data whilst everyone else takes the hits," he snapped, handing the panel back.

"Very well, sir."

"Kaleb!"

Hugo spun, not quite believing his ears. Harvey strolled towards him, waving. She had on a Service-issue vacuum suit and her smile was wide and bright.

"Marilyn," he said, blinking and glancing at Fraser. "I mean, Captain Harvey... what are you doing here?"

"Far be it from me to ignore a Call," she said with an even wider smile and a mock salute. "Especially one with such a handsome return. So..." she stood with her hands on her hips and looked him up and down. "Service all along, huh?"

"Yes."

"The crew too?"

"Everyone."

She shook her head, still grinning. "Should have guessed. Good lord," she let her glance slide from Hugo to a very uncomfortable looking Fraser. "With friends like the Service who needs enemies, huh?"

Fraser stiffened.

"Fraser. To your fighter. Report in to *Assertion* with our status."

"Yes sir." Fraser flung another dark look at Harvey then strode away.

Harvey laughed. "You know, I can forgive myself for not figuring it out. You were always stiff as a board, Kaleb, but never as stiff as that." She gestured after Fraser. "Hey," she said, sobering up. "Can we talk?"

"It's good to see you," Hugo took a step closer to her and lowered his voice. "It really is. More than I can say, even. I wish I could talk -" He trailed off as more shouts and the clunks of sealing cockpits rang out around them.

"It's good to see you too," she said, her snide smile melting into something a little warmer. "Shall we agree to both make it through this so you can answer all my questions?"

Hugo managed a smile of his own. "Not all of them, maybe."

Her smile faltered. "There's one main one. Webb...?"

Hugo felt his spirits slump back down. "Did you hear?"

"I don't know what I heard," Harvey said, face grim. "I heard that he's... alive? How's that possible?"

Hugo shook his head, the hum of fighter engines starting up filling the bay. "There's too much to explain. And even I don't entirely understand. Keep that promise and I'll tell you everything. Or I'll try to."

Harvey's eyes flickered for a moment, then she nodded. "Okay, Kaleb. Commander, even. You better get to your ship."

Hugo nodded, glanced around and then leant forward and kissed her on the cheek. The brief moment when he could smell her skin made him feel strong. He pulled away and made himself turn and head to one of the berthed fighters where a technician was shifting from one foot to another, visibly resisting the urge to tell Hugo to hurry.

Hugo scrambled up the ladder and strapped himself in whilst keying in the commands to raise the engines and seal the cockpit. The tech scrambled away with the ladder and Hugo watched his hands move over the controls as if from a distance.

"Gamma Company," he said, pulling on his headset. "Move out and report in."

The unit reported into his earpiece in a regimented and practised order as he eased his fighter up from the berth and steered it towards the drift shield and open space beyond. They were followed by the brusquer and more garbled reports of the civilian recruits without code names. Harvey was last and he could hear the grin in her voice as she addressed him as Commander.

Hugo pushed thoughts of her from his mind as they left the fighter bay and Command fell away in his rear-view display. A glance at his other screens showed Gamma Company falling into perfect formation around him. The *Assertion* loomed ahead with other companies assembling around her and he headed in her direction, manoeuvring between the milling companies of fighters and fuel ships, repair rigs and communication vessels.

"Commander Hugo, Gamma Company, reporting in," Hugo said over the comm as they left the bustle of Command behind and his hail cue came in from the flagship.

"Nice of you to join us, Commander," Luscombe grumbled. "I have been told we don't have time to question why you are in a fighter and not here at your station so I will store that away for later. Along with many other things we need to chat about. Form your company up at point 5-0-99 and await orders."

As he moved along the underbelly of the *Assertion*, steering his company between the bands of skiffs, fighters and tugs that zoomed through the shadows, he saw a familiar shape up ahead. The *Zero* hung steady in the light beyond the flagship with her three fighters formed up beside her. The fractured light made her hull gleam and he felt a catch in his throat as he realised he knew every scratch and dent in her hull.

There was a sweeping moment of vertigo whilst he struggled with the notion he was in drift around her rather than in her command chair and wondered if he would get to sit in it again.

Hugo keyed in secure comm codes. "Webb? Are we set?"

"Sure are, Hugo. Shall we dance?"

"Fall in and follow me."

"Gotta say, Hugo," Webb said with an edge in his voice. "This is kind of exciting, huh?"

Ø

Webb listened to the silence that was Hugo's reply to his comment with a grim satisfaction stealing through him. He engaged *Father*'s thrusters just as Gamma Company's formation drew level and he pulled in alongside. The others fell in to port and they followed the unit to the rendezvous.

He took a moment to blink at the *Assertion*. It filled his whole screen, a great stretch of silver, blinking lights, busy portals, rows and rows of viewscreens and gargantuan thrusters mounted at her stern. He would have mistaken her for a colony, had she been more battered and possibly with some patched-up breaches in the hull.

The monstrous bridge arched up out of the main body of the ship like a cobra's head. Her guns mounted below were easily each as big as the *Zero*. He swallowed, knowing that another, newer, one of these ships was waiting for them at the strip.

He was so busy staring that Hugo had to repeat his command.

Webb shook himself. "Say again... Captain? Commander? What do I call you, anyway?"

"Hugo's fine," Hugo grunted and Webb couldn't stop his grin. "Be ready. Admiral Wilson's fleet is almost re-grouped. We'll be launching for the strip in four minutes."

"Roger, Hugo," Webb said. "Everyone got that?" His crew all responded with clipped affirmations. Webb hesitated then turned the comm back on. "Look, guys... I know this is weird for you. And I'm sorry. I'm aware I haven't exactly handled this whole thing well. But Hugo's right. This could be the beginning of better things. If we make it through."

Silence replied to him but he blundered on.

"You might get some medals. Or some decent pay. Fuck, you might even get a chance to make your own decisions about your future. Weirder things have happened. Apparently. But... I know it's what he would have wanted for you. What do you say?"

"Sure thing, Commander," Sub replied. "For Webb."

"For Webb," said Bolt.

"For both of you," More said. "And for Hugo."

"Steady, More," Webb tried to make his smile heard in his voice. "Don't you think his head's gonna be big enough after this as it is?"

"Depends how it ends, I suppose Commander."

"Guess so," Webb relented. He paused, chewing his lip and staring at the fighter positions on his display. Then he switched the band to single communication before he could change his mind. "Anita?"

There was a pause before Rami replied. "Yes?"

He took a breath, shook his head. "Look... I... dammit. It's just -"

"It's okay."

"No," he snapped, rubbing his eyes and willing the ache inside his ribs to ease, just for a moment. "There were lots of things he should have said to you, Anita. Lots of things he wanted to say." He paused. Commands from Hugo started to scroll over his screen but he just stared at them, listening to Rami not speaking. "I know what they were... if you want to hear them."

"I think I know already, Commander," she said after a silence. "But...

thank you."

He nodded though he knew she couldn't see him. The ache hadn't shifted, it had just became sharper. Power surges from the surrounding ships showed on his display. He switched the comm back to group transmission, breathed in, straightened his back and put his hands on the controls. "Okay folks. This is it. See you on the other side," he said, impressed despite himself that he managed to say it with a steady voice. He tightened his grip on the controls and told himself again to ignore the feelings that weren't his battling in his brain. He'd made up his mind. They'd already done their mourning for him. He was making things right.

Ø

Hugo took a breath as his fighter got up to speed and allowed himself one moment to close his eyes to be away from it all, then he opened them and slid into his role like climbing back into a second skin. He only let himself check that the *Zero* and her three fighters were in formation behind him once as Gamma Company moved out before being taken over by the command feed from the *Assertion*, reports from his company and the Analyst data already feeding in via murmured commands in his headset and data on his screens.

At maximum speed they came up to the Lunar Strip in less than three hours, but to Hugo it felt like it could have been anywhere between three seconds and forever. The moon hung bloated and pale in the distance, her string of colonies nothing more than glints stretching off into the darkness of space until they looked like no more than extra stars flecked across the blackness.

His screens showed the *Resolution* and her fleet were right in their path, but they weren't even in visual range before Pharos flung her first wave at them.

The flat, toneless voice of an Analyst came through his headset over the pounding of his own pulse. "Alpha, Omega. Sweep 6-6-1 and come up at level 3 engagement. Gamma and Beta counter-approach. Fire at Will. Acknowledge."

"Acknowledged," Hugo muttered as he swept his fighter down and away from the approaching enemy. "Stay tight, Gamma. Engage at 6-8-4." He paused. "Fire at will and listen for commands."

The lights from the unit's auto-acknowledgements all flicked on across his monitors. Webb didn't respond but a scan of his instruments showed the *Zero* hanging just out of formation and then he pushed them from his head.

Pharos's fighters started firing even before they were near enough for accurate hits. He'd seen the technique before, designed to split up formations before they got too close, but Hugo sent a course correction on silent commands through to his company and they missed the bulk of the shots and pulled up as they did so, slamming into the midst of the enemy squadron from below.

He skimmed and pulled, swerved, shot and swept through the formation. His company followed his commands and section by section they started to split the nearest enemy squadron up. His cockpit was occasionally swept white with the light of the fire from the *Assertion*'s cannons.

Hugo shook his head. The flagship's cannons were powerful but the fighters were too manoeuvrable, dodging the *Assertion*'s fire more often than they were hit. But too many of their people had died already at the hands of supposed comrades. He suspected Wilson was trusting in their numbers to negate the need to conserve firepower. Either that or showing mercy was not in the forefront of his mind.

Hugo kept one eye on his screens as he swept back again. Another enemy craft ballooned into a silent fireball on his port side but a glance at his reading showed he had already lost three of his own. One civilian. His heart climbed into his mouth before he realised it wasn't Harvey. He shuddered and re-engaged.

The battle wore on. His pulse stayed steady though sweat was breaking out on his forehead. His scopes displayed his unit as green dots taking out the red dots of the enemy. Out of the viewscreen he saw them as flashes of fire against the blackness of space that flared before being sucked into nothing.

"Beta sweep though 8-5-7, push in on a Lunar heading," an Analyst purred in his ear. "Gamma bank 5-2-5. Engage enemy. Acknowledge."

Hugo ground his teeth a moment.

"Gamma, acknowledge," Luscombe snapped.

"Sir," Hugo growled. "There's a break to port. If we -"

"Bank 5-2-5, Gamma. Engage enemy. Acknowledge."

Hugo ground his teeth some more. "Acknowledged."

He relayed the instructions to his unit and swept them along the edge of the battle, firing as he went. He barked more orders, keeping his unit on its course, wincing when the enemy fighters reflected their move and took out two of his fighters before they'd gained position.

"Hugo?"

"What?" Hugo snapped, pulling his fighter round to avoid an oncoming enemy, pulse cannons blazing.

"There's a break," Webb replied. "Point 7-4... uh... over there! To port. Between you and the *Resolution*."

"Stick to formation, Commander. You've got a bank coming through below."

"I got them," came More's calm voice and Hugo caught the flash of the *Zero*'s heavier guns taking out two of the engaging on-comers, breaking their pattern.

"Hugo -"

"Webb, the break's closing."

"We could still get your fighters through. And the *Zero*."

"What for? The only thing that can engage the *Resolution* is another flagship."

"That's Service thinking. And just what Pharos will be expecting."

Hugo switched his comm feed to order a bank of Gamma to swing round in response to the re-engagement of a new squadron attempting a sweep from above. When he switched it back Webb was still talking.

"Stick to your orders, Commander," Hugo talked over him.

"Since when do you care about orders, Hugo?"

"Since ignoring one got you killed," he snapped.

"That wasn't me," the clone's voice was low and dangerous. "Hugo, three or four good shots could take out her communication rig."

"How do you know that?"

"Webb knew. I know. Seriously, Hugo. We cut the puppet strings and her fleet will fall apart. Tell me I'm wrong."

"Captain, watch out!"

Rami's warning had come just in time. Hugo swore as he swerved out of oncoming fire. "Dammit, Webb."

"Hugo, do it!"

Hugo swore again then switched his comm. "Gamma Company..." he took a breath, checked his instruments then swung his steer stick round. "Follow and flank. Needle formation to point 7-4-0. Acknowledge."

Every Service pilot in his company acknowledged without question which caused a momentary chill to brush through him. Harvey was the only one to pause.

"You sure about that, Hugo?"

"Stick close," Hugo said. "Webb has a plan."

"Why doesn't that reassure me?"

"Move out," Hugo ordered and he banked hard. The battle disappeared from view and yawning, starry blackness filed his viewscreen, looking calm, cool and peaceful in comparison to the blinking chaos of his controls. A glance at his scope showed the remains of Gamma Company tailing him, with the rogue blips of the *Zero* and her three fighters alongside. He sent one more glance over all his instruments, ignoring the cool voice of the Analyst in his ear ordering him to respond, and plunged his fighter into the thick of the action.

He held his breath and willed his control to let his eyes and hands do the thinking. The drift was a tangle of fighters with the *Resolution* insignia across their sides, all pressing forward for a chance to break through. The break in their own line ebbed and flowed but Hugo wove and ducked with cannons on full, his company keeping in a tight cluster behind him and together they blasted a narrow channel through the swarming fighters.

The *Zero* went by on his starboard as nothing more than a flash of light. Its weapons blazed and three enemy fighters that had peeled off from the main engagement to tighten the defence were reduced to so much rubble bouncing off his cockpit. The pale backdrop of the moon gleamed in the distance, Tranquillity glowing in its crater. The *Resolution* hung like a giant insect before them. Some of Beta and Omega that had managed to get this far were engaged around her. She was expertly placed, just far enough towards the moon to be out of range of the *Sincerity*'s and the *Assertion*'s guns but still close enough to get accurate readings on the battle.

"Keep tight and close, Gamma," Hugo said. "Pilots Brian through Jango engage the defensive fleet. Keep in close with Beta. Everyone else..." he took a breath. "Engage the *Resolution*. Concentrate fire on the communication towers and network relays. Co-ordinates and schematics being transmitted." Hugo keyed in the numbers from memory then engaged his thrusters to maximum power before he could change his mind and slammed forward between some approaching fighters, firing as he went.

Three more of his unit were lost in the first few minutes. He pressed on, backing up the fighters drawing up the defences. The *Resolution* was radiating interference, so his readings on the flagship were sketchy, but from what he could tell by eye his unit were landing the hits.

"Concentrate fire," Hugo barked and three fighters swerved to obey. "*Zero*. We need your cannons.... where's Webb?" Hugo asked, scanning his readings

"Sir," More sounded uncertain. "Sir... *Father* made impact with the flagship."

Hugo went cold. "Repeat, *Zero*."

"He cut his comm and *Father* went straight in at speed and took out a whole docking sector."

"Is he okay?"

"I don't know sir," said More.

"Sir?"

"Sub?"

"Sir... I feel I should tell you..."

"Sub," More warned.

"Silence, More," Hugo snapped. "Sub, what's happened?"

There was a pause when they all had to dance away from an incoming wave and let the next wave behind them make a hole in the line before they could swing back round towards to the *Resolution*. "Sub?" Hugo prompted again.

"Webb took some explosives from the hold before he launched. He told me not to tell you."

Hugo swore, long and bitterly. "Idiot," he growled. "Fucking suicidal moron."

"Sir," More started again but Hugo ignored him.

"Webb," Hugo barked into the comm. "Webb, come in. Come in now." Just static returned on *Father*'s comm channel. He tried Webb's wrist panel and still no response. He swore again. "All *Zero* crew, flank Gamma and run interference and defensive manoeuvres. Report in to the *Assertion* and keep in track with the battle plan."

"Kaleb, what are you doing?"

"Marilyn, stick with the *Zero*," he ordered.

"Kaleb," she called again before Hugo could no long hear anything over the blaring of proximity alarms in his cockpit. The *Resolution* loomed closer and closer until he could pick out individual viewscreens in her hull. His readings blurred and buzzed from the interference as he approached the impact site that had once been the starboard docking station.

XX

Webb had expected to feel anger. He'd expected the wash of red that almost blinded him when he had overhead the conversation between Hugo and Luscombe to rise up and swamp him again, make him so charged with the emotion that it gave him energy. He had been concerned that it might cause him to get clumsy or caught before the job was done.

But he needn't have worried.

He didn't feel hot or cold. There was nothing. Just a blank coolness like the drift of space. He knew what he had to do and that was it. It was easy.

He hadn't even felt a pang when *Father*'s chassis crumpled and flame from the engines bloomed and snuffed in the vacuum of the ruined docking bay. His neck was a bit sore from the impact but that was it. The harness and crash frame had done its job, just as Sub had said it would.

He'd already sealed on his helmet and what was left of the controls along with a few determined kicks got the hatch open. He shrugged the pack on his back then launched a wire into the mess of shadow and floating debris that was the docking bay. He pressed the recoil and was speeding through the silent space deeper into the *Resolution*. One body, eyes wide and mouth frozen in a silent scream, bumped past him in the dark then drifted on.

He activated his boot magnets and set about trying to override the breach protocols on the first door he came to. The chilled determination in him guided his fingers and he had the door open in moments. There were alarms blaring in the corridors and people running. Orders scrolled on wall displays. He ducked into the first dark space he could find and shed the vacuum suit. He prowled through the back corridors, the ship's schematics cold, hard lines inside his head and grabbed the first unfortunate technician who happened to pass by on his own.

Webb left his body tucked in a corner of a conduit cupboard. The glassy eyes stared up at him from either side of the bullet hole as he pulled on the Service-issue coveralls.

"Don't worry buddy," Webb mumbled. "Better a hole in the head now than eating drift later." He nudged the technician's legs further into the corner with his foot, not looking at the slack face, then moved out into the busy corridor. No one gave him a second glance.

Part of him marvelled at the efficiency of the activity around him. There was no panic. Every face was calm, every workstation had an occupant and every officer had a headset they were muttering orders into. Everyone was dressed in black and grey and moved with control, even the ones pelting down towards the engineering decks with tools and panels.

Not that it would do them any good.

He got down to the engineering decks and still no one looked at him. The breach he'd caused with *Father* was scrolling in the damage reports but nowhere was there a report to check for an intruder. He guessed they thought no one would be that dumb. Or perhaps sneaking in wasn't the proper ethics of war.

He strolled into the main reactor chamber without any technicians even glancing up from their displays. He paced through the safety hatch and up to the towering metal structure that housed the port reactor. The humming was so loud it made the air feel solid. He took a moment to gawp up at the structure, was caught unaware by the thought that Kinjo would love to see this, then shook his head and bent and shoved the block of high-power explosive as far under the reactor housing as he could reach.

He made a show of pausing at a workstation and tapping in some commands as he left, taking the opportunity to re-route some of the reactor's diagnostic scans, then paced back out of the reactor room and into the teeming corridors.

The river of activity continued to flow by him. He turned towards the bridge, keeping his pace steady but finally starting to feel fire mounting inside him.

The command levels were emptier but still no one gave him a glance. The viewscreens looked out on the battle, but he kept his eyes on the deck. The guarded doors of the bridge were in sight when he heard a familiar voice.

"Governor Cho-Jin, you must stay put," Fitzroy was growling into a wrist panel as he came up behind him. "I'm on my way to Pharos now. All is going as planned. Stay in Tranquillity to centralise communication."

Webb slowed and let Fitzroy overtake him and proceed onto the bridge, the security men nodding him through.

Webb drifted along, putting in a pair of ear plugs, searching inside himself for fear but finding none, until the guards at the door asked for ID. He dropped the stun charge right between them, squeezing his eyes shut. He could still felt the blast ripple through his flesh and had to blink as the effects dissipated, then stepped over the downed guards, pulling out the ear plugs. The double doors to the bridge hissed open as he approached.

The *Resolution*'s bridge was easily as big as the *Zero*'s hold and was almost blindingly bright. Everything was again Service-white and pristine. It made his head ache. No one, not the navigators, gunners, pilots or guards looked up as he slid himself into a tech workstation right at the back of the room.

Pharos was not sat in the command chair but stood in the centre of the deck, feet apart, face set and eyes locked out the viewscreen, even as Fitzroy chattered urgently in her ear. Webb's jaw ached. He made himself breathe slower as his hands on the controls worked their way around the *Resolution*'s system firewalls, but he couldn't tear his eyes off the admiral. He couldn't look away from the way she stared out at the thruster trails and explosions lighting up the darkness of space with nothing in her eyes.

He watched his hands enter the re-route commands and then pulled out his gun.

Ø

Hugo had to make a conscious effort to push aside the creeping chill produced by moving through the corridors of a Service flagship whilst knowing he was in enemy territory. He cursed Pharos and Fitzroy and everything he could think of as he looked around at the Service men and women, clothed as he was, thinking like he did, or like he used to, but knowing that they were fighting and dying for something that, at the end of it all, was nothing to do with them.

He kept his head down in case he was recognised and accessed the first unmanned workstation he came to to try and find out what the hell Webb was up to. The strength of the surge of relief he had felt when *Father*'s cockpit had been empty had unsettled him. But this, along with everything else, he pushed aside. For a moment nothing but Doll's words echoed through his head...

...you might still get a chance to save him...

It wasn't Webb... and yet it was. All the hurt, all the anger, all the bitterness of everything that had ever been done to Ezekiel Webb now belonged to his clone. Hugo could guess what he would do in the same situation. And if he was anywhere near right, he knew Webb would not have planned on surviving.

It was down to Hugo to get him out. To save him.

He stared at the workstation screen with his zero-results search blinking at him whilst system alert lights flashed and alarms sounded around him, then went with his gut and turned aft to try and find express lifts that would take him up to the bridge.

The first moment of real panic rung through the corridors when the ship gave a great shudder and the lights all blacked out. There was a moment of swallowing silence and then the air was storming away. His feet went out from under him. He grabbed out blindly, got a hold on something solid and clung. His ears were filled with a rushing like a waterfall and the air was ripped from his lungs. Muffled screams rang out and objects knocked against him in the dark.

Something struck his head. He bit his tongue and saw stars but managed to keep his fingertips around the handhold. He blinked the hot stinging out of his eyes and spat blood. Just when his fingers were starting to slip, there was a surge that rocked his belly and he fell to the ground.

He sat up, blinking, just as the lights came back on. People were shaking themselves and getting to their feet, some rubbing bruises, others wiping blood out of their eyes like he was. There was lots of coughing. The air tasted thin and the hum of the ship's workings had changed key.

Crew around him gathered themselves and limped on, muttering into wrist panels and headsets, giving or seeking new orders. Hugo got to his feet then froze as he caught a glimpse of one of the displays across the corridor. He made himself stagger to it and stared. The port reactor was gone and had taken most of the stern with it. The results displayed just long enough for Hugo to gather that all external communications, 40% of life support, 25% of the crew and 60% of the power were now gone. Then the screen went blank and the overhead lights dimmed.

He turned and ran, picking his way through dropped equipment and debris. Technicians worked feverishly and were shouted at by officers hovering like crows. The displays flickered back on and someone somewhere cheered but then was silenced. Their course had changed.

"Get back in the system," someone barked. "Get those commands overridden, now."

"I can't, sir," a navigator quavered. "Someone's put in a lockdown -"

"Break through it."

"There's not enough processing power left in the main servers -"

Hugo kept moving, heart pounding. The lights went again. Only emergency lighting came back on. The panic around him fizzled to a frozen acceptance, like ice forming in the air. A few people continued to rush by, but most just stood and stared at the wall displays. He could smell smoke.

When he got to the lifts they weren't working. He swore again and turned about to try and find a service hatch. The order to abandon ship started blaring out just as he found one. He had to press against the bulkhead to avoid being swept off in the throng of crew heading towards what was left of the stern and the escape pods. They hurried but they didn't push and they followed each other like ants moving through a colony. He wanted to scream at them to hurry the fuck up. Didn't they know the *Resolution* was bleeding oxygen? Bleeding fuel? If the stern fires reached the second reactor...

He shook his head and elbowed his own way through the oncoming tide of crew and took the ladders and stairs two and three at a time. After the chaos of the engineering and service corridors, the stillness in the command-level corridors was eerie. The evacuation command was still repeating through wall speakers and the alarm lights were still flashing, but there was no one around. He passed one downed security guard and then another, and pulled out his own gun. The doors to the bridge were closed but not locked. They slid open when he hit the control.

Only one of the guards who had her weapon trained on Webb looked around as Hugo came in. The other two kept their eyes on their target, dressed in Service Technician coveralls with a grim look on his face and a gun pointed at Admiral Pharos. Their focus allowed Hugo to take them out before they even realised what was happening. The one who had seen him opened fire in his direction but he had already managed to get behind a workstation. It exploded into shards of metal and sparking wires. More shots were exchanged and cries rung out and then everything was silent again. Even the alarms and automated announcements seemed muted. Smoke hung in the air.

His ears were ringing and there were fresh spots of pulsing heat in his shoulders and leg where shrapnel or bullets had grazed him. He swiped blood out of his eyes and got to his knees.

The security team were all dead. Fitzroy was propped up in a control chair, hand clutched at his chest and struggling to sit up. There was blood dribbling from his mouth and his already pale skin had taken on a greyish tinge. The only ones standing were Webb and Pharos.

"Stay back, Hugo," Webb grated in a voice Hugo barely recognised.

Pharos looked at Webb like he was an insect caught in her cockpit. The grip the commander had on his weapon caused his knuckles to stand out white and his face looked like it had been cast from steel.

"You destroyed a future today, Webb," Pharos said into the silence. "If your hell exists, it will welcome you with open arms."

"Funny," Webb said, grin sickly. "You seemed rather fond of me at one point. How times change."

She glared down her nose at him. The bridge shuddered around them and the proximity alarms rose in volume. The yellow streaks of jettisoned escape pods arced off and away outside the wide central viewscreen. The white surface of the moon filled the whole expanse beyond. Tranquillity blinked ahead.

"Webb," Hugo said, standing. "You set us on a collision course?"

Webb didn't move. "You shouldn't have come."

"I can't let you do this."

Webb threw him the twisted grin that had been turned on Pharos. "Don't worry. It'll all be over soon."

"Webb -"

"Don't call me that."

"He's right," Pharos intoned. "He doesn't deserve the name Webb. Or McCullough. Despite his blood, despite his life, none of the Lunar greats have manifested themselves in him in any way. They would be ashamed."

"What, the bastard your precious McCullough fathered with some nameless Lunar 1 nobody didn't live up to your expectations?" Webb laughed, clicking back the gun hammer. "And you call me deluded."

Pharos smiled. It was horrible. "You lost, useless fool," she said. "Even now you don't understand."

"I'm about done with your brand of understanding, Admiral."

She shook her head and for a moment Hugo thought he saw sadness creep into the edges of her expression but then it iced over again. "McCullough and I were to build a future. You, our child, were to be that future. But instead you've destroyed it all."

Webb stiffened. His face twisted. Hugo stared at the pair of them. Stared at the way they stood, the same murderous determination in each of their faces.

"No... it's not true..." Webb's voice cracked.

Pharos's smile widened into a mockery of Webb's usual grin. "Oh, my dear boy. If only that were so." She put her head on one side. Tranquillity loomed closer. All the hail lights on the command panel were flashing and warnings scrawled manically across the displays but Pharos didn't even spare them a glance. "I'm still trying to decide whether it was Duran or I who made the biggest mistake. Me, for hiding you on Lunar 1 or Duran for insisting you were retrieved. He knew his chance was over but that our dream could live again, in you. If only he knew how you'd end up ruining everything."

"He had help," Fitzroy growled in the corner, breathing shallow but face twisted in fury.

Pharos's weighted gaze slid from Fitzroy to Hugo. "Yes. You. You who I thought had the flexibility of mind to understand what it was like to straddle opposing sides. To see all angles. To appreciate the necessity of making one's own rules. I'm not even sure which of you has been the biggest disappointment."

"Webb," Hugo said, ignoring the admiral though it felt like her gaze was burning holes in him. "We have to go."

"Yes. Go," Pharos waved a hand. "Go and accept your medals and then run away somewhere dark and spend the rest of your life trying to convince yourself you did the right thing."

"Did you order it?" Webb snapped, taking a step closer to Pharos.

"Order what?" she asked, in a tired voice.

"His death? When you couldn't get him to join you, did Fitzroy put out the contract on his life, or was it you?" For the briefest of moments Hugo thought he saw the barest flicker in the admiral's eyes. "Did you order the death of your own son?" he shouted whilst the hand holding the gun trembled.

Pharos clenched her jaw and the flicker was gone. "Yes," she said, not breaking eye contact for a second. "Better dead than a life spent as less than nothing."

Webb's whole body was shaking. Fitzroy was no longer smiling. Nor was he breathing. The ship shook. Hugo could make out the lines of the skyways and spacescrapers of Tranquillity.

"You took too many wrong turns," Pharos whispered, looking out the viewscreen.

"I guess I take after my mother," Webb's voice shook and choked but he was grinning. The gun fired. Pharos went down. Webb kept firing until she stopped moving. She lay slumped on the deck, one leg bent under her, arms spread wide. Blood trickled in rivulets between the floor tiles. The one eye that remained stared up at the bulkhead. Webb stood over her, still shaking, gun still aimed.

Hugo shook himself and staggered forward, clutched at his commander's jacket. "Webb," he hissed "Help me redirect the ship."

Webb turned his face to Hugo but it didn't look like he was seeing him. His eyes were red. His mouth was open but he made no sound. Some of Pharos's blood was spattered across his face.

"Zeek," Hugo said, taking a grip of his commander's shoulders. "Snap out of it."

"Tranquillity has to go," he mumbled, gazing right through him.

"No," Hugo shook his head, looked right into his eyes. "No, Webb. There are innocent people down there."

Webb's face screwed up into another twisted smile. "All gotta go sometime. Better to die now than live as less than nothing."

Hugo shook him. "Fucking snap out of it. This isn't you."

Webb blinked and tears cut tracks in the dirt and the blood. He looked surprised for a moment then seemed to finally focus. He looked very young. He pulled Hugo's hands off his shoulders. "I'm done, Hugo. It's over."

"Webb..." The commander's jaw tightened. "Commander, we get through this we can find you a new name. A new start. Just... don't let this happen. Tranquillity may have been part of Pharos's game plan, but the people in it weren't."

Webb swallowed a few times, still staring at Hugo. He felt the edges of desperation begin to claw at his insides and he put a hand behind Webb's head and pulled him forward so their foreheads were pressed together. "Please," he breathed. "Don't be like her."

Webb shivered and pulled away. He wiped his eyes on his sleeves, hesitated for the longest moment Hugo remembered experiencing, then went to the nearest control panel. Hugo, heart in his mouth, took a co pilot's chair. Sweat was soon pouring down his face as he wrestled with the controls. Tranquillity was wheeling closer and closer. He felt them gather speed as gravity took hold.

"Re-route all power from the starboard reactor," Hugo ordered. "Get everything, *everything*, into the thrusters."

Webb shook his head. "I don't think it will be enough."

"Do it anyway. Re-route gravity and life support if you have to."

Webb's face was still blank but he nodded and keyed in the commands.

Second by painful second crept by and slowly the controls started to respond. The ship groaned and clanked but gradually and sickeningly slowly, she arced out of her course.

"Ten degrees further," Hugo said through clenched teeth. "Just get her ten degrees further to port. Then we run."

"Hugo -"

"Do it."

Webb pressed more commands and stared out of the viewscreen as Tranquillity fell out of view and the rocky grey of the moon's waste spread before them.

"Right. Run."

They scrambled away from the control panel and ran across the bridge.

They skirted Pharos and Fitzroy's slumped forms and pelted through the doors and down the corridor.

"Shit," Hugo spat when he realised all the command-level escape pods had been jettisoned. "We'll have to chance the engineering levels..." Webb just nodded, looking drained and uncaring but Hugo growled and grabbed him by the jacket and shoved him ahead. "Run, damn you."

They ran. The gravity warped and slipped, making his insides lurch and occasionally causing them to have to stumble along at an angle. It was becoming more difficult to catch his breath but he kept moving, keeping Webb ahead of him. They vaulted down service stairs and ladders, jumping over rubble and careening around corners as fast as their overworked legs and the weakening gravity would take them. He spent precious seconds at a workstation to establish that there were some escape pods left on the next level below before ordering Webb onwards.

They got down a level then skidded to a halt in front of some locked blast doors.

"It's breached," Webb mumbled. "You have a suit. Go."

"This isn't a negotiation," Hugo snapped and shoved Webb towards a workstation. "Strap yourself in."

"Hugo -"

"Fucking stop arguing with me and do it."

Webb sighed and strapped himself into the workstation chair, eyeing Hugo as he pulled up his helmet and sealed it. He took deep breaths of the suit's air and felt his mind clear then set about overriding the breach protocol on the doors. He remembered a time when he didn't even know breach protocols could be overridden. Burying the mixed feelings that thought produced, he slammed in the last code and the doors juddered open.

He stumbled over with the force of the escaping air. He rolled over and over and heard Webb cry out but activated his magnets and his feet clamped to the bulkhead. He felt something in his leg go but didn't let himself acknowledge the pain. Debris flew past him and around the next bend in the corridor towards the breach. The emergency lights flickered off then on again and the ship shook.

He got himself upright and used his hand and foot magnets to crab his way down to the nearest pod and activated the doors. As soon as they were open he turned back and waved at Webb. Webb sat staring down the corridor at Hugo. For a moment Hugo thought he wasn't going to move but then he shook his head and undid the restraints.

The commander tumbled and was pulled down the passage, heels digging into the floor in an attempt to slow his progress but he still collided into Hugo with enough force to knock the wind out of both of them. Hugo clung on and Webb got a hand out to grab the edge of the pod. Together they heaved themselves through and activated the door control.

Everything stilled as the pressure stabilised. Hugo swallowed down bile and scrambled to the pod's launch controls. It shook as its thrusters pulled them away from the *Resolution* and then against the moon's gravity. Hugo clung to the controls until the shuddering steadied and there was nothing but swirling, star-pricked blackness out of the viewscreen. He unzipped his helmet and took great gasps of the pod's air just as the fireball of the *Resolution*'s impact with the moon erupted behind them. The force of the blast sent them spiralling away. The narrow rear viewscreen showed the great ship crumpling against the surface like tin. A mess of metal, flame and white moon dust was flung out past their pod then all was still.

Hugo closed his eyes and breathed. The pain from his leg overrode his senses. His throat and eyes stung and he coughed and wiped blood and dirt from his face and slowly felt his pulse begin to calm.

Webb was hunched on the tiny bit of floorspace with his arms wrapped around one knee, staring at nothing.

"Are you okay?" Hugo said, wincing as he scrambled toward him. Webb didn't respond until Hugo put a hand on his arm then his feverish eyes snapped toward him.

"It feels real," Webb whispered. "I know none of it is mine...these feelings aren't real... but it feels real."

Hugo swallowed. Without thinking he hunkered down next to the younger man who buried his face in his arms and shook. The adrenaline was ebbing, leaving a cold, empty nothingness behind. He wanted to cry too. And kick. And scream. But he just sat next to Webb as he trembled and stared at the bulkhead without seeing it.

Ø

"Hugo. Hugo wake up."

Hugo blinked. The sweet blankness of oblivion fled. His vision blurred and then focused in with a snap that brought with it a crashing wave of pain. He coughed and doubled over, groaning.

"Shit," came a familiar voice somewhere close by then hands were on him, sitting him back up. "You fucking moron. Why didn't you say you were hurt?"

"What's happening?" Hugo gritted. Webb was bent over him, face tight with concern. "Webb, I'm fine. What's going on?"

"We're being hailed." He tried for a ghost of his old smile but it came out looking tired and wretched. "Time to face the music?"

Hugo blinked at him. "I suppose so."

Webb nodded and crawled to the escape pod's control panel. There was a mumbled exchange whilst Hugo blinked at the shadows above him. The pod shuddered and changed course and the *Assertion* appeared in the viewscreen. Webb made a show of steering though the lock the flagship had on them wouldn't be something he could steer out of if he tried.

There was a clunk as the pod docked. Webb bent down and got Hugo's arm over his shoulders and they heaved themselves upright just as the doors hissed open. They held each other and staggered into the heaving docking bay.

"Kaleb," Harvey rushed over to them. "Are you okay?"

"What's happening?"

Harvey shook her head, taking his weight off Webb who she was eyeing warily. "It's not over," she said. "They're without their leaders now, but Pharos's fleet are Service-idiots born and bred. They'll die rather than be taken under arrest for mutiny. But the *Sincerity* has broken through the line, more ships are arriving and they're already planning the move into the strip for clean-up."

"What about Tranquillity?"

"The *Resolution* missed it," Harvey said. "Just. I heard that the impact took out some of the outlying environment controls, but nothing vital. They'll be able to stabilise."

"Good." Hugo straightened up off Harvey but then leant heavily against the nearest bulkhead. "Webb?"

Webb was still stood where he had stepped out of the pod, staring around the docking bay. Damaged fighters were crushed in at every available berth and more were arriving. Medics were swarming over the scene, pushing lifter-gurneys and helping pilots down from cockpits. There was blood and burns and bones jutting out of flesh and the air was filled with gasps and cries. The battle could still be seen raging in the distance out of the docking bay's drift shield and viewscreens. The silent dance of flashes, bursts of flame and the starlight glinting off wreckage seemed to fill all space.

"Hugo," Harvey muttered in his ear. "If I were you I'd get yourself patched up by a medic here and get the hell away. Command is after your blood. Both of you."

"Oh good," Hugo murmured. "Glad we're going to get the credit."

"I'm serious, Hugo. I could get you out on the *Phoenix* -"

"Captain?"

Hugo turned to see Rami and Bolt approaching. Their flightsuits were rumpled and blackened in patches. Rami's hair was plastered to her forehead and her eyes were red but otherwise she was deathly pale. Bolt looked exhausted and angry.

"What?" Hugo asked, so sharply that Webb snapped his attention back. Rami glanced between them all.

"What is it, Anita?" Harvey said, voice low.

"The *Zero*..." Bolt started, then stopped.

"What's happened?" Webb said, voice cracking.

Rami swallowed, glanced at the floor and took a breath. "We lost her."

"How?" Hugo breathed after a silence like stone.

"During the attack on the *Resolution*," Bolt intoned. "She went in for the communications matrix just as the stern blew."

"More? Sub?" Hugo croaked.

Rami just shook her head, lips a thin line and hands clenched at her sides.

"No," Webb mumbled, looking dazed. He brought his hands up and dug the heels of his palms into his eyes. "No..."

Hugo couldn't seem to get his breath. Heat surged behind his eyes and he could no longer see the docking bay or anyone in it. The pain from his injuries drifted away like smoke on the wind and all he knew then was a blackness opening inside him that threatened to suck him in.

He was only vaguely aware of Harvey cursing and stepping in front of him just as armed Service security men hurried up to them, weapons drawn.

"Don't fucking touch them," she hissed. "I'm warning you."

"Marilyn..." Hugo pulled himself back together enough to stand up straight and lay her hand on her shoulder. She was trembling. "It's okay."

"It's not fucking okay," she cried. "In what way is any of this okay?" She gestured wide with her arm, taking in all the twisted metal, wreckage and the people who were burnt, broken and bleeding.

"Ma'am" the largest of the security men muttered. "Please step aside. These men are under arrest."

Harvey stood shaking a moment longer. "This isn't over," she whispered.

"No," Rami put in, hard eyes on the security men. "No it's not."

XXI

As the lights never went off in the brig and he'd had everything, including his wrist panel, confiscated, Hugo had no idea how long he was there. He lay on the bench and stared at the ceiling for hours. He imagined he could hear the flesh knitting over his shrapnel cuts. He spent hours concentrating on the itch and sting of the cut on his face healing, sinking into the feeling of it so that he wouldn't snap and pound his fists bloody on the white walls.

Every time he closed his eyes there were explosions and blood. More's and Sub's faces flashed in front of him, frozen in drift-rictus or with fire eating flesh from the bone. Sometimes he saw Webb's face, still and grey with rain running down it like tears as soil was shovelled over the closed eyes. Sometimes it was Kinjo's, ash-pale with empty, angry eyes.

In the end he kept his eyes open.

Undetermined days passed, marked only by his visits from the brig medic and a guard with ration bars and water flasks. Sometimes he overheard the conversations of the Servicemen as they changed shifts outside his cell. LIL was overthrown. Eventually. But it was a long and bitter process. All the loyal Service troopers had been killed or evacuated from the Lunar Strip in the first hours of the revolution. The thousands that were left were Pharos's soldiers and, just as Harvey said, fought to the end. It didn't matter that the Lunar Strip colonists rose up and denounced them. It didn't matter that citizens took up arms and joined the Service in taking down the revolutionists' strongholds. They fought on.

Lunar 1, the only colony with little Service presence to begin with, was the only colony unaffected, although Hugo heard later that thousands of its colonists went to the aid of the rest of the strip.

It was drawn out and angry and bloody. And so utterly, utterly pointless that occasionally Hugo was racked with bouts of laughter that made his throat burn and his ribs ache and his eyes stream. Then he would scratch at his healing cuts to bring him back into his body and he would gradually calm and lie and stare at the ceiling again.

Hugo had a feeling the Service had never intended for his arrest to stand. Even the best efforts of Rami and Harvey wouldn't have got a mutiny charge expunged and yet there came a day when the medic came to scold him again for undoing his stitches and she wasn't alone.

"Kale," Giles said once the medic had left. "It's over."

Hugo wasn't sure what aspect of his life his brother was referring to, but he felt something shake out of him all the same. With it went a lot of his anger, his fear and his pain until all that was left was a spreading numbness.

Ø

He was back in his uniform and wondered how he had ever come to miss it. It felt restrictive. He stared at the wall over the commanders' heads until someone ordered him to be at ease.

"Where's Webb?" was the first thing he asked.

His mother looked to Luscombe who sighed. "Gone. Vanished as soon as we gave him his pardon."

Hugo swallowed.

"Have you been discharged from the medbay?" the special commander asked, frowning at the angry cut on his face.

"Why am I here?" Hugo said.

"Sit down, Captain," she said. Hugo took one of the straight-backed seats in front of the panel of commanders. Luscombe looked tired but a little wary. Wilson sat up straight with his hands clasped on the desk, looking determined. His mother, as usual, he couldn't read at all.

"We have something important to discuss with you," she said. Hugo didn't answer. His mother's face didn't change though Luscombe frowned. "The colonel has been going over the history of the *Zero* project with me," Special Commander Hugo continued. "It is extensive. And complex. Probably even more so than your time with it allowed you to know."

Hugo still didn't say anything. Part of him wondered where she was going with this but the larger part of him didn't care and wished they'd send him back to his cell.

"Captain?" her voice hardened as his silence lengthened.

"Ma'am?"

"Are you paying attention?"

"You're telling me things I already know," he said, adding a muttered 'Ma'am' when her eyes hardened.

"Whatever has happened, you're still an officer, Kaleb Hugo. Please act like it."

"I'm still an officer?"

"Just," Luscombe grumbled. "Now listen up, will you?"

Hugo inclined his head slightly, though the numbness making his chest tight did not shift.

His mother regarded him for a moment longer whilst Wilson looked amongst them all, uncertainty showing in the lines of his face.

Special Commander Hugo straightened in her chair and continued. "Now, whilst Admiral Pharos concocted the *Zero* project for her own wayward means -"

"To keep her own son an unwitting political prisoner."

His interruption barely caused his mother to pause, "The principle is still sound," she said. "In the aftermath of this uprising, the Orbit is only going to get more fractured. We need the *Zero* -"

"It's gone," Hugo said, the numbness in his chest flaring for an instant then dissipating again as quickly as a fireball in a vacuum. "Most of its crew, too."

His mother pursed her lips but did not blink. Luscombe fidgeted in his seat, once again shooting him a I-stuck-my-neck-out-for-you glare.

"I am aware of the losses," the special commander continued. "But those that remain...you, Lieutenant Rami, Crewman Bolt. Even Dr. Spinn..." She held up her hand. He hadn't been about to say anything but what he thought must have shown on his face. "Between you all, you have years of experience, contacts and... an alternative way of thinking. We need to assimilate the practices of the *Zero* into the essential functions of the Service. But above-board. Well funded. With proper back up and support."

"An official level of the service for undercover operations?" Hugo asked

"Yes," replied the special commander.

"It's a way forward, Hugo," Luscombe said. "And we want you to to run the show."

"It won't work."

"Why not?"

"The only reason the *Zero* managed what it did is because it wasn't Service. It was in drift. Underground. The crew, the ship. None of them were ever entirely yours."

Wilson and Luscombe exchanged glances. His mother kept her heavy gaze on him.

"So show us," she said. "Help us understand. We need proper investigation and processes to bring every level of offender to justice. No more loose operatives dealing out death and judgement under the guise of vengeance."

"If you're talking about the Splinters -"

"Hugo," Luscombe growled, leaning forward. "The Orbit's fucked up. We're fucked up," the other commanders stiffened but Luscombe bulled on. "I know this probably better than you. But this is the first time the Service has been given a big enough kick up the arse to consider that maybe, yeah, better measures should be in place to monitor and resolve it all. You have a chance to make a real difference here."

Hugo stood. "It's not that simple."

"Captain Hugo," Admiral Wilson called just as he reached the door. Hugo turned. The admiral was stood, hands behind his back, eyes open and measured. "I understand you have lost a lot. You may even feel that you have lost your faith." Hugo looked away, his hand on the door panel, but just stared at the metal. "You don't have to believe me," Wilson continued, "but I will tell you that I understand. I will also tell you that what you've lived through makes you special. It makes you strong."

"I don't feel strong," Hugo murmured.

"Those with strength rarely do," Special Commander Hugo said. "It is something they live with. Carry. It makes them bigger than themselves and gives them reasons not to be defeated, but they don't always know why."

Hugo turned. His mother was looking right at him, as were the other commanders. He finally felt something stir inside him. "My ship and two of my crew are gone. Those that are left have been arrested and re-hired too many times already. My commander..." he swallowed, held Erica Hugo's gaze and tried again when he could trust his voice. "My commander was betrayed and killed then betrayed again. And all for nothing. This isn't my fight any more. I don't know that it ever was."

"Kaleb," his mother stood. Luscombe and Wilson watched her come round the table to stand in front of him. He met her eyes as they searched his, not recognising the look in them. "Fighting for a better future is *everyone's* fight."

Hugo felt a trembling start to take him from the feet up. He couldn't find any more words. But his mother never looked away and when she put a hand on his shoulder it was warm. His trembling stilled.

"I believe in you, son," she said.

"The time for taking orders is over for you, Captain Hugo," Luscombe said after a pause. "Time to start building your own destiny. It's up to you if you build it just for yourself, or for everyone."

Epilogue

The wine was good. It tasted sweet and light and danced on Hugo's tongue just as the music from the orchestra rose and fell in his ears and the couples in their fine suits and gowns swung around the polished dance floor. He took another mouthful then tipped his head back and drained the glass earning a reproving look from Harvey.

"If you pass out I'm not carrying you home," she mumbled.

He didn't answer, just carried on staring round the room. "It's wrong, isn't it?"

"What is?"

"This," Hugo said, gesturing around the ball room whilst grabbing another glass of wine from a passing waiter.

Harvey shrugged. "They want to believe things are changing. Is that so bad?"

"Things won't change."

"They will if you make them," she said, sliding up next to him. Her hair had grown out long enough to be mustard-coloured once more and was clipped up from her face with diamond slide. Her gown was rich and black and swept the floor but she stood like a spacer and her eyes were wide and open and knowing. It comforted him. She smiled and took his hand then looked back over the ballroom. "So how many people in this room are you related to?"

Hugo grimaced. "Altogether? About thirty."

"Fuck," she muttered and he felt her hand tighten in his. "Do I have to talk to them?"

"Don't bother," he said with a half smile. "I don't."

His mother stood near the platform spot-lit from the medal ceremony, resplendent in silver silk, talking with his father and Giles and two more of his brothers. Giles saw him looking and raised a glass in his direction. The smile on his face was genuine. Hugo lifted his glass to his brother in return before draining it and grabbing another.

"If you hurl on my dress I'm never speaking to you again."

Hugo smiled, twirling the glass between his fingers and enjoying the burn of the alcohol in his throat. "I think I need some fresh air," he said. "I'm okay," he added, seeing the concerned purse of her lips. "I'll be back."

"You better be," Harvey muttered. "I still have no idea how to talk to these Service types."

"Relax," he said, bending in and kissing her on the temple. "You're going to be great at this."

She muttered something into her wine glass that he didn't hear. He smiled and strolled away, skirting the edge of the dance floor and moving out the arching doors and onto the terrace. The night breeze was cool and real, like nothing any colony system could replicate. Sydney was a stretch of lights blinking below the glittering bands of the skyways and beyond them, the stars.

He ambled further down the terrace, trying to get away from the music and climbed a fire escape to the next level of the Memorial Music Hall. He emerged onto a smaller terrace that was dark, the ballroom beyond it locked up and silent. The breeze was even stronger up here and it swept away the cheerful tune from below out into night. Hugo sighed and loosened his collar, leaning against the wall and closing his eyes.

"Nice suit."

Hugo started, clutching at the wall. He blinked into the gloom and froze. "What are you doing here?"

"I was invited," Webb chuckled, straightening up from where he'd been leant against the fire escape and pacing forward.

"Invited to the ceremony," Hugo mumbled. "For your medal. Not to skulk about on the roof and scare me to death."

Webb shrugged as he came out into the pale light from the skyways.

"Funny, isn't it?" he said "They want to give me a medal for the same thing they arrested me for." His hair had grown long enough to tuck behind his ears. He looked more like the man Hugo remembered first showing him around the *Zero*, though there was something different. There was more tension in his poise, not so much of the easy grace. His smile was still ready, but it was harder.

"You're a hero of the New Age," Hugo mumbled, looking away over the stretch of lights into the darkness on the horizon. "Don't you want to enjoy it?"

"I'll believe in the New Age when I see it," Webb muttered, leaning on the barrier, the breeze ruffling his hair. "Do you believe in it, Hugo?"

Hugo came forward and leant on the rail beside him. He looked into himself, chasing the emotions rolling around his gut like mercury dropped in a bowl. "Yes," he said suddenly. "At least... I believe it's possible."

"'A new vision, a new future, a new Service'?" Webb said with a grin.

"That's the propaganda," Hugo replied. "That's the pretty face."

"And the reality behind it?"

"Me," Hugo said with a shrug. "And Luscombe. Wilson too. Maybe General Ling, though I'm not convinced he has the..."

"... capacity for creative thinking?"

Hugo smiled. "Something like that. There's such a thing as too much honour."

"Any honour," Webb grinned, "is too much honour."

Hugo sighed. "We'll see. Anything could happen."

"If they listen to you?"

Hugo looked at him. "Yes."

"How's that going so far?"

"Still a way to go," Hugo hedged.

Webb grinned again. Then he gestured at his face. "Didn't you want to get that fixed?"

Hugo touched the scar. It still burned sometimes and he occasionally woke up in the night scratching at it just like he had in those waking days in the brig after the battle when it had been fresh.

"For a long time," he fumbled. "For a *very* long time... every time I looked in the mirror... I didn't know who I was looking at."

"Know the feeling," Webb said quietly.

"No matter what happens now though, no matter what they end up making me do... I will know. I will remember the *Resolution*. I will remember what really happened. I..." he paused again, shaking his head. "I couldn't move forward unless I had a way to make sure I never lost my way again."

Webb nodded. "I suddenly have more hope for the future," he said with a more genuine smile.

There was a pause whilst Hugo stared into the night and rubbed the scar on his face without thinking.

"It's hard to believe she's gone," Webb said quietly. Hugo looked at him. He was frowning slightly and staring at nothing. "The *Zero*, I mean. I can't figure out which are my feelings and which are his. But wherever they're coming from..." Webb shook his head.

"Did you hear the tribute?"

"Yeah, I heard it. More's and Sub's too. Along with those of all the other poor bastards that are no longer breathing."

"Things could change," Hugo said, very quietly. "You could help."

Webb shook his head. "I've had enough of the Service for two lifetimes," he said, the edge in his smile harder than ever. "Good luck to you, Kaleb Hugo. And watch your back. Remember what these people do when you don't fall in as they like."

"You could be a part of this," Hugo dogged on. "Very few people know who you really are. Even fewer know what happened to you. You're still your own man and you could make a difference. Rami and Bolt have found places where they can."

"What about Spinn?"

"He's been pardoned in exchange for evidence against Pharos and been shipped off to the *Endeavour* to carry on with research."

"Out of your sight?"

Hugo ground his teeth but didn't reply.

There was a pause. Snatches of violin music wafted up to them. Hugo breathed in the scent of the wind, concentrating of the feel of the metal rail under his elbows and the silence filled with understanding that engulfed them both.

"I'm going to make it illegal, you know," he said a few heartbeats later.

"What?"

"Cloning," Hugo answered. "I'm going to make sure this never happens to anyone else."

"Is that supposed to win me over?"

"No. I just wanted you to know."

Webb nodded. His face was turned away, a shifting plane of shadows in the wan light, but Hugo could tell he wasn't smiling.

"I once told you... him... that I knew soldiers like you. That they didn't last."

"You were right," Webb said with another nasty smile.

"You have a chance to prove me wrong." Hugo looked out over the bay. "It's too late for him..." Hugo paused to steady his voice. Webb's gaze was calm and measured. "And you can't unload what you've been given. But if you go blasting into the future not caring where you end up, like he did..."

It sounded lame even in his own ears. There was so much more he wanted to say, wanted to make this man understand and ask his forgiveness for. He knew at least some of it was what he wished he'd said to the real Webb. The futility of the whole thing welled up in his throat. He nearly turned and walked away but Webb put a hand on his arm.

"Do you want to know the real reason I didn't talk?" The clone's voice was so quiet it was almost swept away in the breeze. "On the *Tide*? Do you know what the real reason was?"

Hugo held his tongue. The hand on his arm tightened.

"I wanted...." he paused, shook his head, pulled away and straightened up. He sighed and looked up at the sky. "I wanted to believe that if I could convince the blade I wasn't made of someone else... that maybe I could make that true."

Hugo swallowed a few times. "You can't."

"I know that. I can't get rid of it. So I have to own it. Is that right?"

"Use it," Hugo said.

For the briefest of moments Hugo dared to hope he'd convinced him. But then he shook his head and the hope evaporated.

"Not for the Service," he mumbled.

"Then for yourself. You have a chance to live the life he could have had. But it's only you that can make it work."

They stared at each other in the darkness. The seconds were swept away in the wind and more music reached them, along with the sound of Harvey's voice calling his name.

"Why did you come here?" Hugo muttered, already knowing the answer.

"To say goodbye," Webb said, quietly. He held out his hand and Hugo took it. It seemed an empty and useless gesture considering everything it stood for. "Both versions of me have said it, Hugo, but it's true. You're a good man. If anyone can drag this Orbit into any sort of New Age, it will be you."

"Thank you. For everything. You saved me."

Webb's grip tightened a moment then his hand dropped away. "Take care, Hugo."

"Webb," Hugo called at the last minute before the younger man disappeared down the steps. "If you ever need help... if you're ever lost or in trouble..."

In the shifting light from the skyways Webb's old grin spread over his face. "When am I ever not?" he said, but his laugh lifted some of the bleakness from his words. "Look after yourself, Hugo. Promise me that."

"I will if you will."

Webb paused and smiled wider. "Deal."

And then he was gone. Harvey was still calling him and the wind brought the smell of the water to him. He looked up at the stars glinting between the skyways and the moon, gleaming and pale, and marvelled at how peaceful it could look.

END

Acknowledgments

So many people have encouraged and supported me to get to this point that I'm quite overwhelmed. I am thankful to every last one of you, whether it was just for putting up with my disappearing into my anti-social writing cave for weeks at a time or suggesting spaceship names, every last one of you helped this happen and have my gratitude.

I would like to thank in particular my parents, Ann and Phil and my brother Christopher for never doubting that one day I would release a book, even when I doubted myself. I'd also like to thank them and my other relatives Adam and Cheryl, Stephen and Linda and Derek and Sheila, for the emotional and financial support that got me through my university degrees which helped me get further towards this goal.

I also want to convey my undying gratitude to the other writers in my life who have never hesitated in answering my questions, offering advice and helping me learn. In particular I have Matt Wesolowski to thank for his unswerving support and encouragement, as well as George Green, Jo Baker, Ray Robinson and Catherine Spooner, my tutors from university who helped me to learn there is always more to learn.

I also want to thank Anna for her eternal enthusiasm and excitement for my projects' success, especially during conversations when I talked of little else and Reg, without whom this book would never have happened.

I would finally like to thank my partner, Andy, who has survived being in a relationship with a writer for eight years and counting which is an achievement in itself and his family, Stuart, Angela, Valerie, John, Gen, Jennifer and Andy who provided everything from encouragement to contributions to writing retreats.

Zero would not have happened without the support of all my family and friends and I shall continue to try and become a better and better writer and make you all proud.

About The Author

J. S. Collyer was born in Birkenhead on the Wirral in England before moving around a lot with her family at a young age. Settling finally in Shrewsbury, Shropshire, she was already an avid storyteller having started to write stories from as soon as she could hold a pencil.

She began reading obsessively when she discovered Star Wars and science fiction in secondary school and went on to study literature and creative writing up to Master of Arts' level at the Lancaster University. After graduating with her MA in 2008 she has stayed in Lancaster with her partner and kept her hand in with short stories and has started a few novels, before finally getting the idea for Zero after deciding to put a fantasy project on hold.

She has always had a taste for narratives that are larger than life and science fiction delivers what she needs. But, though it's true she likes spaceships, lasers and moon rocks, she also likes humanity, sincerity and relating to her characters. They may live on the moon, but they're real and she is committed to creating human narratives albeit usually with a super-human backdrop.

Discover more of her fiction as well as details of previously published work on her blog http://jcollyer.wordpress.com.

Other Fiction Titles from Dagda Publishing

9647892R00206

Printed in Great Britain
by Amazon.co.uk, Ltd.,
Marston Gate.